# WARLOCK

WARLOCK
BOOK 1

DANIEL KENSINGTON

DARKSPACE PRESS

WARLOCK
Book 1

A Harem/Magic School Fantasy

by Daniel Kensington



Formatted with Vellum

# WITCH TITLES

*Witch Titles*

*Magella/Magellae* (male: *Magellus*) - From magi, with a diminutive suffix. A young witch or one not a member of a coven.

*Sororix* - Sister. A witch who is a member of a coven.

*Dominus/Domina Ritualis* - Master/Mistress of the Ritual. The warlock or high priestess of the coven.

*Magistra* - Teacher

*Magistra Prima* (*Prima*) - headmistress of the school

*Magira* - Latinized from the Greek "*mageíra*", a Family head or member of the Witches Council.

*Archimagira* - Head of a Witches Council.

# CHAPTER ONE

*Wake up, Noah.*

"Noah, wake up, dude."

The second voice I knew — it was Alex, one of my foster parents — but the other was a kid, a little girl, which was weird because the only girl in the home was Morgan and she was sixteen, seventeen tomorrow, as her birthday was the day after mine. Maybe Alex and Karen had taken another foster in already? Since I was eighteen today and aging out of the system that made sense, but they usually took in teenagers and the girl had sounded younger — maybe eight or nine.

I pulled the blanket off my head and rolled over — I remembered pulling it over my head when my roommate Chuck got up. He always left the light on — he really had no concern for others.

"Come on, Noah — Karen's almost done with breakfast if you want some before you leave."

"Okay, okay." I swung my feet out of bed and sat up, stretching to relieve the kinks that always came with this bed — it was a holdover from when Alex and Karen took in much younger kids, so wasn't exactly comfortable for my six-foot plus frame. "Who's the little girl?"

"What little girl?"

I rubbed at sandy eyes, finger-combed my unruly hair into some semblance of order, and looked around. Alex was in the doorway of the room, but no one else.

"The one who was telling me to wake up?"

Alex frowned from where he was standing in the doorway. He was thin, in his forties, with a long, greasy ponytail and a mustache trying for handlebar but only managing a bad fu-manchu.

"Dude, that was me." He looked offended. "You telling me I sound like a little girl?"

I rubbed at my face some more and ran a hand through my hair to try and wake up. I noticed the hair was getting a little too long — I usually kept it a little long, but it was now past my shoulders and that was a bit much. I probably should have asked Karen for a haircut before aging out, but there wouldn't be time today.

"No, Alex, sorry — I must have been dreaming."

I blinked a couple times and as I woke up I started to think that was probably true. The voice hadn't been so much heard as ... felt? So, it must have been a dream, and it felt like she'd been telling me to wake up all damn night, which was why I was still so horribly tired, despite normally being a bit of a morning person.

"Breakfast, dude," Alex said, then looked away as though embarrassed. "Then I gotta ask you to pack up — CPS is dropping someone off this afternoon."

I nodded. It wasn't a surprise. Alex and Karen needed the money and the State stopped paying for me today. They'd probably been nagging Child Protective Services for months to set up a replacement for me.

"I know," I said. "I'm mostly packed already — I'll be out right after breakfast."

Alex's shoulders slumped.

"Sorry, dude — it's just —"

"It's okay, Alex. I know how it goes." I stood up and held out my hand. "You guys have been really good to me — thanks for everything, okay?"

"Yeah, dude, no problem. Ah, your case worker left a packet for you — services and stuff. Karen has it downstairs."

Alex took my hand briefly, then left me alone.

I really was grateful to them. I'd been with Alex and Karen since I was thirteen. Other foster homes before that, but Alex and Karen took in mostly teenagers, so when I'd gotten older than the previous home liked, the State moved me. That had happened two other times — first the home I'd started in as an abandoned infant, then a second at five when I started school, then Alex and Karen.

Three families I knew I was never going to see again after moving on.

I got dressed and set my backpack on my bed so it would be easier to finish packing after breakfast, then went downstairs.

My roommate, Chuck, was just finishing his when I came into the dining room, so I got a quick fist bump and a "good luck" as he rinsed his plate and headed out for the day.

"Here you go," Karen said, setting a plate on the dining table.

I sat down to a breakfast of oatmeal and fruit, which was pretty typical for a breakfast here. Not fancy, but it was real food — filling and nutritious. The oatmeal was even fresh made, not from a packet, since that was less expensive when cooking for this many people. Sure, the fruit was barely-thawed from its previously frozen state, but that was another cost issue and it was still real fruit, not some strawberry-flavored candy thing. Despite the distance I felt from Alex and Karen, I couldn't say they didn't provide for us. I'd had food, shelter, clothing… everything you need, right?

"And here's your information packet," Karen said, sliding a heavy manila envelope onto the table next to me. "Mrs. Dexter dropped it off for you early this morning, but I didn't want to wake you. She said something came up and she wouldn't be able to drive you to set up services this morning, but if you scheduled an appointment with her office…"

Karen's voice trailed off — I think she was as familiar as I was with how well scheduling appointments with Mrs. Dexter or any of the other CPS case workers typically went.

"Thanks," I mumbled around a mouthful of oatmeal.

Karen patted me on the shoulder, then returned to the kitchen.

I didn't bother opening the packet or even looking at it — I knew what it contained because Mrs. Dexter, my case worker for most of my life, had explained what I'd get.

All my records from a lifetime in foster care; a birth certificate with their best guess at my birth date, June fourth — "best guess", because I'd been abandoned in a baby drop at a fire station — and lists of services I could sign up for now that I was going to be on my own.

Housing was going to be my first stop, I'd already decided, so I'd head for the shelters first and get signed up, then one of the job placement services, then the financial services. I had about a hundred dollars saved and stashed in my backpack, which would buy me some food for a few days, and if I could find a job then I wouldn't need the welfare services for long.

Mrs. Dexter had talked about taking me around to sign up for everything beforehand, but it never happened. Case workers talked about a lot of things that never happened.

I finished my breakfast, then went upstairs to finish packing.

Everything I owned fit in my backpack now that I'd emptied it of textbooks and other school crap after the last day of school. As far as clothing went, I had seven of most things. Karen was a big believer in efficiency, so all us kids had enough clothes for one week, the time between laundry days: pants on Monday, shirts on Tuesday, underwear and socks on Wednesday. Sheets got washed on Thursday and Friday, because there were so many of us in the house. So, seven of everything, except jeans, because you can wear a pair of jeans for more than one day, Karen said.

There wasn't a lot of variety, and nothing fancy, but I'd always had something to wear, and all of it rolled up tightly and fit inside my backpack.

To be fair to Karen and Alex, some of the other kids had more in the way of clothing because they'd give us each a little bit of money each week. Some kids bought nicer clothes with it, but I'd tried to save as much as I could over the years, which is where the hundred dollars came from.

Yeah, a hundred dollars wasn't much to show for five years of saving, but I had bought things, just not clothes — usually treats for me and Morgan, probably the only person I could really call a friend after a lifetime in foster care. She was the only thing I was going to miss about this place.

I took a last look around the room I'd spent years of my life in, then headed downstairs for the last time.

---

"ALL PACKED?" Karen asked as I entered the kitchen.

"Yep," I said. "Everything."

I set my house key on the counter since I wouldn't be needing it anymore.

Karen held out her arms, so I gave her a hug, and she squeezed me hard.

"You're going be okay, I know it," she said, patting my back.

"Thanks — thanks for everything. Do you know where Morgan is?"

Karen released me from the hug and nodded.

"She's out front — and here's a couple sandwiches I made for you," she said, handing me a paper bag. "Keep in touch?"

"Yeah, thanks."

I nodded, even though I'd seen kid after kid leave with her saying those same words over the years and couldn't remember any of them keeping in touch. Maybe they did with Karen and the rest of us just never heard about it? I don't know — maybe Alex and Karen could have been a bit more parenty if they'd had just one or two kids in the house, but with eight? There always seemed to be some distance.

I'd absolutely keep in touch with Morgan, if I could — she was another babydrop-lifer like I was and had been here as long as I had. In fact, we'd been placed with Karen and Alex within a week of each other and Morgan had quickly become like a little sister to me — an annoying, demanding little sister ... which I guess was probably redundant. We even looked enough alike, with similar hair and eye color, that people often asked if we were siblings.

"Hey, you," I said, finding her on the front steps. I closed the door behind me and sat next to her.

"Hey."

Morgan tried to pass herself off as a tough girl — short, brown hair she colored blonde but never all the way, thrift-store jeans with rips they came by honestly, boots, leather jacket over a loose t-shirt, and fingerless gloves I never saw the point of. I didn't think she pulled off the look, because her brown eyes were too soft and her upturned nose far too cute, but I also got to see the more vulnerable side she never showed anyone else, so maybe I was biased. It was a warm day, so she had her jacket off, but she never went anywhere without it.

She was very attractive, in a tomboy sort of way, and I'd never understood why she didn't date. It was a lot easier for a girl in foster care to date than a guy, not needing to have a lot of money or a more private place to hang out.

"You're going?" she asked, putting her elbows on her knees and looking down at her feet.

"Yeah, I need to get started finding someplace to live and a job. Alex said there's someone new coming this afternoon."

"Great, another asshole," Morgan muttered, then looked at me with wide eyes. "Not you! I meant —"

"I know what you meant," I said, laughing.

She wasn't wrong — most of the guys here were assholes, especially to her. I'd never figured out why CPS had put her here when the rest of the home was all guys — maybe because there hadn't been anywhere else at the time, and once you were placed somewhere it was hard to get moved. If there weren't any serious problems or other reasons, you pretty much stayed where you were.

"You'll be alright," I said, nudging her with my shoulder.

"Yeah, you'll be okay, too."

Our bare arms touched and my skin tingled, like a low voltage current running through us.

"You still got that?" Morgan asked, seeing me rub at my arm.

"Yeah." I frowned. "I wish I knew what it was."

It was a weird thing that started about six months ago — I'd get this almost electrical tingle when touching someone, even when not touching anyone sometimes, and Karen had taken me to the doctor to find out what it was. Probably because if I had some major medical thing, they could postpone me aging out, even until I was twenty-five if it was serious enough. The doctors hadn't figured it out, so I guess I was stuck with it.

My arm was still tingling and I shivered as it spread to cover my whole body.

It wasn't unpleasant — in fact, it was kind of nice — and I always felt better when it happened. Right now, I was feeling refreshed, even after a rough night's sleep, but that didn't keep me from yawning as soon as I thought about how tired I'd been.

"Bad night, too?" Morgan asked.

"Yeah," I frowned. "I kept dreaming about someone trying to wake me up."

"What? Like the rental-'rents trying to get you up early so they could cash a new check?"

I laughed again.

"No, it was more like a little girl — I think she got a bit pissy near the end, though."

A cloud passed across the sun, sending the front yard into shadow and I shivered, then jumped as something landed in my lap.

I looked down to find the neighborhood cat curling up into a ball in my lap and already purring.

"Felicity's going to miss you," Morgan said as I started petting the purring cat.

"Yeah, I'm going to miss her, too."

I scratched at the cat's left ear, just at the junction between her black fur and the white patches that peppered her left side. Her right side was all black, but the left had big, irregular patches of white. I'd never seen a cat with that kind of coloring before. The bell on her collar jingled and she arched her neck up into the scratches.

I'd spent a lot of time scratching Felicity. The cat had been a good friend, at times, listening to the things I couldn't even tell Morgan. There are things a teenage guy can't really talk about with a girl, even if she's like a sister — maybe especially if she's like a sister — but Felicity always seemed to turn up at those times to listen.

We'd never figured out which neighbors owned her, even after Morgan and I once went door to door asking.

"I'm going to miss you, too," Morgan whispered, looking down at her feet again.

"Me, too, boogerface."

"Don't call me that! I was *twelve!*"

I chuckled and shrugged. "Hey, you wipe boogers on your own cheeks, it takes a while for people to forget."

"It was a dare! *Your* dare!"

I shrugged.

She stuck her tongue out at me, then sobered again and we just sat in silence for a bit.

"What about me?" Morgan finally asked.

"What?"

"Am I going to see you again?"

"Of course — we talked about that."

Morgan shrugged. "People say things they don't mean all the time."

I shivered again — between the cloud-covered sun and the damn tingling, which was getting worse, I was wondering if I should have taken a jacket even though it was June. I hadn't because Karen and Alex would probably need all my winter stuff for the next kid and I'd certainly have a job and my own money by the time it got cold enough for me to need one.

"Not me," I said. "As soon as I get a job, I'll get a phone and we'll talk just as much as we do now." None of us kids had cell phones, but the house had a landline. "And by the time you turn eighteen, I'll have my own place and you can come stay with me while you get on your feet."

"That's a long time. What if they move me to another home? Or what if you're busy, or move to another city, or ... you could meet someone and maybe she wouldn't want me moving in, or — I don't know. Anything could happen."

That wasn't likely, given she only had a year more to do, but the facts didn't matter. I could tell she was scared she'd get dumped on the streets like I was, and just needed reassurance, even though her fears were unfounded. It wasn't like I was planning on doing a lot of dating for a while — I needed to get my own feet under me before I even thought about that.

I understood why Morgan was worried, though — we'd watched a lot of kids leave over the years. All saying they'd be in touch, but they never did. Even some guys who'd had the same plan Morgan and I did, but they never followed through. Guys waiting for a call right up until the day came for them to leave — but it never came, and there was no one coming to pick them up. I wasn't going to do that to Morgan, no matter what.

"It's a year from tomorrow, not that long. And I'll find you, no matter what."

"Promise?"

I held up my hand, pinkie extended.

"Pinkie swear."

"I'm *not* twelve!"

"*Pinkie swear!*" I said, sternly.

Morgan stuck her tongue out at me again, but linked pinkies anyway.

"A year and a day," I said. "I'll come get you, no matter what."

That damn cloud finally passed the sun and the yard was warm again. Felicity purred louder, then hopped off my lap and dashed away, collar-bell jingling.

# CHAPTER TWO

The first thing I learned about being on my own was that everything takes longer than you think it will.

The walk from Karen and Alex's to the bus stop took longer, the bus was behind schedule and only got more so during my ride, and the line at the first shelter I went to was much longer than I expected.

The next thing I learned was that there are *a lot* of homeless people in this country.

The first shelter I stopped at had a line, even at ten a.m., and well before I got to the front of the line, they were announcing that they were full for the night. Apparently, you had to sign-up each day, as early as possible.

The second one I heard a couple guys in the first line talking about and saying they always had room — but when I got there, I found out they always had room because they were charging thirty bucks a night. That got you a small room instead of a bunk in some dormitory, but it was still a third of what cash I had — too much.

By the time I got to the third shelter, it was clear that they'd all be full for the night, and it was only noon, so I decided to move on to job placement.

I ate Karen's sandwiches on the way to the first job placement agency and washed them down with water from a fountain in an office building along the way.

Did I mention that everything takes longer than you expect?

Job placement had both a line and a waiting area. First you waited in the line to get the forms you should fill out in the waiting area, where you then waited to be called to turn in the forms.

It's a process, I guess.

---

"NOAH ASHE! Next, please, Noah Ashe! Window eight!"

I hopped up out of my seat and hurried to the window.

The woman there looked me up and down.

"Noah Ashe?"

"Yes, ma'am."

I slid my completed paperwork through the window.

"ID?" she asked, taking the papers.

I pulled out my wallet and handed over my school ID.

"What's this?"

"Um, my student ID, ma'am — I haven't had a chance to go to the DMV and get a —"

The woman sighed, cutting me off. She picked up the paperwork I'd filled out and sighed again.

"You didn't fill out the address."

"I'm, ah, sort of between addresses?"

"Not a problem, what's the address of the shelter you stayed at most recently?"

"I haven't, ma'am, I just aged out of foster care, and —"

She cut me off again with a shake of her head.

"You need an address and you need ID." She handed back my student ID. "That's not even valid anymore." She looked at me and sighed again. "Look, in order to be hired you have to fill out a government I9 form to prove you're here legally and are allowed to work."

"I was born here, though."

At least I assumed I was.

"Doesn't matter," she said. "Federal law, you need to prove it." She rummaged in a drawer and pulled out a form labeled I9. "Here, see? You need either one ID from List A — that's a passport, passport card, or permanent resident card. If you don't have those, then you need one from *both* List B and List C. That's a driver's license or state ID card ... a school ID would work, but yours is expired, or a military ID. Then from List C — that's a social security card or a certified birth certificate."

"I have both of those!" I reached for my backpack and the packet of papers Mrs. Dexter had left me.

"Do you have something from List B?"

My shoulders slumped.

"What you need to do," the woman said, "is go get in a shelter for the night, then first thing in the morning go to the DMV and get your ID, then come back here and I can find something for you. Okay?"

I nodded, not trusting myself to speak. I'd accomplished absolutely nothing all day and all the shelters were probably full — and even if they weren't, the only ones that would have room were the ones that charged, so a third of my cash would be gone.

And I'd still be at square one when I woke up tomorrow.

"Come back tomorrow," she said. "You'll be okay."

---

AT LEAST IT wasn't raining — I could look on the bright side there.

I thought about trying to make it to one of the other service offices before they closed, but a quick check of the bus schedule told me that wasn't going to be possible. And they'd probably require a real ID, too. I wondered why my case worker hadn't made sure I had one before aging out — too busy, I guess. She was always saying how overworked she was.

I decided to just check into the shelter and call it a day, even if it was only around six. I was tired after the long day and sleepless night, and I decided to skip dinner, since I'd had a big breakfast and lunch, to make my cash stretch longer. Maybe the shelter would have a meal? Thirty bucks for the room didn't sound as bad if it came with a meal — and maybe breakfast, too? Did it work that way or not? I kicked myself for not asking questions earlier — if I had, I might have been able to get to the DMV with the shelter address and take care of that this afternoon.

The shelter was a block over from the bus stop, so I decided to cut through an alleyway to get there faster.

"*Hey!*"

Hands grabbed me and pulled me behind a dumpster, slamming me up against the brick wall. My head glanced off the hard bricks and I blinked to clear my suddenly fuzzy vision.

"*Money!*"

"What?" I was so dazed I couldn't really tell what was going on.

"Money! Give me your fucking money, kid!"

I blinked.

The guy had me pinned against the wall, his forearm on my chest and the other hand holding a knife pointed at my face. He had long, stringy hair and a scruffy beard, all surrounding crazy eyes — you know, eyes that screamed, "I'm crazy and I don't care anymore!"

"Come on! Give it over!"

I almost cried. I really did. This was too much. I had less than a hundred dollars to my name and this asshole wanted to rob me? What a fucking birthday.

Anger boiled up behind the despair. Anger at the years in the System. At years of having just barely enough of everything — barely enough food, barely enough clothes, barely enough space to sleep in. At the rest of the System for not having some sort of support ready for me when I aged out. Anger at my parents for putting me in the System to begin with. Anger at this asshole who wanted to take what little was mine.

"Fuck you," I said.

"I'll cut you, man!"

"You think I have any fucking money? I just aged out of foster care, asshole! I got shit!"

The guy scowled and he jerked the knife around.

I closed my eyes, figuring I was going to get cut and not really caring — ERs had beds, right? Probably food, too. What kind of world was it when I was seriously wondering if getting stabbed might be a positive?

My skin started tingling.

*Great — a fine time for a bout of some undiagnosed medical condition.*

I hoped it was both fatal and highly communicable, and that this asshole caught a double-dose of it when he stabbed me.

"Fine."

The guy pulled the knife away from my face and I thought maybe I'd get out of this without losing anything, but then he punched me in the gut with his other hand.

All the air went out of me and I gasped, but the tingling grew stronger.

"Give me the bag!"

He was tugging on my backpack, trying to get it away from me — my backpack that had all my clothes, all my documents, and all my money. Everything I had. What if I had to get a new birth certificate? A new social security card? How long would that take?

"Let go!"

My skin was burning — my vision blurred more as I tugged and tried to maintain my footing.

"*Gimme it!*" the guy yelled, yanking harder.

"*Motherfucker!*" I yelled, pulling back as hard as I could.

My bag came free and as soon as it did, I spun around, thinking if I could catch him one good one with the weight of my backpack, it might knock the knife out of his hands.

"*Get the fuck away from me!*"

My backpack *swished*, not striking anything and the momentum spun me around in a circle again. I fell to my knees, managed to catch a glimpse of the guy running away, then I collapsed face first onto the pavement. My skin felt on fire and my head was spinning.

Through blurry vision, I saw the guy run face first into the opposite wall of the alley, bounce off, then get up and run at it again, blood streaming from his nose.

I blinked, tried to get up, but my arms were weak, head spinning more, and I collapsed again, smacking my head on the pavement.

Not nearly as badly as the other guy, though, because he was running into the wall again.

There was a sickening *crunch* as his head hit the brick, and then I heard a tinkling bell before I passed out.

# THE CHILD

I was in a forest.

Which was weird, because I'd never been to a forest. Hardly ever gone to a park with more than a couple trees, even.

But this was a forest I was walking through.

Sunbeams came through the leaves at an angle and I could hear birds all around. Leaves crunched under my feet as I followed a clear trail that eventually came to the edge of the trees.

Ahead of me was an open space in full sunlight with a block of rough-cut stone offset a bit from the center.

"Come on, Noah, we don't have much time."

I looked down and to my right to see a girl standing next to me. A little girl, maybe seven or eight years old, barefoot and wearing a sack.

"It's called a *shift*, Noah," the girl said, "not a sack."

It was very, very weird that she said this, because her lips didn't move.

"Oh, sorry, I forget sometimes," she said, moving her lips this time.

"It's okay," I said, "I heard you anyway."

I thought I was remarkably calm for having woken up in a forest with a telepathic child — but even though I could think about it being extremely weird, I couldn't seem to *feel* like it was anything but normal and safe. It was like all the fears and anxiety I had from the day of failures and being attacked had been shoved into a box. I could look at them, I knew they were there, but they couldn't affect how I felt.

The girl smiled up at me and the forest lit up far beyond the sunlight, making me feel warm, like strong arms wrapped around me.

"Come on," she said, taking my hand and leading me into the clearing. "We need to talk."

"Are you the one who woke me up this morning?"

"It was yesterday now, but yes — I needed to wake you so we could talk."

We'd reached the stone block, which was waist-height on me. It was maybe eight feet long and four wide, and looked rough and weathered, like it had been there for centuries. The girl hopped up onto it, tucking her sack ... shift under her legs. Her feet were bare and stained green by the grass.

"You woke me up so we could talk but then waited until I was asleep again to do it?"

"Hmph. You're not just sleeping, silly, there are different levels of wakefulness and I needed to make sure your power woke up before you were on your own. Good thing I did, too, because you sure needed it. You just used far too much mana defending yourself in that alley and passed out."

"I don't know what any of that is — and who are you anyway? Other than some sort of manifestation of my subconscious, I guess."

She pursed her lips and scrunched her face up in thought.

"You can call me ... Aurora!" She smiled and the world went warm and snugly again. "It means dawn and it's symbolic of new beginnings, which we're doing, so it's very clever — *and* it's pretty. Do you think it's pretty?"

"It's very pretty."

"Do you think *I'm* pretty?"

She was, now that she asked. She was a beautiful little girl — perfect except for little imperfections that seemed to only make her more beautiful.

"Yes, you're a beautiful little girl."

Aurora's face lit up.

"Thank you! But I'm not a little girl, this is just the best way to appear to you."

"Why's that?" I asked, wondering why my subconscious thought that.

"Because you're a *boy*." Aurora pouted as though that was the worst possible thing I could be. A cloud passed across the sun, throwing the clearing into shadow and making me shiver at the sudden chill. "I've tried all kinds of forms. See, if you were a girl, I'd appear older — really, really old or just a hint of a wrinkle or two, maybe a few gray hairs. Girls respect the wisdom of those forms and listen, but boys don't listen for some reason. So, after that didn't work with boys, I tried appearing the way I really prefer, which is without the wrinkles and gray hair. I'm *very* pretty when I don't have wrinkles and gray hair. Anyway, the girls still listened to me, I think because I'm so pretty and they respect that too, but the boys all wanted to have sex with me, which is *very* annoying — even more annoying than being ignored. Boys are weird."

I was suddenly very uncomfortable with my subconscious.

"Anyway, I got tired of making the boys not annoying, because it's hard to do that and leave them still able to talk to me, which was the whole point in the first place."

I was suddenly very uncomfortable with, and increasingly afraid of, my subconscious.

"So, I tried this!"

Aurora smiled and the sun came out again, warming the clearing and chasing away my concerns.

"Boys listen to me when I look like this," she said with a shrug. "I don't know why — maybe it's a paternal thing? I don't know — I'm more the motherly type, really, but whatever works."

She looked around as though hearing something.

"Oh, we don't have much time. I brought you here because I want to tell you three things — they're very important, so listen to me."

"Okay."

"First, be yourself. There's going to be some strange stuff. It's going to be confusing for you, but you'll be okay, I promise."

*Ah,* I thought, *my subconscious is trying to reassure me after the horrible day I had. Cool — got it.*

"Noah, your subconscious is going to give you ulcers with how *not okay* it's going to tell you things are soon. You don't have a reassuring subconscious at all. *I'm* telling you it'll be okay. Be yourself, do what you feel is right, and you'll be okay, got it?"

"Ah, yeah, got it."

"Good. The second thing is I love you."

My knees buckled. When she said that I felt it. I believed it. Deep in my soul I believed Aurora loved me — that someone really loved me, unconditionally, maybe for the first time in my life.

"Oh, Noah, I'm so sorry," Aurora said, reaching out to take my hand. "I know it's been hard, but you're going to know *so* much love — it'll be sickening, really. Definitely exhausting. I promise. Do you believe me?"

I nodded. I did believe her, and in a second the overwhelming feeling I'd had went away, but it left a warm, secure feeling in my gut.

"Good," she said, then took a deep breath. "The last thing I want to tell you — I need you to do something for me."

"Anything," I said, and absolutely meant it.

"Hush, don't make promises like that — they have too much power. But I do need you to do something very important for me. Maybe it's selfish to use mine this way, but..."

"Use what?"

"Never mind, just listen."

I nodded.

Aurora sighed and looked away. A breeze came up, rustling the leaves and chilling my skin.

"A long time ago, I made a bad mistake." Another cloud crossed the sun and I shivered. "Someone I love very, very much asked me for something and I gave it to her, but she ... she misunderstood what I said. She offered a ... trade, but she didn't need to." A raindrop landed on my cheek and another on Aurora's. "I ... I was busy with something else and ... that's no excuse. It's not." More raindrops fell. "I didn't realize what had happened until it was too late." Aurora's face was wet with rain and her lips trembled. "I couldn't tell her she'd misunderstood, because she'd spent so long thinking I'd done something horrible to her that she wouldn't listen to me anymore. I couldn't reach her at all." The wind swept a torrent of rain across the clearing, soaking me to the skin, but I couldn't look away from Aurora's face. "She's spent so long ... hating me."

Thunder rolled, nearly drowning out Aurora's words. She took a deep breath and looked up at the sky.

"*Stop that!*" she yelled, kicking her grass-stained heel against the stone.

The rain stopped like someone had shut the faucet — one last brush of wind swept my skin before the air went still and the clouds parted to let a ray of sunshine wash the clearing again.

"That's the problem with this form," Aurora said, looking at me again. "Very little emotional control." She frowned up at the sky. "You'd never *dare* do that to the Crone!"

"Who's the —"

"Never mind. Where was I? Oh, yes — so, Noah, there's going to come a time when you're with her and — don't worry, you'll know when, now listen — tell her I wouldn't do that. Please?"

"You wouldn't do what?"

"Just tell her — I wouldn't do that. You'll know when. I promise."

Aurora looked up at the sky again.

"Oops, time for you to go."

She reached out and poked the end of my nose.

"*Boop!*"

# CHAPTER THREE

"Wake up."

A woman's voice this time — young, but clearly an adult, so it wasn't...

*Who did I think it might be?*

I grasped at that thought, thinking there was something important to remember, but it seemed like every time I focused on the thought, the answer slipped farther out of my grasp.

I groaned and blinked. I was really getting tired of people telling me to wake up. I struggled with the last vestiges of sleep, grasping again at what I thought had just been in my head, but the tighter I clutched at it, the more it receded until I couldn't remember a thing about the dreaming world.

"There you go, lad, now drink this and sit up."

Something pressed against my lips — liquid seeped in and I jerked upright, coughing and sputtering.

"*Gah! Awg!*"

"Right, then," the woman said. "Who are you and who must I call to come get you?"

I started to swallow, then stopped at the lingering taste. I looked around desperately for some way to get it out of my mouth.

"You spit that on my floor and I'll dose you again."

I grimaced, swallowed the vile stuff, and glared at her.

The woman was maybe late-twenties or early-thirties. Trim, with a nice figure shown off by the tight jeans and V-neck knit top she wore. Her long dark hair was pulled back and she had startlingly blue eyes that seemed to sparkle, even as she narrowed them to glare at me. I got a glimpse of her finely arched brows and generous mouth before I was distracted, because she was leaning toward me with the bottle of medicine — if that was what it was — prepped for another dose, which gave me an awkward view down the V-neck of her top as the swell of her breasts and gravity pulled it away from her chest.

I swallowed hard and forced myself to look away and take in the rest of my surroundings.

I was in a very soft bed, in a nicely decorated room, with sunlight streaming through the window. It looked like morning sunlight, that sort of soft glow, so I must have been out all night — which made me wonder why I was here instead of a hospital. On top of me was a fluffy, quilted blanket and someone had taken my shoes off, but I was still fully clothed.

I worked my mouth some more to get rid of the awful taste.

"That stuff is nasty," I said, "how's it supposed to make me feel better?"

The woman looked at the bottle in her hand. "Wasn't supposed to make you feel better. It was supposed to make you sit up and do as I say, so you'll not get another dose." She tucked the small bottle into a pocket in her tight jeans. "Done its job, I think."

I groaned again.

"Now, who are you?" she asked.

I took a breath. "My name's Noah. Did you bring me here from the alley? Thank you ... I guess. That guy was trouble." I caught myself, remembering the last sight I'd had of the guy, with blood running down his face and then the sickening *crunch* of his head against the brick wall.

I winced.

"I mean, until he ran away," I added, figuring it might be best not to admit to having seen that. Maybe he'd actually run off after I passed out?

"And not at all bludgeoned to death with a brick wall?" she asked, then chuckled. "No need to dissemble, you're in friendly company. Though I'd expect you to know another witch when you see one." She laid the back of her hand against my forehead. "Did you strike your own —"

She broke off and jerked her hand away as my forehead began to tingle.

"None of that now!" She frowned at me. "What Family taught you such manners?"

I decided I'd try to deal with the "bludgeoned to death" part later and concentrate on the bizarrely less-disturbing "witch" part — what I'd done that was "rude" would have to wait even longer, because as far as I could tell all I'd done was lay in a bed and drink what had to be concentrated car-wash runoff.

"Witch?"

"Really? Very well — *which* Family taught you it was acceptable to pull mana from someone you'd only just met?" She stood up and glared at me. "What are you even thinking? Do you seriously think you could mark *me*?"

"Ma'am, I honestly have no idea what you're talking about. The last thing I remember, I was walking through an alley to get to the shelter and some guy tried to mug me."

I thought about what she'd said already and focused even more on the "witch" part. If she thought she was a witch, then she was crazy, and crazy people were dangerous. I tried to remember any stories I'd heard about crazy witches, though, and none of them ended well for someone who was rude to the witch. I didn't believe she was a witch, but crazy was just as bad.

"I apologize if I was rude," I said, slowly and carefully, "and deeply regret any disrespect or offense."

*Please don't turn me into a candelabra or some shit,* I thought, just in case she really was a witch.

Her gaze softened.

"Well, you did just have a rather bad experience, I suppose," she said finally. "Nearly killed yourself using so much mana — not even enough left to keep your shields up — so I can understand the instinct to pull some from me." She started to pat my hand, then stopped. "Don't worry, I've tried to be polite and not look at you too closely, but there should be enough ambiance for you to restore your shields, at least. Now, who're your people? We'll get you right home and say no more of it."

Definitely crazy — mana, whatever that was, shields, and the way she said "look", with some special emphasis. She said it with a very personal tone that made me want to check under the covers to see if my pants had been undone.

"Um, no need for that — I can just go?" I suggested, starting to sit up.

"No." she said, freezing me in place with her tone. "I'll not have your Family up in arms for me letting you wander off again — bad enough I've brought you to my home. Now, your name?"

"Noah Ashe, ma'am," I said, settling back in the bed. Maybe I could make a dash for the door later — if I could figure out where the door was.

The view through the window showed we were on an upper floor, maybe third or fourth, so I'd have to find her apartment door, then the stairs, then make it out of the building. Once on the street I could probably lose her.

She took a deep breath, which did interesting things to her figure and made me wonder if being "looked" at was such a bad thing. Maybe looking would lead to more —

"I don't know the Ashes," she said. "Is it a small Family?"

"I don't have a family, ma'am — I was in foster care and just aged out today — yesterday, I guess."

She snorted.

"A likely story — so you've run away, then." She sat back in her chair and crossed her legs. "I know the Families can be a bit stifling, but running off isn't the answer. You'll only get picked up by a rival Family and they'll have to hide you away, which will be even worse. There's no room for you to make your own way these days and you should know that."

She stood up.

"If you won't tell me, then I'll look for myself. Your resonants may tell me which line you come from if nothing else."

I clutched the blanket to keep her from pulling it down and "looking" at me ... but not too tightly, since there seemed to be a better than even chance I'd fallen into some sort of crazy-witch-MILF situation and maybe it wouldn't turn out that badly.

Somewhat to my disappointment she just stared at me.

Her eyes went a bit vacant, as though she was seeing something I couldn't, then they widened and she backed away toward the bedroom door.

"The washroom's there," she finally said, pointing to a door on the wall opposite the bed, then laid her hand on the knob of the door behind her. "I'll wait for you in the kitchen — three floors down."

She opened the door and closed it behind her.

I LIGHTENED my grip on the blanket, not quite sure if I was relieved or disappointed.

The last view I'd gotten of the woman had been of well-shaped hips clad in tight denim, sliding through the bedroom door before it closed behind her.

I slid out of the bed and quickly used the bathroom, wetting my hair a bit to get it under control and scrubbing my teeth with a finger to do something about that. Then I returned to the bedroom.

My backpack was on the floor next to the bed, so I checked my few belongings.

Everything was still there, including my cash, even if the backpack was a little worse for wear. One strap was partially torn away from the body and there was a slice across the back where I guess I'd swung it into the guy's knife somehow. I shuddered at the memory — both of the attack and how it had ended.

I considered slipping out the window — there was a fire escape there — but ... free breakfast? Not a thing someone in my position should turn down.

The woman might be crazy, but she didn't seem particularly dangerous, so I shouldered my backpack and left the bedroom.

I hadn't really caught the implications of her telling me to go down three floors to the kitchen, but exiting the bedroom made me realize this wasn't an apartment, it was the whole building. This entire floor was made up of two bedrooms — I could see the second through an open door — and the stairs in the hallway continued up at least another two floors.

The next floor down had a single, closed door off a much smaller hallway, but the one below that was open with a large dining table at the front and a sitting area at the back. The furniture looked old — antique, even — and expensive. The huge dining table had fourteen chairs around it and one wall held a cabinet with pricey-looking dishes. In the sitting room — I couldn't really call it a living or family room, there were just couches, chairs, and a small piano, no television or anything like that.

The clatter of dishes from the stairway reminded me that I should be heading for that free breakfast instead of snooping through the crazy, witch-MILF's house.

"Coffee's on the counter, dear," the woman called up the stairwell, making me jump and hurry downstairs.

This was the ground floor — I could see the street outside through the front window of a smaller, second dining area that filled that space. The buildings across the street were brownstones — *nice* brownstones, ones that clearly hadn't been carved up into individual apartments like so many had.

What did a whole brownstone in a good neighborhood go for? Two, three million? Maybe more?

*Rich*, crazy, witch-MILF.

I rounded the stairs, which continued down another floor to what I assumed would be a cellar of some sort, to see that the middle of the building here consisted of a modern kitchen with an island facing the stairs and the little entryway from the front door. Beyond that toward the back of the building was something I recognized as a living room, with modern, comfortable couches and chairs, as well as an absurdly large-screen TV mounted on the wall above a cabinet with two gaming consoles, several stacks of games, and a variety of controllers.

The scent of coffee, bacon, and griddled pancakes hit me and set my mouth to drooling.

Rich, crazy, witch-MILF was at the stove with her back to me. She'd added an apron, tied at her lower back, which only served to draw attention to her denim-clad butt and the rest of her figure. Her long, dark hair was now tied up in a loose bun, with tendrils falling across her bare neck and making my fingers itch to play with them.

The island had a single place setting, along with a pot of coffee and a carafe of orange juice set in a bucket of ice.

The woman pulled a cookie sheet of bacon from the oven with one hand while she flipped pancakes on the stove top griddle with the other.

Rich, crazy, witch-MILF who can cook.

I shifted uncomfortably as my jeans suddenly seemed too tight and I hurried to the island to hide myself in case she turned around. I set my backpack on the floor next to my stool and laid my hands on the cool marble, trying to get myself under control as images of bending rich, crazy, witch-MILF over that same counter top filled my head.

*What the hell's wrong with me?* I wondered.

I wasn't a stranger to sudden and awkward erections — I was a teenage guy, after all — but this was ridiculous.

As I tried to get control of myself, the woman set the tray of bacon on a cooling rack and turned around. She froze, staring at me, and her eyes went wide at the same time as what I'd previously experienced as a tingling suddenly became a wave of vibration passing through my body.

That blew my control away completely, and I actually hopped off the stool and started around the island despite mentally screaming, *Hey! What are you doing?* at myself.

The woman stepped back against the stove, gestured abruptly, and the vibration stopped, leaving me staggering at the island's corner.

*What the hell was wrong with me?*

I flushed, breathing heavily, a little scared by what had just happened, and moved back to my stool.

"We'll be working on your shields first, dear," the woman said, turning around and transferring bacon to a plate, then muttered, "And my own, as well, it seems. I've gotten too lazy around the house, no doubt."

She busied herself there with the bacon and pancakes, giving me a moment to calm down, and I noticed she'd stopped talking about some family she had to find and was now talking like I'd be here past breakfast to "work on shields" whatever that was.

"Um, ma'am?" I said when I thought my voice wouldn't crack.

"Yes, dear?"

"I don't know your name."

There was another pause and she chuckled.

"I suppose it's been some time since someone within the Veil hasn't known who I am." She turned around and, thankfully, this time there was no vibration or loss of control. "Melaina Seraphina Blackwood — but you won't recognize the name, will you? You really have grown up outside the Veil." She shook her head. "Just call me Mel, dear."

She brought platters of bacon and pancakes to the island and set them down, which distracted me from wondering what the hell a veil had to do with anything.

"How do you like your eggs, dear?"

"Um, scrambled? If that's okay?"

"Perfectly okay, dear."

"Thanks, um, Mel — and thanks for saving me from the alley yesterday. I mean, I guess that was you?"

"Yes, and you're quite welcome. That was not a nice neighborhood."

I added a couple pancakes to my plate and some bacon — the pancakes were fluffy, with a buttery, crunchy exterior and the bacon was thick-cut, crispy and chewy at the same time. I took a quick bite of bacon while I reached for the syrup.

As I crunched and poured, I heard a rapid thumping paired with jingling and a cat hopped onto the island.

Black, save for a series of white spots along one side, and a pink, belled-collar with a name.

"Felicity?"

# CHAPTER FOUR

"It means 'good fortune,'" Mel said, coming over to the island with a plate of scrambled eggs and scratching Felicity's ears.

The cat purred and rubbed against Mel's fingers.

"But..." I tried, but couldn't find words. There were no brownstones near Alex and Karen's neighborhood — the closest were miles away — and none near the alley I'd been attacked in — not like this neighborhood, at least. How could Felicity be here? "What ... how..."

"It's a name, dear, most things have one."

"But ... that's Felicity! I know her!"

"How's that?"

"She's ... she was the neighborhood cat at my foster home. I've seen her ... two, maybe three, times a week for the last five years. I saw her yesterday! How is she here?"

Mel stopped scratching Felicity's ears and narrowed her eyes.

"Where was this?"

I told her the neighborhood and her eyes narrowed even more.

"Felicity Anne Alden, what is it you've been up to?"

Felicity sat, stuck one hind leg straight up in the air, and began grooming herself inappropriately.

"None of that, young lady! I want an explanation."

I'm not sure if I was more bewildered at how Mel seemed to think Felicity could explain or that Felicity was giving off the sense that she understood perfectly well what was being asked of her, certainly had the capacity to comply with Mel's demand, but had no intention of doing so.

"That's it," Mel said, pointing to the stairs. "Go to your room — you're grounded!"

I stared as Felicity stopped grooming, gave Mel a disdainful look ending with a curled lip to show white, pointed teeth, and hopped off the island to dash up the stairs.

"And no internet!" Mel called after her.

Rich, *very* crazy, witch-MILF, *cat lady* who can cook.

I stared at Mel who continued to glare at the stairwell. Eventually she seemed satisfied and turned back to me.

"You said foster care?"

I nodded. "How close are we to Alex and Karen's? How did Felicity get there?"

"When did you go into foster care?" Mel asked, ignoring my question.

"All my life — but what about —"

"I'm sorry, Noah — I can see there's a lot to explain. And I apologize for Felicity, too. Cats do often have a mind of their own, but I can't imagine what Felicity could have been thinking. She should have told me about you years ago, instead she waited until you were lying injured in an alleyway." She shook her head, frowning.

"Wait ... Felicity brought you to the alley? What do you mean she should have *told* you about me?"

Mel nodded. "She was quite insistent about leading me to that alleyway — wouldn't take no for an answer at all."

"She's a *cat*."

"Very much so," Mel said, then sighed. "Too much so at times. I was hoping to let you finish your breakfast before addressing this, dear, but I can tell that's not going to be possible."

"Address what? That you're led around town by a cat?"

The crazy-part was beginning to outweigh the MILF- and cooking-parts and I started wondering if I could make it out the door before the cat lady did anything more to me. I gave my pancakes a sorrowful glance — they'd soaked up the syrup to the perfect squishy consistency and the surface glistened with butter.

"So let me see if I can explain," Mel said. "You've stumbled into a bit of a hidden world, so to speak." She sighed. "I suppose there's nothing for it but to jump right in — the first premise you'll need to accept is that magic is real."

She paused, waiting.

I was honestly expecting something like that, what with her talking about witches.

"Magic? Like spells and ... stuff?" I asked — maybe if I kept her talking, we could keep the worst of the crazy in a box long enough for me to finish my pancakes.

I took two big bites and started chewing while I waited for her to answer.

"Spells are not the whole of it, but yes. Magic, we call it mana, is power — power that most everyone, everything alive, generates and which permeates everything, but only those within the Veil can make use of. Witches, and warlocks in your case."

"You're telling me I'm a witch?"

Mel nodded. "Warlock is the proper term for males, but, yes, you are, indeed, one of us."

I stuffed two slices of syrup-coated bacon in my mouth and wondered if I could get a go-cup for the coffee. Mel said nothing, so I chewed quicker and swallowed.

"You know how that sounds, right?"

Mel nodded again. "I do. You say you've just aged out of foster care? That makes you eighteen?"

I nodded. "Eighteen today ... well, yesterday," I amended, still adjusting to having lost an entire night from being unconscious.

Mel nodded. "That's generally when witches come into their

power these days. Tell me, have you had any odd experiences over the last few months?"

I did *not* say anything about rich, crazy, witch-MILF, cat ladies who can cook.

"Odd sensations, for instance?"

I stopped with a forkful of pancakes halfway to my mouth.

"Maybe?"

"Unexpected tastes, smells, sounds, physical sensations?"

I started wondering if this was one of those cold-reading, psychic scams I'd seen video of online — where a con artist throws out a bunch of possibilities to see what might stick. I mean, if you asked anyone if they'd had odd tastes, smells, sounds, or physical sensations over a span of months, you'd be bound to hit on something, right?

On the other hand, an eighteen-year-old kid with about a hundred dollars in his backpack wasn't a prime target for con artists, and the doctors hadn't been able to find a cause for my tingling sensations. Plus, Mel's blue eyes were absolutely gorgeous and she was completely focused on me to the point that I just wanted to spend the day staring at her ... and eating bacon.

"The last one?" I admitted, transferring a couple more pieces of bacon to my plate.

Mel nodded.

"That's likely how you're experiencing the absorption of mana."

"Mana?"

"Magical power, as I said. All living things shed a certain amount of mana into the environment. As a warlock, you can absorb that ambient mana — it's not much, which is likely why defending yourself yesterday affected you so much. You had only a bit of mana to begin with. What did you use on that man, by the way? Telly?"

"Telly?" The only telly I knew was that I thought it was what English people called a television.

"Telekinesis. Moving things without touching them."

"You think I can move things with my mind?"

"Not your mind — mana and your will." Mel said, then frowned and shook her head. "No, I see you're not going to believe me without a demonstration." She looked around the room, then shrugged. "I suppose I could use something else but this will be so much more fun."

She held her hand out palm up in my direction and then slowly raised it.

And ... I started floating up into the fucking air.

"What the actual fuck?"

"Magic is real," Mel said simply. "The quicker you accept that, the quicker I'll let you down and we can move on to more important things."

The room's ceilings weren't that high, so I was just a couple feet off the floor and the same from the ceiling. I twisted around, trying to see where the wires were — that had to be it, right? She'd trained the cat to distract me, then attached wires to my ... what the hell would she have attached wires to? I was floating — I couldn't even feel pressure on my feet or on my butt from sitting, much less some kind of wiring harness.

"Would you like to spin upside down?" Mel asked. "It can be quite a head rush — especially if I bounce you up and down a bit."

"No!" I said quickly, trying to wrap my head around how I could possibly be floating in midair, but absolutely certain I didn't want to be bounced up and down.

"How about..." Mel gestured with her other hand and a glowing red orb formed there before streaking straight for my face.

"*Argh!*" I screamed, trying to twist out of the way, but the orb adjusted its course and ... blasted right through me to disappear into the wall.

"That's a glamour," Mel said. "An illusion. I can also do an actual fireball if you like."

She was a witch ... a real witch, so of course she'd want to throw a fireball right up front — and I did accept that she was a witch. At least that magic was real, because I didn't have any other explanation for the very obvious fact that I was floating around her kitchen.

"All right! All right! I get it. I believe you. Put me down, please."

"Good boy," Melaina said.

She narrowed her eyes and her lips quirked.

"You're thinking of dropping me on my ass, aren't you?"

Mel sighed. "It's no fun if you're expecting it."

She lowered her palm and my body followed suit until my feet touched the floor again.

I swallowed hard and grasped the counter top — just in case she decided to repeat things, I wanted something solid to hang onto.

"There," Mel said, "wasn't that more effective than me making some dishes fly around the room?"

My knees shook a little bit as I got used to the idea. Sure, I guess it could've been a trick but I really had been floating, so that would be one hell of a trick.

"Yeah, that was effective," I agreed.

No matter what I'd believed in before, I suddenly believed in magic.

Mel smiled.

# CHAPTER FIVE

Mel was silent for a time, letting me think about what she'd just shown me. I didn't look at her, just stared down at the remnants of my breakfast, appetite gone — not because I was upset, far from it. I was confused, but also a little excited — after all, I'd just found out magic was real and, presumably, I could work magic?

Yeah, I accepted it pretty fast, I guess, but what else could I do? I certainly had no explanation for floating in the air. Mel hadn't said anything about me leaving — and the food was good, so why not run with it? This was certainly a better place to stay than any of the shelters.

So, I could either call her a liar and run or stick around and find out more. Even if she was tricking me somehow, what's the worst that could happen?

I mean, aside from being ritually sacrificed to summon a demon or some shit?

The possibility that *I* was the crazy one also occurred to me. I'd been mugged and hit my head on the pavement, right? This could all be some coma-hallucination while I lay in an ER somewhere. But what was the downside of acting like I believed it anyway? I'd either wake up or not ... and I could think of worse ways to spend a coma than fantasizing about a beautiful MILF-witch making me breakfast.

I looked down at the remnants of perfectly crisped bacon and fluffy pancakes.

*Fuck it. Magic or the street?*

"What makes you think I'm a warlock?" I asked finally.

Before answering, Mel poured herself a cup of coffee and gestured at me with the pot.

"Yeah, thanks," I said, grabbing my cup and holding it out for a refill. I was rather proud to see my hand wasn't even shaking.

There was cream and sugar next to the pot, but I felt the need for something strong and bracing.

"Come, let's sit," Mel said, nodding toward the living room.

I followed her there.

The room was arranged with a couch along one wall, a big screen TV, one of the biggest I'd ever seen, on the other, and two chairs set to either side of the couch with a low table in the middle. A cabinet under the television had two game consoles on it. It was hard to picture Mel as a gamer.

Mel took one of the chairs, so I took the other, then she kicked off her slippers and curled up in the chair with her coffee cup cradled against her legs.

"Where to start?" she murmured.

I blew on my coffee, took a sip, and waited. I'd asked one question, but didn't know enough to ask any others. I figured Mel was the expert and I could wait until she'd explained what she thought I should know before asking any more questions.

"Before I get into the details of magic itself, let's talk about what it means to be a warlock," she said finally. "How much do you think you know about witches?"

"Well, we read *The Crucible* last year in English class ... oh, and I saw the movie with those three girls."

Mel sighed.

"So, first, forget everything you think you know about witches.

It's nothing like what you've read in the history books, the fiction books, or seen in the movies. Have you heard of a coven?"

"That's like a group of witches?"

"Thirteen witches." She nodded. "And one warlock."

"Why just one warlock?"

"That will require a bit of history to fully understand, dear, but mostly because warlocks are quite rare and the ratio was, at one time, roughly thirteen to one. That and the moon's cycle drove the structure of covens."

"So, I'm rare? Cool."

Of course, if you're going to have a coma-hallucination, you should be special in it.

Mel chuckled.

"Quite rare, dear. More so than just any warlock, but we'll get to that later." She sipped her coffee, so I took the opportunity to drink some too — it was really good. "Now, I've mentioned mana — that's what we call the power that lets us do magic. It's generated by most living things to one degree or another, and it's done so by what we feel."

"Feel?"

"Yes, emotions, physical sensations, that sort of thing. The mana generated by each has a certain aspect to it that makes it more useful for certain types of magic. Do you follow?"

"Maybe?"

"Let me give you an example. If I were to, say, feel sad, then my body would generate mana with that attribute, does that make sense?"

I nodded and sipped my coffee.

"Mana generated by sadness is most often associated with water magic — likely a connection to tears."

"So a witch feels sad and she can do better water magic?"

Mel nodded.

"Yes, however it's not the same for each witch. I could make very little use of mana generated by sadness, because each witch has what we call resonants — types of mana which resonate with them, which they're attuned to, and each witch has between one and three of these. Sadness is not one of mine."

That made some sense, but it must suck for someone to have to be sad in order to do magic. Hopefully there were some better — what did she call them? Resonants?

I wanted to ask if she could tell how many of those I had and what mine were, but stuck by my decision to let Mel tell things in her own way.

"Two resonants is the most common," she said, "then one, which many consider a very weak witch and is not at all the case, and the rarest is three — there are, I think, only a dozen or two *trinitara* witches alive today. *Trinitara* is what we call those with three resonants."

She sipped her coffee.

"Now, if a witch had the Sadness resonant and experienced sadness, then she would be able to store the mana produced for later — we call this a resonant store, in fact — but if she doesn't have that resonant, then that power associated with the emotion is only available to her for a fleeting instance after it's generated, then —" She flung the fingers of one hand at the ceiling. "— *poof*, it's spun off into the environment and gone. That's what you've been feeling — that physical sensation you've been having? What is it, by the way?"

"Um, sort of ... tingling, I guess."

"Is it unpleasant?"

"No, it, um, feels kind of good, honestly."

"Good. The more mana there is to absorb, the stronger that sensation will be. It's an unhappy witch whose resonants or perception of mana are unpleasant."

"Wait," I said. Something didn't make sense, so I had to ask a question. "You said the tingling I've been feeling was me absorbing that ... floating mana —"

"Ambient."

"Fine, ambient mana, but if a witch can absorb it back and use it, can't they just keep absorbing what they produce? Why do these resonant things matter?"

"Ah, good question, and it brings us to one of the fundamental differences between witches and warlocks. Witches cannot absorb ambient mana, only warlocks can; and, warlocks do not generate mana, only witches do. Well, you do generate a bit, but very little — just enough to keep yourself alive and maintain some very basic shields. And the ambient mana isn't much more for you, unless you encounter someone who's feeling something particularly strongly and shedding a great deal of it, that is."

"So, warlocks are, what? Magic janitors?" I wasn't feeling so special now. "I'm supposed to run around cleaning up all the waste magic?"

Mel grinned. "No, you're of more use than that. So, the coven's warlock, through the magic that binds the coven together, can take mana from the coven's witches, increase it, roughly threefold, and then return it to the coven's high priestess, who then uses it to perform the coven's rituals."

"Oh, rituals, I've heard about those..."

I thought about what I'd heard and wondered if I might be into something bad here. I set my cup on the table slowly and wet suddenly dry lips. I wondered if I could make it to the front door if I needed to.

"What's wrong, dear?" Mel asked.

"These rituals ... is that, um, the Satan thing? Because —"

Mel sighed heavily.

"No, it is not the 'Satan thing'. I told you to forget everything you thought you knew about witches, so you decide to remember the 'Satan-thing'?"

"But —"

"Witches do not worship Satan. Or summon demons. That was a vile slander perpetrated by small-minded fools who saw a coven perform a ritual and insisted it had to be something evil."

It seemed to me that this was exactly what someone doing the Satan-thing would say. "Do you worship anything?"

"The Goddess," Mel said, her mouth fell a little. "In her four aspects. None of which, I assure you, are Satan."

I was still a little skeptical, but willing to hear her out.

"Okay — so no Satan worshiping or demon summoning. Do you summon anything?"

"Warlocks."

"What?"

"A coven's summoning ritual is to summon a warlock. That's what the fools saw and decided it was Satan." She sighed. "Imagine, it's 1610 and you're a witch in a small village. You somehow manage to find twelve other witches from the surrounding villages, but there's not a warlock in sight? At least none you know of. What do you do?"

"Summon one?" I guessed.

"Exactly. The forming coven rushes off to the nearest Grove and, together, use all their power to summon a warlock. One who's nearby feels the call and finds them. He joins the coven and it is complete. Nothing at all nefarious or satanic about it."

I guess that made sense. If witches were rare, and it seemed they'd have to be, otherwise they'd be running everything and not need to keep it a secret, right? So if warlocks were even rarer, then having to summon one with magic made sense. Not like they could post a personals ad on the internet or something back in the 1600s.

"Wow. So, how'd they get Satan out of that? Just not liking a bunch of girls alone in the woods?"

Mel looked away, cleared her throat, and scratched at her neck.

"There ... may be one other reason warlocks are wanted by a coven."

"What?"

"Making little witches."

"Oh."

"Exactly. You see, witches and mundanes — that's what we call people who aren't witches — cannot have children together. Only a witch and a warlock can do that."

It took me a moment to get it — hey, I'd been knocked unconscious the day before and had a lot thrown at me all of a sudden. I was a little slow.

"Wait ... so the warlock —"

Mel closed her eyes. "Yes."

"With all —"

Mel sighed. "Yes."

"*Thirteen* —"

Mel held up her hand. "Yes, please stop, dear. Yes, the warlock typically has sex with all thirteen witches of the coven. Frequently, in fact, as that's typically the way mana is transferred from witch to warlock and back again. That and to increase the chances of a child. Witches have an extremely low birthrate — children are rare and cherished."

This was turning out to be one of the better coma-hallucinations possible, honestly.

"Please wipe that grin off your face," Mel said.

"Sorry, I —"

"It's alright, I understand. You are a young man, after all."

"I still don't see how they get from that to Satan?"

"At the time, it was not encouraged to be an unmarried woman, especially with child; nor was it acceptable to be a man with thirteen wives."

"Oh."

"You see, the witches would still take mundane husbands in the villages — often men they truly did love, quite separately from their coven and warlock — but none of the children would be his. They must sneak away on ritual nights to join the coven, and if a husband were to follow and see ... well, they preferred to think they were cuckolded by Satan rather than Joseph the pig farmer two villages north. Do you see?"

"Yes ... but what about the goat thing?"

"The *what?*"

I cleared my throat, a little regretful I'd mentioned it because of her tone. But I'd seen the movies. "The dude with the goat-head in all the movies. Isn't he —"

Mel set her coffee down, put her head in her hands, and rubbed her temples.

"It was *one* coven — *one*, and fifteen centuries later we *still* hear about it," she muttered, then sighed. "Look, it was a costume. The warlock for that particular coven had a goat costume."

"Um, why?"

"In all times, in all places, some people have had certain ... proclivities. Witches are no different."

I didn't like where this was going.

"Have you ever heard of furries?"

# CHAPTER SIX

"So, then," Mel said, uncurling from her seat and sitting up. "Would you like to begin exploring your own magic, now that I've assured you I'm not leading you down the path to darkness and damnation?"

To be honest, I wasn't entirely sure she wasn't, since I only had her word that there were no Satans or demons or real goat-dudes involved, but I did want to know more.

I nodded and Mel stood up, grabbing her cup of coffee, so I did as well, and she led me back to the stairs and down into the brownstone's basement.

The basement was deeper than I expected, with three flights of stairs before we reached the bottom, which was an open space that must have run the full width and length of the building. The walls were rough stone and the floor was old, worn cobblestones, but the open part at the back was covered in cushioned puzzle mats. Lights lined the walls, leaving the space well-lit, — well enough that I could immediately see there was a circle carved deeply into the mats covering the rear half of the space, with only a couple feet between the circle and the side and back walls. The other half of the space contained shelving and benches with boxes, jars, and cloth wrapped packages, and behind that I saw a maze of pipes and wires.

Mel walked to the rear of the basement, entering the circle and gesturing for me to follow.

I looked around carefully, but didn't see any of those five-pointed stars or anything, so stepped into the circle as well.

"Have a seat at the center, while I set the wards."

I did as she said, lowering myself to sit cross-legged on the mats.

Mel touched her finger to the circle and I noticed it was lined with something silvery. She muttered something, then joined me on the floor, sitting just a few inches away from me.

"What are wards? I don't see anything."

"You will in a moment — that's the first step." She put her hands over her head and stretched, pulling the fabric of her top tightly against her, and I noticed immediately that she wasn't wearing a bra — something made far more obvious by the slight chill in the basement compared to the rooms upstairs. I again wondered what was going on with me — it was the sort of thing I might normally notice, but not as forcefully as I did now. It was as if I had to drag my eyes away from her chest.

"Should I stretch too?" I asked, trying to distract myself.

"Only if you like — I'm simply getting comfortable."

I didn't say that her getting comfortable was making me decidedly uncomfortable.

"Now, close your eyes."

*Thank you,* I thought. I'd been wondering how I was going to concentrate on magic with those hard little bumps staring at me.

"Now stretch out your senses. Think about what you're hearing, feeling, tasting, smelling, seeing —"

"My eyes are closed."

"Yes, but many see mana for the first time with their eyes closed. Fewer distractions."

I nodded — there would definitely be distractions if I opened my eyes.

I concentrated on my senses one by one.

I tasted ... coffee and bacon remnants, which was nice, but not anything unusual.

The basement smelled — not musty, but of earth and stone. Maybe a bit of oil? Was there a boiler?

I tried concentrating on what I was seeing, but it was just the inside of my eyelids.

I must have sighed or made some sound of frustration, because Mel said, "Just relax, dear. Concentrate on what you're sensing, but don't try to force it. Your goal should be to become comfortable with the space and relaxed."

Her voice was very soothing and I thought I might like to sit here for a while just listening to her talk.

I thought I caught sight of a blue glow out of the corner of my eye, but every time I turned my head or moved my eyeballs to look closer, it disappeared.

"Slowly, calmly," Mel said, her voice almost hypnotic. "Wait for it to come to you."

The next time I thought I saw a glow, I stayed still, kept my focus where it was, and the glow grew. Suddenly, like flipping a light switch, the darkness behind my eyelids went blue — a brilliant blue with streaks of white, like lightning crackling across its surface. I realized it was a dome sitting over us, its edges following the carved circle.

"Holy shit!"

"You see something?"

"A big blue dome over us!"

"Those are the circle's wards," Mel said. "It extends below us as well, and keeps us safe within the circle."

"Wouldn't that be a globe instead of a circle?"

"Noah." Mel said, warningly.

"I'm just saying —"

"Do you correct people's grammar on the Internet too? It's been called a circle for thousands of years; we're not going to change the name for you."

"Fine."

"Now, look at me," Mel said.

I did and was nearly shocked into opening my eyes.

Mel was naked.

Well, not naked-naked — more like a bare mannequin. The blue glow and streaks of lightning covered her as well, but like a skintight suit, maybe a wetsuit, that showed her figure but not the details. Even her hair was covered in the same blue-white, but not as individual strands — more like a comic book or video game that drew characters' hair in wide shapes.

"What happened to your clothes?" I asked without thinking.

Then I realized something else I'd heard about witches. I'd asked Mel about Satans, demons, and the goat-guy, but I'd also heard witches were into orgies. Was she naked because there was going to be an orgy? There were only the two of us down here, so could two people have an orgy? Honestly, if there were to be orgies, would that be so bad? I might even be willing to accept a little Satan if it came with a side of orgies. Not the goat ... probably not the goat, but Mel was pretty hot, so —

"I'm not naked," Mel said, giving me a little twinge of disappointment. "What you're seeing are my personal shields, and it's not practical to make them look like clothing, so we just ... cover ourselves."

I didn't think she was really that covered.

Then I wondered what my shields looked like, so glanced down at myself, but I had none. Where my body was supposed to be, was just a sort of shadow — I managed to stop myself from asking why I looked different when I remembered my own shields were on the list of things I had to learn.

"Now I'm going to lower my shields," Mel said. "There'll be two differences — first, you'll be able to see the mana I'm producing and storing; second, I'll be shedding even more of the mana I don't resonate with and you'll be able to start absorbing that."

"Okay."

The blue-white glow around Mel disappeared and was replaced by multiple bright colors and sparkles. Her left side, head to toe, glowed a bright, bubble-gum pink, while her left was a crimson red. Her torso, except for strips of those colors around her sides, glowed grey.

Yes, I know grey doesn't glow, but this did — like a dark steel reflecting light.

Around those colors sparked a dozen others, little dots and threads of colors that appeared, disappeared, and floated away from her body.

Those that floated away from her seemed to be drawn to me, coming closer and closer until they touched and my skin began tingling. Where they touched, their colors changed, becoming a warm yellow that sank into the shadows that filled my form.

"What do you see?" Mel asked.

I described the sparkling and how the colors changed as they touched me.

"What are the bags?" I asked.

"Bags?"

I shrugged. That was the best description I could come up with for the colors filling her. It was like big bags of colored paint stuffed into her shape, filling everything.

"You have these three colors filling you, like bags of paint or colored water or something."

"Oh, those are my mana stores. The size of those indicate how powerful a witch is."

Given that there seemed to be no room left in Mel for those to expand, she must have been pretty powerful. I remembered what she'd said about witches having between one and three of those.

"So, you're one of those, what, tri...?"

"*Trinitaras*, and, yes."

"Oh." I guess that made Mel really powerful, as witches went, and rare. "What do the colors mean?"

"You're seeing different types of mana, different emotions and sensations, as different colors. The change in color you described as you absorb the mana is the refinement I mentioned. You should be filling your own mana stores from that — slowly, since mana loses a great deal of its potency when it's shed."

I turned my attention back to my own shadowy form.

"Why don't I have —" I stopped, noticing something. Deep in my gut were three shapes, about the size of eggs — no, their size was more like those tiny Easter egg chocolates — darker than the shadows that seemed to fill me, but each had a tiny bit of the yellow glow. Not filling them, not even close, even as small as the eggs were — just like they contained a drop, less than a drop, of yellow-colored water. I described it to Mel. "Is that my resonant things?"

"Yes," she confirmed.

"They're ... pretty small..."

Mel laughed.

"Resonants are like muscles, dear — the more you use them, the bigger and stronger they grow. You'll need to absorb enough to fill and stretch them on a regular basis if you want to have more power — and you will want to have more power, trust me."

I nodded. That made sense. I was like a baby warlock, after all, so it was reasonable I'd have just a bit of power. Mel's, on the other hand, looked like she had no more room at all to increase their size.

"How long until I can work up to yours? I mean, your bags are huge."

Mel said nothing.

"Oh, sorry ... I didn't think of how that sounded. I meant your ... mana stores? Not huge bags or anything. They're not huge at all." I paused. "Not that your bags are small," I added quickly. "They're really nice, really, and not —"

"Noah, dear?"

"Um, yeah."

"One of the most important lessons a young man should learn is when to stop talking."

I thought it best to simply nod and keep my mouth shut, especially because Mel appeared to literally have more magic in her little finger than I had in my entire body.

"You see that you have three mana stores?" Mel asked after letting the silence stretch just to the edge of uncomfortable.

"Um, yeah. So, I'm a ... *trinitara*, too?"

"Yes, and that's the reason I was a bit shocked earlier. *Trinitara* warlocks are very rare, even rarer than it is in witches. It's something that makes you special ... but also puts you in a bit of danger."

Of course it did. You certainly couldn't find out witches were real and you had magic without being in danger. No Universe, real or coma-dream, would allow that.

"How?"

"I think we should talk about that later, after we're done here in the circle. You'll be safe here with me for a time, so it's nothing you need to worry about immediately, and you'll be better protected once you have shields of your own."

Part of me wanted to know what the danger was, but another part, mostly the butt cheek that was perched on a slightly higher cobblestone, noticeable even through the thick mat, wanted to get the magic stuff done here so we could move to a nice soft couch.

"Okay," I said.

"Good. Now, first, we'll want to find out what your resonants are. Though you can absorb mana of any type and refine it, you'll gain more from those you resonate with. I'm going to start shedding mana of different types — it won't be as strong as it could be, because I'll have to sort of simulate the emotions and sensations, but it will hopefully help us identify your resonants."

"How will I know? I mean, I'm already absorbing stuff and it's tingling."

Mel chuckled.

"Oh, you'll know. It will be a much stronger sensation and your resonant stores will start filling faster."

I thought about what I'd felt when I came downstairs and my

whole body had vibrated when Mel turned around. Is that what she meant? What resonant would she have been throwing off then?

"Alright," Mel said, "let's get started."

For the next several minutes, sparkling threads of a couple dozen colors and shades flowed from Mel to me. She didn't describe what each one was, we just waited for one of them to resonate with me, but the tingling sensation stayed the same.

"Hmph," Mel said after a time. "I'm running out of what I can reasonably fake." She took a deep breath. "There are a couple more I can try, but it will be harder."

"Why?"

"They're my own, so I'll have to suppress storing them. None of a witch's own resonants are shed — unless she's experiencing something very intense and she's unable to store it all."

"Oh."

"Now a witch's resonants are a rather personal thing, Noah. Even mine aren't widely known, so if you learn one of mine, will you keep it a secret?"

"Sure." I didn't see why I wouldn't.

"Thank you. Give me a moment." Mel's figure shifted and she held one hand out in a fist a few inches from the floor. "Alright —"

Mel wrapped her knuckles hard on the cobblestone and threads of crimson red flowed from her hand. Without thinking, I reached out to them, my hand jerked as they touched it and set off a vibration far stronger than tingling. The red sparked and slowly changed to yellow as it entered me and streamed directly toward one of my egg-shaped resonant stores.

"Yeah!" I said. "Definitely that one. A *lot* stronger sensation."

Mel was silent for a moment. "Are you certain?"

She was rubbing her hand and more red threads streamed toward me.

"Yes, why?"

"That was Pain," Mel said. "Physical Pain — there are other kinds."

That didn't sound fun.

"So, what? I have to get hurt to work magic?" Not fun at all.

"No, Noah," Mel answered softly, "you don't need to feel the pain. The witch does."

"Oh."

I hadn't put that together, but as soon as she said it, I also recognized the implications of her having that resonant and its store being as full as hers was.

"Don't think it's so terrible, dear. Witches find better ways of filling their resonants than you might think at first, especially once the coven-bond begins working on them. But Pain *is* a difficult one — we'll discuss possibilities later, if you like. For now, we should probably get some lunch and pick this up again later."

I didn't want to do that. I now knew one of my three resonants, but it wasn't one I was happy with. I'd much rather end this session with a bit of good news — or, at least, know I shared neither of Mel's remaining resonants.

"I'd kind of like to check the other two," I said.

"My other two?"

"Yeah. I mean, it would be good to know, at least, right?"

Mel took a deep breath. "Very well. It's doubtful we share more than the one, but —"

This time she didn't move — she just sat there and a stream of bubble-gum pink threads streamed off her. I didn't reach out my hand this time, but the threads seemed to make a beeline for me. The effect was the same as before — a strong vibration, maybe stronger than the last time.

"Wow," I said. "That one too."

Mel was silent and still for a long time.

"Um, so what was that one?" I asked finally, worried at how long she'd been silent. How much worse than Pain could this one be?

"That was Lust," Mel said, finally.

Now it was my turn to be quiet.

Lust was ... interesting? And embarrassing.

"So —"

"Don't puff your ego up too soon, dear," Mel said, clearly laughing. "It doesn't have to be *you* the witch lusts after."

"Oh."

"Though it is one of the easier ones to satisfy."

I could see that.

"Or," Mel added, "at least fill, if not satisfy."

I really hoped she had her eyes closed like I did, because my face went red hot.

"So? Now can we have some lunch?"

"What about the other one? The grey one."

Mel chuckled. "That one's unlikely. Extremely so."

"Why? Is it like a female-thing?"

"No, it's not a 'female-thing'." Mel groaned. "Fine, it's quite impossible for you to have that resonant, but I suppose you won't leave it alone if you don't see for yourself." She settled herself. "I'll need you to take the lead in testing this one."

"How?"

"Tell me to do something."

"What?"

"Anything — something simple. Just tell me to do something. Firmly and with intent."

"Um, okay." I wasn't getting it, but went along "Raise your right hand, I guess?"

"Don't ask, dear, tell."

"Okay — raise your right hand," I said firmly.

Mel did. "Keep going, another one." she said.

"Ah, scratch your nose."

Mel did, and I saw steel-grey threads drifting off her and toward me. She made a go-on gesture.

"Clap your hands."

I chuckled as she did. "Should I be saying 'Simon says —'"

I broke off and gasped as the grey threads touched me and an intense electrical jolt ran through my body.

"Argh. That's the strongest yet!"

"That's imp ... are you certain?" Mel's voice was concerned.

"Yeah — definitely. What was that?"

Mel said nothing, then, "Noah, how did you defend yourself in that alley?"

I frowned, wondering what that had to do with it and why she sounded so concerned.

"I don't think I did."

"You did. The alley fairly reeked of mana. What did you do, or say, before the mugger stopped attacking you?"

I shrugged, trying to remember.

"I yanked my backpack away from him ... then I swung it at him ... I think I yelled something like, 'Get away from me', maybe?"

"And when did you start to feel weak and fall down?"

"Right at the end, I guess."

"When you yelled, 'Get away from me'?"

"I guess — why? What is that and what does it mean?"

"That resonant is Control," Mel said. "Witches generate it when they're ... obedient, I guess would be the best description."

"What does that have to do with the guy in the alley?"

"Resonants come with affinities — that's what we call the type of magic a witch, warlock, is most powerful and skilled at." She took a deep breath. "I mentioned Sadness and water magic, for instance, and a witch with the Anger resonant often has an affinity for fire magic."

"Okay, but —"

"Command is an affinity associated with the Control resonant — it's the ability to compel others to obey ... and why you're in even greater danger than I first thought."

# CHAPTER SEVEN

"I normally have just a sandwich for lunch," Mel said.

We were back in the kitchen — I was sitting at the island again and Mel was at the fridge.

After telling me that I was in great danger, she'd stood up and said she'd explain over lunch — and, to tell the truth, I was hungry myself. My stomach growled as though I'd been physically working hard all morning instead of sitting in a basement. I followed her back upstairs. Still, she seemed to be taking my great danger a bit lightly.

"That's fine with me," I said, not really caring as long as it was food, and wanting to hurry up and get to the explanation.

"Turkey or roast beef?" Mel asked, leaning into the fridge, which left me with the sight of her hips and legs as she bent over. Even though I was still seeing her shields, the mannequin-smooth curves were distracting — maybe more so. Mel had told me how to turn it off, but it was so new and cool I didn't want to yet.

"Um, turkey?" I said, trying to tear my eyes and concentration away from her.

She closed the fridge after setting some things on the counter beside it and looked at me. I tried to get my eyes to hers, but I think she caught what I'd been staring at, because she raised one eyebrow and chuckled.

"Those of us with more than one resonant try to keep them balanced," she said, pulling things from the cabinets and bringing them to the island — a couple sealed containers from the fridge, lettuce, tomato, mayonnaise, and a loaf of bread, along with plates and utensils. "If not, whichever resonant is fullest tends to drive our emotions."

She took a slice of turkey from one of the containers — real turkey, sliced thick, and not prepackaged deli slices — along with a large knife, and began dicing some of the turkey into small chunks. As she did that, the implications of what she'd said hit me and I took a closer look at my own mana stores. There was only a tiny bit of mana glowing in each, but the one that had taken in the bubble-gum pink strands was the brightest, containing, maybe, twice as much as the others.

So that must have been what was making me some kind of horny, lust-monkey? My Lust resonant was influencing me somehow? What would the others do if they were fuller?

"I'll teach you how to even things out after we finish work on your shields later."

Mel scooped the diced turkey up with her hand and the knife and dumped it on a plate — she made a quick gesture over it and the scent of warm turkey filled the kitchen, making my mouth water. Then she set the plate at the end of the island and made another gesture.

"Felicity, lunch is ready — and I understand now."

She turned back to me.

"Now, to explain why you're in danger."

She took the bread from its plastic bag and cut four thick slices from it.

"Before Salem, the traditional coven structure worked as well as it could, but —"

"Salem?"

I heard a door close upstairs as Mel put some mayonnaise and what looked like cranberry sauce into a bowl and started mixing it.

"The Trials."

Padding footsteps rushed down the stairs and Felicity trotted over to hop up on the island. She sniffed once at the plate of turkey, then turned her back on us, sat, and stared away with only the tip of her tail twitching. I saw now that Felicity had shields as well and wondered if animals could do magic or if Mel had put them there.

"Yes, Felicity," Mel said, spreading the mayonnaise and cranberry onto the bread. "I understand now why you didn't tell me about him earlier and I apologize."

"*Mrowr.*"

"No," Mel said. "I don't believe I'll apologize for that, since I did give you a chance to explain and you refused."

"*Pfft!*"

"I was not short with you — well, perhaps a bit." She started slicing the tomato. "But you could have told me when you dragged me off to pick him up and saved us all a bit of trouble."

"Mrowr."

"Yes, I'm sure my reaction *was* amusing — but if you play tricks on people and they become annoyed, you have no one to blame but yourself."

"Pfft," Felicity said, but then bent her head to begin shredding her turkey with tiny, white fangs.

"You can talk to her?" I asked.

"Of course, dear," Mel said, laying lettuce and tomato on the sandwiches.

"So, she's, like, your familiar or somet —"

"*Ppfffttt!*"

"Whoa! What'd I say?"

"No," Mel said as though the cat hadn't just hissed at me like she'd like to rip my throat out. "Felicity and I are ... whatever Felicity decides we are on any given day, I suppose. But *not* my familiar — she's rather more independent than that."

"Um, you grounded her." That didn't sound very independent.

Mel shrugged. "If she insists on acting like a rebellious teenager, then she gets treated like one."

"But she can understand us?"

"Oh, yes."

For some reason, that was almost harder to accept than magic existing in the first place, but I made a note to talk to Felicity alone soon. If she really could understand us, I wanted to thank her for being there for me all those years ... and ask her not to tell Mel some of the things I'd shared with her. I'd said some pretty private things to the damn cat, thinking she couldn't tell anyone.

And then I had to blink a couple times at how quickly I'd accepted all this, even a cat who could understand speech.

"Back to what I was explaining," Mel said. "After Salem things actually started to improve for witches. The mundanes eventually tried to deny the horrors they're capable of by writing Salem off to fanatics and hysteria — of course, in order to do so they had to deny our existence as well. The number of clearly innocent women who were killed there ... well, I suppose it made people look at things differently.

"In addition, the New World was very different than the Old. In Europe, privacy was a privilege of the nobility, you see. In the Americas, it was the privilege of the rich. Witches don't have to live in isolated forest huts, you know, we're quite capable of earning a great deal of money.

"Now, a farmer or woodsman can't have thirteen wives, but a wealthy man, the owner of a large estate? He might have his wife, her unmarried sisters and his, perhaps their daughters, and any number of servants — all roles which could be played by the witches of his coven, or come from another to visit, leaving the neighbors and busybodies none the wiser about what goes on."

She finished assembling the sandwiches, made a gesture over them, and slid one to me.

"So, the Families were formed. Rather than one coven being the basic structure, Families formed multiple, cooperative covens, primarily of relations. It was simply easier to transfer the wealth around as necessary and give everyone the protection from mundanes they needed."

I took a bite of my sandwich, surprised to find the turkey was warm, while the lettuce and tomato were still crisp and cold. The spread was more like a sauce — warmed by the turkey and filling my mouth with flavor.

"This is really good," I mumbled around a mouthful — pretty sure it was the best sandwich, maybe the best anything, I'd ever had.

"Thank you, dear." Mel took a bite of her own and swallowed quickly. "The transition to focus on Families had an additional effect, because covens are inherently hierarchical due to the coven bindings — at least twelve of the witches are bound to the warlock, while the warlock may either mark the high priestess or be marked by her."

"Mark?"

"It's a sort of —" Mel shrugged and took another bite of her sandwich. "Well, firstly it's an actual mark — the witches' mark you hear about witch hunters looking for?"

I nodded. I think that had been in *The Crucible.*

"Like birthmarks?"

"Sometimes that's the appearance, yes. It's deeper than just a mark, though. It's a bond between the witch and warlock. A *permanent* bond, and it's what allows the witch and warlock to exchange mana more easily."

I frowned. "Didn't we just —"

"No, dear, that was just ambient mana, not an exchange. An exchange is much ... deeper. Far more intimate."

"Okay — wait, you said permanent? Like marriage, then?"

Mel chuckled. "Marriages can be dissolved, dear, the coven bond is quite literally permanent. Literally literally, not the more common usage these days."

"Oh."

"Yes. Now if the warlock marks all the witches in the coven, then the coven is independent, but if one witch marks the *warlock* then she is the sole high priestess — and yet she is still vulnerable to being marked by another warlock, creating a hierarchy of covens."

I thought about that while Mel chewed another bite of her sandwich. "So, witches have to make a decision whether you want to be independent or part of some hierarchy?"

"It's rarely a decision — at least these days. The marking process itself is an instinctual struggle for dominance, but the Families have taken to planning out their covens with an eye toward that hierarchy. You see, a warlock can give all of a coven's power to the high priestess for a ritual, but if *she's* bound to another warlock, then he can take that power from her and give it to *his* high priestess — and thus, up the chain, to the head coven of the Family."

I chewed slowly. "So, it's a pyramid scheme?"

Mel's brow furrowed and she said nothing as she went to the fridge and returned with two cans of soda, handing me one.

"I'm sorry, this is all we have — it's Felicity's favorite and I really don't have a preference." She took a small bowl and poured some of the soda, setting the bowl next to the cat's plate. "I'll add whatever you prefer to the grocery order."

"This is fine," I said, pondering both the implication that she expected me to be here long enough to need groceries and the sight of a cat lapping up strawberry soda with her rapidly moving pink tongue.

Mel nodded. "A pyramid scheme is not the worst way to describe it, actually. Not to say that all the covens don't benefit from the arrangement to some degree — the Families have a great deal of resources — but most of the power does flow to those at the top."

"Okay, so how does that put me in danger?"

"In three ways: First, as an unmarked warlock, all of the Families will want to add you to their hierarchy — willingly or unwillingly; second, as a *trinitara* warlock, they will want you even more; and, lastly, having the Control resonant with a Command affinity, some will desperately want to obtain that power for their own use ... while others will want to simply kill you."

Mel calmly took another bite of her sandwich, as though she hadn't just described someone wanting to murder me.

"Kill me?"

"Think about it, dear. You have the power to compel others to obey you — likely only mundanes at this point, as you're young and untrained, but with time and growth any witch whose shields you can penetrate and whose will you can overcome will be vulnerable to you. The Families who know they couldn't take and keep you will want to ensure no one else does."

I swallowed hard and pushed my plate aside, losing my appetite.

"That's why Felicity was right not to tell me about you earlier," Mel went on. "My first instinct would have been to bring you here to keep you safe, but ... that would not have done so. I wouldn't have been able to keep others from finding out about you for years ... I'm not a hermit, and wouldn't want to force you to be one." She shook her head. "No, until you came into your power and could shield yourself, it was best for you to remain where you were. Witches aren't entirely insular, but the odds of one crossing your path while you were living as any other mundane and her bothering to look closely enough at you to tell you were a warlock were slim until you came into your power and began absorbing mana. Now it's embarrassingly obvious what you are."

"So, once I learn these shields, I'll be safe?" I asked, feeling a little better.

"No, dear. Somewhat, but not entirely. Even if you can hide your resonants and that you're a *trinitara*, you're still an unmarked warlock and quite valuable for that alone." Mel picked up our plates, seeing that I wasn't eating more, and took them to the sink. "Now, you might wish to join a Family — if so, I can make some introductions for you. What the life lacks in freedom for a warlock it more than makes up for in luxury."

"How's that? What 'lacks in freedom'?"

"Family warlocks don't generally leave the estates. They're kept ... protected."

The pause before "protected" didn't encourage me.

"A Family warlock's duties," Mel went on, "are to harvest mana from his coven and pass it up the chain. Very little else. It's not an onerous or time-consuming job, I suppose, but they do have considerably less freedom than the witches."

"I don't think I'd like that," I said. I'd had enough of being controlled in the foster system — now, as an adult, I was kind of looking forward to doing whatever the hell I wanted without curfews and bedchecks.

Despite this warlock job being to "harvest" mana and Mel telling me that mana exchange was typically done through sex, if I was going to be harvesting power that way it seemed like it should be used by me and my coven — not sent up the chain to some kind of Herbalife executive.

Mel nodded. "Most who weren't raised in the Families wouldn't like it, I think. There are the smaller, more independent Families, of course, but none of them would take the risk of bringing you in unmarked."

"What risk? I thought you said the coven was thirteen witches and the bond was permanent, so if I was part of one and it was ... full, I guess? Wouldn't that put an end to things?"

I wasn't sure how I felt about permanent bonds, but they'd certainly be better than permanent death.

Mel shook her head. "No, there would still be those who feared your Command affinity or wouldn't want anyone else to have it, which would leave you at risk, and many of the more powerful Families would still want to acquire you, even if your resonants remained secret."

"How? If the bond's permanent —"

"It's permanent until a witch's death, which opens up a spot in the coven — and opens the warlock to being marked again."

"Oh."

Felicity strolled over and took the space in front of me now that my plate was gone. She stretched out and rolled over on her side for tummy rubs, which I started automatically.

"Yes," Mel said. "If you don't want to join an established Family — and you'd be quite low on the hierarchy, regardless of your power — then your best course is to form an independent coven of your own and rapidly gain enough power to protect yourself from others. In the meantime, once you learn your shields, there are some things we can do to make you safer."

"Like what?" I asked, running my hand over Felicity's soft fur.

"Well, if you stay here with me — and I won't force you, you're free to leave at any time — people will assume I plan to form a coven with you and that will grant you some protection."

"You're not already in a coven?"

Mel shook her head. "Not for quite some time."

That made me a little sad — from what Mel had told me, the covens were pretty important to witches and I wondered why she wasn't. But the knowledge that covens were permanent until death made it even sadder if she'd once been in one. That must mean her whole coven had died?

"There's a second thing that may keep you safe, but I'll need someone else's help and will have to speak to her first to determine if she's still trustworthy enough."

Mel stacked the last of the dishes to dry and came back to the island, raising an eyebrow at Felicity, who was stretched out as far as she could and purring loudly.

"She likes tummy rubs," I said.

"Oh, I know that," Mel said, the corner of her mouth quirking up. "When you're done with that, let's return to the circle and work on your shields."

# CHAPTER EIGHT

I'd been at Mel's a few days and we were still working on establishing my shields.

We were back in the basement circle and I was sweating and exhausted, despite having done nothing but sit and manipulate my shields all afternoon. Magic was hard.

Mel told me it got easier with practice and concentration, and that soon I'd be able to maintain them without even thinking about it, which would be fine except for my concentration being challenged by Mel doing yoga in the circle as well. She said if she had to be down there instructing me, she might as well get her own activities done.

I think she knew exactly what she was doing to me and was actually trying to distract me to make my shields better.

She was wearing a tight top — well, everything was tight — that ended just below her breasts, leaving her midriff bare until the tight leggings started.

To distract myself from the distraction, I decided to ask a couple things that I hadn't found a good time for since I'd arrived.

"Hey, Mel, do you have a phone?" I asked. I hadn't seen a landline in the brownstone and hadn't seen her use a cell phone at all.

She paused in a particularly distracting yoga pose and cocked her head at me.

"I'm a witch, dear, not a luddite."

I flushed, but how I was I supposed to know? Maybe witches just magic-called each other, though how they'd manage to order a pizza that way I couldn't figure out. On the other hand, I'd seen any number of excellent meals come out of Mel's oven, so maybe witches didn't need to order takeout at all.

"Could I borrow it to make a call later?" I asked.

I'd promised Morgan I'd call her once I got a phone, and since the work I was doing with Mel didn't exactly pay, I wasn't likely to get a phone of my own anytime soon.

Mel frowned. "You may, if you wish, dear, but I fear you'll be disappointed."

Now it was my turn to frown. "Why?"

Mel sighed. "I assume you want to call someone you knew before arriving here, but relationships between witches and mundanes are rarely successful."

"Why?"

Mel unfolded herself from her pose to sit cross-legged, face becoming serious.

"I do understand that modern mores have become quite liberal, dear, but do you really think your friend is likely to be understanding when you have a coven of thirteen women around you?"

I thought about it. Morgan would absolutely give me a lot of shit about something like that, but once I explained ... no, I couldn't do that, could I? Mel kept stressing that witches were only safe because the mundanes didn't believe in them anymore, so telling one probably wasn't allowed. Still, even without explaining magic, the coven itself could be explained away as just a lifestyle preference, right? It wasn't the 1600s anymore.

"Morgan could probably accept that, I think. She'd tease me about it at first ... well, maybe forever, but I don't think it would really bother her."

"So a girl, as well as a mundane? You really think she'd share you with a dozen other girls?"

"What? Oh! No, it's not like that — Morgan's just a friend. Well, more than a friend, but not more like that. Like a little sister."

"Still, dear, how would you explain your new circumstances? Or will you find some way to keep that from her and never invite her to your home?"

I paused — yeah, that would be hard, but I'd promised Morgan to stay in touch and I didn't even have one woman yet, so I'd worry about that if the time ever came.

"I get it, but maybe I can worry about that later? I promised her I'd keep in touch and help her when she ages out next year."

"A promise?" Mel asked. "What sort of promise?"

I shrugged, not really understanding what the difference might be — a promise was a promise.

"Well, I pinkie-swore on it," I said, thinking Mel would probably laugh that off.

Mel pursed her lips. "That is a bit different. A witch's oath is a powerful thing and carries dire consequences if forsaken — the same applies to a warlock." She sighed. "My phone's in the wood box on the table near the front door — feel free to use it any time you like, there's no passcode."

"No code?"

Mel smiled and I decided I probably didn't want to know what would happen to someone who stole a witch's phone.

"Never mind," I said quickly.

Mel slowly folded herself back into a pose that was ... interesting, while I returned to concentrating on my shields.

"Say, Mel," I said after a moment.

"Yes, dear?"

"If witches are real — what about other things?"

"What other things?" Mel asked.

"Like, vampires, werewolves, that sort of thing?"

"Don't be silly, dear —"

I breathed a little sigh of relief, because I wasn't sure I wanted to know vampires and werewolves existed.

"— of course they are."

"What?"

"Most of the things people tell stories about are real — that's where the stories came from. Of course, it doesn't mean that all the stories *about* those things are true, any more than the stories about witches. Regardless, you're unlikely to encounter any of the other races — those of us behind the Veil are somewhat insular."

"The Veil?"

Mel's face fell and she rolled out of her pose to sit cross-legged. She was silent for a long time and I waited, wondering what I'd said.

"The Veil came about shortly after Salem."

"The Trials," I said, having come to understand that witches often referred to the Trials in sixteenth-century Salem simply as Salem or the Trials.

Mel nodded. "Shortly after the Trials, maybe ten years, the Veil began to form. It's a sort of ... curtain across the minds of the mundanes, keeping them from seeing us for what we are. It makes them forget that we're real and dismiss any strange things they might see as their imagination. It's kept us safe for over four hundred years and we all try to keep it that way by not giving the mundanes too much to think about."

"*Rrrowwrr!*"

I flinched as Felicity landed on my back, attacking from behind. The flinch and the impact made me lose concentration and my shields dissolved in shreds of blue-white light.

Mel sighed and rolled onto her back, then lifted her feet and grasped her toes to begin rolling her hips back and forth.

"Start concentrating again and bring your shields up."

SEVEN MINUTES, I thought, later that week. *I can do seven more minutes.*

I was in the living room, idly flipping through the shows available on the multiple streaming channels Mel subscribed to. Mel was in the kitchen — she spent a lot of time there — prepping for dinner. I'd offered to help, but she said I'd only be in the way, and I wasn't going to complain about that, because she was a truly fantastic cook. I'd encountered more flavor in the two weeks I'd been staying with Mel than in years of Karen's cooking.

Tonight's dinner was something called chicken piccata, with garlic mashed potatoes and something-I-forgot Brussels sprouts, and the scents coming from the kitchen were distracting the hell out of me.

I quickly scanned the living room, looking for anything out of the ordinary, because I only had six minutes and thirty-seven seconds left.

My shields had been up and solid for nearly twenty-four hours, and Mel had said once I could keep them stable for that long, despite her and Felicity's attempts to get through them or shock and startle me out of them, then I'd be good to leave the house and exit the brownstone's wards. At least with Mel as an escort, that is.

I was anxious for that — Mel's place was comfortable, but I kind of did want to get out once in a while, and I was *so* close.

*Five minutes, fifty-two seconds.*

I decided to play a game instead of watching something on television, so I turned on one of the gaming consoles and grabbed a controller. Mel had two high-end consoles and a game collection heavy on RPGs, but every time I turned the conversation that way with her, she didn't seem interested. I figured maybe she'd played them too much and gotten a little burned out.

Felicity, on the other hand, seemed fascinated by them. Every time I played, the cat would perch herself on the couch's arm, staring at the screen, tail twitching. Maybe she saw the little figures moving around the screen as some kind of prey?

"*Rroowwrr!*"

I jerked my foot out of the way as Felicity sprang for my ankle from underneath the console.

"*Ha!* Missed me!"

The other reason for switching to a game was that Felicity's preferred method for challenging my shields was a sneak-attack from cover, and I figured she was either under the cabinet or behind the couch. Standing to retrieve the game controller was my best chance to draw her out when I was at least semi-expecting her attack and ready for it.

Now that I'd seen her and avoided the surprise, she couldn't startle me into dropping my shields.

"Five minutes, twenty-six seconds, and you're not going to — *aarrghh!*"

I dropped to my knees, letting the game controller clatter to the hardwood floor, as Mel hit me with an almost overwhelming blast of mana — I have no idea what the spell was called, something to push past someone's shields and take them down, but she'd done it before. Never this strongly, though.

But my shields *didn't* go down this time and I had a chance to reinforce them by pouring what little mana I had in reserves into them. I had little, because I only had access to what Mel decided to shed into the environment. The planned trip, once I could properly maintain those shields, included some places she said would have more ambient mana I could collect.

I flexed my muscles in an unconscious effort to reinforce and expand my own shields to push back against her attack — Mel was trying to get me to keep the shields closer to my skin, but I couldn't seem to get the hang of that. Instead, I expanded them, pushing them several inches away from my body.

"Stop that, dear," Mel said from the kitchen. "You look like you should be hawking refrigerated biscuits."

It was incredibly annoying that Mel was able to continue cooking as though nothing was going on, despite hitting me with a magical attack that sent me to my knees.

"It works," I muttered through gritted teeth.

"*Rroowwrr!*"

Sharp teeth and claws dug into my calf, but I held on, keeping my shields up while I reached down to detach Felicity from my jeans.

"Ah, *fuck*!" I yelled as the cat bit me in the webbing between my thumb and forefinger, and the pressure of Mel's attack increased.

I slumped to the floor, eyes closed, completely ignoring Felicity's continued gnawing while I concentrated on nothing but keeping my shields up.

Just when I thought I couldn't hang on any more, both attacks stopped and I was finally able to take a deep breath.

"Dinner's ready," Mel called.

---

"ARE you sure capers are okay for cats?" I asked.

"*Pft!*"

"I just don't want you to get sick," I told Felicity.

The time living with Mel had me talking to the cat as though she could understand me, too — and I was pretty sure she did. Familiar or not, there was something decidedly weird about Felicity.

For one thing, every meal we had included a plate for her, which she ate at the table with us, and she was currently working her way through a serving of chicken piccata. Next to her plate was a small bowl with a bit of the white wine Mel had chosen for dinner — I had a glass next to me, too, and I was finding I liked it. Every dinner Mel gave a little lecture on the wine and why she'd paired it with the meal, which was interesting.

"She's fine, dear," Mel said.

"If you say so," I said, turning back to my own meal, which was as fantastic as everything Mel cooked. I'd never had anything like the sort of meals I had here — chicken at my former foster home had come in a bucket, mashed potatoes were from a box, and Brussels sprouts never made an appearance, I think because they weren't available in a can. "This is really good."

"Thank you, dear," Mel said. She set her fork down and pushed her plate back a bit. "Now that you can maintain your shields, would you like to go out somewhere this evening?"

"Absolutely — where?"

"I know just the place for you to fill one of your resonants without us being observed by another witch — and I believe young men find it entertaining, as well."

"I'd like to try calling Morgan again before we go, if you don't mind."

I'd tried several times since asking Mel if I could use her phone, but every time I tried calling my former foster home, the line had disconnected after a couple rings. I was at the point where I was thinking of asking Mel to make our second outing be a trip to Alex and Karen's so I could see Morgan in person.

"Of course, dear, just don't say anything about witchcraft."

I paused on my way to the front door to retrieve her phone — like I was going to tell anyone about that?

"No problem," I said. "Morgan would think I was crazy if I mentioned it."

Mel nodded and went upstairs, leaving me in the living room with her phone as I tapped the last few numbers.

This time the phone rang more than twice and at four rings someone picked up.

"Hello?"

It was a male voice I didn't recognize, so probably the new guy who'd replaced me in the foster home.

"Hi, is Morgan home?" I asked.

"Who's calling?"

That was new — in my experience, all the other kids in the home would just toss the phone down and scream the recipient's name before going about their business. Whether the person the call was for picked up or not would depend on if they'd heard their name called the one time. If someone else passed the phone and it hadn't been picked up yet, they'd just hang up the call.

"This is Noah."

"Who's that? How do you know Morgan?"

The questions came quickly and with a little hostility, which started to set me off too. Who did this guy think he was?

"Um, I used to live there — Morgan and I are friends and I'd like to talk to her. Please."

"How do I know she wants to talk to you?"

I took a deep breath and resisted the urge to unload on him. If I did that, he'd probably hang up the phone — then maybe hang out there so he could answer and hang up again if I called back.

"You could ... tell her who's on the phone?"

"Yeah, I don't know if she —"

"Who is it?" I heard Morgan's voice in the background.

"Some guy."

"Noah," I said. "Name's Noah — why don't you just tell her it's Noah?"

"Don't give me fucking attitude, dude," the guy said.

"Give me the fucking phone, Gabriel," Morgan said.

"You want the phone?" the guy, apparently Gabriel, asked, then his voice got dimmer. "Jump for it — come on, jump, little girl, jump, ju — *oof!*"

There was a clatter, a muffled "bitch" that made me look at Mel's front door and think about heading over there immediately, and then Morgan's voice.

"Who is this?"

"It's Noah, who the fuck was that guy?"

"*Noah!* It's been weeks — are you okay?"

I immediately felt guilty, because it *had* been weeks since I left the foster home and even though I'd tried, I felt like I should have done more to contact her.

"I'm sorry — yeah, I'm okay. It's just been kind of crazy since I left."

"Thank God," Morgan said. "You're sure? You're not hurt? Not in trouble?"

"No, no, I'm fine, it was jus —"

"Good, then, *I am so fucking pissed at you!* Weeks! I didn't know if you were hurt, or dead, or what!"

"I'm sorry," I repeated. "I really am. I did try to call a few times, but the calls never connected — and things haven't exactly gone the way I planned after I left."

"Why? What happened?"

"First who was that guy? I asked for you and he started giving me the third-degree."

Morgan snorted. "That's the new foster. Gabriel."

"He sounds like a douche."

"That's ... being kind."

Something in Morgan's voice made me think there was more to it than messing with phone calls.

"Are *you* okay?" I asked. "Do I need to come kick his ass?"

"No, I can handle him — and you're over eighteen, you'd get in trouble if you hit him."

*I wouldn't hit him — I'd use my new-found magic to...*

Who was I kidding? I'd been working on my first spell for a week and hadn't been successful yet. Lighting a candle ... which would have been cool if I could do it.

I couldn't tell Morgan any of that, though.

"All right," I agreed, "but if it turns into something you can't handle, call me, okay? Here, take this number down."

I gave her Mel's cell number. I should probably get a phone of my own, but I had no money and didn't want to ask Mel for more than she was already doing for me — besides, the only person I needed to call was Morgan.

"So, you got a phone? Job and apartment?"

I spent the next hour telling Morgan everything that happened since I left. Not the magic and witches part ... or making a guy head-butt a wall, but everything else.

"So, she's some kind of sugar momma?" Morgan asked when I finished.

"What? No! Nothing like that — she's just helping me out."

"Uh huh," Morgan said with a lot of skepticism. "Why?"

There wasn't much I could say to that, since I couldn't tell Morgan about witches and how warlocks were really important, and Mel wanting to help me so I wouldn't get locked on some Family estate or killed.

"Maybe she just feels sorry for me," was the best I could come up with.

"Well, there is a lot to work with there."

"Hey!"

"What about a job?" Morgan asked. "You didn't say anything about working — or are you just a boy-toy now?"

I decided to stop responding to the bait or Morgan would never let it go.

"No, no job ... I'm sort of doing ... vocational training."

Best I could come up with to describe learning magic. My "job" was almost certainly going to be magic-related, so it wasn't a lie.

"Is that what she calls it? I guess you would have a lot to learn."

I bit my tongue to avoid taking the bait — not least because it did sound like a warlock's main job was having sex with the coven to harvest mana.

"Okay, enough about me," I said. "What have you been up to? Why's the new guy such an asshole?"

"Um, can we talk about that later?"

"Why? Is he there?"

"Yep."

"He listens in on your phone calls?"

"Uh huh."

"Morgan —"

"I can handle it."

It didn't sound like it if she couldn't stop the guy from listening to her on the phone, but I knew Morgan. She wouldn't appreciate it if I pressed or interfered when she wanted to handle something herself.

"I should go," Morgan said, "in case someone else wants to use the phone. You'll call again?"

"Yeah — or you can call me. Um, Mel will answer, it's her phone."

I closed my eyes and winced, because I knew what was coming.

"She won't let you have your own phone? Maybe I should come rescue *you*."

"No, it's nothing like that. I just don't have anyone I need to call other than you, so I don't really need a whole phone of my own."

"I see — what if you have to call her? To tell her you'll be late or something?"

*Not necessary, because I haven't left the house in weeks and when I do Mel will always be with me to protect me from some witch Family dragging me off the street and throwing me in the back of a van or something.*

No, that would definitely not make Morgan less concerned. And would probably result in Morgan coming over to kick Mel's ass.

"It hasn't come up," I said, trying to be as vague as possible.

"Oh." Morgan was quiet for a minute. "Does this change things?"

I frowned. "Change what?"

"You know — later. After my birthday?"

I realized what my current situation would sound like to her with regard to my promise to have my own place where she could stay after aging out, but I wasn't sure how to respond. Would I still be staying with Mel next summer? Would I have my own place? Would I have a coven of my own? That was probably too fast, but what would Morgan think even if I'd found just two or three witches to form a coven with me?

*Hi, Morgan, welcome to my place — here are the other women staying here.*

Mel had warned me about this, and it would be … awkward. But I wasn't going to go back on my promise to Morgan. Aging out alone had been bad enough for me, it was probably much worse for a girl.

"We'll figure it out," I said.

"Oh."

I could tell from her voice that she didn't believe me.

"Morgan, the morning you age out I will be on the front porch waiting for you. You will *not* be alone; do you hear me?"

"I — yeah, I hear you, Noah. Thank you."

# CHAPTER NINE

"Really?" I asked as I exited the cab behind Mel.

"Of course, dear, it's exactly what we need."

Apparently what Mel thought we needed was what the sign euphemistically called a gentleman's club and the guys I'd gone to high school with called a titty-bar. Admittedly, it was one of the upscale ones — probably the one everyone would think of for the most upscale titty-bar in town.

"I don't know," I said, hesitating.

"Trust me," Mel said. "Your Lust resonant will be the easiest one to fill, and there's no place in town better than here to do that." She frowned. "Well, I do know of a few better places, but they'd probably embarrass you."

"Here's fine," I said quickly not even wanting to hear more about anyplace she thought would embarrass me more than her taking me to a titty-bar. "But will they even let me in? I'm only eighteen."

"Right, I almost forgot — let me see that school ID of yours."

"Okay," I said slowly, pulling my wallet from my pocket and extracting my laminated card to hand to her.

Mel ran her finger over the card and handed it back.

"There."

I looked at my card which now looked like a driver's license and said I was a full three years older than I actually was.

"It's a small glamour," Mel said. "It will fade by morning."

"That would have been a useful trick," I muttered, thinking of my first day on my own. Just a simple driver's license would have made everything different.

I tucked my new license back in my wallet and stuffed it in my pocket. Mel gestured at the door.

"Shall we?"

I really didn't want to. It'd been hard enough living with Mel the last couple weeks and not showing how attracted I was to her. That wasn't helped by the fact that she typically dressed in tight or revealing clothing — or the daily yoga/shielding sessions. Even now she was wearing a deeply cut blouse that showed off her cleavage, and every now and then a little glimpse of the lace on her bra, and jeans that could've been sprayed on — along with a pair of heels that showed her legs to their best advantage.

Adding a bunch of dancing, naked women into the mix was not going to help me keep things under control.

But we were here and she was looking expectantly at the door, so I grabbed the handle and opened it for her.

"Thank you, dear. Such a gentleman."

We went in and the thumping bass of the music was like a physical blow. Even in the little alcove at the front, with a curtain and wall separating us from what I assumed was the bar, my insides started pounding and vibrating with the beat.

There was a scantily clad girl at a cash register with a really big guy standing behind her.

"IDs?" She asked holding out her hand without looking up from her phone. "The cover's twenty each."

Mel opened her purse and handed over her ID so I pulled out my wallet and did the same. The guy cocked his head and gave me a look when Mel pulled out two twenties to pay the cover. I guess he was expecting me to pay.

Mel must've sensed I was still reluctant, because she grabbed my hand to drag me through the curtain into the main bar.

It was brighter than I'd expected inside, but still pretty dark. Lights and strobes hit the stages and my attention was immediately drawn to the girls dancing there.

Mel led me toward the largest stage, which had a pole at either end. At the end nearest us a girl who was still wearing at least some clothes was dancing while the girl at the other end was topless. I nearly stopped in my tracks when it looked like Mel was taking us to the seats that were right up against the stage, because there was no way I was going to sit there with her, but she let go of my hand and stopped at a table with four chairs around it a couple rows back from the action.

"Here," she said, pointing at one of the chairs.

At least that's what I thought she said, I couldn't really hear her with the music, but she seemed to be indicating I should sit there. It was still way closer than I'd like to sit. I thought about asking her if we could sit in one of the booths that were around the edge of the bar where it was darker and more...

Then I caught sight of some of the things going on back there and jumped forward to take the seat she was pointing at.

At least the chair had a round, full back and arms that cut off the view, so no one could see me adjust myself as I sat down.

Except the girl on the stage, who was now looking right at me and smirking.

I flushed and tried to look anywhere but the stage.

Mel pulled a chair around the table so it was closer to mine and facing the stage.

"Pay attention, dear," she whispered as a waitress approached. "It's rude to ignore the show."

"Drinks?" a waitress asked, wearing only a little more than the dancers. Stockings, garter belt, and a lace bra and panties. "There's a minimum."

"Please," Mel said. "I'll have a red wine — whatever the bar has opened is fine."

The waitress looked at me.

"Beer?" I suggested.

"You'll have a soda," Mel said.

The waitress looked back and forth between Mel and me and I shrugged.

"Soda," I said, then after the waitress left: "You've been giving me wine with dinner and take me to a titty-bar, but you won't let me have a beer?"

"The bar is educational and a bit of wine with dinner aids the digestion. Now close your eyes, dear."

Take me to a titty-bar and make me close my eyes. This was one of the weirdest outings I'd ever been on.

"Close them. Good. Now look through your shields the way I taught you. Do you see the mana?"

I nodded. I did — and it was pretty amazing. The bar was full of glowing strings being cast off everyone — the dancers, the men watching, even the waitresses. We hadn't been outside Mel's brownstone since I'd learned to see mana and I hadn't realized how much of it was just floating around.

"Wow."

"I told you there was mana everywhere. This really isn't very much, though," Mel said. "We won't be able to fill your stores more than a tiny bit here, but it's useful to learn how — and it will be enough to power your shields and learn a bit of other magic without relying on me."

"Why can't we? Rely on you, I mean?"

"I can't shed enough mana to properly fill a warlock — no single witch can."

"I thought you said a warlock, at least a *trinitara* one, can take mana from any witch, so couldn't we do that?"

"A warlock can hold an entire coven's mana, trebled, but you and I can't risk sharing mana directly — not without being in danger of one of us marking the other — not until you have a full coven, at least."

"Why not?"

"All this nudity and you want a lecture on magic?"

I looked around briefly. Yeah, the girls were naked, but they didn't seem to want to be there, and, honestly, Mel was hotter than any of them and I got to see her all day. True, she wasn't naked, but — I glanced over and caught the sight of her breasts, pressed together by how she was sitting and ... maybe that was worse. Or better. Or something.

"First, what we came here for. Now open yourself up to it and start taking it into yourself."

I wasn't sure I wanted to take anything in the bar "into myself", as I was reasonably certain it would wind up with me needing a visit to the free clinic and end with a shot of penicillin in my ass. Still, I did what Mel told me.

"Now, you see it's just drifting around the room? Like it was in my circle?" she asked.

I nodded.

"Try to imagine that you're drawing it toward yourself — not while it's in someone, you won't be able to touch that, but what they've already shed."

"Could we not call it shedding?"

"That's what it's called, dear."

I huffed, but tried to do as she said.

It was different than at Mel's — there, we'd been in her circle, sitting close to each other, and the mana she shed was already right next to me — here, the mana was farther away and more difficult to influence. After a bit of trying, though, it seemed to be working — the drifting strands, instead of floating up and disappearing in the ceiling or down to the floor, started drifting toward me. As they neared me, I felt tingling sensations where they touched my body before being absorbed.

"Why are only some of them coming?" I asked, watching the strands that, no matter how hard I concentrated on them, never change their path.

"Your influence over mana you don't resonate with is limited. Everything else will drift off into the environment unless you chase after it."

"Oh, okay."

The strands of mana I was able to draw toward me mostly had the pinkish hue I'd learned represented Lust. Which made a lot of sense, given where we were.

I was also getting the crimson-red of Pain, though — those were coming from particular areas of the dancers' bodies, like their feet and ankles, but also from their shoulders when they spun around the poles.

"Okay," I said. "I think I figured out Lust, and the red strings seem to be coming from the dancers' feet and joints —"

"Have you ever tried dancing in eight-inch stiletto platforms?"

"Yeah, that sounds hard." I looked around some more. "This seems ... tawdry."

Mel spread her hands and raised her eyebrows.

"You expected different?"

"I don't know, I've never been to one of these — only seen them on TV and movies. I thought there might be..." I shrugged. "Some kind of show or something."

"That's burlesque, and it's hard to find these days. Chippendale's puts on a good show, but I can't take you there."

"Because I'm a guy?"

"No, because the audience would be full of witches." Mel sat back and crossed her legs. "Now be quiet and watch the dancers while you absorb as much mana as possible." She pulled a bundle of dollar bills from her purse and slid it across the table to me. "Be sure to tip, dear."

I soaked in the energy for a bit. It was a little creepy at first to think about it coming from other people — like I was some kind of energy vampire — but Mel's description of how I could only pick up what they were shedding let me understand that I wasn't taking anything they needed from them.

I guess I was more of an ... energy hobo, going through their magic litter.

After about thirty minutes, I decided to get Mel talking again.

"So, you keep talking about 'marking' like it's a bad thing," I finally said. "If that forms the coven bond, then what's so bad about it?"

"It's not that it's bad, dear, just that it's not something one does without intending to."

"What if you don't intend to?"

Mel chuckled. "It's difficult to explain to someone who hasn't experienced it." She sipped her wine, then gestured at the stack of bills. "This song's almost over, dear, tip the nice girl."

I knew there was no point in arguing or refusing. The first time she'd told me to tip one of the dancers, I'd refused to get up, but then she motioned to the girl who was leaving the stage and handed her a twenty.

Don't get me wrong, it was interesting and I might have enjoyed it more if Mel hadn't been there. Watching. Intently watching.

"You're blushing again," Mel said when I returned from the stage. I don't know how she could tell in the dim, strobing lights. "You're a warlock — you really should try to get used to this sort of thing. This is what witches do."

"Strip?"

I shrugged at her glare, then she grinned.

"Dark of the moon, a few too many meads, a warm, spring night in the Grove..."

That smile, those words, damn — my head filled with images of Mel dancing through a shadowy Grove, casting aside a hooded robe, then hopping up on a stone block and laying back to wait for...

"Balance, dear."

I blinked, shook myself, and looked at my own resonance stores. They were definitely filling at different rates and I worked to shift the energy from Lust to the other two until they were roughly even. I'd definitely experienced how letting one get fuller than the others could affect my thoughts and behavior, so I concentrated on that until my head cleared of naked-Mel thoughts.

"How full are you?" Mel asked.

At first, I thought Mel was asking if we should order food — it had been a couple hours since dinner and I could have gone for some potato skins — but then I realized she was asking about my mana stores. I took a closer look and after balancing things, each was still less than a tenth full.

"Maybe five-percent?" I said. I understood now what she meant about ambient mana taking a long time — at this rate it would take thirty or forty hours to completely fill my stores and Mel's were many times larger than mine.

"That should be enough to power your shields and some basic lessons for a while." She checked her phone. "The stores are still open — let's do some shopping."

# CHAPTER TEN

"Wear the slacks I got you," Mel said, "and one of the dress shirts."

Three weeks and several shopping trips after our first trip to the strip club, my wardrobe was now quite a bit more extensive than it had ever been, but at least Mel had let me pick out most of the things. Even so, while I'd still gravitated toward jeans and t-shirts, it was nice to have a few dressier clothes and I didn't take offense at her reminder that now was the time to wear them.

We'd been back to the strip club several times to keep my mana stores from being completely empty — full wasn't possible unless I made watching topless dancers a full-time job — and I'd mastered at least one of the magical tasks Mel set me.

Lighting a candle with magic was *hard*, at least for me.

Mel said it was because none of my resonants had a fire affinity, but it was the only thing I'd managed so far. We'd tried to figure out what my other affinities might be, with no luck. Pain could have been anything from healing to causing pain — like, making someone hurt without touching them, which weirded me out a bit. Mel said she suspected my Lust affinity was an unconscious thing, probably to make me more attractive than I actually was — I still wasn't sure if she was serious about that or just making fun of me. We already knew my Control affinity was Command, but experimenting with that wouldn't work — Mel wouldn't let me use it on her and neither of us was comfortable experimenting on some innocent mundane.

So, after days of trying multiple types of magic, I'd finally lit a candle — it only took me about a hundred hours of intense, eye-watering concentration and a headache that lasted into the next day.

But it was enough to indicate I was ready for the next step Mel had planned for me: Magic School.

"Students are generally left out of any Family conflicts or maneuvering," Mel told me. "That, plus the assumption that I plan to form a coven with you, should keep you safe enough — at least from the Families. There are few Families that would want to take on both me and Evelina."

"Evelina?"

"Don't call her that," Mel warned. "*Magistra Prima* Evelina Rosethorn — *Prima* of Willowmere College. You should refer to her as *Prima* — and the other teachers as *Magistra* when you meet them."

"Okay — what is that? Latin?"

Mel nodded, looking through my shirts. "Yes, witches in the United States still use Latin for many things — some Greek, a bit of Slavic, and the occasional Celtic influence. A melting pot, if you will."

"People don't really use that term anymore."

"They should." Mel pulled a light-blue shirt from the closet. "This one. Now get changed, she'll be here any moment —" The doorbell rang. "That's her. There's a tea prepared in the kitchen, dear, bring that to the formal parlor once you're changed?"

"Sure."

She left and I changed clothes, then ran a brush through my hair and checked my teeth to make sure there wasn't anything left in them from lunch. Mel seemed to think this was pretty important. I did, too, since it was *magic school* after all. I mean, who wouldn't want to go to magic school? I didn't know how much it cost or how I'd get the money, but getting in was the first step, right? And if I'd learned anything from movies, it was that school bosses were uptight sticklers for protocol and you had to impress them. So, I would.

The formal parlor was the one I'd seen on the second floor that didn't have a TV, so I had to pass it on my way to the kitchen. I could hear the two women's voices, but couldn't see into the parlor through the partially closed pocket doors.

Once in the kitchen I saw why Mel's phrasing had been so odd — "a tea" instead of "some tea" or just "tea."

Not only was there a tray set out with the typical tea things — teapot, tiny pitcher of cream, a bowl of sugar cubes, complete with little silver tongs, saucers and cups — but also a four-tier tower of plates holding little sandwiches, cakes, cookies, and other treats I couldn't identify. My mouth started watering, even though we'd just had lunch a couple hours ago.

I realized it was going to take two trips to get everything to the formal parlor, so I picked up the tower of treats first, and carried it upstairs.

The formal parlor was very different than the living room off the kitchen. That had a comfy couch, a huge TV, and was very comfortable and inviting. The formal parlor was ... very formal. Spindly-legged chairs, tiny tables, and nothing for entertainment other than a piano against one wall. It was clearly a place for conversation, but not relaxing.

Mel's visitor seemed to fit right in with that.

She appeared to be in her thirties, but Mel had made a few comments that made me think it was a bad idea to rely on how a witch looked to guess her age — apparently witches with enough power had some control over their aging. She wore her ash blonde hair up in a tight bun and a lace-edged dress that covered her from wrists to neck to ankles, but really did nothing to hide the fact that she had a nice figure. It was definitely a sexy-schoolmarm vibe.

*Prima* Rosethorn glanced at me as I entered, and frowned, but she didn't say anything. Mel didn't introduce me right away, so I just stayed silent and respectful, setting the sandwich tower on the table between the chairs the two women were seated in, but far enough back so that they could still see each other comfortably, then backed away and turned to return to the kitchen for the tea.

I retrieved the tea tray, then brought it back upstairs and set it on the low table that sat between the four chairs in the room.

The women's conversation had stopped when I entered again, but Mel still didn't introduce me — maybe she was waiting for *Prima* Rosethorn to ask, since she'd said it would be unusual for her to have a warlock in the house, so I decided to lean into the servant role a bit.

I took one of the cups and a saucer and set it on the table off the tray then lifted the teapot looked at Mel's guest.

"Tea, *Prima* Rosethorn?" I asked.

The woman raised an eyebrow and now I could see the corners of Mel's mouth twitch.

"Please," the woman said. "Cream, two sugars, if you will."

Since Mel still didn't say anything, I kept going.

I poured the tea into the cup to what I thought was a good level, added a bit of cream I thought would be the right amount, used the tongs to plop two cubes in, then took one of the spoons to give the cup a quick stir, hoping it would dissolve the sugar. I offered the saucer and cup to Mel's guest, who took it with a small nod.

"Melaina, is there a reason your new footman isn't wearing gloves?" *Prima* Rosethorn asked, turning to Mel.

"He's new and I haven't decided on the livery yet," Mel said, then she laughed and shook her head. "Sit down, Noah, we can pour our own tea — and have some yourself, dear."

"Don't discourage the young man, Melaina," *Prima* Rosethorn said, "there's something to be said for the courtesies." She took a sip of her tea and nodded to me. "A fine effort, young man. The fare is not typically delivered separate from the tea, but a fine effort nonetheless."

"Thank you, ma'am," I said.

Melaina chuckled again. "Evelina, this is Noah Ashe — Noah, this is *Prima* Evelina Rosethorn of Willowmere College."

"It's nice to meet you, *Prima* Rosethorn."

"And I you, *Magellus* Ashe," *Prima* Rosethorn said with a nod, then returned her attention to Mel. "I wasn't aware you were planning to start a new coven of your own, Melaina, and I'm afraid I don't know the Ashes." Then she shook her head. "No, never mind, none of my business." She smiled. "Too much dealing with students makes one think one has a right to know everything. And with the new term starting next week, we've little time. I really should get back to the school." She took a sip of her tea, then set the cup back on the saucer. "So, where's the girl?"

Mel raised her eyebrows, waited a moment, then extended her arm to point at me.

I raised my eyebrows too, because I'm not a girl.

"Yes, I've met your young man, what does that —" *Prima* Rosethorn looked at me, then frowned and blinked rapidly.

"Oh, dear," she muttered.

"Indeed," Mel said, leaning forward and fixing herself a cup of tea.

She sat back and took a sip, and the whole time *Prima* Rosethorn simply stared at me.

The *Prima's* face fell and her eyes widened, then she looked back to Mel.

"No."

Mel took a sip of tea both before and after smiling and nodding with raised eyebrows.

"No," *Prima* Rosethorn said again, but Mel simply sipped her tea. "Absolutely not. It's unthinkable — there hasn't been a warlock at Willowmere for over a hundred years."

"There hasn't been a warlock at any college in over a hundred years — they're kept under lock and key."

"Exactly, and what do you think will happen when the Families find out about him? The lengths they'd go to bind him? He should be hidden away until you have a full coven, or at least until you've marked him." She shook her head. "The last place he should be is as the only male in a college of four hundred fifty girls, those same Families' daughters."

"I don't intend to mark him," Mel said.

I was still trying to parse what *Prima* Rosethorn had said. I'd understood that warlocks were rare, I'd understood that warlocks were kept under wraps by these Families, so I'd understood that any magic school, like Willowmere, would have a lot of girls ... I just hadn't put that together with *me* going there until *Prima* Rosethorn had said the words "four hundred fifty girls."

*Prima* Rosethorn's face went white and she stared at me.

"You don't intend to — you didn't acquire him from a Family, did you. Not even a small one. He's unaffiliated? From the outcasts?"

Mel shrugged. "Unknown."

"Unknown? How?"

"He was orphaned — or, at least, left in the care of the State as a babe."

*Prima* Rosethorn's brow furrowed. "I *am* sorry, young man," she said before turning back to Mel. "This simply isn't possible."

"The Families will all find out about him eventually in any case," Mel said. "The idea of keeping him hidden until he's both acquired his own coven and learned enough magic to wield it successfully in his own defense simply isn't feasible. Just introducing him to witches who might join that coven exposes him — while Willowmere provides both the opportunity for those meetings and extends him the protections of the school as well as my own."

"I'm sorry, but I can't. Even if I were willing, this year's class is full, and you know we have a policy of no exceptions to the admissions quota, for quite good reasons."

Mel set her cup down on her saucer with a muted *clink*.

"I'm afraid I must insist."

*Prima* Rosethorn's eyebrows rose. "Insist? Really?"

"He's a founder's legacy, Evelina, so I'm afraid you'll have to find room."

I kind of felt sorry for *Prima* Rosethorn as Mel seemed to be dropping bomb after bomb on the poor woman — and enjoying it immensely, if I'd learned to read her face right. I had no idea what a founder's legacy was or how it applied to me, but it certainly had an effect on the *Prima*. She closed her eyes and rubbed her temples.

"And how is that, Melaina? I like to think you would've told me if you were ever pregnant, and even if not, that's not the sort of thing that could possibly remain a secret for so long."

So that explained what a founder's legacy was if Mel was one of the founders of the school. But the school was at least a hundred years old, so that couldn't be — maybe Mel's family had been founders and she still had this legacy thing? I still didn't see how it applied to me unless Mel was straight up lying about it.

"Not directly — but given his particular set of resonants, it's almost certain I'm in his ancestry somewhere."

"*What?*" The word was out of my mouth before I'd even consciously processed what she said.

Mel and I were related? Was she just saying that to try getting me into the school, or could it be true? How would she know when I didn't even know my parents' names?

Both women were staring at me, *Prima* Rosethorn with curiosity, but Mel's face was first questioning and then sorrowful.

"Oh, Noah, dear, I'm sorry. I didn't think of how that would strike you. I've lived alone without any family for so long, I'm not very used to how other people might feel about it."

"But, how?" I wanted to know how we might be related. Had Mel known my parents? Or at least known someone she thought could be my parents? And why hadn't she told me this before?

"We'll talk about it later, dear, I promise, but I assure you, the relationship is certainly *very* distant, which is why I didn't think it would have much meaning to you."

I didn't care how distant the relationship might be if there actually was one. I'd spent my whole life not knowing even a single blood-relative, so any was a shock.

"For now," Mel asked, "can you wait until later?"

I wanted to say no and demand we talk about it now, but I also didn't want to have that conversation in front of *Prima* Rosethorn, so I nodded and sat back in my chair to watch the two women begin sparring again. I still didn't know how much this place cost, or how I was supposed to pay for it. I assumed Mel had some plan for that, because she must certainly know that I had no money to speak of. The idea of her paying for my college made me a little uneasy, but maybe if we really were related?

"Well," *Prima* Rosethorn said, "as you say, uncertain and quite distant, even if so."

"The school's charter makes no allowances for the distance of the relation so long as it can be reasonably proven," Mel said. "I should know, I wrote it. And, as I said, his particular combination of resonants makes it almost certain — certain enough, that I believe I simply must insist."

"Insist again? Well, what are these resonants you're so certain of? And why?"

"Lust and Pain," Melaina said then hesitated.

She'd told me to keep my third one secret, both to hide the fact that I was a *trinitara* and had the feared Control resonant, so I didn't think she was going to share that with *Prima* Rosethorn.

"Neither of those is particularly rare, Melaina, even if they were prevalent in your line."

Mel sighed. "Evelina, may I ask you to keep something confidential?"

*Prima* Rosethorn sniffed. "After all the time we've known each other, you have to ask?"

Mel nodded. "And an oath on it, if you don't mind."

"What on earth would —" She stopped and shrugged. "Never mind, if you feel it's necessary, you know I will." She took a deep breath. "By my power, by my Grove, and by the Goddess I love with all my being, nothing I learn here today will be disclosed by me to any other. Is that sufficient?"

Mel nodded, then sipped her tea again.

"And Control," Mel said.

*Prima* Rosethorn opened and closed her mouth several times trying to get a word out.

"You want me to take an untrained, *trinitara* warlock with Lust and Control resonants into a school with four hundred fifty young witches? Can you even imagine how perilous that would be?"

In the immortal spirit of Sir Galahad, I was certainly open to experiencing a little of the peril she described. I was pretty happy Felicity hopped up in my lap at that moment, because it hid the sudden bulge in my pants.

*The only guy on an all-girls campus? Absolutely count me in.*

"I'm sure we can find ways to avoid any of that."

I managed not to blurt out that I did not want, in fact, to avoid any of that, but I did sit forward a little bit to listen more closely.

*Prima* Rosethorn glared at me, very different than the cordial woman I'd served tea to, and I wondered if she was going to blame me for her getting trash-talked, blind-sided, beat-up, and generally trounced by Mel.

"But a *trinitara*, Melaina? If that gets out —"

"The only ones who know he's a *trinitara* are in this room."

*Prima* Rosethorn snorted. "A secret on a campus of young women? You must be joking. He'll be outed on the first day — Introduction to Spellcasting alone will do it. He'll have to partner with another witch and —"

"I'll teach the class," Mel said, leaning forward to take a plate and daintily pick a triangular sandwich from the tea tray.

Both *Prima* Rosethorn and I stared at her as she sat back and bit a small corner off the sandwich.

"What?" *Prima* Rosethorn asked as I took in the implications of that.

Mel was willing to come to this school with me and teach? It had to be just to keep me safe, since she was constantly talking about how irritating witch society was to her and how she and Felicity had everything they needed here. I felt myself tear up and quickly scrubbed at my eyes. What she'd done for me already was more than anyone else had in my entire life.

"I will come to Willowmere," Mel continued, "and teach the class. Introduction to Spellcasting, yes? I'll partner with Noah myself for the exercises, since it would be awkward for any of the girls even if he wasn't a *trinitara*. You've been trying to get me to teach again for decades, Evelina, will you really give up the opportunity over some silly concerns?"

*Prima* Rosethorn sat back and narrowed her eyes.

"You'll teach all of the first-years," she said finally, then when Mel nodded: "*And* an advanced class for the seniors, as well as the same in each of his following years."

"Of course. Part of the reason for me being there will be to keep Noah safe. The school's immunity from Family conflict *and* my presence will certainly do that, don't you think?"

"What I think is that the Families will stop at nothing once they find out about him, and they will." She raised her chin and narrowed her eyes. "You'll teach the four years, regardless of what happens to him. Even if he's taken by a Family and is no longer enrolled."

"Agreed, so long as you do everything in your power to keep him safe."

*Prima* Rosethorn bristled and her eyes flashed.

I suddenly had to wonder which of the two witches before me might actually be the stronger ... or scarier.

"*No one* touches my students."

"That's what I'm counting on," Mel said. She popped the rest of her sandwich into her mouth. "Noah, dear, why don't you take Felicity downstairs while Evelina and I discuss the admissions and housing? It will be quite boring, I assure you."

"Okay."

Felicity hopped off my lap and padded out of the room, while I followed her.

## CHAPTER ELEVEN

I WENT DOWN A FLOOR, GRABBED A SODA FROM THE FRIDGE — Felicity *mrowred* and wound along my ankles as I closed the fridge, so I grabbed a small bowl to pour her a little of the soda. I'd never seen a cat drink soda before getting to Mel's, but Felicity had some with nearly every meal, so I figured Mel knew what she was doing.

Back in the living room, I grabbed one of the game controllers, then sat on the couch.

I tried to get into the game, but it was difficult because I kept thinking about what Mel had said about us being related. I'd spent my entire life without that sort of connection and she'd just laid it out there like it was nothing.

"*Mrowr!*"

"Stop it!" I said, batting her paw away from the controller. The cat seemed to get very upset by the way I played some games. "If you want to play, get your own controller."

"Mrowr."

I sighed and set the controller down on the coffee table, then sat back on the couch. Felicity hopped into my lap and rolled over for belly rubs.

"Is that all you wanted?" I asked, running a hand over her soft fur.

Felicity purred.

"Yeah, I guess this is better than a game anyway." I sighed. "So, what do you think, Felicity? Am I getting too wound up about maybe being related to Mel?"

"Mrowr."

"Yeah, maybe."

Having lived with Mel for a couple months now, I was more and more convinced that Felicity wasn't just an ordinary cat. At first, I'd thought Mel's habit of talking to her like a person was odd, but over time it really seemed like the cat could understand what was said to her. Maybe not really understand, but at least understand the tone and respond accordingly.

Thinking back, that had really been the case for all the years that I'd known Felicity.

I'd spent hours sometimes telling her my troubles and stuff that happened in my life when I'd had no one else to talk to and she'd always responded appropriately. If I was sad, she comforted me. If I was happy, she'd be playful.

Probably she just understood people's tone of voice and mood enough to go off that. I'd heard pet owners describe that sort of thing, so maybe it was just the way with cats and dogs.

"It's just ... I've always dreamed of meeting my family, you know?"

"Mrowr."

"Not my parents, I mean, since they left me in a baby-drop like an overdue library book, but ... someone?"

"Mrowr?"

"Oh, well, I shouldn't complain, I guess. Things have gone a lot better for me than I expected — what with finding out I'm a warlock and everything Mel's done for me."

"Pfft!" Felicity squirmed in my lap.

That usually meant I'd been rubbing too long in the same place and I was about two strokes away from the cat trying to gut my forearm with her claws, so I moved my hand slightly.

"That better?"

"Mrowr."

"You're right — I should shut up and concentrate on rubbing you properly. That's more important, isn't it?"

"Mrowr!"

Felicity planted her hind feet in my stomach and stretched the length of my legs, head and forepaws stretching past my knees, to expose more of her belly for scratches — which I accommodated, switching to both hands.

I heard footsteps and a moment later Mel and *Prima* Rosethorn came down the stairs and into the living room.

"We've settled all the arrangements," Mel said. "I'll tell you the details in a moment, dear, but Evelina is heading back to Willowmere to get things settled there."

"Oh, thanks! Um, thank you, *Prima* Rosethorn —" I nodded at Felicity, still in my lap, and hoped she wouldn't be offended that I didn't get up. I still had healing scratches from the last time I'd tried to displace the cat so I could go to the bathroom.

"You're welcome, young man," *Prima* Rosethorn said, "though you might not thank me later."

I kind of wanted her to expand on that, but instead she looked at Felicity, pursed her lips, and turned to Mel.

"You know, Melaina, you really should —"

"Felicity is fine," Mel cut her off. "She has her own will."

"Hmph," *Prima* Rosethorn said, then turned back to me. "I'll see you in a week, *Magellus* Ashe, when the new school year starts."

With that, Mel walked her to the door.

When Mel returned, I saw that she'd stopped in the kitchen. She had a bottle of wine, a bowl, and two glasses, pausing to open the wine, fill all three, and setting one glass and the bowl on the table before sitting in one of the armchairs.

"It's early for a drink, so soon after tea, but I feel the need for fortification," Mel said.

She kicked her shoes off and curled up in the chair. It was a sexy pose, even with the more conservative dress she had on — or maybe because of the conservative dress. She was completely covered, save for her bare feet and ankles curled around her butt. The sexy effect was only made more so when she reached up and pulled the pins from her hair and shook her head to let it fall down in a messy tangle.

"Evelina is so very formal," Mel said, scrubbing at her hair with her fingers, which mussed it even more. "I much prefer how casual mundane society has become these days."

"What was that she called me? Magallous?"

Felicity pushed harder on my stomach, stretching herself until her front paws reached the coffee table, then rolling over to step from my lap to the table, and began lapping at her bowl of wine. I shook my head, thinking that couldn't be good for a cat, but Mel treated it as something entirely normal.

The glass for me was new, though, since Mel had offered me a single glass with dinner, but shut me down any other time I suggested I have alcohol outside of that.

"*Magellus*," Mel said. "It's a title for young warlocks — rather like Mister in today's parlance. *Magella* is the term for a young witch."

"Oh, okay."

Mel closed her eyes and took another sip of her wine. It was clear she was thinking about something, so I waited for her.

"First," she began, taking another drink, "I am truly sorry that I didn't take into account how you might react to finding out we are likely related. Witches track familial lines to a degree most mundanes would consider absurd — and I assumed, being raised as a mundane, a relationship of such distance wouldn't be meaningful to you."

"Does that mean you know for sure we're related?"

I wasn't sure how that could be, given that I didn't even know who my parents were, but I wanted it to be.

Mel shook her head and I felt my shoulders slump.

"No, not to an absolute certainty, I suppose. Only that it's very likely given your combination of resonants — Control is extremely rare and your particular combination I've only seen in my line. That means it's very likely that we are, but I can't be certain how. Quite confused as to how, actually. I do wish you knew your parents, though — I'd dearly love to trace your family history. Perhaps find..."

She shook her head.

"What's past is past and should remain so," she muttered, taking a long drink of her wine.

"However, we are related," she went on, "however distant it is, I do believe we are."

I swallowed hard, staring at her.

"So ... maybe an aunt? A cousin? Maybe we could take one of those DNA tests and —"

Mel chuckled, but her eyes seemed sad.

"More distant than that, I'm afraid, but also more direct. Far more of both."

"That still —"

Mel shook her head sadly.

"No, I'm afraid at that degree of remove, there's as much relation as nearly any two random people — at least at the genetic level. But I am certain I'm back there somewhere — and that is ... more important to me than you can imagine."

Mel was silent for a time, staring into her wine, then she must have seen the disappointment on my face, because she leaned over and laid a hand over mine.

"Genes can't give a hug, Noah. Witches bear longer connections." Mel sat back and closed her eyes. "I can understand your desire to connect with family, but I also won't lie to you about how closely we might be connected. But, please, know that I do care for you — both Felicity and I."

I nodded, not trusting myself to speak. I don't think I knew until the possibility we were related came up how very much I wanted that — not necessarily with Mel, but with anyone. Even the tenuous feeling of family that came from a foster home was gone for me now, and I seemed to have latched onto Mel for that. Maybe I shouldn't have, but there are some things you don't have a choice in.

"So," Mel said, "the good news is that you are admitted to Willowmere and should begin preparing for that — as well as for having a roommate."

# CHAPTER TWELVE

We took the train to a magic school.

It was disappointing.

The platform wasn't hidden and the only food service was a cart with stale egg salad sandwiches expiring today — luckily Mel had packed us sandwiches she'd made herself.

A cab took us from the station, out of town, and dropped us at the end of the school's long driveway that ran for nearly half a mile between two streams with massive willows on the far side of each, then ended in a wide expanse of manicured grass around the school buildings. The driver made a circle around a heavily planted open space to stop at the far side of the circle.

The school itself seemed to consist of three main buildings around that open, grassy space with the driveway on the fourth side. There were a few other buildings around, but those three and the open quad were the focal point.

"We're rather later than most," Mel said as the cab pulled to stop. "The majority of students will have arrived earlier today or over the weekend."

It was late in the afternoon, in fact, and I only saw one other car dropping someone off, and she hurried toward one of the buildings towing a rolling suitcase before our cab even came to a complete stop. Aside from her, there was no one visible except for *Prima* Rosethorn waiting for us.

We got out of the cab and retrieved our luggage from the trunk — I had luggage now, a small rolling suitcase as well as my new backpack, while Mel had a larger case and a carrier full of Felicity. The cat hadn't objected to getting into the carrier, but she was clearly not happy about it.

"Melaina," *Prima* Rosethorn said. "*Magellus* Ashe. Welcome."

"Thank you, Evelina," Mel said.

"Thank you, *Prima*," I echoed.

"*Mrowr! Pffft!*"

Mel chuckled. "I'm afraid I should hurry to my rooms — Felicity isn't fond of traveling like this."

"Well, it's her own fault," *Prima* Rosethorn said. "If she'd only —"

"*Rrrowwrr!*"

"Really, I should hurry, Evelina."

"Oh, very well — your rooms are in the administrative building — 313. You recall how to get there?"

"I do, thank you." Mel turned to me. "I'll see you in class tomorrow, Noah."

I nodded, swallowing. I'd never liked new schools and this one was particularly new and a more intimidating place than a public school.

"Okay, Mel."

"*Magistra* Blackwood," *Prima* Rosethorn corrected me. "The teachers here are referred to as *Magistra*."

I nodded quickly as Mel chuckled.

"I understand, *Prima* — I'll see you tomorrow, *Magistra* Blackwood."

Mel patted my arm and strode off, pulling her suitcase with Felicity's carrier balanced on top.

"For you, *Magellus* Ashe, you will find your room in the residence building there." She pointed at the building to the left side of the quad. "You're on the fifth-floor with the other first-years — room 506. I trust you can find it?"

"I'll do my best, *Prima*."

With that, she strode off as well, leaving me alone on the quad.

---

THE QUAD WAS EMPTY, but the residential building wasn't.

The bottom floor was a common area of sorts, with lots of seating and rooms with televisions, gaming consoles, and study cubicles. There was more to the rear of the building, but the stairs were just inside the doors and I was headed to the fifth floor.

The bustle of activity ceased as I came through the doors and a couple dozen girls stopped what they were doing to stare at me, then quickly began whispering to each other.

That wasn't unexpected — I was the only guy at an all-girls school, so of course I'd be an oddity. I did wonder if there'd been a rumor mill to let them know I was coming. Regardless, I just kept walking, trying not to make eye contact with anyone — I figured there'd be enough drama tomorrow and didn't need any before classes started.

Right now, the only one I wanted to make a good impression on was my ... roommate.

Not that I minded sharing a room with someone, I'd done that all my life, but, well, this was going to be different.

I went up the stairs — five flights — because there didn't seem to be an elevator. Luckily my bag wasn't that heavy and I was able to just carry it by the handle. My room, 506, was about halfway down the hallway on the left-hand side.

I entered the room, which had a narrow entry space. There was a bathroom to the right as I came in. The entryway was flanked by closets, then opened up into the main room with a bed on each side and two desks at the back just in front of a large window on the back wall.

One of the beds was occupied, but all I could see from my angle by the door was a pair of sock-clad feet at the far end. The socks were brightly striped in a rainbow pattern and the toes twitched as the door shut behind me.

I took a step.

The socks, I saw, connected to a pair of jeans.

"Is that the feral warlock who's going to ravish us all?"

I paused, wondering what tone to take as the only guy at an all-girls school.

My new roommate's tone sounded like she was teasing, rather than hostile, so I thought a little riposte wouldn't be amiss, but then who knew? Maybe I'd get hauled up before the *Prima* for sexual harassment?

I decided the striped socks and her tone made that unlikely. Anyone who wore something that bright had to be fun.

"Ravishers R Us, at your service. Ready for all your ravishing needs, day or night." I tossed my pack toward the end of the unoccupied bed and stepped into the room to stare down at my new roommate.

She was cuter than I'd expected, with a round face, button nose, and a lopsided grin. Long red hair tied back in a pony tail and green eyes, with a scattering of freckles. Petite, too — she'd probably give Morgan a run for her money on shortness. She wore a blue t-shirt with a pink unicorn and a rainbow on it.

"Noah Ashe," I said, holding out my hand.

The girl narrowed her eyes and stared at me for a moment, then took my hand, using it to pull herself up and stand.

"Samantha Prescott," she said. "Call me Sam — and keep your ravishing business elsewhere, I like girls."

"What a coincidence, so do I."

Sam grinned.

I sat on the edge of what I assumed was going to be my bed and

Sam followed suit on hers. I noticed that the t-shirt wasn't as sweet as it first appeared, since the rainbow seemed to be a result of the unicorn farting. I had a feeling I was going to get along well with my new roommate.

"So is that what everyone's saying?" I asked. "That I'm going to ravish everyone in the school."

"Only the foolish – others think they'll be the ones to mark you and be heroes to their Family for bringing in a fresh warlock."

"Great," I said, "that marking thing again."

Sam shrugged. "It's pretty important" she said. "Who you get marked by or who you mark, is pretty much the biggest event in a witch's life."

"Well, I guess I haven't known about it long enough for it to be that important to me."

"That's right, I heard you were *completely* feral."

"Feral?"

Sam grinned. "That's just what we call it when a warlock comes out of the outcasts and isn't bound by a high priestess yet."

"Well, I have no intention of ever being bound to one, so I guess I'll stay feral."

Sam's grin fell. "Really?" Her brow furrowed. "What are you going to do then?" She held up a hand before I could answer. "Not that it's any of my business, but don't you want to be part of a coven?"

I shrugged. "I don't really know. I'm so new to this, but I know I'm not going to let somebody take control of me."

Sam looked down at her feet. "Yeah, I get that."

Clearly there was something about control in her own life, but I wasn't going to go there, having just met the girl.

"Well," she said into the awkward silence, "that backpack doesn't look like it has your books and stuff in it. Did they not get any for you?"

"The *Prima* just told me the room number and sent me up." I shrugged. "She didn't say anything about books."

"You're going to need them by the first class tomorrow morning."

Sam hopped to her feet. “So, we should go pick them up now — the supply office closes in an hour. Did you get your schedule yet?”

I shook my head.

“They’re really throwing you to the wolves, huh? Yeah, even the staff has been talking about you. I don’t think they expect you to be here long, which is probably why they put me in here with you.”

“Really. Are you my punishment?”

Sam chuckled “I think we’re punishment for each other. They probably figure that whoever your roommate is they’re going to try to mark you or you’re going to try to mark them, and I’m no great loss to my Family if that happens.”

I frowned “Why do you say that?”

“I’m a onesie.”

“A onesie?”

Sam chuckled. “Crone’s wrinkles, I’m going to have to teach you everything?” She held up one finger. “A onesie has one resonant. Most witches have two. The really powerful have three.” She shrugged “Onesies don’t have a lot of power. That’s why my mother sent me here. She thought maybe the staff could help increase my power enough so I’d be useful to a coven. If not, I’ll wind up just a servant.” She put on a very serious voice that was clearly mockery of someone. “And that would be embarrassing to the Family and Mother.”

“That seems harsh.”

“There aren’t enough covens to take any but the best and most powerful witches. Nobody wants someone who isn’t powerful. And I have a crap resonant, too, so I’m not holding out much hope.”

“What’s your resonant?” I asked, wondering what could be considered crap by witches when it allowed them to do magic.

Sam stared at me for a moment. “Asking what someone’s resonant is just like that? That’s pretty fucking rude.”

“Oh, shit,” I said, “I’m sorry. Mel told me not to ask things like that, but I forgot.”

Sam stared at me a moment longer, then grinned “I’m just

messing with you. Well, it is rude and a lot of people might get upset at your asking that but mine's pretty much an open secret, so I don't mind."

She took a deep breath.

"I got stuck with Love." She grimaced. "And not, like, friendship love or family love that might be useful, but fucking romantic love. What're yours? If you don't mind telling me ... and even if you do, since you asked about mine. Fair's fair."

Why did I even ask that question? Mel had told me not to tell anybody I had three resonants, but I really didn't want to start my relationship with a new roommate with a lie. Especially because Sam seemed really cool and accepting — something I figured I'd need here.

"Um, Lust and Pain" I said quickly, feeling a little weird about saying that first one to some girl I just met.

If I just told her the two and left one out, that wouldn't be the same as lying. It would just be an omission. Control was the big issue, so I couldn't tell Sam about that.

"Oh!" Sam said. "Those two should be ... fun? Do you know your affinities yet?"

I shook my head. "You?"

"No, I have such a tiny bit of mana to work with that nothing's shown up yet."

"Oh. So, what's so bad about having Love as your resonance anyway?"

Sam began ticking things off on her fingers. "I'm a lesbian. In a society where we don't mix much outside of our Family. And each coven is even more insular. And the Families all reward children, especially male children. So, my dating pool, assuming I could join a coven, is basically twelve girls who all want to get pregnant. My odds of falling in love with someone I can actually have a relationship with are somewhere between slim and you're-kidding-right. If it was the kind of love you have for a friend, I could work with that, or even love of family ... even though I kind of hate my Family."

"Um, yeah, I can see where that would be a problem, but are you saying you can't date outside the coven? Even the, um, mundanes?"

"It's frowned upon — crossing lines like that. And a mundane? Some Families want to forbid that outright. They all remember the times before the Veil when we did that and it bit us on the ass. No one wants to get serious with a mundane. School's different, though — there's a mundane college on the other side of town and a lot of the girls find dates there. No one expects a college fling to get serious, so there's no risk of falling for someone you have to dump when you join a coven." She sighed. "But that doesn't help me, because a college fling you know's going to end isn't true romantic love."

I thought about what Mel had said, about how the witches used to marry normal people — mundanes — but couldn't get pregnant. They'd get pregnant from their warlock, but sometimes the mundane husbands found out and that caused trouble for the coven. It kind of made sense that they wouldn't do that now but it was also easier to get casual sex these days than it was four hundred years ago.

"You know, you don't have to marry someone to have sex anymore, right?"

"Yeah, but covens are such tight knit groups that something casual with somebody you don't know as well doesn't seem as good — at least to me. Witches are kind of conservative in a lot of ways." She shrugged. "Anyway, let's go get your books and schedule. Actually, there's a mailbox outside the door — maybe your schedule's in that."

I opened the door and found the box hanging on the wall beside it that contained an envelope with my name on it. I shut the door again and opened the envelope. There were several papers inside that I'd look at later, but Sam was right about a class schedule.

Noah Ashe - 1$^{st}$ Year, Fall Semester

9:00 - 10:00, Lecture Hall 1, *Magistra* Nightingale:

HIS 101: Foundations of Magical History - An introductory

course exploring the origins and development of magical practices and societies throughout history.

10:00 - 11:00, Room 207, *Magistra* Blackwood:

CAS 101: Introduction to Spellcasting Essentials - A beginner's course covering the basic principles of spellcasting, including foundational will and intent, mana channeling, and spell theory.

1:00 - 2:00, Room 109, *Magistra* Fallowell:

POT 101: Basics of Potion Brewing - An entry-level course focusing on the fundamental skills and knowledge required for potion making, including ingredient properties and simple brews.

3:00 - 4:00, Room 204 / Elemental Grove, *Magistra* Cassian:

RIT 101: Elemental Ritual Practices - A foundational course introducing students to basic ritual magic, focusing on elemental and seasonal ceremonies and their significance in magical practice.

"GIMME," Sam said, bouncing on her bed and holding her hand out, wiggling her fingers until I handed it over. "Let's see ... yeah, we have the same classes in the morning, but not the afternoon. I don't have a rituals class, because I'm probably never going to be in a coven, so I got stuck with Remedial Mana — then I have Potions 204. If I don't get a coven, I'll probably spend my life mixing shit for one."

"Remedial Mana?" I asked.

Sam made a rude noise.

"Yeah, it's a baby class for onesies who can't generate much mana," she said, voice going suddenly bitter. "All about 'use what you have to your fullest ability' and shit. Magic for faster floor mopping. Let's go get your books."

Once Sam had her shoes on, she led me out of the room and back down the stairs.

"First-years are stuck on the top floor," she explained. "The higher grades get the best rooms on the lower floors. Seniors are on the bottom, but in that wing that sticks out the back of the building.

The rest of the bottom floor is the cafeteria, school store, and the common rooms."

"So, no secret passwords to get to our room?"

Sam chuckled. "The senior girls hate jokes like that. So, watch it."

We left the dorm building and crossed the quad to the admin building. Sam took me to the right after we entered and down a long hallway to a door that had the top half open. The room behind was full of shelves covered in books, boxes, and plastic bins.

"Good afternoon, *Magistra* Hennessy," Sam said as we arrived at the counter. "I've got a new student who just arrived and needs his books."

*Magistra* Hennessy looked to be in her thirties. Whatever her age, she'd reached it well. Her dark hair was pulled back in a bun, and the rest of her was dressed ... well, slutty-librarian is about the only way to describe it. A white shirt. with a couple too many buttons undone that showed off some impressive cleavage, and a very tight skirt that ended just above her knees.

She tilted her head back so she could look down her nose at me.

"Ah, yes ... the feral."

I had a feeling I was going to be met with a lot of comments like that.

*Magistra* Hennessy held out her hand.

"Schedule?"

I handed mine over and she turned to the side of the counter and lifted a plastic bin from a shelf there, then started putting books in it.

"History. Spellcasting. Brewing. Rituals," she said as she set each one down, then put my schedule back on top and slid a pen and another paper toward me.

"Sign here," *Magistra* Hennessy said, adding some notebooks, pens, and pencils to the bin, followed by a laptop. "These are quite valuable and will be costly for you to replace. I suggest you refrain from ... tree climbing or mud puddles or whatever it is you fellows do."

I chuckled. "Don't worry, I'm not twelve."

*Magistra* Hennessy sniffed. "All males are twelve."

---

ONCE WE GOT BACK to the room, I started unpacking and Sam offered to help me put my things away.

Each bed had a set of drawers in its base as well as the two closets off the entryway.

I looked around the room and realized there was going to be some awkwardness with a girl for a roommate — well, probably a lot of awkwardness, but one thing needing immediate attention.

"Um, how should we handle changing clothes?"

Sam grinned and jerked her head at my midsection.

"What? You don't want me seeing the package?"

I flushed. "I thought you were gay?"

Her grin widened.

"Doesn't mean I can't look. I like girls, sure, but I'd rather go to a Chippendales show than the typical strip club. The show's a lot better."

Mel had said the same thing and I started wondering how many witches were in the typical Chippendales audience.

I shrugged. My question had been more for her comfort than mine. I had a decent physique and the "package" was, if an internet search for the average was to be believed, a decent bit above. Still, even after just a couple hours of knowing Sam, I had the feeling she was fucking with me again.

"Okay," I said, grabbing the bottom of my shirt and starting to pull it up.

"Whoa, boy!" Sam said "You're gonna have to get a lot better at recognizing when I'm not being serious with you if we're gonna be roommates. I don't think you're Chippendales caliber and *I'm* not putting on a show for you either."

"Ah, so it's *your* package you're worried about being seen?"

Sam narrowed her eyes.

"You think there's something wrong with my package?" she asked.

The deeply buried, lizard-part of my brain started sending danger signals.

"Um, I'm sure your package is fine."

Sam sighed. "Who am I kidding?" She put her hands to her chest. "I can't even pad these things to a B."

"Oh, I'm sorry — too far? I didn't mean to make you feel bad. I think you're cute."

Sam glared at me.

*Drop your tail and run!* my inner-lizard screamed.

"Cute." Her tone was icy.

I realized I'd stepped in it somehow.

"Cute isn't good?"

"No, it isn't. Most girls kind of want the same thing that a guy wants in a girl. Beautiful. Voluptuous. Unbearably sexy," she sighed. "Cute. Cute is a sentence to life in the friend zone."

"Oh, it's like being a nice guy?"

"Exactly! When someone says a girl is cute, that means she's looking at her like a little sister, not someone to smush muffins with."

"Smush muffins?"

"It's a thing."

"Well, if it's any consolation — if you were into guys —"

"No. Just no. You don't have a muffin and what you do have is ... singularly unattractive."

"Hey!"

"Am I lying? Do you think they're attractive? "

I sighed "No, you're right. They're kind of ugly."

"So, you can understand why I don't want to see one on a daily basis."

"Alright. So, what are we going to do?"

"Well, I'm okay with just changing in the bathroom every day."

"That works — I'll plan on doing that too."

"Good. Come on, let's go get some dinner."

We left the room and started down the stairs again. I realized I was pretty hungry and looking forward to a magic school welcoming dinner.

"So, is there, like, a great hall for meals?"

"A great hall?"

"Yeah, with long, wood tables and benches and floating candles with platters of food everywhere?"

Sam rolled her eyes.

# CHAPTER THIRTEEN

It was not a Great Hall.

It was a cafeteria.

Much like the cafeteria at every school I'd ever been to. Linoleum tile floor. Metal tables, with metal benches attached, that folded up in the middle so they could be rolled out of the way. There was a curtained stage at one end, because the place seemed to double as an auditorium, and a cafeteria service line with hair-netted women standing over stainless steel steam tables.

"You know," I whispered to Sam as we approached the end of the serving line, "for being a magic school, this place lacks a certain something."

"Well, you'll see magic in the classes when they start tomorrow."

She pulled out her phone and checked the time.

"Whoops. We're a little bit early," she said as she pulled me away from the line off to some benches nearby.

"How are we early? There are people in line."

"It's only a few minutes after six," she said. "We can't get into line until quarter after."

"What about them?" I asked, gesturing at the line of girls already waiting.

"They're upper-grades" Sam said. "First-years can't get in line until the upper years have had a chance to get in line before them."

"Geez, my public high school wasn't this bad."

"Oh, when it comes to cliques and privileges, I bet mundane high school doesn't have a thing on witches."

We waited a few minutes, then Sam checked the time again and led me to the end of the line.

"Now we can get in line. If someone from an upper grade comes down after us now, then they have to go to the end of the line like anybody else."

The line moved forward and built up behind us as more and more late arrivals joined.

I grabbed a plastic tray and some silverware, then set it on the metal rails that hung in front of the Plexiglass-screened steam tables. The food, when we got to the serving area, didn't look too bad — and as we got closer to the food, I realized it actually looked pretty good.

At least everything was identifiable — back in my high school, they'd served a thing that we really couldn't tell if it was meat or cake. We just called it meatcake and it tasted exactly like you'd think meatcake would taste.

One big difference between Willowmere's cafeteria and high school was the women serving the food. They were all clearly witches, because they looked to be between twenty and forty, and all extremely attractive. I wondered why such attractive women with magic powers would be working in a school cafeteria, but Sam had said that she might wind up a servant somewhere, so maybe the onesies who couldn't gain enough power to enter a coven did all the more menial jobs in witch society?

That seemed kind of shitty, to be honest.

We slid our trays down the line and I had mine loaded up with a plate of roast beef, mashed potatoes, both with gravy, some green beans that looked pretty good — they weren't all gray like they'd come from a can, these looked fresh — a fresh roll, and a slice of apple pie for dessert.

Sam got some kind of fish and a salad.

At the end of the line there were coolers with drinks, so I got a soda and Sam got a bottled water.

Then we reentered the cafeteria and it got really quiet as everyone stopped what they were doing to look at me. I'd been so busy chatting with Sam in line that I hadn't paid much attention to the other students — now that I was walking, I had to look up and could see all the girls staring at me.

"Follow me," Sam said and started off through the space between the tables.

I hurried after her and it seemed like every set of eyes in the cafeteria was focused on me — no one was eating, no one was talking, they were just staring, moving only their heads to follow my path.

Off to one side near the stage there was a completely empty table — the cafeteria wasn't nearly full yet, but all the other tables still had many of their seats filled, so it seemed odd that this table was entirely empty.

Sam led me to the end farthest away from anyone else and set her tray down. I followed suit and sat opposite her on the hard metal bench.

"Ashamed to be seen with me?"

Sam grinned. "Maybe it's you who should be ashamed to be seen with me," she said. "This is the onesies table."

I looked around the cafeteria, and this time as I scanned the other tables the girls started dropping their eyes back to their food and to resume eating — and whispering. There was a lot of whispering.

"Let me guess, all the onesies have to eat at this table, because everyone else is a Mean Girl and won't let you sit with them?"

Sam nodded. "Got it in one."

"Schools are all the same."

"Yep."

Two girls approached our table with full trays, glanced at me, then looked at Sam, then hung their heads and sat at the far end of the table. The weird thing was they both looked the same, like twins, only they clearly weren't the same age.

I glanced at them then cut my roast beef and took a bite, chewing and swallowing before I commented.

I nodded toward the two girls. "Does that mean I'm the outcast of the outcasts?"

Sam narrowed her eyes and glared at the two girls.

"Brittany!" she snapped, and pointed to the bench beside her. "Stop being a silly twit and get over here."

The younger girl, who'd sat on my side at the far end, jumped and looked at Sam with wide eyes, then at me with even wider ones, then back to Sam. Sam just continued to glare at her until the girl looked down, swallowed, and slowly stood up.

She carried her tray around the end of the table to Sam's side, paused to bend over and whisper something to the older girl as she passed, then came down to our end and slowly sat next to Sam, keeping her head down and not looking at either of us.

The older girl watched us for a minute, then sighed and brought her own tray down to sit next to the younger girl.

I was on one side of the table and the three girls were on the other, and I wondered why everyone seemed to want to have nothing to do with me — I mean, yeah, I was the only guy here, but these girls couldn't have lived in isolation their entire lives. They had to have seen a guy before, right?

"Brittany, Hannah," Sam said, "this is Noah. He's a freshman and my roommate."

The two girls remained silent and still, not even picking up their silverware to resume eating.

Now that they weren't at the other end of the table, I could tell that they really did look the same. Brittany's dark hair was cut shorter than Hannah's, and she was slightly slimmer — not in a way that meant Hannah was overweight at all, but that Hannah was clearly the older one and her curves had filled out more. Brittany still had a certain coltish look to her.

"Oh, Mother's stretch marks, girls, he's a guy, not a werewolf. He's not going to go for your throat if you make eye contact! Say hello."

The girls glanced up at me in unison.

"Hello," they said together.

Then they looked down at their plates again, but at least they picked up their silverware and started eating.

"Better," Sam said. "Noah, this is Brittany and Hannah — Hannah's a senior and Brittany's a freshman like us. They're sisters, if you hadn't figured that out." She glared at the two girls and gave a disgusted sigh. "And apparently, they think that you're going to try to have your way with them right here on the cafeteria table."

Both the girls blushed, and I began to wonder if these witch Families might actually be so insular that the girls here really *hadn't* ever seen a guy before.

"I wouldn't do that," I said, taking a sip of my soda.

The two girls looked up at me and I grinned.

"I'd wait until I could get them somewhere alone without witnesses," I said.

*"Eep!"* Brittany jumped and hunched over. Hannah looked like she was about to run away.

"He's kidding," Sam said quickly.

"I heard Cassandra say he —" Hannah started to say.

"Cassandra's an idiot," Sam said. "She doesn't know anything and you shouldn't be listening to her."

"I *was* kidding," I said. "Sorry, it's just you girls act like you've never seen a guy before."

"We've seen guys before — you're not a guy," Hannah said.

I frowned. "I'm not?"

"You're a warlock," Brittany said.

Hannah nodded and Sam shrugged and nodded as well.

"A regular, mundane guy can't suck us dry and leave us a mummified corpse," Brittany said.

"*What!*"

"He's not going to do that," Sam said.

"But he could," Hannah said. "Even if he didn't mean to."

"What the hell are you talking about?"

"Girls, you're scaring him —"

"*He's* scared?" Hannah asked.

"Nobody's been drained for, like, two hundred years or something like that," Sam said.

Sam's reassurance did not reassure me, and it looked like it hadn't reassured Brittany or Hannah either.

"Nobody's had a feral at Willowmere in that long, either," Hannah said, then she flushed and looked at me before lowering her eyes again. "Sorry, I didn't mean to call you that."

She clearly had meant it, but I shrugged it away anyway. It probably wouldn't be the last time I head a slur thrown my way here.

I looked around.

The food line was getting shorter and four new girls had joined our table, sitting at the far end like Brittany and Hannah had to start.

I chewed thoughtfully for a minute, then had to ask.

"So, are you serious about that draining thing?"

Sam leaned forward and said more quietly, "Okay, so if a warlock takes too much mana during a harvest, he can completely drain the witch — but that hasn't happened in a really long time. It usually happened during marking anyway, if the warlock lost control of himself, but the Families have put an end to that. The covens are much better managed now."

"Because we learned what we were doing and now keep the warlocks under better control," Hannah said. "No offense."

"I don't plan on draining anybody," I said, raising my right hand and putting my left over my heart. "No ravishing, no draining. Solemn vow."

Brittany and Hannah looked at each other and Sam raised an eyebrow.

"Really," I said. "I wouldn't know how."

"Which one?" Sam asked.

My roommate had an evil grin on her face.

"I admit I understand the fundamental concepts of ravishing," I said, feeling my face heat up, "but draining, I have no idea what that even is."

Further discussion was paused as I noticed the cafeteria go silent again.

*How do they manage to finish a meal with all the drama?* I wondered, looking around to discover that everyone wasn't staring at me.

This time the focus was on one of the first tables where a girl stood frozen halfway over the bench with her tray hovering a couple inches over the table. An older blonde girl on the other side of the table glared at her.

"Little onesie doesn't know her place," the blonde girl said loudly enough to carry all through the cafeteria.

"Crone's bunions, did no one tell her where we're supposed to sit?" Brittany whispered.

"I can't believe her cousin didn't tell her," Hannah whispered back.

"Well Cassandra is going to give it to her now."

"Who's Cassandra?" I asked.

"The blonde," Sam said. "The high and mighty priestess-wannabe Cassandra Blake."

The blonde girl, Cassandra, narrowed her eyes further.

"Well, what are you waiting for?" Cassandra asked.

"I ... I don't know what I did to make you mad, I'm sorry," the other girl said.

Cassandra raised a hand above the table.

"Go sit where you belong," she said, wiggling her fingers at the other girl.

The girl's tray leapt out of her hands and everything on it would've wound up on her chest if she hadn't jumped back in time — as it was, the tray, and the girl's entire dinner, crashed to the floor upside down.

"Better clean that up little, onesie," Cassandra said, then picked up her fork and resumed eating. "We don't want the stench around here anymore."

And, just like that, everyone in the cafeteria went back to their own food, completely ignoring the girl, who was staring down at the remains of her dinner. She glanced at Cassandra, swallowed hard, and knelt to start trying to scoop the mess back onto her tray.

I frowned. "Isn't anyone going to help her?"

"Cassandra will just target anyone who tries," Sam whispered. "Interrupting her fun just makes her madder."

I shook my head.

Bullies just made me mad — I'd hated them since elementary school. Something about this scene irritated me even more, though, and I felt an oddly strong urge to go help the girl. Before I realized it I was moving, spinning my legs over the table's bench and standing.

"What are you doing?" Sam asked.

I took my plates and soda off my tray and set them directly on the table. I thought if we had two trays it would be easier for me and the girl to clean up that mess.

Without answering Sam, I took my tray and walked over to the other table — predictably, the cafeteria got really quiet and I could feel everyone's eyes on me, but I kept my eyes on the kneeling girl. I didn't want to raise my gaze and make eye contact with the blonde, Cassandra. That would just either encourage or antagonize her.

I could still notice, though, that Cassandra had some seriously enviable breasts. Her long blonde hair hung over her shoulders and draped her figure a little until you were close enough to see how the buttons of her blouse were straining.

I knelt beside the other girl. She had dark hair and was a little taller than Sam, I thought, though it was hard to tell with her crouching on the floor. I caught a glimpse of brown eyes before she quickly ducked her head and stared at the mess on the floor. It was hard to tell what her figure was like, because she was wearing pretty loose and baggy clothes.

"Hey," I said quietly, "you hold your tray still and I'll use this one to scrape things onto it, okay?"

"A onesie and a feral on their knees cleaning," Cassandra said. "How appropriate."

"Just ignore her," I whispered, pushing the mess toward her tray. "I'm Noah."

The girl glanced up at me then back down and her face turned red.

"Rachel," she whispered.

"Scrub it good, onesie," Cassandra said. "Service is going to be your life, after all."

I took my own advice and ignored her, but Rachel's shoulders stiffened and I heard what might've been a sniffle.

I clenched my teeth to keep from saying something. It was just so *meaninglessly* mean — what could this girl have possibly done to warrant that kind of bullying?

The truth, of course, was that the only reason bullies needed was weakness — they only respected someone stronger.

And since witches saw their resonants as strength, it kind of made me want to whip my three out. Mel had said *trinitaras* were so rare that Cassandra almost certainly wasn't one, so I wondered what she'd say to finding out I was.

Mel would probably kill me if I disclosed the most important secret she'd told me to keep before the first day of classes even started — so I clenched my teeth harder and turned my attention back to cleaning up Rachel's spilled food.

Most of the mess was picked up — there was just a thin layer left on the floor and I saw a woman approaching with a bucket and mop, so I stood up and took Rachel's elbow to help her stand with her tray full of food and dishes.

"And ferals should just be put down," Cassandra said.

I glanced at her. If she'd been a guy, this would be the point where we'd start squaring off. I'd done that with bullies enough times to know the pattern, but I couldn't very well smack Cassandra. It wouldn't have the same effect as on a guy, and would probably get me in a load of trouble.

If I knew more — anything — about magic, I might have tried some of that. I assumed that was how her finger flicking had upended Rachel's tray, so there seemed to be some magic use allowed between students. Unfortunately I really couldn't do any magic except the candle-lighting — and I didn't think setting Cassandra on fire would fall under whatever "acceptable magic use" policy Willowmere had.

No, Cassandra was trying to show everyone she was top dog by saying mean things so that's how we'd have to fight her — and, after years of tutelage by Morgan, who could make a bully seriously rethink her life-choices, I had some material to work with there.

They might call me "feral" and whisper behind my back, but I was still the only guy at an all-girls school and there was no way my opinion didn't matter to them a little bit.

I turned my back and led Rachel two steps toward the cafeteria serving line and trash cans, before pausing like I'd just noticed something.

I turned back to Cassandra.

"You know, you're not nearly good-looking enough to get away with being that nasty."

# CHAPTER FOURTEEN

Sam made it through the rest of dinner, the walk back to the dorms, and into our room before she threw herself onto her bed and started laughing hysterically.

"I ... can't ... believe ... you said ... that ... to her ..." She managed to get out between giggles.

"Rachel, you can come in if you want," I said, "but close the door so nobody hears Giggles here and runs to tell Cassandra she's being laughed at."

"In your room?" Rachel asked, eyes wide.

"Up to you," I said. "Sam's here to keep me from ravishing you and it looked like you wanted to say something."

After the exchange with Cassandra in the cafeteria, I'd walked with Rachel to the garbage cans to dispose of her tray and then back to the food line. The doors to the serving area were closed, but not locked, so I pushed one open. The staff was already moving trays of leftovers from the steam table and cleaning up, and they glared at us as we entered — but a few seconds later the woman with the mop and bucket came in and whispered to another woman who seemed to be head of the kitchen.

They were all much friendlier after that, and got Rachel a new tray with a fresh plate of food and two slices of pie.

"That's an extra one for you," the kitchen head said giving me a nod. "Glad to see someone take that witch down a notch."

I had to grin at that — it seemed Cassandra hadn't made any friends with the staff either, and if she treated all the witches with just one resonance as she had Rachel, I couldn't blame them. I also got the feeling that "witch" was sometimes used as a euphemism for something else.

Rachel had been quiet all through dinner, but she followed Sam and I back to our room afterward. She was staring at the floor and her face was bright red, making me regret the ravishing comment. Rachel seemed very shy and it didn't seem fair to embarrass her.

"I — I just wanted to say thank you again," Rachel said.

"No problem," I answered. "I was glad to help."

And I was. I'd probably made a mortal enemy of Cassandra and her little clique, but they just as probably weren't people I wanted to be friends with anyway. In fact, I kind of liked the onesies — at least Sam, Rachel, Brittany, and Hannah. The rest, four of them, had stayed at the other end of the table. The five of us at our end had a good time getting to know each other, and the three girls I'd first met had quickly gotten over their initial wariness of me — at least most of it. Sam, of course, had none of that and treated me like we'd already been friends for years.

"Did ... you ... see ... her ... face?" Sam managed to get out.

"No, I didn't look back at her."

"It was fantastic!" Sam cried, gaining a little control of herself. "You hit the nail right on the head with her — she's made so many mods to her body that she must have issues with how she looks."

"Mods?"

"Yeah, she never looked like that when we were at summer camp together," Sam said. "And it's not just that she's older — her nose is smaller, her lips are bigger, that hair color never occurred in nature, and the boobies are definitely enhanced."

I blinked. "That's a lot of plastic surgery."

For some reason that started Sam off laughing again and I looked at Rachel to see if she could tell me what was so funny.

"Witches don't need plastic surgery," Rachel said, "don't you know that?"

I shrugged. "I think I'm gonna get pretty tired telling people here I know nothing."

Sam laughed some more.

"Oh, well," Rachel said, "once we come into our power we can do a lot with our bodies. We don't get as sick as most people, and we can sort of change our appearance."

"Wow." I wondered if I'd be able to do things like that too. "So, she used her power to..." I cupped my hands at my chest in a rough approximation of how I remembered Cassandra's was.

Rachel flushed red and looked at her shoes.

"And if you look at her ears," Sam said, "you'll see that they're just a tiny bit pointed — she is *so* pretentious."

I sat on my bed while Sam regained her composure and sat up as well. I gestured for Rachel to come on in and sit down too.

She came farther into the room, but then hesitated looking between the two beds. We did have desk chairs in the room, but the desks were at the end of each bed with the chairs beyond that, so Rachel bypassed the beds and took one of those.

We spent about an hour comparing schedules and talking about what we knew about the teachers — most of that was Sam and Rachel, because I didn't know any of the teachers. Until we started talking about Mel's class.

"Mel's really nice," I said when Sam asked Rachel who *Magistra* Blackwood was.

"Who?" Sam asked.

"Um, *Magistra* Blackwood," I corrected myself.

Sam frowned. "You know one of the teachers?"

I shrugged. "Yeah — um, I know Mel. Not really well, we just met over the summer, but I know her."

"Mel?"

"Oh, yeah, she told me to call her that, but I'll try to remember it's *Magistra* Blackwood here."

Sam grunted. "Huh. I've never heard of the Blackwoods, other than the one, and I thought I knew all the Fam —"

Her eyes grew wide and she stared at me.

"Mel what?" she asked.

"Blackwood?"

"No," she snarled at me, eyes still wide and starting to bounce up and down on her bed like she'd been plugged into a wall outlet. "Mel is short for what?"

"Oh, Melaina," I said.

Sam's eyes widened even more and she looked at Rachel whose eyes were also wide but had added an open mouth.

"Melaina ... Blackwood?" Rachel asked.

I nodded. "Yeah —"

"Melaina *Seraphina* Blackwood?" Sam demanded.

I nodded again.

Sam reached across the space between our beds and grasped my upper arms tightly, shaking me until my teeth clacked together.

"You ... know Melaina *Seraphina* ***Blackwood***?"

I nodded — which was easy because she already had my head going like a bobblehead.

"What's she really like?" Rachel asked quickly.

Apparently, Mel was a big celebrity in witch society and the rest of the evening was the two girls asking me every question they could think of about Mel, not all of which they believed my answers to.

"The Blackwood *cooks?*" Sam asked.

"Yeah, she's really good at it. Best food I've had in my life."

That went on until there was a chime that seemed to come from everywhere at once, and then a voice.

"Lights out in twenty minutes. Twenty minutes until lights out."

"What was that?" I asked, jumping because the voice, too,

seemed to come from every part of the room. I looked around, but didn't see any speakers in the ceiling or walls.

"Lights out," Sam said as Rachel hopped up, hurriedly said goodbye and rushed for the door. "I'll change first, but there's probably only time for one of us to shower tonight — do you want to go now or wait until morning?"

"Ah, morning's fine. But what the hell was that voice."

Sam hopped up and began pulling pajamas out of the drawers under her bed.

"What?" she asked, giving me an incredulous look as she headed for the bathroom. "The school announcements?"

# THE CRONE

The forest again, so I knew I was dreaming.

Then I frowned, because I remembered Aurora and the previous dream I'd had here, but I also remembered *not* remembering the dream when I was awake.

Had the previous dream actually occurred, or was remembering it part of this dream? Did our dreaming selves have memories our waking selves didn't? That would be weird.

I looked around for Aurora, but didn't see her.

"Come on, boy, I don't have all night."

I turned back to the empty bit of forest where I'd just looked and found an old woman.

Very old. Wrinkled, hunched, head so bowed it seemed a strain for her to crane her neck enough to look me in the eye. She did, though, with a pale blue, rheumy gaze.

"Well?" she said, raising her right hand, which gripped a gnarled cane, and gesturing toward the clearing.

"Who are you? Where's Aurora?"

I had a feeling I was going to wind up liking the little girl a lot more than the old woman.

"I'm Viera. The Child's already spoken to you — it's my turn."

"Maybe I don't want you to have a turn," I said, backing away.

My heel came down on something sharp and I looked down to see what I'd stepped on.

"What the hell! Why am I naked?"

I quickly covered myself with my hands and backed up farther.

Viera cackled — I couldn't even call it a laugh, definitely a cackle.

"If you don't want to be naked in your dreams, boy, then exercise some discipline with them." She gestured toward the clearing again. "Come on, then, no one cares about your twig and berries." She lowered her gaze. "Or branch ... I'll grant you branch."

I felt my face go hot and tried to cover myself more completely.

"Come on, boy, to the Grove."

"Why?"

Viera raised her eyes to mine again and scowled.

"Because you can walk there or I can grab you by whatever's handy and drag you," she said, glancing pointedly at my hands.

"Okay, okay," I muttered, edging my way around her and back to the trail, then walking toward the clearing. "The other manifestation of my subconscious was a lot nicer."

There was a loud swish then a sharp pain on my ass as she smacked me with her cane.

"Don't be cheeky."

I skipped forward quickly, turning my head to keep an eye on her.

"What do you want?" I asked, figuring I should let my subconscious get this message across as quickly as possible so I could escape from its cranky, stick-wielding old woman manifestation.

"Same as the Child," Viera said, following me to the block of stone. "A gift and a geas."

"A what?"

"Which didn't you understand? Gift or geas?"

"I'm not an idiot," I said.

"The thing about this form, boy, is I have a lot of self-control —

but that comment tests even me." She set her cane on the stone block and leaned against it. "Aurora gave you her gift and her geas, an obligation, and now it's my turn."

I thought about my dream with Aurora, but didn't remember any gifts — yeah, she'd asked me to tell someone something and I'd agreed, so I guess that was an obligation.

"I don't think she gave me anything..."

"Love and reassurance aren't gifts?" Viera asked. "Though why she'd waste her geas on such a silly thing, I don't know."

I remembered the feeling of being unconditionally loved and immediately regretted my words. That had, indeed, been a gift, and I wanted to apologize to Aurora for ever doubting that. The feeling had been so overwhelming that a simple thank you didn't seem nearly enough.

"She knows, lad," Viera said, almost kindly, making me eye her warily.

"Okay, thanks — so you want something from me?"

Aurora had just asked me to pass along a message, I wasn't sure I really wanted to know what this old woman wanted me to do.

"And a gift," she said, reaching toward me and touching my forehead lightly with a finger.

I wanted to move away, but seemed rooted in place. Viera's touch was dry and cool, the skin of her fingertip thin and papery.

"There," she said, withdrawing her touch.

"Um —"

"I know, I know, you feel no different, and you likely won't notice it, but I've given you a bit of strength. We know you'll need it and it'll come to you when you do. Now, the geas — return my family to me."

"What?" I was asking that a lot, but this seemed like a really big task when I didn't know who the hell she was.

"My family's lost their way — I want the little fools back. Even the annoying ones." She frowned. "That's most of them these days, to tell the truth."

I shook my head. "How am I supposed to —"

I broke off and leapt back as Viera's cane slashed through the space I'd just left.

"Hey!"

"Don't be a fool, boy, you should know full well."

"Well, I don't!"

Viera sniffed. "Well, you'd better figure it out, hadn't you? That's my geas — bring my family back to the proper path. Fail at your peril."

"That's not fair!"

I didn't know what kind of peril the old woman might have in mind, but I was pretty sure it was peril I didn't want.

"Fair? Boy, you should find the one who told you life would be fair and kick him right in the fork. He lied to you."

"But how am I supposed to do that if you won't tell me who your family is or what path you're talking about? This doesn't make any sense!"

The old woman chuckled. "Oi, did the right bastard tell you life would make sense, too?" She raised her cane. "It'll come to you, boy. It'll come." She glanced up at the sky. "Time to go — fare well."

"Wait, can I ask you a question?"

"Of course."

"Are there more of you?"

She tapped me in the chest with her cane.

# CHAPTER FIFTEEN

I WOKE UP EARLY THE NEXT MORNING TO THE ROOM'S ALARM clock going off.

I crawled out of bed, slapped the stop button, and whispered, "Sam? You awake?"

The shadowed form in her bed rolled toward the wall and disappeared under a blanket.

"Sleepy-time," Sam mumbled.

"The alarm went off — we need to get ready for class. Sleepy-time is over."

"Snoozy-time!"

I chuckled. "All right, I'll hit the shower — but I'm turning the room light on as soon as I'm done."

"*Snoozy!*"

I grabbed my clothes and went into the bathroom, closing the door before I turned the light on. I quickly showered and brushed my teeth, then dressed and opened the bathroom door. Our room was every bit as dark as when I'd entered the bathroom.

"Sam? I'm turning on the light."

"Snoozy-time!"

"Snoozy-time is over."

I turned on the room's light.

"I hate you! You're *mean!*"

I chuckled again. "You'd hate me more if I let you be late for class the first day."

Sam dragged the blanket off her face, grumbling, and glared at me.

"How can you be functional this early?" she asked.

I shrugged. "I don't know — I've always kinda been a morning person."

She struggled her way to her feet and went to her closet.

"I knew you were some kind of pervert," she mumbled, heading for the bathroom with a pile of clothes.

I took a moment while Sam was dressing and doing whatever else girls do in the bathroom to go through the books and supplies I'd picked up yesterday.

It was pretty basic stuff — a couple of notebooks, a few pencils, and most of it fit in my backpack once I'd unpacked all my clothes.

I busied myself with arranging two notebooks and four pencils in my backpack along with my books so I could pretend I wasn't watching as Sam came from the bathroom, sat on her bed and drew on her socks. Her t-shirt was pastel-colored cartoon bears ... involved in some improbable and possibly illegal acts.

"Okay," she mumbled, sliding on her shoes. "Let's get some breakfast."

---

THE CAFETERIA SMELLED like bacon when we arrived.

There was less of a line than there had been for dinner, and Sam explained that breakfast and lunch were more casual than dinner, since the cafeteria was open longer to accommodate the different class schedules.

"Dinner's the only meal that everyone's out of class all at once," she said, grabbing a tray.

I took a tray for myself and we made our way down the line.

"Breakfast is anytime from five to ten," she went on, "and lunch from eleven to two."

The options for breakfast looked every bit as good as dinner the night before, maybe better.

The steam trays held bacon, sausage links and patties, fried potatoes, and fake scrambled eggs, but there was also an omelet station serving real eggs any way you liked, and, beyond that, pancakes, French toast, waffles, and a variety of breads and pastries. A table to the side held a crock of oatmeal, with a variety of dried fruits, and the coolers held a selection of juices and milk.

Sam made her way to the coffee urns next to the juice and poured herself a cup that was about equal parts coffee, milk, and sugar. I grabbed a cup of black, a glass of orange juice, and then had my plate loaded up with bacon and sausage before throwing on a couple pancakes and smothering the whole thing in syrup.

Sam got a bowl of oatmeal with every dried fruit and nut available.

"All that meat is going to kill you," she said. "The first bodywork you're going to have to concentrate on is clearing your damn arteries."

"Wait — are you saying witches can eat anything they want then just magic it away?"

"Mother's sigh, really?" my roommate huffed. "Just because you can use magic to fix something doesn't mean you should break it in the first place."

We reached the onesies table, which was still apparently a thing despite the more casual atmosphere of breakfast, and found Rachel already there.

Sam set her tray down and looked at Rachel's plate, which had more syrupy bacon on it than my own did.

"Really?" Sam commented.

"Mwut?" Rachel asked around a mouthful.

I went to the side of the table opposite Sam and sat next to Rachel.

"Sam's opposed to bacon," I told her, cutting my pancakes into bite-sized pieces.

Rachel's eyes went wide.

"But bacon's good!"

"You're damn right, bacon's good," I said, holding up my hand for a fist bump.

Rachel flushed red, but touched her fist to mine.

"I'm not *opposed* to bacon," Sam said. "I just don't have so much magic that I can repair the consequences of —" She gestured at our plates. "— eating an entire pig for breakfast."

I speared two slices of bacon with my fork, folded them over, and stabbed a couple bites of pancake before shoving the mess into my mouth.

"I'm sorry," Rachel said, "I can move down there if it bothers you."

"It doesn't *bother* me, I just —"

"What bothers you?" Hannah asked as she and Brittany joined us.

"Bacon," I told her.

"Oh," Hannah said. "I'm a sausage girl."

Hannah speared a sausage link and stuffed it in her mouth. I refrained from commenting.

"You're all going to have heart attacks and I'm going to laugh," Sam said, putting her head down and staring at her oatmeal.

After that we all chatted about other things, including comparing schedules to see who was in what classes, then it was time to go to our first class.

As we were all standing up, Rachel's plate slipped from her hands and landed in her lap — upside down, of course, so that her heavy skirt was covered in syrup.

"Oh, no!"

"Oh!" Brittany said, then hurried around the table to help. "I'll take your tray — you hurry back to the dorms and change for class."

"Thanks," Rachel said, hurrying away.

What I was glad she hadn't caught sight of was Cassandra and a couple other girls looking our way and laughing. I caught Sam's eye and nodded their way.

"Do you think she did something?" I asked.

Sam frowned as we picked up our trays and backpacks.

"Maybe? I'm not sure what Cassandra's affinities are — we're kind of far away, though, unless she's more powerful than I think she is. You need to be careful of her, though — she's not going to forget what you said at dinner yesterday."

"Well, if Mel and Felicity couldn't get through my shields, I don't think she will."

Sam frowned and avoided looking at Cassandra's table as we made our way to the doors.

"She doesn't necessarily have to get through your shields to do something. Look what she just did to Rachel — if she did it."

Out of the corner of my eye I could see Cassandra watching us walk by.

"I'm pretty sure she did," I said.

"Watch out, onesie!" Cassandra called. "I think the feral's after you!"

Under cover of the laughter that followed, I leaned into Sam and whispered.

"You said everyone already knows you're gay, right? Mind if I use it?"

Sam raised an eyebrow.

"Okay?"

I turned back to Cassandra.

"How does it feel to be at the bottom of the list for both the only guy in school *and* the lesbian?"

"I REALLY HOPE I don't have to insult Cassandra at every meal," I said as Sam and I exited the residence building and made our way across the quad to the classrooms.

"I'll share some things about her from summer camp that could give you some new material," Sam said. "There was a bathroom incident she probably still thinks about before falling asleep."

Our first class was in a lecture hall on the first floor of the building. Rows of tiered seating rose from where we entered, with a podium and whiteboards filling the bottom.

Sam led me up the steps to the last row.

"Let me guess, another onesie thing?"

"Yeah, but also by choice." She slid her backpack under one of the desks that lined the rows and pulled out her chair. "We learn pretty quick not to let anyone sit behind us."

She froze and caught her lower lip between her teeth.

"Um, you don't have to," she said, not looking at me. "You have two resonants. You can sit anywhere you want, if you —"

"What? No way. I'm sticking with the onesies —" I caught sight of Rachel and Brittany coming through the door and waved to get their attention. That, of course, caught the attention of others and the whispering and pointing started again as more and more girls filed into the hall. "You girls have been nice to me, which is more than I can say about the rest of them."

Brittany sat next to Sam and Rachel sat next to me after giving me a little questioning look and getting a nod. Rachel had changed her shirt as well after the syrup incident and the loose, baggy top was open enough for me to catch a glimpse of creamy, white cleavage as she sat.

I felt a swelling in my pants and double-checked my resonant stores to make sure they weren't unbalanced again, but they were fine, so it was just me perving on my new friend.

I dragged my eyes away before Rachel could catch me staring — the poor girl was so shy and quiet that her head would probably explode if she knew I'd been checking out her boobs.

Just then the class quieted as *Prima* Rosethorn entered the classroom, causing everyone to go quiet and hurry to their seats before she reached the podium.

"*Magellae*," the *Prima* began, then looked at me. "And our singular *Magellus*, welcome to your first year at Willowmere. Before *Magistra* Nightingale begins class, I wish to make a few special announcements while I have you all together here."

"I bet the west wing is closed to students who don't wish a painful death," I whispered to Sam.

"*Magellus* Ashe," the *Prima* said sharply, "is that something you wish to share with your peers?"

I had no idea how she heard me — I barely moved my lips, and I'd kept the volume really low.

"No, *Prima* Rosethorn," I said quickly.

"Good," she said, then scanned the rest of the room. "Firstly, I wish to address the matter of *Magellus* Ashe. I realize that his presence has come as a surprise to most of you, however, I wish to stress that having a warlock at Willowmere is not in any way unprecedented. Willowmere College has a long history of inclusivity, and having a warlock in our midst should be met not with rumor and speculation, nor with trepidation, but with an eagerness to learn about others and more broadly widen your experiences."

There was a sudden bark of laughter, quickly muffled, but I couldn't see which girl had laughed. *Prima* Rosethorne didn't seem to have that problem.

"*Magella* Patterson, would you care to share what it was you found so amusing?"

"No, *Prima*! I'm sorry," a girl called out.

"Well, I believe it was *Magella* Simmons who made the comment, perhaps she would like to share?"

I could see the girls now, because everyone else in the class had turned toward them. The one who'd laughed had her head hung low and the girl next to her also had her head bowed, but covered her face with her hands.

"*Magella* Simmons?"

The girl with her hands over her face responded with a muffled, "No, *Prima*, I'm sorry."

"Pity," *Prima* Rosethorn said, "as I believe it was quite relevant to my next topic. Perhaps I should share instead."

The *Prima* raised her hand and twirled her finger, and suddenly a girl's whisper filled the lecture hall.

"*I'd sure like to expand some experiences with him.*"

The hall erupted into quickly stifled laughter as *Prima* Rosethorn glared around at the girls then focused her stare on me and frowned.

Sam had turned to me and opened her mouth, but quickly closed it — along with clenching her fists and hopping up and down in her seat as though there was something struggling to get out of her, but she didn't want *Prima* Rosethorn to broadcast it to the whole room.

"There will be none of that at Willowmere this year," *Prima* Rosethorn went on. "That sort of fraternization with an uncontrolled warlock, no matter how tame or how great you think your self-control is, carries a great risk of it turning into an attempt at marking." She narrowed her eyes. "There will be no marking of any student, at Willowmere, no matter what your mothers may have told you. Even the attempt to do so, even if *unintentional*, will result in both students' immediate expulsion with prejudice."

There was a rustling sound as the class took that in.

I wasn't sure what prejudice meant, but the threat of expulsion was pretty clear, and I was okay with the rule. Yeah, it was fun to fantasize about being the only guy in an all-girls school, but the reality was I knew there'd only be drama and more if I were to date any of the other students. Being roommates with Sam and friends with Rachel and the others would probably spark enough rumor and drama to keep all of us busy for the year. I was perfectly fine with keeping those activities to partners from the mundane college like Sam had told me the girls did — if I could even manage something like that. I could just imagine the small talk.

*What's your major?*

*Oh, I don't go to the same college you do, I'm at the all-girls school.*

I did want to know what *Prima* Rosethorn meant by "no matter what your mothers may have told you", though. That sounded pretty odd.

"On a less dire note," *Prima* Rosethorn went on, "I am pleased to announce an addition to our faculty for this year."

I resisted the urge to whisper something about a new defense against the dark arts teacher to Sam.

"Several classes, including your Introduction to Spellcasting Essentials class, to Willowmere's great honor, will be taught by *Magistra* Melaina Seraphina Blackwood."

There were shocked gasps from the class, followed by a wave of applause as Mel entered the lecture hall. I rose with the rest of the class and clapped, though I was confused — based on the reaction Mel was a much bigger deal in the witch community than I knew, even after the intense questioning Sam and Rachel had put me through the night before.

"Wow," Sam said. "I can't believe we're going to be taught by The Blackwood herself."

"Is she really that big a deal?" I whispered. Our chat about Mel the night before had all been me answering their questions and not getting any of my own in.

"The Blackwood? Oh, yeah! She's one of the Powers."

"Powers?"

"Shush," Sam hushed me as the class settled down and resumed their seats.

Mel approached the podium and nodded to the *Prima* who stepped aside.

"Thank you, *Prima* Rosethorn, for that kind and flattering introduction." She looked around at the assembled students. "I will not take too much of your time. I'm sure *Magistra* Nightingale is eager to begin putting her class time to good use. I just wanted to say that I am honored to have the opportunity to teach at Willowmere, and looking forward to meeting each of you later on in class. I plan on teaching at Willowmere for the next several years, so will be seeing all of you through to graduation."

# CHAPTER SIXTEEN

We all left the lecture hall with a long list of books *Magistra* Nightingale expected us to read over the next week.

None of the other students seemed particularly worried about it, and when I asked Sam, she mentioned that all of the texts were things that the witch Families usually had their kids read long before coming to Willowmere.

Rachel tugged at my sleeve.

"I've read them all, I can help you ... if you want," she said.

"Thank you — I think I'm going to be a little overwhelmed with all the stuff you guys know, but I'd never heard of before this summer."

We split up after that, with Sam and I heading for Mel's class and the other girls heading for theirs. We'd finished comparing schedules during lulls in *Magistra* Nightingale's history lecture and found that, while Sam and I had Mel's class together in the morning, Rachel and I had the same afternoon schedule. Sadly, Brittany and I didn't have any classes together after the first of the day.

Mel's class was on the first floor as well, and was in another, but smaller, lecture hall, with tiered seating, and a large open space instead of just a shallow podium at the bottom.

Sam and I took our seats in the last row, and I grumbled a bit because I'd really have preferred to sit closer for Mel's class, but I didn't want to leave Sam sitting alone or with one of the other onesies who were still avoiding me.

"Is you having to sit in the last row a rule or just something everybody expects?"

Sam shrugged. "It's not a school rule, but breaking it just causes trouble."

I grumbled again but took my seat. Yeah, I wanted to sit up front, but I also didn't want to sit somewhere Sam couldn't or wouldn't.

Once everyone had taken their seats, Mel came in and there was another burst of applause — not as loud because only about a third of the freshman were in this class.

"So why is Mel so notable?" I whispered to Sam.

"Sshh," Sam shushed me. "I don't want to miss anything she says — and I can't believe you call her 'Mel'."

"Thank you, everyone," Mel said, motioning with her hands for silence. "I appreciate the reception, but there's no need to greet me with applause every time I enter a room. You shouldn't treat me any differently from any of your other teachers."

She left the podium and began pacing in the open space while casting her eyes all over the lecture hall.

"This class will be very hands-on with your mana, as you learn how to manipulate it, store it, and use it in your spells. In addition, we'll be working on improving and strengthening your personal shields beyond what you may have been taught in your Families. Shielding your power is important for a number of reasons — especially in the event of conflict, where you may be targeted with offensive spells."

One of the girls in the second row raised her hand.

"Yes, *Magella*...?"

"Fiddlestone, *Magistra* Blackwood, Helena Fiddlestone."

"Your question, *Magella* Fiddlestone?"

"Who would we be fighting? My mom said there hasn't been open conflict with the Patriarchy in decades."

"That's true," Mel said. "The last large-scale conflict with the Patriarchy occurred in nineteen fifty-four. However, there are always skirmishes and smaller attacks, as they haven't forgotten about us — and we have certainly not forgiven them. And there are the inter-Family conflicts to consider, as well."

"What's the Patriarchy?" I whispered to Sam.

"What?" she looked at me, bewildered. "How do you — right, you know absolutely nothing." She glanced at Mel who'd resumed talking. "Later?"

I nodded. Of all the teachers I didn't want catching me talking or ignoring her in class, Mel was at the top of the list.

Mel took a stack of papers from behind the podium and gave them to the first girl in the first row to begin passing around.

"These are some more recent historical texts and analyses that I'd like you to begin reading. While I'm sure *Magistra* Nightingale has already assigned you more reading than you'd prefer —" She waited for a few chuckles to subside. "— It's my understanding that she starts with and focuses on the history of witches in the Americas, beginning with our first arrival here. These sources are all more recent and detail the conflicts we've had with the Patriarchy since the last major battles. I also like to stress that this list is not exhaustive. There have been many unexplained disappearances of witches and even some warlocks over the last seventy years."

Another girl raised her hand. "Yes?" Mel said, raising her eyebrows.

"Katrina Cartright, *Magistra* Blackwood. Are you saying the Patriarchy was responsible for those disappearances?"

Mel shook her head.

"There is evidence that the Patriarchy was responsible for some of those disappearances — not all, by any means, but I do think every witch —" the corner of her mouth quirked up, "— or warlock should know how to defend themselves in the event of an attack."

The papers being handed out came to me from Sam, so I took one and tried to hand it to the girl five seats away from me in the back row, but she shied away like I had something contagious, so I set stack on the desk two seats away from her and returned to mine.

"As we'll be working on shields, and doing so often requires opening or dropping your personal shields for observation by someone else, I'd like you all to start giving thought to who in the class you might like to pair up with as partners — someone that you trust to be that open with, and to keep the secret of your resonants if you wish. There'll be oaths sworn to that by all of you — and before you mutter about that, you'd best get used to it. There are a great many secrets you'll keep after your stay here — or suffer the consequences if you don't.

"Now, if the girl you'd prefer to partner with happens to be someone in one of the other timeslots for this class, please let me know after class and I'll work with *Prima* Rosethorn to adjust your schedules so that you are both in my class at the same time." She glanced at me. "*Magellus* Ashe, since you are the first warlock to attend Willowmere in some time, there may be some reluctance amongst your peers to make themselves so vulnerable with you, so you may work with me directly on those exercises."

I started to nod, but wasn't really thrilled at the idea of being singled out for special treatment — I knew why, and that it was the only reason Mel was teaching here, but I didn't have to like it. I thought it would just set me farther apart from the other students. But Mel was certainly right that working with one of the girls would be awkward even if I wasn't trying to make sure no one knew I was a *trinitara* — and working that closely with one of the witches would certainly expose that.

I noticed Sam was sort of squirming next to me, so I glanced at her and saw that she looked ... disappointed?

"I could work with you," Sam whispered. "I mean ... if you didn't mind working with a onesie. I know it's not the best —"

She trailed off, leaving me to think about why she was offering, because she looked hopeful now. I bet most of the other girls wouldn't want to partner with her because of her being a onsie and — a quick look at our last row confirmed it — there was an odd number of onesies in the class, which would leave one of them having to find a partner amongst the girls with more resonants.

I couldn't partner with Sam because she'd find out I was a *trinitara* — but if I didn't partner with her, now that she'd made the offer, and she was hoping to partner with me instead of someone else in the class, then she'd be upset with me, and maybe hurt, and I had to live with her. The whole situation was made worse because I wouldn't be able to tell her *why* I couldn't partner with her. Explaining would have the same result as partnering with her in the first place — unless I lied to her, and I didn't want to do that either.

"*Magellus* Ashe?" Mel asked, brow furrowed and clearly wondering what I was doing. "Do you have something to add?"

I leaned close to Sam's ear, even turning my face so I was facing the back wall.

"Can you keep a secret?"

"What?" Sam was frowning at me now.

"If I told you something — something serious — like, life-threatening serious, could I trust you to keep it a secret?"

It was an abrupt decision, I knew, and probably stupid. After all, I'd only known Sam for ... less than a day and here I was thinking of telling her a secret that Mel told me could get me killed?

Sam was quiet for a second, which was heartening because that meant she was actually thinking about it.

"*Magellus* Ashe?"

Sam nodded.

"So long as it wouldn't hurt anyone I care about," she said, "I'll tell no one the secret you speak of — by my power, by my Grove, and by the Goddess I adore, I swear it."

I met Sam's eye and returned her nod. She'd just sworn the same oath *Prima* Rosethorn had when Mel told her, so if it was good enough for Mel it should be good enough for me. I turned back toward the front of the class.

"Thank you, Me — I mean, *Magistra* Blackwood, but I think Samantha and I would like to work together, if that's all right?"

"Really?" Mel said and there was some other murmuring in the class.

I nodded, but the look on Mel's face told me she didn't approve.

"If that's all right?" I repeated.

"Let's discuss it after class, *Magellus* Ashe."

And that only caused more murmuring.

I gulped, but nodded.

The rest of the class was like the first day of class anywhere, except for the topic being magic — Mel passed out more papers, a syllabus, yet more reading material, and exercise instructions for merging shields rather than dropping them, as that would be the first exercise for the partnered witches.

At the end of class, the girls started shuffling out, but Sam and I made our way down the steps to where Mel still stood at the podium.

Mel waited until the last of the girls was nearly at the door then looked at Sam.

"Would you mind waiting outside, *Magella* Prescott? I'd like to speak to *Magellus* Ashe privately on this matter."

"Of course, *Magistra* Blackwood," Sam said and headed for the door. "I'll wait for you outside, Noah, and then we can get to lunch."

Once we were alone Mel raised an eyebrow.

"Making friends already, dear?"

I shrugged. "At least I got a roommate I like."

Mel nodded.

"That is good," she said. "But with regard to a partner in my class, the exercises we'll be doing will require letting your partner see your resonants. From that she'll know you're a *trinitara* and might be able to deduce your primary affinity." She took a deep breath. "It's best if we put off anyone finding out that you're a *trinitara* with Control as long as possible. And by as long as possible, I hope that to be somewhat later than the first day of class."

"I understand — but Sam asked to partner with me and if I told her no and then didn't explain why..." I shrugged.

"I see." Mel pursed her lips.

"She promised to keep it a secret."

Mel's face went cold and she looked at the open doorway where Sam was standing.

"You've already told her?"

"No," I said, "I asked if she could keep a secret and she said she would. She said the same thing *Prima* Rosethorn said when you asked her to keep it a secret."

Mel's eyes came quickly back to me.

"What did she say?"

"The power, tree, goddess thing."

"Grove," Mel corrected me. "She made that oath without knowing what secret she was to keep?"

"She said so long as it didn't hurt anyone she cares about."

"Well, you seem to have made an impression," Mel said. She took a deep breath. "Very well, then — I won't gainsay that oath, breaking it would be far worse than anything I could do. If you want to tell her and partner with her, I won't object."

"Thanks, Mel — um, *Magistra* Blackwood."

"Just Mel when we're alone, dear," she said, laying a hand on my arm.

"Thanks, Mel," I answered, rushing out to catch up with Sam.

"So, what was that about?" Sam asked as I closed the classroom door behind me. Then she paused. "Sorry, I mean, if it's really private. You don't have to tell me, I'm just curious."

"She just had some advice for me."

"Well, if The Blackwood is giving you advice, you should probably listen."

"Why's that?" I asked. "I mean, why is everybody so impressed by her — I like her, a lot, but why is she such a big deal to witches? What did you mean earlier when you said she was a Power?"

We started walking, heading for the cafeteria.

"She's a Power in her own right."

"What's that?"

Sam looked at me. "I keep forgetting you know nothing."

"Hey!"

"You know nothing, Noah Ashe," she said, grinning.

"Just remember what happened to the girl in the show who kept saying that."

"A fictional death isn't going to keep me from good teasing material. Get used to it or join the archery club."

I held up my hands. "Okay, I do admit I know nothing about this witch shit."

Sam's grin grew wider. "It's good you know your limitations."

"So, what's Power in her own right mean?"

"It means that Melaina Seraphina Blackwood has no coven — she doesn't need one."

"Why?"

"The way I've heard it, and her history is really murky, is that she's outlived at least three major covens, through most of the wars with the Patriarchy, and she's now so powerful that she could defeat most covens all on her own."

I thought for a minute — hadn't Melaina said at the beginning of the class that open war with the Patriarchy had ended in the fifties? And *three* covens?

"Wait, how old do you think she is?"

Sam shrugged. "I don't think anyone knows — except her. We know she was at Salem, of course, and I've heard —"

"Wait, what do you mean she was at Salem — like, she visited there?"

"No," Sam said, "she was at Salem. During the Trials. She saved a half dozen real witches from the Trials."

I blinked. "That's impossible."

"Really? Witches do live a long time. The more power we produce and use, the longer we live. The Blackwood has *a lot* of power."

I thought about the way Mel's resonant stores completely filled her body, but still —

"Are you telling me that witches can live for hundreds of years?"

"Not, like, *many* hundreds, usually. Not most of us — usually around a hundred or two, maybe a hundred fifty is pretty normal. Baba's probably the oldest witch we know of, but she's a major exception."

"Baba?"

"Baba Yaga — nobody knows for sure when she was born, but at least eight hundred, I think."

"Eight hundred years?"

"Oh, no, sorry."

"That's a relief."

"I meant eight hundred AD. But that's when stories about her started and she was already powerful then, so she was probably born a few hundred years earlier."

I tried to take that in. I guess I should've expected it, given that Sam said witches can monitor their bodies and even modify them somewhat like Cassandra had. Staying healthy to over a hundred probably wasn't much of a stretch, even if I thought a hundred and fifty was. But if Sam was serious about Mel being at Salem during the witch trials, that would be a whole other level. I didn't want to even think about this Baba person.

"Are you really saying Mel's hundreds of years old? She looks like she's thirty... Thirty-five tops."

Sam grinned. "Don't let her hear you say that."

I shook my head.

"There are Family records and histories of Melaina Seraphina Blackwood arriving in Salem and trying to get the real witches out of the Trials — and other mentions of her a lot earlier than that. Rumors about her being way older."

"But, how?"

"She was already very powerful when she arrived in Salem, so must already have been part of a really powerful coven in the past." Sam shrugged. "I think some of the matriarchs — the heads of Families — are a few hundred years old. My mother's only ninety-two. But The Blackwood is ... another level."

"What? Your mom's in her nineties? How old are you?"

Sam swung her bag into my shoulder.

"Hey! Never ask a girl her age!"

I took a look around the quad. As we made our way over to the dorm building and the cafeteria, I wondered how old the rest of the girls at the school were.

"Sorry, it's just —"

Sam grinned. "I'm just teasing you — I'm eighteen, the same as you. It's not like we grow up slower, it's just that as we come into our power, we gain more control over things and use it to keep ourselves looking young and living longer. You know the saying, 'live hard, die young, leave a beautiful corpse'?"

"Yeah."

"Witches don't do the middle part — we pretty much look twenty or thirty something until we croak. The whole 'crone' thing never happens. Patriarchy propaganda ... except for, you know, the actual Crone."

I gave a little sigh of relief. It was one thing to be the only guy in the girls school — it would be another thing to be the only eighteen-year-old guy in the school full of, like, fifty-year-olds or something.

"So, what's the secret?" Sam asked.

"Um, later? Tonight, when we're back in the room?" It wasn't something I thought I should talk about out in the open.

"Okay, but it better be good."

# CHAPTER SEVENTEEN

The potions classroom looked like my old high school chemistry class and not the shadowy den of brews and alchemy I was hoping for.

Chest high tables with four stools, two on each side. Each had a stainless-steel sink and a couple gas taps. Shelves lined the walls with an assortment of beakers and other glassware, as well as jars of what I assumed were ingredients — at least those looked like something magic, as they were clearly bits of plants and other things, not sterile chemicals. There were even bunches of them hanging from the ceiling.

Each table already had a pair of burners and some beakers in place, along with small ceramic dishes with some sort of ground plant.

Rachel and I took an empty table near the back of the room and sat, waiting as the other students slowly filtered into the room. I struggled to keep a straight face as girl after girl entered the classroom, saw the two seats available at our table, and then desperately scanned the room for a free seat anywhere else. Eventually, all the other seats were filled and the last two girls to arrive stared at our table like it was some unknown level of hell, before finally coming over and sitting down.

"Hi," I said, smiling and holding out my hand. "I'm Noah, this is Rachel."

"Katrina," one said, after a long pause, then the other, "Sylvia."

Sylvia had active bitch face, in the sense that she couldn't seem to look in my direction without crinkling her nose like she was smelling a sewer, but she was still attractive like all the witches were. A sort of dirty blonde hair, unruly in a very specific and time-consuming way, and dark eyes — I couldn't tell the exact color of her eyes at that distance.

Katrina was the better looking of the two, with long, chestnut hair and eyes I could tell were hazel even across the table.

Neither took my hand, so I withdrew it, but didn't stop smiling.

Rachel was looking at Sylvia.

"What?" the other girl demanded.

"Sorry," Rachel said, "I just thought you were a second-year, and this is a —"

"Shut up," Sylvia said, turning her back on us to stare at the front of the class.

"Ah, cool," I said, quickly figuring out why someone in their second year would be in a first-year course — she must have failed this class the first time around. "At least we've got someone at the table who's been through this before and can tell us what's coming."

Sylvia's neck went red and I caught Rachel giving me a small smile. I returned it, because, damn it, it was only the first day and I was already sick of my friends being treated like shit by these witches.

"Attention! Attention!" a voice called out. "Pay attention, *Magellae*."

The room stilled, but I couldn't tell who was speaking — it didn't sound like the school's weird public address system.

"Thank you, everyone. Now, I am *Magistra* Fallowell, your potions teacher this year, and we're going to jump *right* into things."

The voice was high-pitched, almost childlike, but I still couldn't see who was speaking. It seemed most of the girls in the class couldn't either, because all but the first row of tables was looking around, while those in the first row were focused on the front of the room.

The teacher must have been there, but too short for us to see her from the back tables? Mel had said all the things out of fairy tales were as real as witches — did Willowmere have any of those ... I didn't want to call them creatures, surely, if one was a creature, but couldn't think of what else to call them.

"Hey, Rachel," I whispered. "Is she a gnome or something?"

"A *gnome, Magellus* Ashe?" the voice asked from the front of the class.

*Fuck, was I ever going to remember all the teachers seemed to be able to hear everything in the classroom?*

I was half afraid *Magistra* Fallowell would answer that question and tell me they could read our minds, too, but she didn't — instead, the most gorgeous, less than five-foot tall, woman rounded one of the tables and came up the aisle toward me. She was short, yes, but had a figure more defined than Marylin Monroe and a face that needed no makeup to put all others to shame. Her long, black hair shone in the classroom lights, swaying back and forth as she walked — and it was long, almost as long as she was tall, but it was forgotten as soon as I saw her eyes, green as emeralds.

I'd thought all the witches were extraordinarily beautiful, but *Magistra* Fallowell was head and shoulders above all of them ... no pun. Her eyes drew me in and nothing else mattered.

"Do I look like a gnome, *Magellus* Ashe?"

"No," I murmured, "you're beautiful."

*Magistra* Fallowell's eyes went wide. "What?"

"You're the most beautiful woman I've ever seen."

"Oh, Maiden's nips!"

She spun around, hiding her eyes from me and my heart broke for a moment, until I watched her gorgeous hair swing as she strode back to the front of the class — but then she went behind the front row of tables, cutting off my view. I started to get up to rush to the front of the class so I could see her again.

"Will someone smack him out of it?" *Magistra* Fallowell called. "I'll just be a moment."

Rachel punched me in the jaw.

"*Ow!*" I exclaimed, holding a hand to my face and turning to glare at her. "What was that for?"

"*Magistra* said — and you deserved it," she answered, glaring back at me.

"What — why?" I suddenly remembered what had happened and what I'd said. All the girls in the class were staring at me, most of them giggling. What had come over me? I mean, yes, *Magistra* Fallowell was gorgeous, but how could I say something like that to a teacher?

It was then that the object of my highly inappropriate comments ... and more inappropriate thoughts, if I was to tell the truth, and thank the witches' Goddess I hadn't verbalized any of *those*, came back into view.

"*Magistra* Fallowell," I stammered, "I'm sorry — I don't know what —"

"No, no, *Magellus* Ashe, it's I who owes you an apology." She spun around, taking in the entire class — and not incidentally spinning that gorgeous hair, which, thankfully, didn't have nearly the same effect on me as it had before. "*Magellae*, let this be a lesson to those of you with passive affinities — no good comes of being lax in shielding their effects." She began pacing the classroom. "Now, let's open the containers of herbs I've laid out for you."

"What the hell just happened?" I whispered to Rachel, figuring if *Magistra* Fallowell heard and called me out for it, then she could damn well explain it to me herself.

Sylvia turned around to answer me.

"*Magistra* Fallowell has a double Allure affinity," she said like she was talking to an idiot.

"A double what?"

Sylvia sighed. "Her resonants are Passion and Longing — both gave her Allure. She can cause an unbearable attraction in someone if she puts her mind to it." She sneered at me before turning her back. "Or the weak-minded even if she doesn't."

*Magistra* Fallowell was ignoring us while the class opened the vials of herbs.

"So, it wasn't my fault," I whispered to Rachel. "Why'd you hit me so hard?"

"You didn't even *try* to resist it," she said, still glaring at me. "You just went all drooly-faced."

"I didn't drool." I wiped at my chin. "Did I?"

"Your herbs, *Magellae, Magellus*," *Magistra* Fallowell called from the far side of the room.

I hurriedly opened my jar as Rachel did the same.

"Who can identify this herb?" *Magistra* Fallowell asked.

Rachel raised her hand along with a handful of others.

"*Magella* Stimpton?"

"Peppermint, *Magistra*," a girl answered.

"Close — very close, but not correct. *Magella* Winthrop?"

"Watermint, *Magistra*," Rachel said.

"Correct — and the properties of watermint?"

"Soothing to the skin and stomach, and ... um, ah —" Rachel cleared her throat, "um, love, plus protection and purification in rituals."

"Indeed — but don't get too excited, *Magellae*, watermint's love affinity is quite weak. It only offers a bit of a ... nudge to whatever feelings must already be there. *And* the target must willingly accept the potion from the giver's hand —" She grinned, showing perfectly even, perfectly white teeth. "Meaning, your prey must know you are the giver and consume it knowing it came from you — so no sneaking around. But today you will be using watermint for its main purpose — creating stomach tonics for *Magistra* Fallwhistle's infirmary — this is one of the simplest potions, one which we can complete, for the most part, within our class time, and provides a fine introduction to potion making. In the cabinets beneath your tables, you will find the other necessary ingredients and implements, please get them out."

"We're making a potion on the first day?" I whispered to Rachel.

"It's an easy one," Rachel said, nodding. "Probably something everyone's already helped brew at home."

There was a rustle and clatter as everyone got their materials out. I hopped off my stool and moved it away from the table so I could access the cabinet underneath, and pulled out a tray covered with things. There were two sealed bottles of clear liquid, two containers of white crystals, a ceramic mortar and pestle, and a medium sized beaker.

"Very well," *Magistra* Fallowell said when the class settled down again. "Fill your beakers with five hundred milliliters of water and place them on the burners, but do not light them yet. Then add twelve grams of salt to your mortar and grind it to a fine powder. Scales are also in your cabinets."

There was another flurry of activity as the girls and I complied. I saw others tasting the two white crystals to see which was salt, so I figured it was safe and did so too.

"The salt's to purify the implements," Rachel whispered as we all ground the salt. She hung her head a little and blushed. "All of us know that from home, but I thought ... you know, with you not growing up with ... us..."

"Thanks," I whispered back, happy she'd thought of me enough to tell me.

"It's probably overkill, since the watermint has purifying properties, too, but it's important not to let your potions get contaminated."

"Gotcha," I said. "What happens if it gets contaminated?"

Rachel shrugged. "A null potion, an unexpected effect, fire, mostly-small explosions, whatever."

"Now, dispose of your salt, everyone," *Magistra* Fallowell called. "You may just dump it in the sink."

The sink was on my side of the table, between Rachel and I, so we could just turn and dump our salt there, but Sylvia and Katrina had to lean all the way across or come all the way around the table. They chose the former ... and they were both wearing loose, open-necked shirts that gaped open and gave me a view down both their shirts. My gaze automatically went back and forth between them before settling on the Katrina-view.

Sylvia's were okay — all the witches were gorgeous — but hers had the hard, too-full look some porn stars have. Katrina's were the sort of soft, pillowy visions that made me want to nestle in and take a nap.

Katrina must have seen my head gymnastics, because she blushed and lowered her gaze as she sat back — at least there were a few positive reactions to me here.

"Now rinse your mortars and pestles," *Magistra* Fallowell said.

I had to chuckle as all the girls who'd leaned over to empty their salt now had to hop off their stools and go around to the other side anyway, but I quickly held my hand out to Katrina and gestured for her to give me hers, then I got them under the water right after Rachel finished hers. Katrina gave me a flirty thanks and I was starting to think this was a lot more like what I'd thought being the only guy in an all-girls school should be like when Sylvia elbowed me in the kidney as she went back to her stool.

I grunted and had to look away from Katrina, which was disappointing, but *Magistra* Fallowell was already moving on to the next instruction, so I had to hurry and rinse my own mortar and pestle to catch up.

"Next into the mortar, six grams of sugar and eleven grams of watermint. The watermint, we'll be infusing with an intent to sooth; the sugar, with changing sourness to sweet. It's described as a sour stomach, after all."

"Infusing?" I whispered to Rachel.

"Putting mana in it."

Okay — that made sense and I assumed it was like casting a spell such as the candle-lighting I'd mastered — readying your mana, pouring your intent into it, and releasing it.

In fact, that was the next thing *Magistra* Fallowell had us do. Ready some mana — not too much, she said, because we were only fixing and enhancing the affinities of the ingredients — then infuse that mana with our intent to sooth and sweeten into the mixture. While we did that several times to, as she called it, "set things," we lit our burners and heated our water. Then in went the rest of the sugar, followed by our sugar and watermint mixture and we boiled that down to a syrup.

Finally, the syrup got mixed with the liquid in the other bottle, which turned out to be vodka — something about absorption.

That was it, apparently, other than to let it sit for a couple weeks then strain out the watermint leaves. It was ready enough, though, for *Magistra* Fallowell to grade us, and she started going around the room immediately.

"Well, that was kind of cool," I said, pouring the last of the mixture into the bottle we'd use for it to steep in.

As I looked up, I caught Rachel slipping a smaller bottle of green-tinged liquid into her backpack, and noticed that her potion bottle was less full than mine. I wondered if she wasn't feeling well and didn't want to go to the infirmary for some reason, but didn't have time to ask, because *Magistra* Fallowell was at our table and asking to sample my potion.

I handed it over kind of proudly — it was my first potion, after all, and I was pretty confident I'd gotten it right.

*Magistra* Fallowell took a sample with a glass straw and placed a drop on her tongue — which, honestly, wasn't fair for someone that good looking to do to a guy.

"Hhmm," she said, frowning. "Inert, I'm afraid, *Magellus* Ashe — perhaps you didn't rinse your mortar and pestle well enough and some salt got in. Too bad."

My shoulders slumped — I'd been so certain I'd gotten it right, but maybe I hadn't rinsed mine well enough after taking care of Katrina's. It'd serve me right for getting sloppy over a pair of boobs and some pretty eyes.

Then I noticed Sylvia, who was pointedly looking the other way, but her shoulders were shaking as though she was holding back laughter. I thought back to when we'd been rinsing things and quickly checked the table by my burner. There was a bunch of white powder there with specks leading back to Sylvia's seat — had she dumped some of her salt into my beaker when we'd been cleaning? Had she sabotaged me?

Just then, *Magistra* Fallowell moved on to check Rachel's potion, but as Rachel moved to hand it to her, she knocked her whole tray of equipment — bottles and all — into the sink and dropped her potion bottle, too.

"Oh, no!" she cried, grasping for it, but that only upended it, dumping her whole potion into the bottom of the sink.

"That is unfortunate, *Magella* Winthrop," *Magistra* Fallowell said. "See me one evening this week after classes and you may brew a new one for half credit."

# CHAPTER EIGHTEEN

Rachel was in my Rituals class, too, so we walked there together.

This room was open in the middle, with the desks in two rows on three of the walls, with the fourth wall covered in whiteboards. The open space in the center had a large circle painted on the floor, its edges right at the crowded desks.

Rachel and I took seats and, again, all the girls entering after us looked at me and made a point of sitting at least two desks away from me.

I hefted my backpack off the back of my chair and set it on the desk next to me.

"At least we have lots of room," I whispered to Rachel, who giggled, covering her face with her hand, then sobered and straightened up as the teacher entered.

"Good afternoon, *Magellae*. Sit down. Settle. Pay attention." Her strong accent made her speech rapid and clipped, as though each word or two was its own sentence. She looked at me and sighed. "Good afternoon, *Magellus*, as well."

I started to answer, thinking if she'd singled me out it was only polite, but she moved on quickly.

"I am *Magistra* Cassian. Rituals. Notebooks out."

There was a rustle of backpacks and paper as everyone got out notebooks.

"Take notes. Listen, then write. I give no handouts, no slide decks. Silly waste of time. Now, who can tell the three states of mana?" She looked around the room and some girls had their hands up, but she pointed at a girl who didn't. "*Magella* Lee?"

"Um, raw, generated, and refined, *Magistra*?"

"'Um', not state of mana. Say what you mean, nothing else. Wasted words are wasted time. Wasted time is wasted life. Next, what is raw mana?" Again, hands went up, but she pointed at me. "*Magellus* Ashe?"

I froze for a bare instant then tried to answer in as few words as I could.

"Don't know."

The class erupted in laughter until *Magistra* Cassian snapped her fingers.

"Correct," she said. "You do not." She glared at the class. "Never laugh at truth, *Magellae*. Never laugh at ignorance. Former cannot be changed; latter can be; neither care about your opinion."

She strode to the center of the circle.

"Raw mana is energy created by life. All life, to single cell." She pointed at me. "What is raw mana, *Magellus*?"

I jumped, not expecting her to call on me again, but answered quickly.

"Energy created by all life, even a single cell, *Magistra*."

She nodded, then scanned the class again.

"First ignorance, then knowledge. This why you are here. Are any of you not ignorant?" She pointed to the door. "Those may leave, nothing for them here."

When no one moved, she pointed at Rachel.

"Generated mana, *Magella* Winthrop?"

"*Eep!*" Rachel jumped, then quickly said, "Generated mana comes from our body processing raw mana through our experiences, emotional and physical. It's how we feel those things and it's what we use for spells and rituals."

"Correct, but too many words." Her eyes scanned the class again. "Only write necessary words. 'Eep' not on quiz. Next, refined mana. *Magella* Carston-Burke."

"Mana that's been taken and returned through a warlock," a girl in the back row on the other side of the class said.

"Correct." *Magistra* Cassian walked to the whiteboards and slid one aside. The one revealed had the outlines of two people drawn on it in black marker. One was clearly supposed to be female, with a bit of an hourglass figure and the other, blockier one, seemed to be male.

She picked up a marker and quickly shaded parts of the female figure.

"Raw mana — life." She grabbed several colored markers and spotted multicolored dots throughout the figure. "Experiences. Love. Hate. Pain. Pleasure. Calm. Chaos. All you experience is raw mana transformed. More, you experience *because* raw mana is transformed. All life is transformation. All is change from that to this. Understand?"

There was a chorus of "Yes, *Magistra*," as we all scribbled to copy down the diagram.

"Good."

She took up the black marker again and drew two circles inside each of the figures.

"Resonant stores —" She filled about a third of the circles in the female figure with two different colors. "— capture mana, but only the resonant —" She made a bunch of different colored sparkles outside of the figure. "— others drift away. Then —"

"Excuse me, *Magistra* Cassian?"

I looked up from peppering dots in my notebook to see a girl across the room with her hand raised. The girl next to her was staring at her with wide eyes and rapidly shaking her head back and forth.

"Yes, *Magella* Patterson?"

"Isn't all this sort of, um, basic? I mean, ah, we all know all this — maybe not the feral," she glanced my way, "but the rest of us do."

The girl beside her stopped shaking her head, closed her eyes, and put her head down on her desk.

"You are not ignorant," *Magistra* Cassian said, then pointed at the door. "You may leave."

"What, but —"

"If I have nothing to teach you, leave."

"I wasn't saying that — we're here to learn about rituals, not baby stuff."

The girl next to her slowly slid her desk away from Patterson.

"Who taught you baby stuff?" *Magistra* Cassian asked.

"My mother and aunts —"

"Beverly Patterson is your mother?"

"Yeah, and she —"

"Ask to see grades from my class. D-student should not teach." She glared around the room, then focused on Patterson again. "Stand up."

"I —"

"Stand up."

The girl stood and nervously looked around, but none of the other girls would even meet her eye.

"Can witch use mana not of her resonant?" *Magistra* Cassian asked, tapping at the colored dots within the figure.

"No, they're shed into —"

"Not these!" The rapid tapping moved to the dots outside the figure, then back to those inside. "These!"

"Well, I guess — before it's shed, but it's so little —"

"Little equates to nothing, *Magella* Patterson?"

"No."

The girl's shoulders slumped and she looked down. I think she'd figured out she was in for a very bad time.

"Witch uses mana other than her resonants only in the moment,"

*Magistra* Cassian said, looking around the class again. "Once shed, mana is no longer hers."

I felt pretty good for already knowing that. My trips to the strip club, and Sam talking about how she could only use the mana she was generating at the time because she couldn't fill her Love store, had already taught me this.

*Magistra* Cassian turned her back on the girl and faced my side of the class, eyes locking on mine. "*Magellus* Ashe, others can make use of mana once shed? Yes, no? *Do not sit down, Magella Patterson!*"

I jumped at the shout, but *Magistra* Cassian didn't even turn back to ensure the girl was standing — which she was, having hopped back out of her seat — and was still staring at me.

"Yes, *Magistra* Cassian," I said, hoping she wouldn't ask about the details of how I knew, because I really didn't want to tell the whole class about sucking up mana at a strip club.

"A warlock can absorb that mana from the ambient environment," I added, grateful Mel had given me a little information about it.

"*Ew*," several girls said, as though I'd just described going through their trash cans for food.

"*Magella* Patterson," *Magistra* Cassian said, turning back to the girl. "Ambient and non-resonant mana can be used in ritual? Yes? No?"

To the girl's credit she thought about it for a moment before saying, "No?"

"*Incorrect!* And reason your mother failed class."

I leaned over to Rachel.

"I thought she got a D?" I whispered.

"Fail my class, *Magellus* Ashe," *Magistra* Cassian said without turning around, "you take again." Her eyes scanned the rows of girls. "And again. And again. Keep in mind."

She returned to the whiteboard.

"All," she said, drawing a wide circle around the female figure, "is available to the warlock in a ritual. Why important to know, *Magella* Patterson?"

"I..." the girl's shoulders slumped. "I don't know, *Magistra*."

*Magistra* Cassian nodded as though the girl had said something profound.

"Excellent. You may sit down and learn."

*Magistra* Cassian glared around the class for a moment as though daring anyone else to question her — when no one did, she nodded.

"*Magella* Winthrop," she said, "your Family practices difficult rituals, yes? Can you answer question?"

Rachel shrank in her seat. I slid a hand onto her desk and touched her arm in encouragement. She glanced at me, swallowed, then sat up straighter.

"If a coven underestimates the power necessary for a ritual and doesn't have enough to complete it, the results are ... disastrous. So, drawing on the ambient mana in the Grove might be the only way to finish the ritual and ... survive."

*Magistra* Cassian nodded.

"Yes," she said. "In major working gone wrong, tiny bit of mana could make difference." She paused, raising her eyebrows. "Even raw mana?"

The class went still and silent, no one moving.

Except me, because I didn't know what the hell she was talking about. If we — well, the girls — had all this raw mana that only filtered through their experiences in dribs and drabs, wouldn't it make sense to try and access it?

"That ... that's forbidden," one of the girls said.

*Magistra* Cassian nodded again.

"Is. Why?"

No one spoke, but Rachel slowly raised her hand.

"Yes, *Magella* Winthrop?"

"*Magistra*, unfiltered, raw mana is too much for a witch to control. It's too powerful, too wild."

"Correct, *Magella* Winthrop. Last time we know of coven

attempting to use raw mana in ritual was 1908. Was Siberia. Mundanes believe it some sort of comet, maybe asteroid. But no crater. Witches know truth. Still sense wild mana loose there. Destruction two thousand square kilometers."

The class was very still.

"So. If ever tempted, you may think on this class and thank me."

*Magistra* Cassian returned to the whiteboard and tapped the female figure's mana stores.

"So — now we have mana. Time for ritual, yes?" She looked around the class. "You. *Magella* Wainright. Time for ritual?"

"No, *Magistra*."

"Why?"

"Rituals need refined mana, *Magistra*."

"Yes! Not all of answer, but yes. Also, one witch? Not enough mana for ritual. Only covens do ritual. Days, weeks — harvest mana, give to priestess, harvest mana, give to priestess. Fill her." She held her arms out from her body like she was a huge ball. "Fill to burst like purple girl in chocolate movie." She tapped the male figure on the board. "So — warlock good for two things. One is take mana to priestess. Other make *Magellae* blush and not listen to learning."

She grabbed a yellow marker and an eraser, then erased the colored mana in the witch figure's stores.

"So. Warlock take mana and increase. Only in coven."

She drew yellow lines to the warlock figure's stores and filled them in.

"Increase — how much? You, *Magella* Smythe."

"Three-fold, *Magistra*."

"*No!*" *Magistra* Cassian threw the yellow marker to the floor. "Is not exact. Is thumb-rule. Different each warlock, each witch. Know your coven — know how much mana your warlock increases. Important for ritual. Never do ritual from thumb!"

She retrieved her marker and dusted it off.

"How warlock take mana and give to priestess? *Magella* Wainright."

"Um, sex."

That got me a lot of looks and a lot of giggles before *Magistra* Cassian exploded again.

"*No!* No. No. No." She started pointing around the room. "All you girls, all the time — sex, sex, sex. *No!*" She held up a finger then slowly brought it down to touch her other hand. "Touch. Fingertip as good as — what famous Warlock Bard say? Any other part belong to man. Touch needed to transfer mana. What increases power? Intimacy."

A couple hands went up and *Magistra* Cassian sighed.

"What's the difference?" the girl *Magistra* Cassian pointed at asked. "I mean, we all know we're going to join a coven and have sex. Isn't that just it?"

"This the problem with covens today. Families think so smart. Pick covens — piece, piece, piece. This resonant match! This girl be high priestess! Use spreadsheet like coven is business!" She shook her head. "Coven is not business. Coven is family. You pick coven with love, with heart — coven is friend, coven is lover, coven is sister. Coven is not spreadsheet!"

*Magistra* Cassian paused while she looked around the room. I followed her gaze and saw a lot of confused looks, which I didn't understand, because what *Magistra* Cassian had said made a lot of sense to me. If I was going to be tied to thirteen women for life, shouldn't we love each other?

"Girls not listen." She shrugged. "Families not listen. Maybe too late." She took a deep breath. "Tomorrow, we talk circle, Grove, and altar. Questions?"

"*Magistra* Cassian?" one of the girls asked. "You said a warlock can only refine power within a coven. I heard a *trinitara* warlock can exchange mana with any witch and even refine raw mana, is that true?"

"Yes? No? Raw mana very dangerous. Doesn't want to be controlled, wants to be free. Outside ritual? Maybe. Exchange with any witch? *Trinitara* warlock in full coven? Yes, take, give, any witch.

No worry. *Trinitara* warlock without full coven?" She chuckled. "You in coven. *Trinitara* warlock almost always mark. Take strong witch to mark *trinatara. But* — you never meet. Three, four, *trinitara* warlock in world now? I don't know." She laughed. "See? I am ignorant, too. No shame."

---

IT WASN'T until dinner that I had a chance to ask someone to explain the whole Patriarchy thing Mel had mentioned in class. The food was just as good as the night before, and the cafeteria was just as stare- and whisper-prone toward me, as well.

I settled in with my dinner, lasagna and breadsticks with a salad Sam made me take, then asked the girls about it. The witch in the serving line had even asked me which piece of lasagna I wanted — gooey middle or crunchy edge — and given me one of the two corners left when I pointed, a choice she hadn't been giving the girls ahead of us.

"Okay, so what is this about war with the patriarchy?"

I was a little afraid I'd now fallen in with some feminist cult. Not that I was opposed to feminism, I just thought some people went too far with it — past equal and into just hating on guys.

"What about it?" Hannah asked.

"What is it?" I said. "The only patriarchy I've heard of is, like, women's salaries and glass ceilings and stuff like that."

"You have to remember he knows nothing," Sam told Hannah, then turned to me, spearing a cherry tomato from my salad and popping it into her mouth and chewing. "No, it's not a bunch of old men secretly controlling the world to keep women down and in their place."

I nodded. That was good to know.

"It's a bunch of old men secretly controlling the world to keep witches down and in their place," Sam went on. "Women in general are just collateral damage."

"They lost a lot of power after Salem," Rachel said. "Once the Veil started taking hold and people stopped believing in witches and other things, they couldn't use fear as much to control people."

"So, wait, what?" I was having trouble wrapping my head around it being an actual thing. "It's a real thing?"

Sam nodded.

"Sort of? It's the Patriarchy of Delphi — they formed in opposition to the Oracle there." Sam shrugged. "Maybe they got tired of the Oracle saying 'I told you so.'"

"What do they do?"

"Everything," Brittany said.

"Everything harmful to witches," Hannah added.

"They didn't have much power until Rome took over," Rachel put in. "The Greeks never really listened to them. Things really started getting bad with the *Veneficiis*."

"The what?"

"The *Lex Cornelia de Sicariis et Veneficiis*," Hannah said. "Roman law in 200BC that —"

"Eighty-one BC," Rachel corrected.

"Whatever, ancient times are all the same."

Rachel looked a little offended at that, but Hannah went on.

"It started as a law against poisoners and assassins, then they used it for women accused of witchcraft."

"It always starts with the poisoners," Brittany added. "They did that whole mistranslation thing with the Christians."

"That was later," Hannah said, "it started with the Romans."

"Yeah, the Romans really had it in for us — Augustus, Tiberius, Constantine. They all had edicts against witches."

"Assholes," Sam muttered.

"Then came the Synod of Elvira, the Council of Ancyra, the *Canon Episcopi* — every couple hundred years there'd be something new and more witches died."

"What are all those?" I asked.

"Those were all from the Church," Sam said. "See, what the

Patriarchy would do is infiltrate mundane institutions and try to twist them against us."

"My grandma says the Christians were pretty cool in the early days," Rachel said.

"Don't get me wrong," Sam said, "it wasn't all Christians, they were just the ones in power in Europe and that's our history. The Patriarchy fucked things up all over the world, though."

"Things got really bad later," Hannah said.

"Yeah, the Middle Ages were rough. The Inquisition, the *Malleus Maleficarum*, then later the Würzburg and Bamberg trials, Pendle, and finally Salem."

"They were a lot less active after Salem," Sam said. "That's when the Veil was created."

Mel had talked about the Veil, something that hid witches, and other things, from the mundanes, making most people think such things didn't really exist.

"How was that created?"

Sam shrugged.

"It was —" Rachel cut herself off and looked down at her plate.

"What?" I asked.

Rachel shrugged. "I'm not supposed to say — it's just a family story."

"Why can't you say?"

"It's a privacy thing. I think there was an oath."

"Oh."

Rachel looked around at the rest of us, all of whom, including me, were looking disappointed. I wanted to know as much witch history as I could and this seemed like a big deal.

"I can say ... somebody did something."

Hannah snorted.

"It was a ritual," Rachel went on, "and someone sacrificed something big. That's all I can say."

"I heard that too," Sam said, "but never any details."

"Anyway," Rachel said. "The Patriarchy started losing a lot of influence after that. They still get people worked up once in a while, though, and attack us directly when they can."

"Yeah," Brittany said, "and every time they start something innocent mundanes take the brunt of it. Those Satanic daycare center hoaxes in the eighties?"

"Patriarchy," Hannah said, while the other girls nodded.

# CHAPTER NINETEEN

"So, what's the big secret?" Sam asked.

I was cross-legged on my bed in pajamas while she'd just come out of the shower and our room was filled with warm, moist air scented by some sort of fruity wash. Her hair was wrapped in a towel and the rest of her was covered by a fluffy white robe.

Well, mostly covered, since she drew one leg up onto her bed so she could begin painting her toenails, which exposed a lot of leg — I was pretty sure she had some pajama shorts on under the robe, but the expanse of exposed skin led me down thoughts of — I had thoughts, okay?

Sam cleared her throat and I jerked my gaze back to her face.

"You are such a guy," she said, returning to applying the tiny brush to each toenail. "Secret?"

I nodded at her toes.

"Are you going to do that the whole time?"

Sam held up the bottle and brush.

"This is what girls *do* when they're sharing secrets." She nodded at my bare feet. "Unless you'd like me to —"

"No, thanks," I said, quickly tucking my feet under my blanket.

Sam laughed.

"You should consider it — help you fit in."

"I'll pass."

"Hmph. So ... secret? Or are you having second thoughts? It's okay if you are."

I was having second thoughts, but not because I didn't trust Sam to keep it secret — I was afraid of what might happen to our new friendship. Mel made such a big deal about the Control resonant and Command affinity that I was worried, even if Sam kept it a secret because she'd promised, she might still decide she wanted nothing to do with me.

"No second thoughts," I said. "Just worried."

Sam frowned.

"Must be something serious — come on, tell me."

"Probably easier to show you — we have to do the shield-sharing exercise Mel gave us anyway."

Sam's eyebrows went up.

"Something to do with your resonants?" She held up her nail polish and brush. "Can I finish this and let it dry a little or should I wipe it off?"

"Go ahead and let it dry."

I wasn't sure if waiting was better or worse — on the one hand, it put off Sam maybe being scared of me or something; on the other, it gave me more time to worry about it.

"Good — so in the meantime, what's up with you calling *Magistra* Blackwood 'Mel'? Last night you told Rachel and me about having dinner with her and stuff, but not how you know her in the first place."

"Oh, that." I realized that, yeah, Sam and Rachel had been so busy asking me about Mel that they hadn't bothered to ask how I knew her, so the topic of me living there for the last few months never came up.

"'Oh, that.' Yeah, oh, that. You're on a first name basis with the most powerful witch in the Western Hemisphere and you say, 'oh, that'."

"The whole hemisphere? Really?"

Sam nodded. "Maybe the world? Baba's probably more powerful than The Blackwood, but nobody's seen her for decades, so she could be dead. Anyway, how? Spill it!"

"She, um, got me into the school. I was sort of staying with her over the summer after I got out of foster care."

Sam stopped painting.

"You say 'I stayed with The Blackwood over the summer' pretty damn casually, too. How do you even know her and how could she get you into Willowmere? All the spots are taken years in advance, the only thing that —"

Sam stared at me for a moment.

"You're a *Blackwood legacy*? How? The Blackwood doesn't have any living family — that's part of the whole ... thing about her."

I shrugged.

"She said we were probably related — distantly. Very distantly."

"But close enough to be a legacy admission? Crone farts!" She screwed the cap back on her nail polish, stared at me for a minute, then frowned. "Wait — that's *not* the secret?"

I thought about it for a minute — Mel hadn't told me not to tell anyone that, just not about the Control and Command things. And being a *trinitara*, which was along the same lines. She hadn't said anything about our relation being secret.

"No, I think she expects that to come out."

Sam raised her hands in the air and slammed them down into her mattress, leaning forward with wide — and a little scary — eyes.

"You have a secret bigger than *being a Blackwood legacy*?" She grabbed up a cloth and began scrubbing at the polish on her toes. "Oh, Maiden's tears, fuck the toes I need to hear this!"

She wiped the last of the polish off her toes, then swung her feet off the bed and leaned toward me, holding out her hands.

"Gimme! I want to know whatever this secret is."

I put my feet on the floor and took her hands.

"Okay," she said, "here's how this works. We push our shields out, then as they touch think of them merging, rather than pushing the other back. Like soap bubbles, okay?"

I nodded and closed my eyes.

"You still have to close your eyes? Shit. Sorry, I didn't mean —"

"It's okay," I said. "We've established that I know nothing, remember?"

"Still sorry. I shouldn't have said it like that." She took a deep breath. "Ready when you are."

"Okay."

I slowly expanded my shields away from my body, watching as Sam did the same. The lightning-striped blue grew off each of us and touched. I could feel the pressure of her shields on mine like a light touch, but instead of resisting it, I willed mine to open, spreading to the sides with hers so that our shields formed an open conduit between us.

It was surprisingly easy. Much easier than I'd expected and probably the easiest work I'd ever done with my shields. The edges where our shields met and merged were seamless, with streaks of white running across the blue, uninterrupted from my side to hers.

"You're good at this," Sam said. "So, what am I looking for..."

Her words trailed off and I waited, swallowing hard and clenching my jaw in the hopes she wouldn't freak out.

"Mother's milk ... you're a *trinitara*?"

I nodded.

"Of course you are. *Trinitaras* ran in the Blackwood line. Run, still, I guess," she added quickly, then paused.

My heart was hammering in my chest, waiting, but even as our joined shields allowed Sam to see my resonants, I could now see hers and I frowned, then my shoulders slumped as I realized what I was seeing.

Sam's resonant, her only one, was so small and dark. Like an acorn buried deep inside her, too deep to ever see sunlight. I suddenly understood what it meant when she said she was a onesie with a useless resonant — not just that she didn't have much power, but that she'd never felt what that resonant store should hold.

I met her eyes with mine and something of what I was thinking must have shown on my face.

"Shit," Sam muttered, pulling her hands from mine and crawling back into the corner of her bed.

Our shields snapped apart and I could no longer see into her core.

"Sam, I'm —"

"Don't you dare say you're sorry! Don't you fucking dare." She crossed her arms over her chest as though to keep me from seeing it again, then took a deep breath. "It's nothing I'm not used to." She barked an angry laugh. "That's just me — the littlest onesie, right?"

Something deep inside me wanted to move over to her bed and put an arm around her to comfort her, but I knew that wasn't what she wanted. Maybe she needed it, but she sure didn't want it, and I didn't know her well enough to force the issue.

"Okay, I won't," I said instead.

Sam sighed.

"No, I'm sorry," she said. "It's not fair to take it out on you — you didn't have anything to do with it." She laughed again. "Aren't we a pair? Goddess-cursed power bookends — from nothing to everything."

"I don't think I have everything," I said, a little defensive at the thought.

"No? You're a Blackwood *trinitara* — any Family matriarch would cut off her left tit to get you to join."

"Why would I want —"

"They'd give you anything you want, okay? Crone's piss, my mother would probably kill her warlock and mark you herself if you wanted to be at the top of the Family."

"Come on —"

"No, really — okay, maybe not." She paused, thinking, then

nodded. "Yeah, she would. Most of the Family heads would, I think. You could ask for anything ... *anything* and they'd give it to you."

"I don't want anything from them," I said.

"Why not?" Sam looked genuinely puzzled. "The most powerful warlocks have ... everything. What do you want?"

I thought about what Mel had told me life was like for a warlock in the Families.

"I want to be able to go to a movie," I said.

Sam shrugged.

"And? Every estate I've ever seen has a bitching home theater — we get all the new stuff, even prereleases."

"I want to go to a movie at the mall and have a cinnamon bun after."

"Oh." Sam frowned. "No, you can't do that — they'd dart you like an escaped gorilla."

"There's an image I didn't need."

Sam finally uncrossed her arms and moved forward to sit on the edge of her bed again. I guess she'd gotten over the embarrassment of me seeing her resonant and my reaction — at least for the moment.

"So, what do you want to do if not join a Family?"

"Mel thinks I should form my own coven and try to get powerful enough that we can defend ourselves from the Families."

"That's nuts — there hasn't been a warlock-led coven in a hundred years, maybe more."

I shrugged.

"That's what Mel thinks I should do."

Sam thought it over and pursed her lips. "A Blackwood *trinitara*? Maybe it works." She gave it some more thought. "So, what's your third resonant? It's hard to tell with warlocks because you refine the mana and it all looks the same."

Now it was my turn to be silent and think. Maybe I shouldn't tell her? If she couldn't tell on her own, then she wouldn't know, right? Or I could tell her it was something else — something innocuous.

But she'd trusted me. She'd sworn an oath — a pretty big one — to keep my secret, even knowing me for less than a day. Lying to her or refusing to answer would be like a slap in the face after that.

"Come on," Sam said, "it can't be more embarrassing than mine." She grinned and cocked her head. "I showed you mine," she half-sang.

I took a deep breath. "Control."

Sam's face went blank, then she grinned and shook her head.

"Nuh-uh," she said. "Not buying it."

"Yeah-huh," I said. "And a Command affinity," I added, wanting to get it all out there and ... well, if Sam didn't want to have anything to do with me for it, so be it.

Her eyes went wide and she shook her head harder while I tried to look as innocent and harmless as possible. I even edged back on my bed to lean my back against the wall.

"That's impossible," Sam said. "The Families bred Control out of every line — all of them. There's no one left with it except ..." Her mouth hung open. "Crone's saggy tits ... except The Blackwood. I don't think most people even remember she has it most of the time, because there's no Blackwood line anymore."

I nodded.

"Sam, I wouldn't ever..."

"I think I know that." She drew her legs up and hugged her knees. "You just told me something that could literally get you killed, you know?"

I nodded.

"Why?"

Sam's tone was pretty serious when she asked, so I tried to give her the best answer I could.

"I was really worried about coming here — more worried about having a roommate. A girl roommate." I shrugged. "Then I walked in here and you were so cool — about everything. Getting Hannah and Brittany to sit with us at dinner — it was like you were going way out of your way to make me feel okay here."

I had to look away, because she was staring at me so intently.

"So, when you said you'd partner with me in Mel's class, I couldn't think of any way to tell you no that wouldn't hurt you — and I didn't want to do that. I don't ever want to do that."

I realized I felt about Sam much the way I felt about Morgan. Protective. Not only wouldn't I hurt them, but God help — Goddess help, I suppose I should start saying — anyone who did try to hurt them.

"You swore a pretty big oath — I don't really understand it, but Mel says it's a big deal — to keep my secret without knowing what it was. Why shouldn't I trust you just as much?"

The room went silent as we both sat there, then Sam took a deep breath and scooted forward to sit on the edge of her bed again.

"Okay," she said, biting her lower lip. "Make me do something."

"What?" I couldn't have heard that right.

Sam bounced up and down.

"Nobody's seen a Command affinity in two hundred years! Make me do something!"

"Are you serious?"

"*Yes!* This is the coolest thing ... *ever*. Make me do something!"

"Are you sure?"

"Make. Me. Do. Something," Sam chanted, bouncing in time to her words — which made her robe fall open, giving me a quick glimpse of bare skin under it.

"Oops!" she cried, pulling it closed, then waved a finger at me. "But not anything like that! Make me do something that isn't, you know, creepy."

"Something not creepy," I muttered.

Sam seemed completely serious and I didn't think she was going to change her mind, so I decided I'd have to do it. She was asking me too, so it wasn't like I was forcing her to do something. On the other hand, I hadn't ever used my Command affinity on purpose. Only accidentally, and that had wound up killing a guy — which was probably a good argument for learning how to use it so it wouldn't trigger accidentally again and wind up hurting somebody else.

"I'm not sure I know how," I admitted.

"Really?"

"I've only used it once, that I know of, and that wasn't on purpose."

"Wow, okay."

I didn't really think it was worth a "wow", since we were freshmen in a magic school. There were probably lots of things the first-year witches here had never done, right?

I shrugged.

"Okay, okay," Sam said, grinning. "So I'm the guinea pig. Have you done *any* spells?"

"Um, I can light a candle. Mostly."

"Stop looking so embarrassed — that's more than I can do most days. So ... what you want to do is basically the same as lighting a candle — or it should be."

"Should be?"

"How am I supposed to know for sure? No one's had Command for a a long time — for all I know you have to sacrifice a chicken first. But we'll treat it as the same and give it a try."

The chicken thing bothered me a little, because Mel hadn't mentioned that. "What things do we have to sacrifice a chicken for?"

Sam blinked. "Really?"

"Don't look at me like that — this is all pretty new to me, so for all I know chickens are a regular thing."

"Only for dinner," Sam said, sighing. "This *should* be a lot like lighting a candle — just don't set me on fire."

"No promises."

"No fire," Sam said firmly. "I know where you sleep." She grinned. "But the principle's the same — gather a little of your mana, I'm not sure how much you'll need, so maybe start with a little more than you'd use to light the candle, then you fill it with your intent. Just remember the intent is whatever you tell me to do — no *poof*."

"No poof," I agreed.

"That's it?"

"Well, magic that affects something else has to get there, so then you fling it at me."

"Fling?"

"Make the mana with your intent get to me somehow. Sometimes touch is easier, but, yeah, you just ... make it go at me."

I took a deep breath. "Okay, if you're sure you want me to?"

"*Make me do something!*"

I decided to hurry up and try, before someone in another room heard Sam and came to investigate. I gathered up some mana — not a lot, since she was sort of cooperating and I figured it wouldn't take that much — and pushed it toward her.

"Put your right hand on your head," I said, feeling the mana take on my intent and flow out of me ... where it hit Sam's shields and splashed into nothing.

"Oh, I felt that!" She frowned. "But I didn't put my hand on my head."

"Mel said I'd have to use enough power to get through a witch's shields, so I guess I didn't use enough."

"Here — I'll drop my shields so you don't have to use too much mana. I know it's hard for you to recharge here — though if we're working together for class, I can probably let you absorb everything I shed. Not like I can use it."

The blue glow of Sam's shields died, exposing her resonant to me again, but she didn't seem to be thinking about that.

I formed the mana and filled it with my intent again, releasing it as I repeated, "Put your right hand on your head.

"*Eep!*" Sam shrieked as her hand rose and planted itself on top of her head. Her arm tensed, muscles and tendons standing out as she struggled. "This is *so cool!*"

She started moving her arm and fingers, but her palm stayed on her head.

"*Grrrarrghh!*" she snarled, straining to move her arm, then gasped and relaxed.

"You're taking this pretty calmly," I said.

Sam shrugged, then tried pulling her head away from her hand instead of moving her hand, but that didn't work either.

"It'd be harder for you if I was resisting with my magic, right? Instead of just physically?"

"I think so — Mel said something about a contest of wills."

"So, it's not really that different from the coven bond — just outside the coven and more deliberate. And it doesn't make me *want* to obey, just physically do it. Cool."

I started to ask what that meant, but all Sam's squirming made her robe gape open again.

"Let me go! Let me go! *Let me go!*" she shrieked, clutching at her robe with her left hand.

"Okay, okay," I said, laughing and covering my eyes with one hand. I released my hold on the mana I'd sent at her. "You can move your hand again. Let me know when it's safe to look."

"Hmph — okay, you can look now." She'd gotten her robe back together, belted it tightly and was now looking at her hand and flexing her fingers. "That was so weird."

She bit her lip again and stared at me.

"What?" I asked.

"I have a secret, too."

"You like girls?"

Sam reached over to my bed and smacked me.

"I'm serious," she said.

"Okay, okay, I believe you — but, Sam, it wasn't a trade, you know? I told you my secret so we could be partners in Mel's class, not so you'd tell me one."

"I know — but, I want to tell someone. I want to tell you." She looked down at her feet then back at me. "My mother didn't send me here to learn — well, yes, to learn, but not in the classes. She thinks there's probably a book in the library that would ... help me."

"Help you what?"

Sam gave me a look that said I was being stupid.

"Oh, the power thing?" I asked.

"Yeah, the power thing. She's not sure of the name of the book, but she told me who wrote it, and she's certain it should be in the library and would help with what she calls my 'condition.'"

"I don't get it — why'd you have to come to Willowmere as a student for that? Couldn't she just ask the school to let her read it?"

"It's in the forbidden section of the library."

That perked me up.

"The magic school has a forbidden section in the library?"

"Noah! I'm serious."

"So am I — this is the first time the magic school has seemed like a magic school to me — other than the actual magic, of course. I'm talking aesthetics and ambiance." I caught Sam's look. "Okay, okay, I'm sorry. It is a big deal and I shouldn't joke about it."

"Hmph. Anyway, if I get caught — or even if I don't, but if there *is* something that can increase my power they'll figure out how I did it, so I'll probably be expelled for that. I just wanted you to know — in case I disappear or something."

I thought about what it must be like to have so little power in a world where others used it so casually — like Cassandra using it to flip Rachel's tray, while Sam had barely enough to maintain her basic shields. After merging shields with her I could tell that even I had stronger ones than she did.

"What can I do to help?"

# CHAPTER TWENTY

Three weeks into the school year, and we'd all gotten into routines.

Each of the grades had somewhat different schedules.

As first-years, freshmen, we had classes on Monday, Tuesday, and Wednesday — giving us two days during the week and the weekend to work on the assigned reading, essays, and practical exercises. There were a lot of those and we'd all been pretty busy for the first weeks of school — which isn't to say we had no free time, just that we were being given a lot of work to do.

Hannah, who was a senior, said the workload would be less after the Christmas break, which she called Solstice. After that we'd have more free time and be allowed to leave campus to go into town. I guess the idea was to get everyone focused on their schoolwork first, then lighten things up a bit. She also kept saying, "Of course, there's Halloween," which I didn't understand, but everyone else seemed to think it was a big deal.

It was a Saturday morning after breakfast and we all went to the library, which wasn't my favorite thing, but we had a history paper for *Magistra* Nightingale due on Monday.

After about an hour, I noticed the other students in the library were leaving — packing up their books and heading out.

Rachel began doing the same.

"What's up?" I asked.

"Tryouts," Rachel whispered.

"Tryouts for what?"

"You should go, Noah," Sam said. "It'll be fun."

Rachel looked at me a little expectantly.

"What are we trying out for?" I asked — I could think of quite a few things I'd encountered or heard of in the witches' world that I didn't want to try out for.

"Not for you," Sam said. "You have to be a junior or senior to play."

I shrugged. "Well, as long as I don't have to do any of the trying out, I'll come with you, Rachel. Are you coming, Sam?"

Sam caught her lower lip between her teeth and looked around at the swiftly emptying library. "I ... I think I'll stay here for a bit. Maybe I'll catch up with you guys later, okay?"

I looked at her for a moment, suspecting something was up. "You go ahead, Rachel," I said. "I'll be right there."

Rachel nodded, gathered up her stuff, and headed for the door with her shoulders hunched and her eyes never leaving the floor. I really wished there was some way to give her more confidence — she was such a sweet girl, and smart. Always ahead of the rest of us in class, but never speaking up.

"Are you going to do something stupid?" I asked as soon as Rachel was out of earshot.

"No, I'm going to do something smart."

"You're going to try to sneak into the forbidden section, aren't you?"

Sam shrugged. "It's the perfect time — most of the staff will be going to the tryouts."

The forbidden section turned out to be a locked room on the second floor of the library — just a typical, wood-grain door — and

Sam and I had watched some of the teachers go in there, so we knew the librarians kept the key in an unlocked drawer in the main reception desk.

"If you get caught —"

"I won't. I've been planning since I got here — most of the staff will go to watch the tryouts. So, there won't be as many librarians — maybe none. If I can get them to leave the desk unattended, I can just grab the key and I'll have all afternoon in there. This might be my best chance to find that book."

"It might be your best chance to get expelled."

Sam shrugged.

"My mom keeps asking if I've made any progress. I need to do something soon."

I sighed. Not only did I not want her to get in trouble, I wasn't sure I wanted her to find that book — I mean, those books must be locked up for a reason, right? Probably because they were too dangerous for the students. On the other hand, she was my best friend at Willowmere.

I looked around the library. There were still one or two students around, but most had left, and I couldn't spot any of the staff except for one of the librarians, *Magistra* Whitman, at the reception desk where Sam needed to get the key.

"You want some help?"

Sam bit her lower lip and lowered her head.

"Do you mind?"

"I wouldn't ask if I minded. I still think it's probably dumb, but I'll help if I can."

"Thanks." She pulled a book from her backpack and showed it to me. "This is from the opposite end of the library — I was going to ask *Magistra* Whitman to help me find it, but couldn't figure out how to stay at the desk while she went looking. If you were to say you're going to the tryouts and ask if she could find it for you while you're gone..."

"Sure," I said, "I can do that."

I pulled out my notebook and made a note of the title and author.

"Say it's for *Magistra* Fallowell's potions class," Sam said.

"Got it," I said, packing everything into my backpack and standing. "Just be careful, okay?"

"Hmph" Sam said, "you're worried about me — you really do care."

I punched her in the shoulder. "Of course, I care ... if you got expelled, they'd probably give me Cassandra as a roommate."

Sam laughed. "It would serve both of you right, I think." She nodded toward the door and held up a fist. "Get going, I got sneaking to do."

I bumped her fist and headed for the reception desk.

"Hi, um, *Magistra* Whitman?" I asked, pulling the folded paper from my pocket.

"Yes, *Magellus* Ashe?"

"Um, I need this book for *Magistra* Fallowell's class," I said, handing over the paper, "but I couldn't find it on the shelves — could you tell me if someone has it checked out?"

"Of course." She took the paper and typed at her computer for a moment. "Hhmm — it should be there, unless someone's taken it to study with here in the library." She looked around the library. "With everyone gone to the tryouts, possibly it's on a return cart — did you check there?"

"Um, no, sorry." I jerked my head at the doors closing behind the last of the students headed to the tryouts. "I was sort of, ah..."

*Magistra* Whitman smiled and I felt bad about deceiving her like this, but Sam needed to get that key.

"Why don't you run along to watch the tryouts and I'll check the return carts for you. Come back later today and I should have that book."

"Thanks! I really appreciate it."

"Go enjoy yourself."

# CHAPTER TWENTY-ONE

I caught up with Rachel outside, and we joined the groups of girls heading toward the back of the administration building.

"So, who's trying out for what?" I asked.

Rachel laughed — and I had to smile with her. Her own smile was lovely, and laughing made the corners of her eyes crinkle. She was really adorable.

I noticed two girls ahead of us were carrying cases that were almost as long as they were tall, but really narrow and had a flared base. I stared at them for a moment, growing excited.

"Do they have brooms in those cases?" I asked. Maybe, finally, I was going to see something that would be the way it should be at a magic school. Thoughts of a game that was played on flying brooms ran through my head. But Rachel only laughed louder. She stumbled and almost dropped her books.

"Brooms? No, no brooms."

"Well, are they something cool at least?"

Rachel shrugged. "We think it's cool."

I saw she was having trouble with her stack of books. "Here let me carry some of those for you," I said, reaching over and grabbing a few off the top of her stack.

"Thanks," Rachel said, the moment of laughter gone and she was staring at the ground again.

We made our way between the administrative and classroom buildings into the field beyond. I'd never been back here, and was surprised to see a little sports stadium. There were bleachers on either side, one end had a scoreboard, and both sides of the bleachers were rapidly filling with students and teachers as more and more came out of the dorms to join the line heading for the tryouts.

Sam had been right about the staff coming as well, and I saw nearly every teacher I could recognize as we got closer. The teachers were all clustered around the side of the field, which was a little bit bigger than a football field.

Even the cafeteria staff was there, manning booths, handing out the typical game day food.

Rachel and I stopped at the burger stand, where we got burgers, fries, and soda, before heading into the bleachers.

At least the bleachers weren't too tall — just one level of them — so the onesies rule about sitting in the last row actually worked out well for this, as the top row gave an excellent view of the field.

It looked like two teams of girls, one wearing blue jerseys and one wearing red jerseys, were warming up — doing stretches, and jogging around the field. I finally got to see what was in the cases ... and it wasn't broomsticks.

They were sticks with a little triangular net at one end.

I'd seen them before and I frowned trying to think of what that sport was called.

"La Croix? Is that what this is called?" I asked.

"You're thinking of lacrosse, this is spellstick."

"Spellstick? What kind of name is spellstick?"

Rachel glared at me. "Mundanes play a game called football with an egg that only gets kicked once in a while — *we can play spellstick!*"

"Okay, okay — so what's the difference between lacrosse and ... spellstick."

"You'll see," Rachel said.

We sat down and started eating, so I reached over and stole one of Rachel's fries just to see what she'd do.

"Hey! You got your own!"

"Yeah, but stolen fries are better," I said stealing another one.

"Hey!"

She reached over and snagged one of mine, quickly popping it into her mouth.

"You're right, they are better."

I looked over to find her smiling while looking at me, and gave her a smile back, but she immediately turned bright red and looked down at her feet again, which didn't stop her from reaching over to steal another one of my fries.

We ate our burgers while the warm-ups continued, stealing fries from each other and sharing quick smiles.

The bleachers got crowded, but not really full — I guess if Willowmere had a team, then there must be other magic schools that did too, and for real games there'd be a home side and a visitor's side. For the tryouts, everybody split up and had more room — or maybe the sides were for the red or blue teams and people were sitting on the one they supported.

The teams lined up on the sidelines, and I noticed they'd set up nets on the field, about the size of a soccer net, which made me frown because I thought real lacrosse used a smaller net or something.

"They're getting ready," Rachel said excitedly — probably the most excited I'd ever seen her.

I didn't get her excitement, though — I mean, how exciting could a bunch of girls running around chasing a ball with sticks be?

The teams lined up on either side of the field, all looking toward the open end of the field opposite the scoreboard, and I saw that the bleachers and field perfectly framed a huge willow tree. Everybody in the stands stood up and Rachel hopped to her feet and motioned for me to stand as well. As soon as I did, the school's weird magic speakers started playing music and the whole crowd started singing.

IN THE GROVES *of ancient lore, where the willows weep and sigh,*
*Stands our mighty Alma Mater beneath the moonlit sky.*
*With the Child's faith and innocence, the Maiden's charm and grace,*
*The Mother's strength and wisdom, the Crone's all-knowing face.*

RISE, *rise, fair Willowmere, in shadows and in light,*
*In the Goddess's four aspects, we will find our might.*
*Forward, onward, strike them down, with mana pure and clear,*
*For the honor of the Goddess and our fair Willowmere!*

"HOLY CRAP, YOU'VE GOT CHEERLEADERS?" I asked as the song ended and a troop of short-skirted, sweater-wearing, pom-pom waving girls ran out of the crowd and began waving their pom-poms and screaming.

"*Maiden! Mother! Child! Crone!*

"*Kick their ass and send them home!*

"*Gooooooo Willowmere!*"

The crowd went absolutely batshit, yelling, clapping, and stomping their feet until the bleachers shook. If they were this worked up over tryouts, I was a little afraid of what a real game would be like.

The cheerleaders ran off the field and players ran out, taking up positions. One of the teachers in a referee shirt went to the middle of the field and tossed a ball the size of a softball onto the grass, then stepped back quickly and blew her whistle.

One player from each team started running for the ball.

A blue player got the ball first, but a red girl was there in a moment and threw a shoulder into her chest — actually lifting her off the ground and flinging her backward a good ten feet.

"Oh, shit!" I exclaimed.

"Told you it was fun," Rachel said.

"Yeah, but they're not even wearing pads!"

"Pads are for pussies," Rachel muttered, staring intently at the field.

I looked over at her, my eyes wide with surprise, and she flushed bright red, but never took her eyes off the field.

The red player had the ball in her net and was running toward the opposite goal, but angling toward the side of the field. Blue players were converging on her, and other red players were moving into position. I figured it would be like hockey or basketball with a couple of passes, then in for goal.

I was pretty wrong.

The red player with the ball must have found the line she liked, because she wound up with her stick and flung the ball at the blue net. I thought that was going to be it, because the net was the size of a soccer goal but the ball was so much smaller. I didn't think the goalie would have a chance ... which she didn't, but not for the reason I thought.

The ball moved faster than it had any right to — there was a loud *crack* and I lost sight of it for a second. The blue goalie was moving around in front of the goal, which was unnecessary because the ball turned into a fiery streak that dissipated into ash before it got close.

A whistle blew.

"Penalty red," the referee called out, her voice echoing through the stands. Even though I didn't see any speakers. "Damage to the ball."

"Tone it down, Belinda!" Rachel screamed, then turned redder and looked down at her feet — but just for a second because she quickly raised her eyes and stared intently at the field again.

It was hard, but I kept myself from laughing at how intense the normally shy and reserved girl had become on the game.

The referee had a new ball in hand and this time, instead of placing it on the ground at midfield, she tossed it toward a blue player who caught it in her net.

The blue player started running toward the red net and quickly accelerated to a speed I thought no human could possibly attain.

None of the red players were in a position to stop her, but just as I thought she had a clear line for the goal, one of the red players waved a hand and a wall of fire erupted in the blue girl's path.

"Holy shit!" I yelled.

"*Yeah! Fry her ass!*" Rachel screamed.

I thought that might be what actually happened, as the blue player was going too fast to avoid the firewall, and she didn't even try to. Instead, she leapt into the air, twisted, and flung the ball from her net toward a teammate. Before she got to the firewall, I saw another blue player wave a hand at her and she went through the wall of fire, coming out the other side in a cloud of steam.

She emerged from the steam in a huge bubble of water, hit the ground rolling, and tumbled a few times before jumping to her feet soaking wet. The blue player who got the ball was already angling toward the other side of the field, but there were more red players there.

Two of them converged on the girl with the ball, who wasn't as fast as the last one, and swung their sticks. One hit the blue player's stick with a kind of twisting motion that popped the ball right out of the net. The other one, while still running, swung her stick like a lumberjack at the blue girl's legs.

"What the fuck?" I exclaimed as a loud *crack* echoed through the stadium and the red girl's stick, as well as the blue player's leg, cracked and bent at odd angles where they shouldn't have.

"That should be a penalty," Rachel muttered.

"No, shit, it should be a penalty — she broke the girl's leg!"

Rachel glanced over at me. "Not the leg — the defense was offsides."

I stared at her for a moment. "What? You can just break another player's leg?"

Rachel's attention was back on the field as the ball, after being tossed out of the girl with the broken leg's net, was rolling free on the turf.

Rachel shrugged. "She'll get better."

A red player got to the ball first, scooped it up, and tossed it to a teammate before a blue player ran into her and the impact slung her a good thirty feet before she hit the ground and rolled.

"Ooo, Strength affinity," Rachel said. "We need that on the team."

Now the girl with the ball was running, but as she did, pillars of earth erupted from the field around her — she dodged through them getting closer and closer to the goal. At first, I thought the pillars of dirt, which erupted and then fell back to the ground, leaving no trace, were an attack by the blue players, but then I noticed that they were always between the girl with the ball and someone on the opposing team. It looked like she might be doing it to block the other team from seeing her or getting close to her.

Closer to the goal, she twirled her stick and flung the ball at the net — in a normal sort of throw that a real person might make, not some kind of sound barrier breaking freak.

The ball headed toward the upper corner of the net, and I didn't think there'd be a way for the goalkeeper to get to it, but she waved a hand and a wall of ice rose from the ground. The ball bounced off, and there were cheers from the other set of bleachers.

"*Review!*" Rachel screamed. She jumped to her feet, waving her arms and screamed again, "*Review!*"

The call got taken up by other girls on our side, and I could hear boos from the other bleachers.

The referee's whistle blew, and her voice echoed across the field again. "Challenge, red team," she called. "The play is under review."

The ice wall disappeared, but then I had to blink as glowing images of all the players appeared on the field and started moving around as they had before the whistle. A ghostly image of the girl with the ball, running through translucent pillars of dirt, made its way toward the goal. She threw the glowing image of the ball, and then the ... replay stopped as the ball neared the lines marked in front of the goal. The referee walked over to the goal and squinted along the line, then twirled a finger. All the ghostly figures slowly moved forward as an image of the wall of ice started slowly creeping up from the ground in front of the goal.

The referee twirled her fingers back, then forward again.

The images rose again, and the referee kept looking at the ball from several angles.

She twirled her fingers and the image of the ball moved forward and then back and forward and back again as the wall of ice grew and retreated.

More screams erupted from our bleachers, but I couldn't tell what anyone was yelling except Rachel, who kept yelling, "*Penalty shot!*" Over and over again.

There were boos, louder than before, from the blue bleachers.

The referee walked back to the center of the field and started talking over whatever the announcement system was, her voice echoing through the stadium.

"Upon review, the ball had not crossed —"

I could barely hear the referee, even with her voice amplified, over the sudden cheers from our bleachers and the boos from the blue bleachers.

"— the six-yard box before the defensive block. Penalty, blue team! Penalty shot!"

"*Yeah!*" Rachel screamed, jumping up and down.

"What the actual fuck?" I asked.

Rachel looked at me, eyes wide and bright, and a grin splitting her face from ear-to-ear.

"The goaltender can't use defensive magic until the ball gets within six yards of the goal," she said.

"You can break a girl's leg, but you can't cast a spell until the ball moves someplace?" I asked, bewildered.

Rachel shrugged. "It was just a shinbone," she said, "it's not like she got her skull cracked. She'll be fine by the time the period's over." She pointed toward the sideline on the other side of the field. "See? She's already up and around."

I looked where she pointed, and saw the girl with a broken leg standing and hobbling around as though testing her leg with a teacher nearby.

"This is bizarre."

"This is *fucking spellstick*!" Rachel yelled, going back to cheering as the red team took their penalty shot and had it blocked again by the blue goalie's ice wall.

The game went on like that for another forty minutes, with spells being thrown around that, frankly, terrified me. Even for me, having made a dude bash his head against a brick wall, these girls were fucking brutal. At least seven of them had to be carried off the field over the course of the game, and all seven came back to play just as hard.

In the end, red managed to score one goal, when the girl who'd first taken a shot and vaporized the ball — I think her name was Belinda — managed another shot that blasted straight through the blue goaltender's wall of ice, the back of the net, and hit one of the posts holding up the scoreboard with a loud *clang*.

But because the ball was still in one piece, that was legal.

The blue team didn't manage to score a point, but did manage to send more red players off the field than red did blue — and judging from the reactions of the crowd, that was at least as important as scoring a goal.

The game ended in both sets of bleachers cheering while the girls who had just been, as nearly as I could tell, trying to kill each other, lined up to shake hands in the middle of the field.

As we stood up with the others to exit the bleachers, Rachel glanced over at me. She was hanging her head again and wouldn't meet my gaze.

"What did you think?" she asked, quietly.

"That was the most brutal thing I've ever seen — I've seen MMA fights with less blood."

"I know," Rachel said, grinning. "Wasn't it great? With the new players from this game, I think we're going to have a great team this year." She hopped up and down as she walked. "I can't wait until third-year when I can try out!"

"You want to play?"

"Hell, yeah."

I had trouble imagining Rachel playing such a violent game — at least the Rachel I knew from classes and hanging out. The Rachel I'd just seen at the game could probably take down a whole team on her own.

I walked Rachel back to her room so I could help with her books, moving along slowly with the huge crowd all trying to get back to the dorms. The whole way from the sports field she talked nonstop about spellstick. How the Willowmere team had done last year — and the year before that — and before that. Rattling off statistics, win-loss records, who was the best player each year, everything, but as we got closer to the dorms she quieted until she was back to her usual, shy self.

"Thanks for watching the game with me," Rachel said quietly, as we neared her door.

"Anytime, it was fun — brutal and terrifying, but fun. I'll have to learn the rules so I know what the hell's going on next time."

Rachel entered her room and started to close the door, but stopped, with only her head poking around the door's edge at me.

"I, um, my Family, that is, has a box for the Banshees — that's the Boston team," Rachel said so quietly I could barely hear her. "Would you, um, maybe like to see a pro game, once the season starts?"

"Yeah, I'd really like to see another game ... with you," I said.

Rachel's eyes widened as she stared at me. Then she looked away. "Um, okay, I'll get the schedule, and we'll figure out what game we can make it to, then I'll let my mom know."

"Great, it's a date," I said, grinning.

Rachel's eyes grew wider and she slammed the door shut with a startled, "*Eep!*"

# CHAPTER TWENTY-TWO

Sam was back in our room when I returned, sitting at her desk with a large, leather-bound book.

"How did you like the game?" she asked as I shut the door.

"It was fun, but Rachel's a little freaky at these games — there was one point where one of our players got knocked out, but there was no penalty, and I thought Rachel was gonna run out on the field and kill the referee."

Sam giggled. "Really? I can't picture that."

I grabbed a soda from our fridge and sat at my desk.

"You need to come to the next game with us — it shows a whole other side of that girl."

"Wow. So, there is something that gets her wound up — but there won't be any games until the season starts in second semester."

"Oh, and apparently her Family has a box for the Boston Banshees and she invited me to see a professional game with her."

Sam raised an eyebrow. "She asked you?"

"Yeah."

"I think she has a crush on you."

I shrugged. "She might —"

"And how do you feel about that?" Sam asked with a serious expression on her face.

I shrugged. "She's cute," I said, "but she's so shy. It's hard to tell what she's really like."

"She is cute," Sam agreed. "And she's got that tight little butt."

I almost choked on my soda.

"How can you tell anything about her butt? I've never seen her in anything but those baggy clothes that just hang there."

"Trust me," Sam said, nodding sagely. "I am very knowledgeable about girls' butts. I'm surprised it's a skill you don't have."

I waited until Sam was taking a drink of her own soda. "I'm more of a boob guy."

Soda sprayed onto the desk.

"Oh, really?" Sam asked dabbing at the soda on her shirt with a tissue. She looked down at her chest. "I guess I'm out of luck then?"

"I didn't say they had to be big."

Sam flushed and looked away.

"Okay, this conversation is getting a little weird."

She turned back to the book she was reading and I flopped down on my bed.

"You're the one who brought up butts — I was just talking about going to a spellstick game." I kicked my shoes off and pushed them over the side of the bed to *thunk* onto the floor. "Is that the book you were after?"

"Yeah," she said, turning a page. "And I found what I needed — but it's not going to be easy."

"You found it already?" I sat up again — that was big news.

"I think so. I found this potion, which says —" She leaned over the book. "— 'Take you this draught, drained in all, and trebled by each essence shall your power be.'"

I thought about it. "So — your power will triple? That's not bad."

"Triple for each addition of the essence, which I can add three times — at the new, first quarter, and full moons."

"Very cool."

"Yeah, but the new moon is tomorrow and I, um, don't have any essence to start brewing it."

"Well, where do we get some essence?"

I had visions of us having to sneak off campus to visit a dusty, dimly lit shop full of exotic ingredients. Maybe we'd even have to convince the shopkeeper to sell us the essence, because there were, like, witch laws about using it or something.

"Um, essence usually means..." She flushed bright red and grimaced. "Well, it usually refers to Essence of Life, which, um ... well, it symbolizes power and creation, which is, I guess, why it's used in this potion..."

"Yeah, so where do we get it?"

"Yeeaahh," she said, drawing it out, "so, um, the Essence of Life goes along with, um —" She laid her hands over her belly. "The Cradle of Life?"

Sam was being so evasive that I was wondering if this essence stuff was something we'd have to either steal or cost so much we'd never be able to get any.

"But where? Is it expensive or something?"

"No, it's pretty cheap, usually. Free, even." She clenched her fists and shook them, clearly frustrated. "So, the *Essence* of Life — enters the *Cradle* of Life — and *creates* life."

"You mean *real* life, like an egg and — oh."

"Yeah."

"So, the essence is —"

"Yeah."

"And you have to put it in this potion and —"

"Yeah."

"Ew."

"Yeah."

It occurred to me where the only place to get "essence" at an all-girls school would be.

"You had *this* to talk about, but me talking about boobs was weird?"

"It's not like we have to *do* anything, I just need ... it."

"Sam —"

"What? Like you have something you're planning to use it for?"

"Well, no, but it's..."

"And don't tell me you don't have any — you spend more time in the bathroom than I do."

"Hey!"

"It's true — not like you have to shave your legs, so I'm sure you're doing something in there!"

Something about her tone made me look at her closer and I saw that her hands were shaking, fingers tapping quickly on her desk, and she was looking down at the book, not meeting my eyes.

I got off my bed and took the few steps to Sam's desk, but she kept her eyes on the book in front of her, not even glancing at me.

I knelt beside her, resting my right arm on the desk.

"Hey, what's up?"

"What's up? What do you think is up?" she asked, still not looking at me.

I laid my hand over hers to still the tapping, but could still feel her trembling.

"I think you look really upset and I don't know why. Sure, I was giving you shit, but you know I'll help you, right?"

"You will?"

Even at that she didn't look at me.

"Of course I will — I mean, it's weird and a little nasty, but I'll do it for you. So, what's really wrong?"

"I don't know if I want to do this."

I shrugged. "So don't — I certainly wouldn't drink something like that."

"Not that — the potion cooks for so long and has so many other ingredients that it's really nothing. And it's certainly not the worst thing that could go into a potion."

I almost asked, but decided I didn't want to know. "Then what?"

"All my life it's been about power, power, power," she said so quietly I could barely hear her. "After we found out I was a onesie ... my mom hardly spoke to me. She brought in experts and all these exercises that were supposed increase my power, but none of them worked. I did them all — I did everything she asked of me, but none of them worked."

A tear ran down her cheek then dropped to land on her lap, so I squeezed her hand harder and put my other hand on her back. What kind of mother could do that? I mean, what kind of mother could toss her kid in a baby drop, either, but this seemed just as shitty.

"I've done *everything* she told me to. Almost everything — everything I could. I mean, how does a twelve-year old convince herself she's in love with someone?" She shrugged. "I couldn't do that, but I couldn't lie to her, because I clearly wasn't generating any mana. Who yells at a twelve-year old for not falling in love, Noah?"

*Okay, shittier. Say what you want about foster care, but nobody there ever fucked with my head like* that.

"I don't know if I want to do this anymore."

"Do what?"

"This," she said, waving her hand at the book. "Maybe I should just accept I'm a onesie and live with it. I'm good at potions, I could do that instead of being in a coven. I might have to have another witch imbue the ingredients sometimes, but a lot of them would be willing to do that if it meant not having to do the brewing themselves."

"Okay."

"But I don't *want* that! I'm a witch, damn it! I want to be in a coven and do rituals and dance for the Goddess under the new moon! It's not *fair!*"

Even I knew suggesting life wasn't fair wouldn't be the right response. I did decide, though, that the mood might need some lightening.

"So, this —" I waved my hand at her book. "Jizz-juice potion, does it —"

"Oh, Crone's tits! You did *not* just call this ... *ew*, I might have to drink it and now that name's going to be stuck in my head!"

She smacked me on the chest with both hands, but I noticed they weren't shaking anymore. I started laughing and it only took that to set Sam off and we laughed for several minutes, making up more and more outrageous names for the potion.

"Wizard's whizz!"

"Conjurer's cream!"

"Sorcerer's sauce!"

I held up my hand to pause her and be sure she listened. I knew I had the winner.

"Magic-Man Milk," I said calmly.

Sam fell out of her chair, slammed her head into the wall, and cracked her knee on the bottom of her desk.

"Ow! Oh, Goddess," she laughed. "You can't make me cry from being sad, laughing, and hurt all at the same time! My eyes are confused!"

I rubbed her knee while she rubbed her head until she stopped giggle-crying.

"Better?" I asked, standing up and offering her my hand.

"Yes," she said, taking it and pulling herself to her feet.

"Good — so, this ... potion, does it have to be used right away or does it keep for a while?"

"What? I don't know." She ran her finger down the recipe in the book. "It says a year and a day, but I can't tell if it gets weaker and weaker until then or just expires and stops working — this is a translation and the wording is weird."

"Okay, so make the potion, stick it in a drawer, and decide later if you want to drink it or not."

"Yeah, I guess I could do that."

"Good," I said, holding out a hand. "Got a cup?"

# CHAPTER TWENTY-THREE

A few days later, Sam was on her bed studying for her potions class, which was a lot more complicated than mine, given the glimpses I'd seen of her textbook. The big potion she was making, which was currently simmering on a hotplate by our room's window, was even more complicated.

And stinky, which was why it was by the open window.

I set my own work aside — an essay on the use of willow switches dipped in spring water as purification before a ritual — and checked the time. It was a Thursday, so we didn't have classes, and I'd been waiting for later in the afternoon to try and call Morgan again.

"Hey, Sam, can I borrow your phone?"

She tossed it toward me, not taking her eyes from her book. "Calling your girlfriend again?"

"I told you — not my girlfriend. More like a little sister. She's the closest thing to family I had in foster care."

"Uh huh. Do you want me to go downstairs?"

I shook my head, leaning back against my pillows while I tapped Morgan's number into Sam's phone. I still didn't have one, for all the same reasons — I was on campus all the time and the only person I wanted to call was Morgan, so why should I bug Mel to get me a phone when I could borrow Mel's or Sam's?

Morgan had tried calling Mel's number a couple times since I'd come to Willowmere, but, with Mel teaching classes and us living in different buildings now, we hadn't connected. Morgan called, Mel would tell me and I'd call back, but we hadn't been able to connect yet — that it was the new guy, Gabriel, who seemed to always answer the phone made me a little suspicious of that. Maybe Morgan was going out more, or maybe Gabriel was lying through his annoying teeth when he said she wasn't home.

It was getting to the point where I was thinking of asking Mel to take me back into the city one weekend to check on Morgan and make sure she was okay.

As for Sam's question, it was her phone and to study somewhere else she'd have to go downstairs. That seemed a lot to ask of her, especially when Morgan and I didn't really have any private discussions to have.

"Hi," I said as someone picked up — and, sure enough, I recognized Gabriel's voice. "Is Morgan home? This is Noah."

"Noah who?"

I ground my teeth. Since the asshole asked who it was every time I called, I'd started just telling him — after which he started asking for a last name. I wondered if, eventually, he'd be demanding I email him a copy of my ID for each call.

"Noah Ashe. Her friend. I've called before."

"Yeah, yeah. She's not home."

"Okay, could you give her a message?" I wanted to leave Sam's number for Morgan so she'd have a better chance of reaching me when she called back.

"What am I? Her secretary?"

*Apparently, yes, since you answer the fucking phone all the time.*

"I'm not saying that, I just —"

"Is that for me?" I heard Morgan's voice ask.

"Hey! You said she wasn't home!"

"It's that Noah-guy," Gabriel was saying. "Are you sure you want to —"

"Give me the fucking phone, asshole!"

There were sounds of a scuffle then a door slamming.

"Noah? Is that you?"

"Yeah — Morgan, what the fuck is going on over there?"

"It's been weeks again! I called like six times, why didn't you call me back? *Fuck!* You did, didn't you?"

"I tried a couple times after every time you called."

"That *asshole*! It was always Gabriel who answered, right?"

"Every time," I agreed.

"I'm going to *kill* him!"

"Do you want help?"

"No, I've got it handled — I just *hate* him. Everybody here does. Mike bought an extra-long cord for the upstairs phone so we could take it in the bathroom because that *creep* listens to everybody." Morgan took a deep breath. "Never mind him — how are you?"

"I'm good — really good — but before that let me give you a new number to reach me at."

"Oh, good, you finally got your own phone — let me find a pen. Okay, go."

I gave her Sam's number, then had to explain.

"It's not my phone, I still don't have one. You're the only one I call."

"Your ... whatever she is has two phones?"

"Um, no, this is my roommate's phone."

"You moved out of that woman's place and got your own? That's good."

"Not exactly," I said.

Yeah — I had a lot to catch her up on, since the last time we'd talked had been before I knew I was coming to Willowmere.

"Not exactly good?" Morgan asked.

"Not exactly moved out of Mel's. I'm sort of at college."

"College? Sort of? Did you get a job? Noah, is that woman paying for this? She must want something if she is. Are you sure —"

"Hey!" I cut her off. "It's not like that. Yes, Mel got me into the college and, yes, she's paying for it, but she doesn't want anything like that."

Not that I'd object if she did, but I really didn't need those thoughts in my head. I had plenty from hundreds of hot witches my own age surrounding me every day — even if Mel was significantly hotter than all of them.

"Look," I went on, "I really am okay. Better than okay, I'm really happy — and you'd like Mel."

"So, I can meet her?"

"Of course. I want you to."

"When? This weekend? Sorry — that's probably too soon ... I miss you."

*Shit.*

"I miss you, too." I thought of how to phrase it, since we weren't allowed to leave campus until the second semester, and that wasn't normal for a mundane college. "We're really busy, though — lots of classwork. It gets better in the second semester, though — at least that's what they tell me."

"So not until next year?"

I could hear the disappointment in her voice, but Sam was waving an arm at me mouthing something.

"Solstice break," she whispered after I failed to lip read a few times.

"What? Oh! Hey, Morgan, Sam just reminded me that we'll be off for Solstice ... I mean Christmas, and I'll be back in the city for that. How about —" I thought quickly about it. "— the day before Christmas? Not Christmas Eve, but the twenty-third? I'd like to see you before Christmas."

I'd have to come up with a gift that would make up for how unavailable I'd been.

"That's three whole months ... sorry, forget I said that, you must be really busy."

She was still disappointed, I could tell, but I couldn't think of any way to meet her sooner. We weren't allowed to leave campus on the weekends and there wouldn't be a Thanksgiving break, even for Thanksgiving Day. I'd asked Sam about that and she just scowled and stomped off, muttering, "Fucking Puritans," so apparently it was a touchy holiday for witches.

"I miss you, too."

"Okay," Morgan said. "So, tell me about college."

## CHAPTER TWENTY-FOUR

"Hey, guys, look at this!"

Rachel was more excited than I'd ever seen her outside of a spell-stick game and as she set her breakfast down and sat next to me, I could swear there was even heat radiating off the girl.

She ignored her breakfast and waved a piece of paper at us.

"What is it?" Sam asked.

"Yeah," Brittany agreed. "We can't see it with you waving it around like that."

"Look!" Rachel cried loudly enough for girls at nearby tables to look over. "Look! Look! *Look!*"

She slammed the paper down on the table.

We all leaned over to get a look.

*Invitation Only Spellstick Tryouts*

The top read in big, bold letters, then:

*Congratulations! You have been selected to try out for the Willowmere Junior Wyverns. Try outs are one day only, Saturday, September 28th, during the scheduled Wyverns practice. Come prepared with stick and spells!*

"What's Junior Wyverns?" Hannah asked. "I've never heard of that before."

"It says!" Rachel said, bouncing up and down. "Right here!"

She pointed to a paragraph at the bottom of the page.

*The Willowmere Junior Wyverns will be a select group of players from the lower grades. You will practice with the team, travel with the team to games, and act as the Wyvern's practice squad.*

"Oh, wow," Brittany said.

"I know, right?" Rachel cried, bouncing up and down. "Practice squad? That means we'll really get to play the team — not all out or anything, but almost like real games!"

"When's practice?"

"This afternoon! I can't wait!"

Sam sniffed and looked around, frowning.

"Did one of you turn your curling iron up too high? I smell burning hair."

"*Eep!*" Rachel hopped up and grabbed the paper before running off. "I need to go ... practice for the tryouts! Yeah, practice!"

"She didn't even eat her breakfast," Brittany said.

Sam shrugged. "Probably too excited. Are you sure you didn't smell that?"

"Maybe you're having a stroke?" Hannah offered. "Isn't that a sign of a stroke?"

"I thought that was when you smell burning toast," I said.

"Maybe it's Rachel's toast?" Brittany suggested, pointing at the other girl's abandoned tray.

Sam sniffed. "I don't think so." She shrugged. "It's gone now."

Brittany put a tentative finger on Rachel's plate. "So if it's not stinky, does anyone else want some?"

We all shrugged and Brittany pulled Rachel's plate over next to hers.

"You know you can go get more food if you want, right?" Hannah asked her sister.

Brittany shrugged. "That would be greedy — this is not being wasteful."

"What are you guys doing today?" Sam asked. "Other than watch Rachel try out for the team?"

"We're going to tryouts?" Hannah asked.

"Of course we are," Brittany said around a mouthful of Rachel's eggs.

I nodded. "I know I am."

Hannah shrugged. "Okay. I'm not much into spellstick, but I'll come cheer her on — she was so excited."

"Yeah," Brittany said. "Let's get a whole cheering section." She glanced down at the other onsies at the far end of the table. "I'll go talk to them — since they still think Noah's going to eat them or something."

"I know some seniors who don't usually go to games," Hannah said, "but I think they'll come if I say how excited Rachel is about it — they like a good underdog story."

"Yeah," Sam said, "I think I could get a few girls from my Potions class to come — they're always asking me for help, so they can pay me back today."

The girls turned to look at me and I shrugged. "I only know you guys."

"Aw," Sam said, making tiny-violin finger motions.

I laughed — yeah, I didn't have a lot of friends at Willowmere, but I thought I had some good ones and that's better than quantity.

"You guys are all I need," I said.

"Nah," Hannah said, "you need nine more."

Brittany and Sam froze, staring at her, but it took me a minute. The five of us — the four of them — and nine more would be thirteen witches. A full coven.

Hannah's eyes were wide and I could see a red line slowly rise up from her cleavage to turn her face bright red.

"I meant ... that was a joke ... right? I didn't mean..."

"I think someone's got the warlock-wants," Sam said.

"Yeah, sis," Brittany said. "Are you finally over that mundane guy from last year and ready to settle down?"

Whatever that was about, it sent Hannah's face from bright red to bloodless white.

"I need to do homework," she said, standing and leaving her tray behind to hurry out of the cafeteria.

Brittany sighed. "I shouldn't have said that."

"What's that about?" Sam asked.

"She had some fun thing going with a mundane last year, then something happened and she got all moody about it — I thought she was over it, but I guess not." She stood up. "I should go apologize."

I looked at the three abandoned trays with half-eaten meals.

"Don't you run off," I told Samantha, "I'm not cleaning all this up by myself."

Sam laughed. "Okay, but then I'm going to round up some support for Rachel. What are you doing?"

I grimaced. "I have reading to do for Rituals."

Sam laughed as we got up and started loading everybody's trays onto our own.

"Try not to get too worked up."

I liked Rituals, I really did. It was the big magic, like setting the wards around a whole building or calling on the Goddess for favor in some endeavor or even just asking Her to make Her will clear so the coven could please Her. It was cool. I enjoyed reading the Rituals textbook.

Except that it had pictures.

Apparently, all the rituals had very specific places for the witches to stand and stances they had to take for the ritual to work. Like raising the chalice exactly right or being at cardinal points around the altar and stuff.

So there were pictures.

And apparently clothing was optional at a lot of rituals.

My college textbook had more skin in it than most porn magazines.

"Too late," Sam said, staring at my crotch.

I set my tray down and quickly turned my back on the cafeteria, trying to think about Potions recipes — there was nothing that could turn me off quicker than Potions class, even if Katrina was really cute and our flirting had...

*Damn it!*

I tried thoughts of baseball, but that just made me think of spellstick because it was a better game and thoughts of spellstick were all about super-hot witches in what was effectively combat — my reaction was probably perverse, but years of Xena reruns had messed me up, I think.

Sam patted my arm.

"My work here is done — almost time for the next essence addition. Cup's on the bathroom counter."

# CHAPTER TWENTY-FIVE

I wasn't completely brain dead and had the ability to think a little bit, so I asked Sam if I could borrow her phone again, which she agreed to. She usually left it in the room and she'd given me the passcode.

"What are you going to find?" she'd asked when I'd been surprised at that. "My secret girlfriend?" She'd frowned. "Let me know if you do — I could really use a secret girlfriend."

So I went back to the room and took my Rituals textbook into the bathroom for a few minutes, then got Sam's phone. I opened the window a little more, because Sam's potion was coming along and the smell hadn't improved at all.

I leaned back against my pillows and called Morgan — I was trying to stay in touch more. We could have emailed, I suppose, but Alex and Karen only had one computer and it was right in the middle of the living room, so no privacy at all and they limited its use to mostly school stuff anyway.

Besides, Morgan and I had always talked and it felt weird to type at her.

"Hello?"

"Hi, Gabriel, it's Morgan's friend, Noah Ashe. The one she told you last time to give her the fucking phone or she'd set you on fire in your sleep?"

"No need to get pissy with me."

I smiled to keep my tone light, even though I was wondering if Sam knew a potion to make this dude's dick shrivel up like last Halloween's Twizzler.

"No pissiness from me, Gabriel. I'm just reminding you — I know Morgan can be a little testy at times."

"Yeah, it seems like that little bitch is always on the rag or something."

"Ha! Ha, ha! Very funny. Too true."

*Dude, I am going to stuff your Twizzler in a rat's cage one day. The big ones from the subway that carry knives and whole pizza slices around.*

"So is Morgan home?"

"Yeah, yeah. *Hey, Morgan! Call!*" He came back on the line and his voice was a lot friendlier than I'd ever heard it. "Hey, so I heard you left right before I came here?"

"Yeah."

"Where are you at now? Things working out for you?"

What the fuck was this? Were we buddies now or something? This guy was just bizarre.

"I'm doing okay," I said, not wanting to piss him off again, since he was acting as gatekeeper between me and Morgan. Maybe once Morgan was out of there, I could track the little shit down. Maybe take Rachel and let her use his head for a spellstick ball or something.

"Still in town?"

"Um, no, not exactly."

"Yeah? Where at?"

Then Morgan arrived.

"Thank you for not being a dick, Gabriel, now give me the phone."

I heard shuffling and a door closing.

"Noah?"

"Yeah, it's me. Things okay?"

That had become my standard opening.

"Yeah — I just can't wait to get out of here."

"I know. A few more months."

Morgan sighed. "So how are things with you?"

I spent a few minutes catching Morgan up on events since our last call — what I could, at least. I ended with how excited Rachel was for the chance to get on the spellstick team — changed to lacrosse, of course — and how the other girls were going to put together a cheering section for her.

"That's really nice of them." She was quiet for a minute. "Um, Noah, do you know any guys there?"

"What?" I managed to get out before my throat constricted.

Shit, I hadn't even thought of that — even sanitized of magic, I'd been telling Morgan about my life not even thinking that I hadn't seen a dude in person for weeks.

"It's just that all you ever talk about are these girls. I'm not complaining, they sound nice and everything, but what are you doing up there, putting together your own harem?"

I choked, coughing to get a little air. "What? No! No harem! Why would you ask that?"

"Geez, I was kidding, but if you're going to have a seizure over it, maybe there's something to it. So what's the deal? Are all the guys fraternity assholes or something?"

"I just ... don't have a lot in common with the guys here."

I existed, the guys at Willowmere ... didn't. That's a big hurdle to overcome in getting to know someone.

"Okay, it's just a little weird, don't you think?"

"My friends are weird? What about your friends?"

Morgan was quiet for a minute, then she sighed. "I don't have any friends other than you."

"So who's got the weirder friends?"

Another sigh. "I do."

I laughed and Morgan joined in a second later.

"Did you spend the last three calls only talking about girls just so you could make fun of me for not having friends?"

"Would I do that?"

"Yes, you fucking would, you asshole."

I laughed again. "Well, I didn't — it was just a happy coincidence."

Morgan's suspicions successfully redirected, we spent a good hour talking. Mostly about kids we both knew from school and the other fosters at Alex and Karen's — stories about the new guy, Gabriel, were conspicuously absent.

Soon, it was a little after twelve.

"Hey, I need to go," I said at a break in the conversation. "Rachel's tryouts are in an hour and half — I should get some lunch and head over there."

"Oh, yeah, can't keep your harem waiting?"

"It's not like —"

"Do you make them wear those little I Dream of Jeannie pants?"

"I — I —" I honestly couldn't come up with anything to say, since my head was filled with images.

"You're thinking about it!" Morgan laughed. "Good luck getting that look off your face before you see them all!"

# CHAPTER TWENTY-SIX

I THINK I MANAGED TO KEEP THE LOOK OFF MY FACE AT LUNCH — or, at least, no one noticed because they were all busy making fun of Rachel's lunch.

"Grilled chicken?" Sam asked.

"Are those vegetables? I don't think I've ever seen Rachel eat a vegetable."

"How'd they even get a scoop of rice without the cheese sauce?"

"I need to eat right!" Rachel protested, turning her nose up as she crunched on steamed broccoli. "Lean protein, complex carbs, and natural sugars." She swallowed the broccoli and started peeling a banana. "I need to be at my best!"

"She's right, guys, leave her alone," Hannah said. "She needs to keep her head on right."

"Thanks," Rachel said, quickly eating her banana.

She had a case with her spellstick ... stick? Whatever, she had it on the table next to her and was eating with one hand so she could keep the fingertips of the other on the case. She rinsed the banana down with the last of her water — another new thing, since I'd never seen her drink anything but soda.

"I'm so nervous," Rachel said as we all stood and dropped our trays off at the counter.

"You're gonna do great," Brittany assured her. "You've got your own stick and everything."

We left the dorms and started walking to the spellstick field.

"Yeah," Rachel said, "but I've never really played — I've played at playing, but I haven't really played before. Not with spells and everything. What if the other girls have more experience? What if I freeze up and can't cast a spell? What if I cast the wrong spell? What if I trip? What if —"

"Whoa, there," Sam said, skipping in front of Rachel and stopping her with hands on the other girl's shoulders. "Deep breath. Good, now: Who's been watching spellstick games her whole life?"

"Me."

"And who's memorized the entire spellstick rulebook?"

"Me," Rachel said quietly.

"And who knows every play in the Banshee's playbook?"

"Me," Rachel whispered.

"You know everything about this game. Everything. The other first- and second-years aren't going to have any more time playing than you. They've never played with real spells, either, and there's no fucking way they know more about this game than you. Now, who's going to rock this tryout?"

"Me," Rachel said, voice a little firmer.

"Who's going to be the best middie out there?"

"Me," Rachel said.

"Who's going to be out there leading the Junior Wyverns the first time they kick the seniors' ass?"

"Me!"

"Alright, then!"

We all slapped Rachel on the back and we started walking again, Rachel with a much more confident stride. She was almost marching, shoulders back and head higher than I'd ever seen the shy girl hold it.

Rachel marched into the stadium like she owned it.

One section of the bleachers was almost half full. When we came in the girls there waved at us and Hannah and Brittany waved back.

The team was already suited up and on the field running drills while their coach walked the sidelines, blowing her whistle and yelling instructions.

Rachel set her case on the bottom bleacher bench and unzipped it. She slowly pulled her spellstick stick out and I swear I was half expecting her to kiss the thing or something.

She took a deep breath, squared her shoulders and walked over to the sidelines, while the rest of us went over to the group in the bleachers.

"Remember," Hannah was telling the girls there. "When it's Rachel's turn, really turn it up."

All the girls nodded, grinning, but Brittany was looking around, a frown on her face.

"What's wrong?" I asked her.

"Something's not right," Brittany said.

"What?"

"I don't know."

"Is somebody going to get hurt?" Sam asked.

Rachel was still waiting for the coach, who'd glanced at her a couple times, then gone back to yelling instructions at the players.

"What's going on?" I asked Sam.

"Brittany's a precog," she said. "She thinks something's wrong."

"Precog? Like precognition? Seeing the future?"

Sam nodded.

"I'm not very strong," Brittany said. "I just get feelings sometimes — and something's wrong."

"Like what?"

"Oh, no," Sam whispered. She looked around. "Oh, no, no, no, no, no."

The spellstick coach was talking to Rachel now, and Rachel looked so happy I didn't even want to look around to see what was bothering Sam. Rachel was grinning like her head was going to split in half and she was bouncing up and down with excitement.

"What is it?" I asked Sam.

"Where are the other girls?"

"What?"

"The other girls for the tryouts," Sam whispered.

She started for Rachel, but it was too late as I realized what she meant. The team was on the field, the coach was on the sidelines, the girls Hannah, Brittany, and Sam had rounded up to cheer for Rachel were in the stands ... but that was it.

Rachel was the only one here to try out and I watched her smile fade as the coach must have been telling her that.

Telling her there were no tryouts, there were no Junior Wyverns, and everything Rachel had been so excited about was some kind of cruel joke.

"Rachel!" Sam yelled, but the other girl was already gone.

She dropped her stick, left it right there on the sidelines and ran.

Sam ran after her and that's when I heard the laughter.

From up in the bleachers, in the top row where I hadn't noticed them before, Cassandra and four of her little cliquemates were pointing at where Rachel had left the stadium and laughing.

"Oh, Goddess," Brittany whispered while Hannah, I guess, was explaining what had happened to the girls who'd come to support Rachel.

I turned my back on Cassandra and her friends. I couldn't see them laughing — if I did, I was going to do something I'd regret, I knew. Girl or not, I found my fists clenching.

To try and distract myself from what I wanted to do to Cassandra, I walked over to the sidelines to retrieve Rachel's stick. The coach was still there, frowning.

"Was that some kind of trick?" the coach asked me.

I picked up Rachel's stick and brushed the grass and dirt from it.

"Yeah," I nodded.

"That's..."

"Yeah," I nodded again. "It's exactly that."

I turned around and took Rachel's stick back to its case, set it inside, and slowly zipped it closed.

"What's wrong, feral? Didn't your little onesie make the team?"

I closed my eyes.

*Don't even look at her*, I told myself.

I picked up the case and started walking, head down.

"What? No clever comeback? Not going to insult me again?

I had to look. I couldn't help myself.

Cassandra and her friends were halfway down the bleachers, all of them laughing and smiling.

I looked at Cassandra ... and all my anger went away.

I was just sad.

These girls lived in a world with *literal fucking magic*. Their families had more money than ... anyone. Cassandra was as gorgeous as any of them — perfect teeth, perfect nose, perfect figure, especially if you liked boobs right on the edge of too much, and even her stupid, pointed ears were perfect.

All that, and she was still being mean and cruel.

What had to be broken inside her to make her do something like that to anyone, much less Rachel?

"I hope it gets better for you," I said.

"What?" she asked, laughing.

"Whatever it is inside you that makes you so ... broken."

"Oh, *I'm* broken? Not your defective onesies?"

I shook my head. "Rachel's probably the kindest, gentlest girl at this school. She'd never hurt anyone." Well, maybe on the spellstick field ... if she ever went near one again after this. "To do that to her?"

I shook my head again and walked away.

"Whatever it is that made you so angry and cruel — I'm sorry and I hope it gets better."

RACHEL WAS in our room with Sam when I got back.

I set Rachel's spellstick case by the door.

She was curled up on my bed with her head in Sam's lap, still crying.

I sat on the floor by Sam's legs and wrapped an arm around Rachel's back.

"Did you kill her?" Sam asked in a whisper.

I shook my head, rubbing Rachel's back.

"Did you throw her off the fucking bleachers?"

I shook my head.

"Well, what did you do to her?"

"I told her I was sorry for whatever it is that made her so angry and cruel and I hope it gets better."

Sam was silent for a minute. "Remind me not to piss you off. Cassandra's going to hate the idea of someone feeling sorry for her."

Rachel sniffed. "It was Cassandra?"

I nodded. "Yeah."

I kept rubbing Rachel's back while Sam stroked her hair.

"I hate her," Rachel whispered.

"Don't say that," Sam whispered, stroking her hair.

It nearly broke my heart, because I couldn't imagine this sweet girl hating anyone.

I scooted across the floor and got Sam's laptop from her bed, then went back to my spot on the floor and opened it up, starting a web browser and going to the video site where the witches posted their spellstick videos.

"What are you doing?" Rachel whispered.

"We're going to watch a spellstick game."

Rachel shook her head. "I don't want to."

"Are you sure that's a good idea?" Sam asked.

"This is our thing," I told Rachel. "You come to our room and we watch spellstick and you make fun of me for not knowing the rules." I clicked play. "Are you going to let Cassandra take our thing away from us?"

# THE MAIDEN

Again with the forest — I was beginning to feel a bit like Scrooge, except I was the one visiting the spirits.

I didn't even bother looking around, just started walking down the path to the clearing — that was going to be where I was wanted anyway. I just hoped it was Aurora and not Viera this time.

It turned out to be neither.

As I entered the clearing, I initially thought I was alone, but then I saw a figure at the clearing's edge to my right.

Taller than Aurora but standing straighter than Viera.

*Great, a new one*, I thought.

The sun was lower in the sky this time, so I had to blink as I changed course and walked toward the woman. Closer, I saw that she was young — my age, maybe — with long blonde hair bound back with a ribbon. She wore a rough, loose-fitting blouse, hardly laced in front, and a long skirt that stopped just above her bare feet.

Had Viera worn shoes?

I couldn't remember — I thought the old woman's cloak had been too long to tell.

Then, as she drew even closer, I stopped walking and simply

stared. It wasn't just that she was beautiful — it was that she *was* Beauty. As though she embodied every meaning of the word and more.

I stood still and simply watched her approach me, each step like the most sensuous dance I'd ever seen. Her golden hair caught the sun and sent beams of light sparkling through the clearing. Her eyes caught those beams and glowed. Mere steps away, the scent of flowers overpowered me, as though every blossom in the world had suddenly opened, ready to accept —

The vision of loveliness placed her fingertip underneath my jaw, setting my skin afire, and I stopped breathing — until she shoved my jaw up sharply, causing my teeth to clack together on my tongue.

"And *that's* why I can't use this form, even though it's my favorite." She stepped back and glared at me. "*Boys*."

"How many of you are there?" I asked after I'd recovered myself.

"Just four. The Child, the Maiden, the Mother, and the Crone — don't call her that, she doesn't like it."

I vowed to remember that, because I didn't think I wanted to know what Viera would do to me if I called her a crone.

"You're the Maiden?" I asked.

She nodded. "I am." She caught her lower lip between her teeth and lowered her eyes, lashes fluttering. "For now?"

My vision blurred, narrowing to just the sight of perfect, white teeth pinching a luscious, pink lip. My heart pounded and blood rushed — pain exploded in my right shin.

"*Ow!*" I cried, grasping my leg and hopping away from her. "What was that for?"

"Because you need to think with your brains, not your balls. Not even two questions and you're falling all over yourself — have some self-control, will you!"

I started to apologize, since she was right — I couldn't seem to concentrate when I thought about her ... then I paused and frowned.

"No," I said, then waggled my finger at her. "Oh, no no no."

"What are you talking about?"

"*You* did the lip thing. And the —" I fluttered my lashes at her. "— thing. And the whole, 'Oh, yes, I'm the Maiden ... for now?' thing. You know *exactly* what that does to a guy and you did it on purpose — you don't get to complain when you get exactly what you asked for!"

She stared at me in shock for a moment, then her face collapsed into a horrifying scowl and she glared up at the sky.

"*You hag!*" she screamed, then looked back at me, furious. "You've seen that utter *witch* already, haven't you?"

"What —"

"Don't deny it! I can smell her arthritis cream on you from here. What did she give you?"

"What —"

"Viera! What gift did she give you?"

"Um, she said strength, I think?"

Her face froze, still in a scowl — which didn't change how beautiful she was. Frankly, she could yell at me all day and I'd be perfectly ... I shook myself, blinking, and scowled back, but she'd already turned her glare back up at the sky.

"Strength against wiles? Really?" She stomped her feet, pumping her arms with her fists clenched. "Do you have any idea what that's going to do to my girls? And that's *persistent* — it'll take us *ages* to breed that out of the line!"

She stomped over to the stone block and hopped up on it, muttering to herself.

"Um, do you have a name?" I asked, edging around to put the bulk of the stone between us.

"Call me Aveline," she said, face still angry but not so much so that it made me think I was about to be struck by lightning. "And I am quite cross with you."

"Sorry?"

"Oh, it's not your fault, I suppose." Aveline sighed. "It's just Viera being Viera. Always so *smug* — like she knows best." She took on an older, snide tone. "'Look at me, I'm so much older. I have more *experi-*

*ence*. I have *perspective*.'" She glared up at the sky again. "Well, I'd rather lack *perspective*, than *moisture*, you dried up old bag!"

She hopped off the stone and came over to me, making me back up a couple steps.

"Fine, let's get this over with since it's not going to be any fun." She started speaking rapidly. "Hello, Noah Ashe, I'm the Maiden and I have for you a gift and a geas. The geas is I want you to teach my children to have fun again — they've become a bunch of stodgy, stick in the muds —" She spoke to the sky again. "— just like some others I could name!" She looked back at me. "Got it?"

"How am I supposed to —"

"I don't know — tickle them or something — but I want to see some fucking joy, understand?"

"Um, okay, I guess." My dreams were just getting weirder and weirder.

"Good. Now for the gift —" She pursed her lips. "Fine, the old biddy wants to make it hard for my girls? Resistance to wiles? Hmph. Let's double-down — I'm going to give you some of *my* power, and they're still going to wrap you around their little fingers, just see if they don't."

She slipped a hand behind my neck, pulled me close and tilted her head. Our lips met and...

# CHAPTER TWENTY-SEVEN

"Wake up, it's Halloween!"

I groaned and tried to dig farther into the corner between my bed and the wall where I already was because of Sam turning on the damn light.

"Go away, it's Sunday!" I was a morning person usually, but one day a week I liked to sleep in. Apparently, that was too much to ask.

"Halloween!" Sam yelled, pressing on my mattress to bounce me up and down.

I groaned again. Then I tried to think, what day was it?

"It's the first — Halloween is the *thirty*-first."

"*Halloween month!*" Sam grabbed my arm and dragged me toward the edge of the bed. "Come on, you're going to need a big breakfast to keep up your energy today!"

"You have got to be kidding me."

The light and the lingering scent of Sam's potion slowly cooking on a hotplate in the corner finally drove me to get out of bed. The potion had been simmering for over two weeks and the smell hadn't improved a bit.

Sam pulled my arm again, dragging me to a sitting position, then shoved a pile of clothes into my arms.

"Get dressed while I brush my teeth!"

She barely gave me time to brush my own teeth before dragging me out of the room where I shared looks of sympathy with a couple groggy first-years whose roommates had suddenly also had manic-breaks.

Downstairs, it seemed like the whole school was trying to get breakfast at once, which I'd never seen before — the girls usually straggled in over the course of several hours. Now, though, the cafeteria was bustling with activity and everyone seemed to be shoveling their breakfast into their mouths as quickly as they could.

"I hope I get cobwebs," Sam said around a mouthful of pancakes — a little drip of syrup escaped her mouth and dribbled down her chin and I resisted the urge to reach out and swipe it away with my finger. "I can pull a mean cobweb."

"What are you talking about?"

"Decoration teams," Rachel said as she and Hannah joined us. "I want animatronics."

Hannah snorted. "You're too short for animatronics — you have to be tall enough to get the heads on."

"They have ladders," Rachel muttered eating a spoonful of yogurt.

"Did I miss assignments?" Brittany asked breathlessly, setting her tray down so quickly she almost dumped her milk all over the table.

"No, they'll do them after."

"After what?" I asked. "What the hell is going on?"

The cafeteria went dark, and like someone had thrown a switch on them too, every girl there went completely silent — even the constant cafeteria background noise of silverware on plastic trays ceased.

"*What time is it?*" an amplified voice screamed into the silence.

"*Halloween!*" Every fucking girl in the cafeteria screamed back at the top of her lungs, making me cover my ears against the assault.

*"What! Time! Is! It!"*

*"All! Hallows! Eve!*

*"What time! Is it!"*

*"Samhain! Samhain! Samhain! Samhain!"*

The girls chanted, clapped, and stomped to the rhythm filling the dark cafeteria with sound. I looked around in amazement, half-expecting them to drag a rope-bound virgin out on the stage for sacrifice. Then the crowd went silent again as a booming bass cord cut across the chant.

The lights came on.

Flashing, strobing, floodlights, and spotlights in all colors.

Which was extremely odd, since they were coming from places I could have sworn there were no lights just a minute ago.

Then, to music worthy of a multi-level marketing promotional video, the bounciest girl I'd ever seen bounced onto the stage. Her ponytail bounced, her skirt bounced, her boobies bounced...

What? You'd notice too.

"Hi, everybody, I'm your All Hallows Eve event coordinator this year, Cassia Lightfoot!"

*"Hi, Cassia!"*

"Yes, those Lightfoots! And no, I won't!" Cassia yelled with a cocked head and wide grin.

All the girls laughed.

"Won't what?" I asked Sam.

Sam shushed me.

---

"YOU KNOW," I said, lifting the left leg of a twelve-foot, hydraulically wired skeleton just a little bit more so we could line it up with the pelvis we were attaching it to. The quad was filled with other witches doing similar work — or pushing crates and boxes from wherever they were stored, to as far as I could tell, everyplace on campus. "I would've thought witches would take Halloween a little more seriously."

"Oh, we take it seriously," Sam said sliding a cotter pin in place to hold the leg on.

We got started connecting the hydraulic lines between the leg and torso.

"You know what I mean — there's a robotic werewolf over there, at least three pallets of fog machines, and I'm pretty sure that was a real dead body that went by a minute ago."

The last of the lines went together with a click.

"Look," Sam said as I stood and offered my hand to help her up. She took it and I pulled her up, then she dusted the seat of her jeans off. "Witches were persecuted for centuries. We were hanged, burned, beheaded, drawn, quartered, drawn *and* quartered —"

"I get it —"

"We were stuck with pins, dunked in ponds, weighed against ducks —"

"That was a movie," I said.

"Whatever. The point is, this *is* a serious time for witches. It's a time when we remember and honor the memories and spirits of those witches who were tortured and murdered simply for being what we are. It is a somber, reflective —"

"With werewolves?"

"You're Goddess damned right with werewolves!" Sam said, grinning. She threw her head back. *"Aaarrooo!"*

*"Aaarrooo!"* the call got taken up by every witch around and passed across the quad and through the school buildings in an expanding wave.

"Seriously, it's a time where we celebrate being free from that. We celebrate that, after those centuries, even millennia, of persecution, the mundanes have finally forgotten about us." She gestured at the giant skeleton. "That their thoughts of us have been reduced to this — that the more garish and ridiculous the decorations they put up, the more ridiculous and unbelievable the idea that we exist becomes."

I nodded. "Okay that makes sense —"

Sam shoved me hard and laughed.

"You are so easy! Lighten up, it's the free candy. Half the school is going to glamour themselves down to twelve years old and hit that rich neighborhood on the southeast side of town."

---

I LOST count of how many animatronics we assembled during the course of the day — there were skeletons, werewolves, some kind of thing that was mostly fabric on a wire stretched between the roof of the admin building and the dorms, and enough fog machines to run a rock tour.

All around the quad and along the path to the athletic field different booths and scenes were being set up. By the end of the day, I was practically an expert on all the hardware — we had animatronics that were pneumatic, hydraulic, electric, and some powered by a box I was pretty sure was just magic, but couldn't figure out if we were using magic for some of these why all the things looked so typically fake.

"Why the physical displays? Couldn't the teachers just glamour up something?"

Sam stared at me for a moment. "How would that be any fun?" She frowned and cocked her head at me as though I just said the dumbest thing she'd ever heard. "Besides, we don't want them to look real, we want them to look like Halloween."

"What's the difference?"

"You'll see," she said. "Here, hold this head while I pull the wires out, they're all stuck down in his chest cavity."

By the end of the day, the campus had been transformed. It looked like some kind of demented fair or amusement park.

There were booths and displays absolutely everywhere, and it looked like an entire medieval village had been erected on the spell-stick field, complete with animatronic cows and sheep, — all of which mooed and baaed in distress every time the roaming pack of werewolves got too close.

The werewolves were actually a little scary — I knew that underneath, they were just six of those four-legged robots from some company in Boston, but they'd been covered in fur, and had articulated tails and a head whose muzzle was pulled back in an eternal snarl.

They roamed the campus with a team of witches carrying laptops hurrying after them and every hour or so they'd start sniffing the ground and then chase one of the students until she managed to get inside a building. The handlers said they were "calibrating" the things, but I was becoming more and more certain that the robots were doing it on their own.

Dinner that night was the most subdued I'd ever seen the Willowmere cafeteria — everyone was exhausted, and that included me. Even the bouncy Cassia Lightfoot looked tired and failed to bounce when she took the stage midway through dinner, but she did manage a little excitement.

"*Fantastic* job today everyone!"

"Thanks, Cassia," came the subdued reply.

"I'm thrilled to report our status is — *done!*" There were some muted cheers. "So, enjoy your dinner and get a good night's rest, because starting tomorrow we're going to be busy, *busy*, *busy!*"

"How can we be busy if we're done?" I asked Sam. "And done with what? What's all that stuff for?"

"It's for *Halloween*," she whispered back, "now shush."

"And!" Cassia was going on. "I'm thrilled to say our bookings are now at *eighty-six percent!* That's a new record for the Willowmere Witch Fest — and it's going to be the best one *ever!*"

"The what?"

Rachel finally took pity on me, I think, and explained while Cassia went on and on about the great job everyone had done.

"You've heard of stuff like the Halloween Nights some amusement parks put on?" Rachel asked.

"Well, yeah," I said — I'd never been to one. Not many amusement park visits in foster care, after all. "So, the college does some kind of haunted house or something?"

"This is what we do," Rachel said. "Nothing too scary —" I'd debate that, having seen the utterly terrifying robot werewolves. "— just fun stuff and a little history thrown in."

"Why? If we're trying to keep witches secret, doesn't that do the opposite?"

"I told you all day," Sam cut in. "It's about making the mundanes *not believe in us* — and if they somehow start to, then make them think we're not so bad. Think about it — would you have believed the college putting on a month-long Halloween Faire with all that camp was full of real witches?"

"Nope," Rachel said.

"And if you *did* find out later that they were real witches, would you think they were that bad after they gave you popcorn and cotton candy every year?"

"And let you ride the werewolves?" Rachel put in.

"And make candy potions," Hannah said.

"And play hide and seek with the 'witch' in the village," Brittany said.

"But most of all it's fun," Sam said.

DINNER ENDED EARLY and we all went to our rooms — it was early, but we were tired.

About an hour before curfew, there was a knock at our room's door.

"Come in," I called.

Sam and I were both in my bed — no, not like that, we were just watching videos on the same laptop and it was the easiest way to do it. We were each tucked into a corner with the laptop in the middle opposite us, so we could see the screen. Hardly even touching each other, except when one of us stretched a leg too far.

The door opened and Rachel came in. She smiled at me — well, almost, before ducking her head so I couldn't see that she was smiling. Then she looked at Sam.

"Oh," she said. "I didn't know you'd both be here, Sam, I thought you were going to the library — sorry, I can come back later."

"Too tired — but don't go, it's fine," Sam said. "We're just watching stupid stuff — time to stop anyway. Come on in."

"Okay," Rachel said, but she seemed to be a little hesitant — more so than usual, even. She came over to the bed and I saw she had a plate with a cupcake on it. "I was just in the cafeteria and they only had one left, so I thought you might —"

"*Dibs!*" Sam called, launching herself forward and nearly knocking the laptop off the bed as she grabbed the cupcake. "Ooo, mint frosting!"

"Hey!" I protested as she took a huge bite, swallowed, and stuffed the rest in her mouth.

Rachel was staring at her, eyes wide and mouth slack.

"You owe me for last week when I gave you my pie," Sam told me, "so get over it."

"You said you didn't like pie!"

"I don't, but I do like cupcakes." She licked frosting and chocolate crumbs off her fingers. "Thanks, Rachel."

Rachel didn't move.

Sam frowned. "You okay?"

"Um," Rachel said, "oh, no." She covered her mouth with her hand and backed away. "I, um, have to go now."

She spun around and dashed from the room, and if it wouldn't have been so out of character for the shy girl, I'd have sworn I heard a muttered, "fuck."

"What's up with her?" I asked.

"I don't — oh, no," Sam said, groaning and smacked her forehead with one hand. "She wanted to give *you* the cupcake. Maiden's blush, I told you she has a crush on you — and I messed it up. Crap."

"You think?"

"Yeah, that's why she said she'd come back later. She only brought one. For you."

I wasn't sure how I felt about that — I liked Rachel, she was fun and I got a kick out of teasing her, as well as watching her go ballistic at spellstick games. She'd been coming to our room to watch spellstick with us — with me, maybe — about every other night since Cassandra's horrible trick. On the other hand, I wasn't sure if I liked her in that way, you know? She was cute and sweet, but I thought I was too new to the whole witch culture thing to start dating. Did the witches even call it dating? They probably had some weird name for it.

"What should we do?"

Sam sighed. "I'll talk to her tomorrow — maybe drop a hint or two about something more special than a cupcake she can do for you. It'll be okay."

# CHAPTER TWENTY-EIGHT

The first two weeks of Halloween-month went by and I was exhausted, but the witches seemed to only get more and more energized.

The class workloads had been reduced, cutting most of the homework and long reading assignments, focusing mainly on in-class lectures and exercises, but everything about the Halloween Faire took their place. Throughout the day there was maintenance on the displays, restocking the booths, and making sure the werewolves were plugged in and recharged — then, about an hour before dusk every day, everyone got ready for the evening's activities. Costumes repaired and donned, fog machines on, food stands fired up, and the werewolves released.

Then the buses and cars started arriving, dropping their passengers at the head of the drive and parking along its length. Kids from kindergarten to high school — a couple hundred every night — ran through the faire, eating, drinking, riding werewolves, running from werewolves, finding the witch hiding in the village (who always gave the finders treats), and all manner of other events.

I, and most of the first-years, were tasked with restocking the stands and emptying the trash cans throughout the night, with a select few shadowing the more senior students in their roles.

Even the dinner hours had been pushed earlier and later, with the cafeteria remaining open from lunch to after midnight, so that students could eat before or after their work, or both, as well as picking up a quick snack on our breaks. Rachel and I had just finished restocking a cotton candy stand and were heading to get some food before our next assignment.

"I'll catch up with you in the cafeteria," I said, as Rachel and I entered the dorms. "I want to check in on Sam."

"Is she sick?"

"She said she wasn't feeling like working today — but she didn't seem sick."

"Okay," Rachel said. "Ask her if she's hungry? You could bring her something from the cafeteria."

"Like a cupcake?" I teased.

Rachel blushed and bit her lip.

"Um, was she okay? After the cupcake, I mean?"

"Why wouldn't she be?"

"No reason! It *was* the last one, though, so maybe it had been sitting out too long or something?"

"No, she's been fine all month. She just didn't feel like getting up today."

"Oh, okay, good."

I realized I hadn't seen Rachel and Sam at the same time except for class and meals. She'd stopped visiting our room to show me spell-stick videos and wasn't dropping by to hang out at all. I hadn't really thought about it, since we were so busy with the faire, but she hadn't been to our room all month.

And Sam seemed to be asking about her all the time. It was weird, now that I thought about it, but we'd been so busy with the Halloween Faire that I hadn't noticed until now.

Rachel headed for the cafeteria while I started climbing the stairs.

I opened the door to our room and saw Sam's rainbow-sock clad feet at the end of her bed.

"Hey, roomie," I called softly. "You doing okay?"

I eased the door shut so it wouldn't slam if she really wasn't feeling well, and walked into the main room.

Sam laid on her bed, frighteningly still, with her eyes closed and black froth covering her lips.

---

"SAM!"

I dropped to the floor and knelt beside the bed, reaching for her wrist and leaning over to hold my cheek next to her lips to see if she was breathing.

I couldn't feel either breath or pulse.

"Help! Somebody, I need help!"

She wasn't breathing and her heart wasn't beating — I tried to remember the CPR class from high school. I pressed my fingers into her chest searching for the notch at the bottom of her rib cage and put both hands there one on top of the other, pressing hard. The instructor had said that — press hard, press harder than you think you need to, press as hard as you can.

I tried, but I saw Sam's body just sink into the mattress as I pressed.

"Help!" I yelled again.

I didn't know if there'd be anyone to hear me — everyone was probably in the cafeteria for lunch or working on the faire.

I dragged Sam off the bed onto the harder floor, cradling her head so it wouldn't fall and slam against the floor, then I straddled her hips and put my hands on her chest again, pressing down as hard as I could.

*What did they say? How fast? Some stupid song, right?*

I remembered then, and almost cried at what a silly, stupid thing it was to have to remember in a situation like this.

"Uh," I muttered to myself, pressing hard, "uh, uh, uh, staying alive, staying alive."

"Oh, Goddess! What are you doing to her?"

I looked up and one of the other freshmen was standing in our doorway eyes wide and hands at her mouth. I'd seen her around but didn't know her name.

"Help! He's killing her!" she screamed.

"No, something's wrong, it's CPR!" I yelled, trying to keep the beat going.

Two more girls came to the doorway and shrieked.

"Go get the nurse!" I yelled.

"Get off her!" one of the girls yelled, stepping into the room.

She rushed over and shoved me, throwing me off the rhythm — I pushed her away roughly, and fumbled trying to find the right hand-position again before I finally got it and could restart compressions.

I looked up at the crowd in our doorway, and met one of the girls' eyes who looked more sensible than the rest.

"You!" I yelled. "Go! Get! The nurse!"

The girl's eyes flew wide and she shoved her way through the other girls.

I paused briefly to check Sam's pulse again, but there was nothing.

I had to think for a second before continuing, to remember whether I was supposed to do breathing, too. Some movies showed that, but what had the instructor said? I thought I remembered it was just the chest compressions, stick with those.

I started pressing again, putting my whole weight behind it, feeling Sam's thin frame under my hands. It seemed to go on forever, but couldn't have been that long because the girl wasn't back with the nurse yet.

All of a sudden, I felt Sam twitch and her head moved — she coughed and I took my hands away.

I looked up at the girls in the doorway — all of their eyes wide — and didn't see the nurse yet.

How long had it been?

It didn't matter.

I got off Sam — she coughed again but her eyes still didn't open.

I started to slide my hands under her body — if the nurse hadn't gotten to us yet, then we go to the fucking nurse — but I caught sight of something on Sam's desk.

It was a potion bottle, but empty, and there was a black residue in the empty bottle that looked like whatever it was around Sam's lips.

My heart sank, and I knew she'd finished that damn potion — the full moon had been two nights before — and then taken it without telling me. Maybe she thought I'd try to stop her or disapprove.

I scrambled over and grabbed the bottle, putting it in my pocket, before I reached under Sam again to lift her. I figured the nurse would need to know what she'd taken, and the bottle would have to do because I didn't know where she'd put the book she'd stolen from the library.

I lifted Sam and headed for the door.

"Get out of my way!" I snarled.

The girls scattered, moving away from the doorway and putting their backs to the wall to clear a path.

I hurried down the hallway then started on the stairs.

Sam might not have been very heavy, but I wasn't a big muscular guy and I felt the strain in my arms and my knees started twitching before we got to the third floor. By the time I reached the first floor, I was panting, but not going to give up.

I kicked open the door to the dorms and started for the administration building where the infirmary was.

Now we were on the quad and word was spreading so girls were coming out of both the cafeteria and the classroom building to see what was going on, as well as all those already on the quad setting up for the faire.

Halfway across the quad *Magistra* Fallwhistle, the nurse, hurried out of the administrative building.

"Can you get her to the infirmary?" she asked, rushing up to us.

"Yeah," I panted.

"What happened?"

"Potion... More power... She took..."

"You know what potion?"

I shook my head. "Book... Somewhere... In room ... maybe."

A girl rushed up to us.

"Let me float her," she said, hurrying along with me and the nurse.

That didn't make any sense to me — but I couldn't think of anything except putting one foot in front of the other and getting Sam to the infirmary.

"I'm a telly," the girl said tugging at my arm. "Let me float her."

"Noah, let her help," the nurse said.

I panted, finally understanding and slowed so the girl could get her power under Sam. My arms fell to my sides as her weight left them, and I staggered after her and *Magistra* Fallwhistle.

A couple girls rushed ahead of us to open the doors to the administrative building, and we burst in to rush through the students and teachers in the hallway toward the open infirmary door.

"Put her on the first exam table," *Magistra* Fallwhistle said.

Sam's body floated over and settled onto the exam table. I rushed over and felt at her neck and wrist to make sure her heart hadn't stopped again.

*Magistra* Fallwhistle took the empty potion bottle I handed her and unscrewed the top, sniffing at it.

"A potion to increase power, you say?"

I nodded, trying to catch my breath.

*Magistra* Fallwhistle grunted, and set the bottle on her desk. She came over and laid her hands on Sam's forehead and stomach, then closed her eyes.

"Goddess — well, she's gotten that," she murmured. She opened her eyes and looked at me. "Did you know about this?"

I shook my head. "I knew she was thinking about it," I said, "but I didn't know she was going to take it today."

"And you didn't think to tell a teacher?"

I hung my head and my face flushed.

Mel burst into the room and a moment behind her was *Prima* Rosethorn, closing the infirmary door quickly behind her to cut off the gazes of the growing crowd.

"What happened?" *Prima* Rosethorn demanded.

*Magistra* Fallwhistle jerked her head at her desk. "The girl brewed a potion to increase her power," she said. "*Magellus* Ashe said there's a book somewhere in their room — can you send someone to search for it? I need to know what potion."

While the *Prima* turned to do that, Mel strode over to the desk and lifted the potion bottle. She wet a finger with her mouth ran it along the residue inside the bottle, then returned the finger to her mouth to taste the potion.

I knew it was wrong, I knew it was the wrong time, but my body didn't know either of those things, and the image of Mel sucking the potion off her fingertip and the knowledge of what I'd given Sam to use in the potion flashed through my head. Without me willing it, I felt my dick twitch and harden in my pants.

Then I thought of the sort of grief Sam would give me if I told her how that inappropriate thing happened — and prayed she'd be okay so we could spend hours laughing about it.

I collapsed to my knees beside the exam table, eyes scrunched tight against tears.

"I know the potion," Mel said, stepping up to the table.

"What was it?" *Prima* Rosethorn asked.

"Not a good one," Mel said, then looked at me. "Did you give her something for the potion?"

I flushed again and nodded — it was embarrassing as hell, but I wanted Mel to know the truth so she could help Sam.

"How much?" Mel asked.

"I —" I couldn't understand the question — it's not like we weighed it or anything.

"How much?" Mel repeated. "How many times did she add it?"

I flushed even hotter. "Three," I said.

Mel looked at the potion bottle she held. "Was it all in here? Did she drink it all?"

"I think so."

Mel cursed under her breath.

"Melaina, what is it?" *Prima* Rosethorn asked.

Mel turned to stare at Sam.

"Evacuate the building and close the faire."

# CHAPTER TWENTY-NINE

"Evacuate?" *Prima* Rosethorn asked. "You can't be serious —"

"If it's the potion I think it is, then the girl drank an entire batch that was meant to be shared amongst a full coven."

I looked up, shocked. That didn't seem like something Sam would do deliberately, and she was too smart to make a mistake like that. A moment later, *Prima* Rosethorn echoed my thought.

"I can't imagine how she could make a mistake like that — she's one of the best potions students we've seen in years."

At that point, Sam's body began to shake as though she was having a seizure. *Magistra* Fallwhistle and Mel grasped her on one side and I grasped the other to keep her body on the exam table.

*Prima* Rosethorn hurried over to assist.

"Melaina?" *Prima* Rosethorn asked.

"I imagine she found the English translation," Mel said, "and Samantha didn't understand that the instruction 'and you shall drink it, all entire, in a single round' was meant for the plural you — thirteen witches of the coven — and not one singularly foolish little girl."

*Prima* Rosethorn grunted. "Still... We should be able to contain..."

"The boy's a *trinitara*, remember?" Mel said.

"He's... What? What..." *Magistra* Fallwhistle looked at me with wide eyes.

"What does he have to do with it?" *Prima* Rosethorn asked.

"This potion requires essence," Mel said, "which can be added up to three times — Samantha chose three."

"I see," *Prima* Rosethorn said. She stared at Sam, then at me. "Yes, evacuate..."

She left the exam table and hurried over to the door.

Sam's shaking had subsided a bit, so we all stepped back from her, though I stayed close and took her hand.

I was having trouble accepting that they were actually evacuating the building. This was too surreal.

*Prima* Rosethorn returned and came over to us.

"Noah, please go with the others — the staff will be assembling everyone at the far side of the playing field."

I shook my head. "I'm not leaving Sam."

If they were assembling on the far side of the playing field, that meant they were evacuating the dorms and classrooms too? What the hell was going on?

"Young man, this is not the time to —"

"I need him," Mel said, interrupting *Prima* Rosethorn.

"Melaina —"

"If you want a chance to save the girl," Mel said, "I need him. The only chance Samantha has is to drain off that mana — he is an unmarked, *trinitara* warlock. He can drain anyone."

"Thirteen trebled," *Prima* Rosethorn said. "There is no way he can contain —"

"If it can save Sam, I'll do it," I interrupted.

"Neither of you should be so confident in your place that you feel free to continue interrupting me," *Prima* Rosethorn said. "You may be a Power in your own right, Melaina, but you well know I am not to be trifled with either. What you propose, when it fails, would treble the power unleashed yet again." She shook her head. "No, I can't allow it."

"I'll do it — if Mel says there's a chance, I'll do it. I don't care."

"You will die, *Magellus* Ashe."

"You think I'd be living if I let my best friend die when there was a chance I could save her?"

*Prima* Rosethorn's nostrils flared.

"You and I will be having a conversation about just whose school this is, Melaina Blackwood," *Prima* Rosethorn said, striding toward the door. "For now, I'm going to have everyone moved back to the edge of the forest, then return to strengthen the wards on the building." She paused, hand on the doorknob, not looking back. "Good luck."

---

"WHAT DO I HAVE TO DO?" I asked Mel.

Instead of answering me, Mel turned to *Magistra* Fallwhistle.

"You should go with the others."

"I won't leave a patient," *Magistra* Fallwhistle said.

Mel started to argue, but then paused and simply nodded at the other woman.

She turned to look at me.

"Noah, *Prima* Rosethorn was not exaggerating the risks. You may not have the capacity to do this — likely not. If you don't, you'll die. Even if successful, it's going to be unbelievably painful for you."

"Is there any other way to help her?"

Mel shook her head.

I nodded.

"Then what do I do?"

"Samantha's body has been compelled to produce far more mana than anyone's should — not only that for an entire coven, but enhancing that as well. She's creating a huge amount of mana that her body simply can't process fast enough and it's rapidly burning her up. What you'll have to do is draw that mana off, refining and storing it yourself."

*Magistra* Fallwhistle was shaking her head. "*Magistra* Blackwood — this is incredibly dangerous. He's eighteen years old and has no coven, his mana stores can't possibly contain the amount of mana I felt in the girl. Not to mention the dangers of marking."

Mel shrugged. "Being marked is not, I think, a fate worse than death — and if we do nothing, Samantha's death is assured. I believe we can avoid any marking, however, as the connection won't be too intimate and with Samantha being unconscious, she may not resist enough to trigger the boy's instincts. Regardless, the real danger will be if Noah can't contain the refined mana."

She came around to my side of Sam's bed and laid a hand on my shoulder.

"Noah, I'm not exaggerating that this will be the most painful, dangerous thing you've ever done. Your mana stores are still new, barely fully formed, and you're going to have to stretch them to the utmost."

"I don't understand, but I'll do it."

"You need to understand, or I can't allow it. Think of your mana stores like muscles, dear. Exercise builds muscle, just as stretching and expanding your stores with more mana makes them larger — and, just as with muscles, that building causes damage and pain. That's what the soreness after exercise is — your muscles have been stretched and torn, damaged, and then rebuild themselves, adding new muscle as they repair the damage. In the case of your stores, this will be like taking your body to a professional body builder's state in a matter of minutes. What should take years, possibly decades, all at once."

"Okay, I get it — unbelievably painful and dangerous. Let's go."

It's not like I wasn't scared — I was. What Mel described sounded horrible and I was imagining having the aftereffects of years, decades, worth of workouts inflicted on me at once. No matter how scary, though, I couldn't say no — not just because I cared about Sam, but because I was partly responsible. I'd helped her get the book, I'd given her the ... essence — this was partly my fault for helping her and I had to fix it or I'd never forgive myself.

Mel straightened and grasped Sam's shirt, pulling it open and snapping the buttons. They hit the tile floor with clacking that seemed oddly loud.

"Put your hands here —" she took my left hand and put it on Sam's chest just above her bra. "— And here." She put my right hand on Sam's stomach just below her bellybutton.

"You and Samantha have been partners; you know her shields?"

I nodded.

"You need to get inside them, whatever that takes."

I nodded again, then closed my eyes and concentrated on seeing our shields like we did in class.

Sam's shields seemed stretched and hard, more like a shell than something she wore.

I opened my own and let my power reach out — there was no give like there usually was. Every other time I'd touched someone's shields — Mel's, Sam's, even my own — they had a pliable feel. Sam's didn't. It was like the difference between touching a basketball and a bowling ball. I let my power creep along her shields, looking for any way in — any crack or crevice in the hard shell. I felt around — Sam always made her shields a little bit ... bigger over her chest. I'd teased her about it over and over. That always left a gap between her shields and skin, so I concentrated there, putting more and more pressure on the hard shell around her until I felt it give.

There — I let my own power enter the tiny crack and pull it apart just a bit — I exerted more force and felt the hard shields around Sam stretch a bit. More force, and more stretching. If I could just get a bit inside them, she wouldn't be able to keep me out.

Suddenly, Sam's shields cracked and I could see her.

I gasped, shocked. With the talk of enhancing power, I'd expected something bright — even too bright to look at. But Sam was full of darkness — a greasy, oily darkness that flowed through her and filled her.

Filled her too much, because it felt like she was ready to explode.

"What do you see?" Mel asked.

"It's like she's filled with oil," I said. "Too much, it's like it's going to explode."

"That's the raw mana," Mel said. "She should've filtered it through her own emotions, but it must've been too much, too fast, and overwhelmed her before she had a chance."

"Raw?" *Magistra* Fallwhistle asked. "You didn't say it produced *raw* mana — what are you thinking? He can't draw that off! No one can!"

"He can," Mel said. "He's of my line."

"What difference does that make?"

"We were always close to the Goddess," Mel said. "Closer to the source."

"What should I do?" I asked, interrupting a lot of stuff I really didn't care about in that moment.

*Magistra* Fallwhistle backed away, staring at us like we were crazy.

Mel nodded. "I want you to connect your resonants to hers."

"But she only has one —"

"Look closer, you can see the space for three — the other two?" Mel asked. "They're dormant, but should be there."

I looked closer, trying to see beyond the inky darkness that filled Sam and thought I saw what Mel meant. They weren't that much smaller than her active resonant store, testimony to how little mana she'd actually generated and stored over her life.

"Okay, yeah, I see them I think."

"You can still connect to those — you're going to be pulling that raw mana out of her through her resonants," Mel said. "Take it into yourself and filter it through your own — you don't have to think about that, it will happen automatically as you draw it into your own stores."

"Connect? How do I do that?"

"It's a bit different for everyone — it'll depend on how you visualize your power and interact with it. Just think about connecting and trust your instincts."

*Great,* I thought. *I get to improv saving my friend's life.*

I thought about it, picturing Sam's resonants and trying to will a connection to them. I thought I was getting nowhere, but then I had the oddest feeling. It was like sliding inside something warm and welcoming. And I felt it three times.

And, dammit, my dick twitched.

It felt like what I imagined sex would feel like.

I could feel Sam surrounding some part of me — three parts of me.

I groaned.

"I take it you've got something?" Mel asked.

I nodded, not trusting my voice, because it felt so good, and I hoped Mel and *Magistra* Fallwhistle couldn't tell what I was feeling. If she could, Mel didn't give any indication.

"Now I want you to think about that raw mana in Samantha and draw it toward yourself. Much as you do with ambient mana. Like you're sucking it out through those resonant connections." She paused. "Noah, raw mana is very volatile. It doesn't want to be controlled, but you must convince it."

"Convince it?"

"Mana comes from the Goddess," Mel said. She had the same sad look she always got when she talked about the witches' Goddess — like she was talking about some old friend who'd died or something. "She'll help ... if you ask her. Now start to draw it into you."

I groaned again, because before Mel had even finished speaking, I'd begun to do just that. It was like draining an ice-cold bottle of soda on a hot summer day, except the bottle never emptied and you never needed to breathe. It just went on, and on, filling me, satisfying a craving that never lessened.

"Draw it into yourself," Mel said, "and fill your resonants." She paused. "Noah, whatever it feels like now, it's going to hurt soon." I could hear her swallow and lick her lips before continuing.

I groaned again, because the thought of Mel licking her lips and swallowing made my dick twitch again, and I realized it was completely hard. Beyond hard — and I worried that it might burst through the fabric of my trousers that it was already straining against.

Then I realized that Mel and *Magistra* Fallwhistle were right across the table from me and could see whatever tent I was making in my pants.

Then I realized I didn't care if they could see that, because I'd be perfectly happy to strip down and let them have a look at it without anything in the way before bending them both over *Magistra* Fallwhistle's desk and —

*Whoa, where is that coming from?* I thought.

I drew my attention back to what was happening and not just reveling in the sensations, and saw I'd already, I guess instinctively, begun filtering the raw mana I drew from Sam into my own resonants — starting, it seemed, with Lust which was filling rapidly.

"Remember to try to keep them balanced," Mel said. "You'll feel any one of your resonants less if you keep them in balance — too much in one and it will affect you."

I tried to concentrate on the flowing power and divert about equal amounts to each of my resonants. Gradually the Lust eased and I felt my erection, not soften, but not seem like it was going to start dragging me around the room looking for satisfaction.

"Your resonants are going to fill, Noah. And then they're going to stretch — you're going to think that you can't take anymore, but you must endure. Remember, your resonants are like a muscle, if you use them, they grow — you're just going to use them a lot in a very short time. Do you understand?"

I nodded.

"You need to take it all, no matter how much it hurts. Until there is nothing of that raw mana left in Samantha."

"All of it? Won't that hurt her?"

"No, she'll be fine so long as you're connected to her, and we'll be sure she's okay before you withdraw. We just need to get all of the raw power out of her and let her own system recover. So long as you can hold it, we'll be fine."

"And what if I can't?"

"There are things we can try if that happens, but don't worry about it right now."

"I'm already kind of worried about it — so what if the other things don't work?"

Mel shrugged. "Then the world's conspiracy theorists will have a wonderful time explaining the lack of a crater."

I thought about it for only a moment before realizing that none of what could happen would make any difference to me now.

"Okay."

The pain came quicker than I thought it would. I tried to keep my resonants balanced, but soon couldn't concentrate enough to think about it as they filled and stretched and I felt that I was going to burst apart.

It was the worst pain, the worst anything, I'd ever experienced. Like my entire body was swollen, skin tight and about to split. I thought I clenched my jaw, but couldn't tell with everything else I was feeling.

The pain grew and went on and on, until I started to think I might rather die than continue — but that would mean Sam died too, and I wouldn't allow that. I remembered what Mel had said — convince it? Ask the Goddess? Would the witches' Goddess, if she was real, even listen to me? Did I have a choice?

I'd never prayed before — my foster parents weren't much on religion and likely wouldn't have taken us to a church, even if any of us had wanted to go, so it's not like I had a template to work from.

*So, um, Goddess?* I thought. *Hi, I'm Noah — you probably know that, right? Omniscient or something? Anyway, I need your help — Sam needs your help. I don't know if you're real, but I know Sam believes in you — she talks about you all the time. Yeah, mostly it's swearing by your nipples and farts and stuff, but that's just Sam, you know?*

Another wave of pain ran through me and I tensed up. I think I might have popped something in my brain, because I smelled fresh grass. And flowers, and earth, and fresh-baked bread. Did that mean I'd had four aneurysms?

When that wave passed, or not passed, but I'd taken it enough to get used to it for a second while I waited for the next, I kept praying.

*Sam loves you and trusts you. And Mel — she looks so sad when she talks about you, like she's lost a part of herself — I don't know what's up with that, but I know she believes in you and loves you, because no one could look that hurt over someone they don't love.*

I nearly screamed. It felt like someone had stuffed a balloon covered in broken glass inside me and was inflating it more and more. Three balloons. I didn't even want to look at my resonant stores, because I was sure they were about to burst.

*Please help me? Please help her?*

I remembered what the girls had told me about the Veil — that there'd been a ritual and a sacrifice? Did the witches' Goddess demand that? It didn't feel right, but —

*If you need to, you can take me instead? I'm okay with that — just, please, she's my best friend and ... I love her.*

I did scream then — it was too much. My insides were being ripped apart.

I couldn't do it — I couldn't take any more, and Sam was going to die. I was going to die. Probably Mel and *Magistra* Fallwhistle were going to die, because I was too weak.

"Hold it, Noah," Mel said from the other side of the exam table.

I heard *Magistra* Fallwhistle beside her. "You should never have let him try this."

My eyes were clenched shut and I felt tears rolling down my face.

I screamed again, then there were hands on me.

Someone laid a hand atop each of mine where they laid on Sam's body. Someone else stroked the back of my neck and brushed back the sweat-damp hair that had fallen over my face. Lips brushed my cheek where the tears streamed. Arms looped around my waist, holding me tight.

The pain didn't lessen — it grew, but my strength grew with it.

I don't know how long that went on, it seemed like forever, then it eased, but only in the sense that things weren't being stretched any further, they'd only stopped.

"Hold it, Noah," Mel whispered. "You can hold it."

I shook my head, I had to let it out somehow or I was going to explode.

"You can do it, Noah."

It was like trying not to vomit or the last few feet to the toilet when you had to go really bad.

"I ... can't..."

"Very well — *Magistra* Fallwhistle, please rush to the cafeteria and get me a five-pound box of salt," Mel said.

"Salt?" both I and *Magistra* Fallwhistle asked at the same time

I didn't know what the hell Mel could want with salt at the time like this — just the thought of salt made my stomach churn, as though the mana was filling my physical body as well and wanted out any way possible.

"I need to create a circle to help him contain this," Mel said. "Please, hurry, I don't know how much time we have."

I heard the clatter of *Magistra* Fallwhistle's heels and then the infirmary door slammed.

"What ... circle?" I asked trying to distract myself from what I was feeling.

"What? Oh, there's no circle needed. I just wanted to get her out of here so there are no witnesses."

"Witnesses? What about the other witches?" There had to be others — there'd been too many hands on me to just be Mel and the nurse.

"We're alone now, Noah, and that's good because no one can know what's about to happen," Mel said. "Now, listen carefully, dear.

When they ask you, tell them that you had nothing to do with this. It must have been an effect of the potion, but it certainly wasn't anything you did. Do you understand?"

"No..."

"I'm going to have you do something — I'm nearly certain you can, the ability runs in my line, our line — but it is *not* something anyone, anyone at all, can know of. It's not a greater secret than your Control resonant, but very close." She paused. "No, it is a greater secret — Control will just make them want to kill you. This? For this they'll do anything to have you."

"That's not comforting."

"We'll claim it was an effect of pulling the wild mana through Samantha's resonants, not what you are about to do. Do you understand the gravity of this?"

I nodded. I really didn't, because I was having way too much trouble concentrating, but I trusted Mel. I did hope, though, that the secret shit that could get me killed or worse would just come all at once instead of being dumped on me over and over again.

"Tell me," Mel said. "When they ask, what do you say?"

"I don't know how it happened, maybe it was the potion, I didn't do anything," I repeated stiffly, trying to control the power struggling to get out of me.

"Good," Mel said. "Now, I want you to push the power you've taken back into Samantha."

I shook my head — immediately regretting it, because my vision spun. "That will... There's too much."

I blinked after a quick glance at my own resonants — they'd stretched and grown to the point that they nearly filled half my torso. Sam's resonant was ... so small. She couldn't hold even a tiny fraction of what was trying to escape me.

"I know. You need to push it into all three of her resonants and expand them as well."

I shook my head. "No, she only has one."

"You're going to open the others."

"What?"

"Pushing that mana back into Samantha is going to open her other two resonants."

"I can do that?"

"You are of my line, dear. I honestly don't know how — I thought all my children had perished long, long ago — but you are. You can do this, but no one other than the three of us, you, me, and possibly Samantha if she ever questions it, must ever know."

"Why?"

This made no sense — if a warlock could open up dormant resonants and make a witch a *trinitara*, wouldn't that be good?

"Noah, a free warlock is desirable to the Families, a *trinitara* more so. A warlock with Command would be valuable to the Family that binds him. A warlock who can fill that Family with *trinitaras*? At will? He is a danger to the balance of power. It would terrify them — every Family except his would band together to destroy them all. It might even be enough to bring the other races into the conflict. It would be bloody war behind the Veil and could well spill over into the mundane world."

"Ah, fuck," I moaned in the most bizarre question I could ever imagine myself saying. "Could I not just be a normal warlock?"

"There are no normal warlocks of my line, dear. Get used to it."

Another wave of pain ran through me. "Never mind, just tell me what to do before I spew mana out of every orifice, please?"

"Listen carefully, Noah," Mel said. "You have a decision to make about Samantha's resonants — the ones that you open are going to mirror your own."

"What does that mean?"

"When you connect your resonants to hers, her primary will cancel out whatever's connected to it — it will just accept the mana since you've refined it. But opening her dormant ones will set their resonance. You need to make a choice — you're Samantha's friend and you know her best of either of us, so you have to decide which of your three resonants you'll mirror into her."

I'd have complained about that, too, but the pain was growing to much and I needed to get this done.

I thought about that choice. Lust was a no-brainer; Sam would love having that — especially paired with the Love she already resonated with. I grinned as I thought of her finding some hot young thing with big boobs and a tight ass and really falling in love with her to fill two resonants to the brim.

The other was a harder decision.

Finally, I decided that Sam would never want to face the sort of fear and wariness that came with the Control resonant. She loved other people too much to be able to take it.

Our resonants were already connected that way, as I'd first set my primary, Control, against hers.

"Okay," I said.

"You're sure?" Mel asked. "This is a fundamental change for her. Make your best choice."

I nodded.

"All right, now start forcing the mana back into her — try to keep it equal, as you did taking it from her. Keep her in balance so that her resonant stores expand at the same rate. There's going to be resistance, but you need to push against it. It's going to hurt her as much as taking it in hurt you, so do it quickly and don't draw it out — and stop when you feel you can contain what's left. Don't give her more than you must."

"No pressure," I muttered.

"And, Noah?"

"What?"

"This is going to feel quite different for you, dear. Try to contain yourself."

"What, worse?"

"Not exactly. Stop dawdling, dear, and get started."

I grumbled, but started pushing power into Sam, and then groaned with both the easing of the pressure I felt and the sensation of the power flowing out of me into her. Mel was right — it was very different.

This no longer hurt, at least for me. It was like a long, drawn-out orgasm — only I was feeling three of them, one for each resonant, and I began to really understand the witches' fascination with their rule of three.

I started to wonder what it would be like to do this while also having sex — and then realized that's exactly what the covens did. The orgy-thing suddenly made a lot more sense. If the amount of mana being transferred had been a normal amount, instead of ripping me, and now Sam, apart to stretch our mana stores, it would have been the most intense pleasure I'd ever known.

I felt Sam shudder, and almost stopped, but Mel said, "Until you can contain what's left easily. Don't stop, no matter what, until you reach that point."

I grunted and kept going.

The pressure inside me eased and I could start to think better. The sensation from filling Sam didn't ease though, if anything the absence of that pressure and swelling of my stores made the other things I was feeling more intense.

Sam was shuddering beneath my hands.

"Oh, fuck," I moaned.

Mel cleared her throat, but didn't say anything else.

I opened my eyes, no longer needing to concentrate on not exploding, and saw how this was affecting Sam. Her face was contorted in pain and her whole body was tense and straining. She was dripping with sweat — streams of it running off her face and body. The sight made me want to stop, but I didn't think I could contain the amount of mana I still had inside me.

In fact, part of me wanted to fill her more — I wanted to be inside her, filling her. My eyes locked on her open shirt and exposed skin, causing that urge to grow, but I knew Mel would stop me if I started stripping our clothes off. And that neither Sam nor I would ever forgive me if I did that, so I pushed down the urge.

Then a new feeling erupted in me. My jaw ached and I longed to bend over and latch my teeth on that creamy flesh — somehow, I knew if I did that, I could pour more mana, more power, into Sam in a way that would be ... exquisite. I growled and bent forward.

"*Ow!*"

"That's the marking urge," Mel said after pinching my earlobe hard. "Resist it."

"What the hell?"

I was pretty sure my ear was bleeding, but I didn't want to break the physical connection I had with Sam to check.

"It would have come when you were drawing the mana out of her if she'd resisted — luckily, she's unconscious and didn't. Now you should have enough self-control to avoid it."

Marking. Yeah, I didn't want to come out of this with a coven — not without Sam's consent. I tried to relax my jaw and not think about it as I continued to push mana into her.

Eventually, things eased until I felt I could draw a breath and I slowed the flow of power into Sam. I looked at her and she had three bulging, glowing resonance stores, each the size of a baseball.

I stopped the flow. My knees buckled and I had to catch myself with my elbows on the exam table to hold myself up.

I looked up at Mel.

"Is it enough?" I asked.

My vision darkened to a small oval of her face as she nodded, then it all went away.

# CHAPTER THIRTY

"I don't object to anything Noah did to me," Sam was saying. "Whatever it was."

Which was very odd because she had not been with Rachel and I at the park when zombie bugs attacked and we had to run to the Eiffel Tower during a thunderstorm so they'd be fried by the lightning that...

"And you, Melaina," *Prima* Rosethorn said, "you maintain you have no knowledge of how the girl's had two new resonants added to her?"

"It's not a known effect of that potion — on the other hand, no one's ever taken so much of it before."

Now the zombie bugs were really going to be in trouble with both Mel and *Prima* Rosethorn to fight them.

"Well, *Sororix* Prescott is on her way, and we'll see what she has to say about things."

"I'm an adult," Sam said. "My mother has nothing to say in the matter."

"Oh, I'm sure your mother will have a great deal to say about a great number of things — and she is still your guardian, young lady. Until you've joined a coven, at least."

I was beginning to think there was more going on here than the zombie bugs, so I tried to turn my head and see what the others were doing, but that just made me groan.

"Look out for the zombie bugs," I muttered.

"Ah, he's awake," *Prima* Rosethorn said, and I heard people moving closer to me.

I opened my eyes and squinted up at the infirmary's bright lights.

"Did we beat the zombie bugs?"

"What are you talking about, *Magellus* Ashe?"

I had a sudden clarity that I most likely had not just come from fighting zombie bugs beneath the Eiffel Tower with Rachel ... who, if my hazy recollection was correct, had been more interested in getting me to eat a mint-frosted brownie than helping me with the bugs anyway. I took a moment to refile that as a dream, rather than a memory, which let me remember the last thing I'd been doing.

"*Sam!*" I cried out, struggling to sit up.

A hand grasped my shoulder to push me back down, I think it was Mel, because both she and *Prima* Rosethorn were beside my bed now — I was on one of the other infirmary beds — but I shrugged it off and swung my legs over the side.

"Noah, lay back down," Mel said, but I ignored her and hopped off the bed ... which, honestly, was a really bad idea.

My knees started buckling but I managed to stagger to Sam's bed where I could at least use it to hold myself up. My head was spinning and hurt like hell.

Sam looked almost as bad as I felt.

Someone had put an exam gown on her, so at least she wasn't still wearing the shirt Mel had torn open, but her hair was a lanky mess, still damp with sweat, so I assumed I hadn't been out too long. There were still black flecks from the potion around her mouth, and she looked ... small. Smaller than just short-Sam small.

"I'm okay," she said, but even her voice was smaller and she looked away from me, turning her head on the pillow.

*Shit,* I thought — she might have just told Mel and *Prima* Rosethorn she didn't object to what I'd done to her, but was she really pissed at me?

"Sam?"

"Come on, dear," Mel said, putting an arm around me, pulling me away then supporting me as she led me back to my bed. "You've both been through something very traumatic and you need rest. Both of you."

I did, really — I collapsed back on my bed and closed my eyes.

"*Magellus* Ashe," *Prima* Rosethorn said, "I do need you to tell me what happened first."

"He needs rest," Mel said.

"The school is in an uproar, the night's faire has been canceled, and *Sororix* Prescott is on her way to question us about what happened to her daughter. In addition, there are rumors already spreading about *Magellus* Ashe being a *trinitara* and, reportedly, having some unique ability to open a witch's dormant resonants. We *must* be able to put those rumors to rest with the truth, no matter what that may be." She took a deep breath. "So, *Magellus* Ashe, what exactly did you do to *Magella* Prescott?"

"He saved my life," Sam said, "isn't that enough?"

"No one is discounting that," *Prima* Rosethorn said, "but I do require an answer. Tell me everything that happened, from the time I left this room."

I opened my eyes and caught Mel's gaze — who could probably make a fortune playing poker, because her face was entirely unreadable. I took a deep breath.

"Mel told me how to connect to Sam's resonants and pull the mana —"

"How did you get through her shields? Let's start with that."

"Oh." At least that was easier to answer. "I got them to crack a little bit, then I was able to get inside — our shields merged after that. Maybe because we'd been working together so much?"

"How, exactly, did you get them to crack? That is not a skill for first-years."

"Um, her shields always have a ... well, a hollow spot, so I —"

"A hollow spot where?" *Prima* Rosethorn asked. "If our students aren't being taught proper shielding, I'll have to address —"

"Crone's piles!" Sam yelled. "I make my boobs bigger, okay? Is that what you want to hear?"

*Prima* Rosethorn turned away from me, but I could practically hear her eyebrow go up.

"Tone, *Magella*."

"I'm sorry, *Prima*," Sam said. "I just..."

"I understand." *Prima* Rosethorn turned back to me. "And then?"

"Um, I got inside her shields and there was all this ... raw mana, I guess? So, Mel had me connect to her resonants."

I really hoped *Prima* Rosethorn didn't ask me to describe that — the feelings were still very fresh and I didn't want to talk about it where Sam could hear me. At least not in front of the teachers — maybe when we were alone, we could talk about it and she could tease me about how that was the closest I'd get to sex with her or something ... if she still wanted to talk to me at all, that is.

"And how many active resonants did she have at that point?"

"Um, one, *Prima* — just her regular one. The other two were ... dormant, it's called?"

"Yes, what happened next?"

"I ... pulled the raw mana from Sam into me."

"I imagine that's when Samantha's resonants opened," Mel said. "Having raw mana pulled through them like that."

*Prima* Rosethorn sniffed. "I see. Is that what happened, *Magellus* Ashe?"

"Um, yeah, I think so? I ... it was hard to pay attention just then."

"No doubt."

I flushed and cleared my throat. It was clear *Prima* Rosethorn knew *exactly* what I'd been experiencing at that point.

"What happened next?"

"Well, there was a lot of the raw mana and it took a while to pull it all, then it was ... too much? It hurt a lot and I didn't think I could hold it all and I didn't want to blow up the school, so —" I heard a muffled sob from Sam's bed. "Sam?"

"I'm fine."

She didn't sound fine, and what I really wanted was for Mel and *Prima* Rosethorn to leave so we could talk — if she wanted to talk to me. If she didn't, I wanted to know that so I could get moved to another room. I'd already done enough to her and didn't want to put her through any more.

"Go on, *Magellus*."

I shrugged. "There's not much more, I think. Mel had me push the mana back into Sam and I ... passed out?"

*Prima* Rosethorn stared at me for a long time.

"I see." She nodded quickly. "So — we can say the opening of dormant resonants was, in fact, a side effect of taking the potion, releasing an uncontrollable amount of raw mana, which was then drained by a *trinitara* warlock. A set of almost certainly unique and quite dangerous circumstances and quite unlikely to be repeatable."

"Repeatable?" I asked.

"Some will be quite interested in the result of this incident," *Prima* Rosethorn said. "The book in question has already been found and secured. Relaying the unique and dangerous circumstances will, hopefully, prevent anyone with another copy from experimenting."

Mel cleared her throat. "I think it's worth mentioning that, had Samantha been even slightly more powerful to begin with ... the outcome would not have been desirable. This was only successful due to her having so little mana of her own at the start."

"Yes, perhaps —"

*Magistra* Fallwhistle came into the infirmary, interrupting.

"*Magistrae* — *Sororix* Prescott is here asking to see her daughter."

"I'll speak to her and then show her in," *Prima* Rosethorn said, leaving with *Magistra* Fallwhistle.

"I'll just be a moment," Mel told them, then waited for the door to close before speaking to me quietly. "Noah, I'm afraid you being a *trinitara* is going to be common knowledge soon. There's no easy way to explain what happened to Samantha without disclosing that — there'd be questions about how a third resonant could be involved at all if the warlock only had two. I'm also not certain *Magistra* Fallwhistle hasn't said something about it already."

"I kind of figured that," I said.

Mel nodded. "I'm afraid things are going to change for you, dear."

"How?"

"You're now known to be even more valuable than simply an unaffiliated warlock. I'd expect the desire to recruit you to join a Family will increase. I imagine there'll be even more pressure from the girls' Families for them to get close to you and certain ... offers may be made."

"Offers?"

Mel raised an eyebrow.

"Oh, offers, yeah."

"Just be careful, dear. And a bit wary."

# CHAPTER THIRTY-ONE

Sam's mom sat by her bedside for about an hour, and never stopped talking.

I heard far more than I wanted to of the gossip in the Prescott Family. Sam seemed to feel the same way, because she kept throwing me desperate looks, but I could only shrug helplessly.

Finally, *Sororix* Prescott stood up.

"I really must get back, Samantha," she said. "I'm so glad you're not harmed. And even helped, it seems. A *trinitara* witch! Imagine that. Perhaps now you can be of real value to the Family."

I felt a little surge of anger that Sam had gone through so much to gain more power because she thought it would make her more favored in this woman's eyes, and still she says something like that.

*Sororix* Prescott bent a little toward Sam who was reclining in the exam bed, stopped, smiled in a way that seemed to hurt her, then leaned in and gave Sam a hug.

She held that for a moment, then hurried to the door pausing long enough to turn around and give Sam a little wave, then she was gone.

Then Sam and I were alone for the first time since ... it happened.

I watched her from my bed, wondering if she was okay with what I'd done.

Sam stared at the door for a long time.

Then she suddenly pulled her knees up and bent forward to bury her face in her arms and started crying.

*Shit,* I thought. *Is she upset about what I did? I don't know if I should go over and console her or not.*

Sam sobbed again and I couldn't just sit by even if it was me she was angry at.

I swung my legs over the edge and stood up, then took the few shaky steps over to stand by Sam's bed. Her shoulders shook more as she heard me there. I lightly set one hand on her back and she felt so small, like the ordeal we'd just been through had made her shrink into herself.

"Sam, I'm sorr —"

Sam turned toward me wrapped her arms around me and buried her face in my chest, sobbing.

I kept one hand on her back and stroked her hair with the other.

Something told me to keep quiet and let her get it out, so I stood there, and stroked her hair as she sobbed harder.

After some time, the sobs got farther and farther apart, then were finally reduced to little hiccups.

"Do ... you know ... the last time ... that woman hugged me?" Sam asked between hiccups.

"No," I whispered.

Sam took a deep breath and let it out slowly. Then another.

"I was seven. It was right before the testing ... the testing that showed I was ... a onesie. I barely saw her after that."

I held her tighter. She breathed deeply again.

"Do you know what she told me before she left?"

"What?"

"She said, 'You should have enough power to mark that feral now.'" Sam shuddered. "I did all that. I nearly died. I nearly ... killed you." She shuddered again and hugged me tighter. "All so I could have enough power that she would love me again, and she just wants *more!*"

Sam tried to control the sobs with another deep breath, but failed.

"Why won't she love me, Noah?"

I couldn't say anything to that, but I did know I wanted to have Samantha's mother in front of me right then so that I could point her at a brick wall and tell her to get away from me. Instead, I just held Sam and stroked her hair until she stopped sobbing and pulled away from me to sit back in her bed.

I pulled a chair over to sit next to her, and she took my hand as I sat down.

"I'm sorry," she said.

"It's okay — that's what friends are for."

Sam shook her head. "No, I'm sorry about your shirt — I snotted it."

I looked down and sure enough my shirt had a big wet slimy spot on it. It looked so ridiculous and disgusting, that I had to laugh, and that set Sam off laughing too in that sort of hysterical laughter that comes when you just had a bout of crying.

Sam kept laughing for a minute, then sobered. She looked away from me, licked her lips, and started to say something, but she stopped and frowned.

"What?"

She swallowed hard. "I want to ask you something... but I don't..."

"You want to ask me something that you don't want to ask me?"

She shook her head. "I want to ask you something, but I don't want to screw up ... you and me."

I smiled and squeezed her hand. "Sam, you're the best friend I've ever had — I would happily strangle any number of strangers if you ask me to. If I know them, we'll have to talk about it a bit. If it's your mother, I'll pay you cash money."

Sam chuckled. "No strangling."

"So?"

Sam took a deep breath.

"I want you to mark me."

---

"IF ... if you want to, I mean," Sam whispered. She folded her hands in her lap and stared down at them. "You said you wanted to start your own coven and I have three resonants now ... I'm not as useless as I was and —"

I reached out and pressed my fingers to her lips.

"That's your mom talking and she's a bitch," I said. "You're not any more useful now than you were before." Sam's lips twitched beneath my fingers. "Okay, yeah, that didn't come out right."

I wished I'd made that mistake on purpose, because it got a smile out of her.

"Anyway," I said, taking my fingers away from her lips. "I haven't really thought about the coven thing, because of what *Prima* Rosethorn said about getting expelled."

"Not now," Sam said. "Not here. I don't want to get expelled either. Not now." She looked away. "I was thinking, maybe at the Solstice."

"Christmas? How does that not get us expelled?"

Sam grinned. "So that's a yes?"

I laughed. "Of course it's a yes — if you really want to."

She nodded. "I do. You said you want to be an independent coven and I want to be part of that — my Family, my mother —" She shook her head, grin failing. "I just can't anymore."

I put my hand over hers. "So how does Christmas keep us from being expelled? And why not Halloween if it's about a holiday?"

"Samhain, and that's ... more about fun — that's why we stay here at school. Some covens will work their darker rituals on Samhain, but the winter solstice is more spiritual. The spring equinox is about rebirth, but the winter solstice is about the promise and hope of that rebirth — it's the longest night. It can either be the darkest time, or the most hopeful."

I nodded. "Okay, but how does doing it then keep us from being expelled?"

"We'll be on solstice break," Sam said. "She can't expel us for something we do when we're not at school — on solstice break our mothers, well, The Blackwood for you, will be responsible for us." She paused and looked away. "If... If you really want to, that is. I don't want to force you into it. Or make you feel like you have to. It's just if I'm in a coven, then I belong to the coven and not to *her*."

I paused to think about it. I'd learned enough about the covens to know that the whole marking thing was a big deal. Sam and I would be tied together forever ... and that really didn't bother me. If I wanted to live in the witches' world, I was apparently going to have to be tied that way to a whole coven, and I couldn't think of any witch I'd rather start that with than Sam.

"*Prima* Rosethorn might not be able to expel us, but she still won't be happy," I said, brow furrowed. "And your mother will be pissed. Mel, too, probably."

"Yeah, but pissing off my mother's a bonus. I'm a little scared about pissing off The Blackwood, though."

"I get that — I can handle Mel, I think. Are you sure though? You're okay to be tied to me, basically, forever?"

"Do you not want —"

"Stop," I interrupted her, realizing we were going round-and-round trying to be sure the other one really wanted to. "You're my best friend, and I don't see that changing. Do you think there's any chance we're not going to be part of each other's lives? Because if you do, I'm going to have to smack you."

Sam's eyes clenched shut and she turned away from me.

"You bastard, I was done crying."

She turned back to me.

"Thank you."

I cleared my throat.

"Um, does this mean we're gonna — you know?"

"*Ew!* Yeah, it does. Let's not make it weird though."

"I'm just going to point out, saying *ew* about it makes it weird."

# CHAPTER THIRTY-TWO

"Noah Ashe and Priscilla Hearst," the school's intercom voice interrupted *Magistra* Nightingale's class. "Please report to *Prima* Rosethorn's office."

I looked around the lecture hall to find all eyes on me, including *Magistra* Nightingale's. It was a week after Sam and I got out of the clinic and things were back to normal ... except for the part where everyone now knew I was a *trinitara* and that Sam was now a *trinitara* and the whole school was back to staring at us both and whispering.

"What did you do?" Sam whispered.

I shrugged. "I don't know — I don't think I did anything."

"*Magellus* Ash," *Magistra* Nightingale said. "If you could perhaps comply more expeditiously it would reduce the disruption to my class which I find already excessive."

I hastily stuffed my notebook and pens into my backpack and stood.

"Sorry, *Magistra*," I said, hurrying down the steps and closing the door quietly behind me.

I spent the walk to the administrative building trying not to think about why I might be summoned to *Prima* Rosethorn's office.

I couldn't think of anything I'd done recently, but that didn't mean I hadn't violated some obscure magic rule that made little or no sense to me. There were, after all, quite a lot of them.

*Prima* Rosethorn's receptionist didn't even have me sit, she just waved me into *Prima* Rosethorn's office, and I wondered if the first thing I should do was ask to have Mel present. Even though I was eighteen, one of those obscure magic rules seemed to be that a witch not in a coven wasn't really treated as an adult, but rather had their Family, or head of Family, act as some sort of guardian. Since Mel was my sponsor at the school, she was the closest to that and *Prima* Rosethorn seemed to treat me as her ward rather than an adult.

I decided to wait and see exactly what it was about before asking for Mel to be there, because I didn't want to interrupt the class she was teaching over what might be nothing.

*Prima* Rosethorn wasn't at her desk, instead she was in her office's seating area, sitting with two other people around a low table that had a tea set and a tiered tray of cakes and small sandwiches.

I started to feel a bit of relief, because nothing could be too bad if it came with tea, right?

"You sent for me, *Prima*," I asked, noticing that another student was one of the people sitting there. Priscilla — Hearst, I guess? I'd never really learned her last name. She was part of Cassandra's clique, but seemed to be more of a hanger-on and hadn't really given me or the onesies any serious trouble.

"Yes, *Magellus* Ashe," *Prima* Rosethorn said, rising. "This is *Sororix* Hearst, Priscilla's mother. She's asked to have a word with you."

The look on *Prima* Rosethorn's face said she was displeased about something — I didn't know if that was *Sororix* Hearst asking, or the fact that it involved me. I wracked my brain trying to think of anything I'd done to Priscilla that might have pissed her mother off, but couldn't come up with anything. If it was Cassandra's mother, then I'd understand, because the snide remarks and my comebacks hadn't ceased at all there.

*Sororix* Hearst rose too and approached me with her hand out.

"It's so nice to meet you, Noah," she said. "May I call you Noah?"

I took her hand, which she presented in that sort of halfway between a handshake and expecting it to be kissed. I didn't kiss her hand — I briefly clasped her fingers between mine and released it, which seemed to satisfy her.

"Um, sure, it's nice to meet you too, *Sororix* Hearst."

"Please, call me Carla."

I nodded, not sure how I felt about that, since her smile seemed very fake and all my senses seemed to be screaming that there was something very odd about this and I should be careful. I didn't think I'd said or done anything to Priscilla that her Family might complain to *Prima* Rosethorn about, since I really hadn't interacted with her that much — most of my conflict with that group had been straight with Cassandra.

"Please, have a seat with us," *Sororix* Hearst said, waving her hand at an empty seat as her smile grew even wider. "I believe you know my daughter Priscilla already?"

"Not really," I said, taking a seat. "Hi, Priscilla."

"Hi," Priscilla said faintly, looking down at her feet — which was pretty unusual for her, as part of Cassandra's clique she was usually just as bold as the rest of them. She seemed almost embarrassed, and I really wanted to know what was going on.

"Really?" *Sororix* Hearst asked, retaking her own seat and staring at Priscilla with narrowed eyes and thin lips. "I was certain you two would've had time to get to know each other by now."

Priscilla mumbled something and I noticed she was looking at me with wide eyes and a sort of pleading expression.

Now I thought I understood. Priscilla's mom, like Samantha's and others, had probably told her daughter to get close to me in the hopes that she could mark me and drag me into their Family, but Priscilla hadn't. I don't know if that was because she didn't like the idea of doing it, or if she just didn't like me enough to try, but either way I was angrier at her mother for that kind of bullshit than I could be with Priscilla, and it didn't seem fair for her to get in trouble for it.

"What I mean, *Sororix* Hearst, is that I really haven't had time to get to know many people here yet — this is all so new to me, and there's classes, and coursework, and I really only had time to speak to Priscilla a few times, not really enough to get to know her well."

"I see. And, please, again, it's Carla."

"Um, sure, okay."

*Sororix* Hearst smiled again, which was sort of frightening, and motioned at the table.

"Would you like some tea?"

"If I may," *Prima* Rosethorn interrupted before I could decide if I wanted tea or not. "*Magellus* Ashe is unfamiliar with our ways, so he should have a bit of background. Noah, *Sororix* Hearst has asked to speak to you on a matter ... fairly typical within the school. Part of Willowmere's mission is to foster connections between the various witch Families — but I will stress that you are under no obligation to accept the Hearst's proposal."

"What proposal?"

*Sororix* Hearst smiled again and pulled out a tablet. She flipped open a stand on its back and set it on the table with the screen facing me. The screen lit up with an image of a house ... a mansion really, with a curved gravel driveway leading up to a front porch that would do a state capital proud, with white columns and what I was certain were marble steps.

The place was three stories tall and I couldn't begin to count the number of windows.

"I'll get right to it, Noah, since I'm sure you don't want to miss any more of your classes than necessary. This —" she said, gesturing at the tablet, "— is just one of several available properties the Hearst Family has to offer. As you can see the entry drive is wonderfully Classical."

She clicked some sort of remote I hadn't seen her holding, and the picture changed to what I assumed was the home's entryway — more marble, a sweeping curved staircase up to the second floor, and a view through to the back wall of the house which was entirely glass and looked out on a long pool surrounded by landscaping.

"This stunning entryway gives access to the East and West wings of the main house, as well as the grand staircase to the upper floor and the master suite. The East wing consists of an exercise room —" the picture changed to an "exercise room" that looked more like a gym where the membership would cost four figures a month. "— a full home theater —" The theater looked like it could easily seat fifty or more people.

*Sororix* Hearst went on to describe the game room, family room, kitchen, chef's kitchen, casual dining area, breakfast nook, and a formal dining room that was larger than many restaurants I'd seen.

"The formal dining room, as you can see, has seating for fifty-six, allowing you to host three full covens in addition to your own — it doubles as a wonderful space for dancing, music, and, with the addition of some portable staging, any reasonably sized theater production."

I blinked at that. "Allowing you" — me? What the hell was going on here? I wanted to interrupt and ask, but *Sororix* Hearst was still going on showing picture after picture of the pool area (massive), hot tubs (four), the formal gardens (something out of a British period piece), the kitchen gardens (which could surely feed a small village), and then moved on to the master suite.

"This home's master suite is designed to provide all of the luxuries a warlock and his high priestess might wish. The main bathroom —" I had to wonder if she meant that the suite itself had more than one bathroom, or if it was the main bathroom for the house. "— has dual showers, including waterfall ceiling heads in both, as well as steam. Also, a Jacuzzi tub located at the very end of the wing with floor to ceiling windows offering a gorgeous view of the mountains — this property is in Colorado, by the way."

I thought I might get a question in here, but *Sororix* Hearst went on quickly, overriding my mumbled start.

"His and hers day-closets flank the bath, allowing quick access to daily wear. There is, of course, a lady's closet on the other side of the bedroom, offering ample storage for evening wear, jewelry, and other necessities, as well as a private lady's bath."

I guess that answered my question about what main bath meant, but since the main bath seemed to have two of everything, I didn't understand why a coven's high priestess might need her own bath less than a hundred feet away from the main one.

"Off the rear of the main building, flanking the pool and gardens on each side, are the living wings. Each has a total of twenty-six bedrooms, allowing space for a full coven and any children on one side, as well as ample room for visiting guests on the other."

*Fifty-three bedrooms? It's a fucking hotel!*

It seemed like her presentation was winding down, because she paused just long enough for me to get a question in edgewise.

"It's very nice," I said, "but I don't understand why you're showing it to me?"

*Sororix* Hearst blinked then giggled.

"Oh, Noah, you are so refreshing." She reached forward across the table and patted my knee. "I'm attempting to recruit you to the Hearst Family, of course."

"What?"

"It seems Priscilla, has not had time to speak to you on the matter. You must know that, as a warlock from outside the Families — and a *trinitara*, no less — we will all be trying to entice you to join ours?"

"Um, Mel — I mean, *Magistra* Blackwood — said that was something, but I really —"

"Well," *Sororix* Hearst interrupted. "Some Families may try to entice you in other, more devious, ways, but we Hearsts believe in being direct and upfront. I would like you to see the obvious advantages in joining our Family, and this lovely home is just one of them. There are also properties available in California, Wyoming, Florida,

New York — though not in the city — and Hawaii, if this one is not to your liking."

"I like it, I mean, it's a great house, but I don't —"

*Sororix* Hearst nodded. "Of course — as a young man you have far more pressing and urgent concerns than real estate. So, I would ask you to consider some of the other enticements we might offer to get you to join our Family, such as..." She gestured at her daughter. "Priscilla."

"What?"

"Mom!"

"Hush, dear, mother's bargaining."

*Sororix* Hearst leaned forward, giving me a great view down her dress to impressive cleavage that I would've appreciated a lot more she hadn't just offered up her daughter like some kind of bargaining chip.

"I want you to know, Noah, that you have the Family's blessing to ... engage with Priscilla as you will."

"*Mom!*"

"Should she manage to mark you in such an encounter, you would of course be joining the Hearst Family, but, if she turns out to be so weak-willed that you mark her —"

Priscilla put her hands over her face and doubled over to rest them on her knees.

"Maiden's tears," she muttered.

"Should you mark her," *Sororix* Hearst went on, "I assure you there will be no ill will from the Hearsts and we ask only that you do give our Family due consideration as a home for your new coven. And if she is not to your tastes, I can assure you that Priscilla, though young, is not the *loveliest* witch the Hearsts have available. If you find her not to your liking, there are many others to choose from."

"*Mother!*"

*What the absolute fuck?*

"Joining our Family as an unrelated warlock *trinitara*, you would, of course, have your pick of any unattached Hearst witches who strike your fancy in order to fill out your coven, as well as our full support in recruiting from other Families, as well."

She looked at me expectantly.

I looked from her to Priscilla, who was still doubled over hiding her face in her hands, to *Prima* Rosethorn, who was glaring at *Sororix* Hearst with lips so thin I could barely detect the crease of her mouth.

*Prima* Rosethorn met my eyes and sighed.

"There is that tradition of recruitment at Willowmere, Noah," she said. "And a policy of allowing representatives of the Families to speak to students about such things." She scowled. "It has been some time since that involved a warlock, of course, and we appear to be in need of updated guidelines in that regard."

"Pish, Evelina," *Sororix* Hearst said. "There's little point in dancing about things. Clear, direct, and right to the point." She turned to me. "Please don't think I require an answer right this minute. Take your time, get to know Priscilla, do ... whatever young people do these days."

"Um, thank you? I definitely need to think this over ... and I should probably speak to Mel, Melaina, *Magistra* Blackwood, about it?"

"Yes," *Prima* Rosethorn said, "it would be quite appropriate to speak to your sponsor and guardian on the matter."

"Of course," *Sororix* Hearst said, "please, take the tablet with you — it contains descriptions of all of the available properties, as well as some of the other perks and benefits of being a Hearst. Priscilla, why don't you run along with Noah back to class?"

"Thank the Child," I thought I heard Priscilla mutter as she jumped to her feet.

"What was that?"

"Nothing, Mother. Noah, you have history now, right?"

I stopped myself from saying I was a first-year and all first-years have history first thing in the morning, but I figured Priscilla was trying to impress her mother by knowing my class schedule.

"Yes, you remembered," I said.

Priscilla and I didn't quite get into a race to see who could reach the door first, but perhaps we should have, as *Sororix* Hearst called out before we could escape.

"Oh, Noah!"

Priscilla and I both paused, fingertips just inches from the door handle.

I caught sight of Priscilla's face as I turned back to the room — her eyes were scrunched shut as though she was in physical pain.

"Please, no, please, no, please, no," she whispered.

*Sororix* Hearst was still standing, a wide smile on her face.

"Even if you're thinking you wouldn't like to join the Hearst Family, please, do ask Priscilla about our generous stud fees."

---

"I AM *SO* SORRY," Priscilla whispered as soon as we were on the quad.

"It's okay."

"No, it isn't — I'm so embarrassed. I can't believe she ... she..." Priscilla grabbed my arm and stopped walking. She closed her eyes and her face was bright red.

I looked back at the administrative building and saw a figure in *Prima* Rosethorn's window.

"Is that your mom watching us?"

Priscilla glanced back and then away quickly.

"*Crone's boils!*" She started walking again, pulling me along. "Please, don't tell anyone about this. Just make something up, or just tell them that my mom asked you if you'd like to join the Family and no more? Please don't tell them my mom suggested we, you know."

"I'll try," I reassured her, but I wasn't too confident about that because Sam had a way of either figuring out what I didn't want to say or figuring out some way to get me to say it.

"Thanks. And thanks for not telling my mother that we've never talked."

"No problem, and thanks for not ... you know."

Priscilla giggled. "Trying to seduce and capture you for my Family?"

"Yeah, that would've been awkward."

"I know, right? It's like every girl in the school got the same instructions from her mom, and we're really weirded out about it."

"Really?"

Priscilla nodded. "Yeah, I mean, we all know we are probably going to wind up in a coven with a warlock we don't know very well, that's normal —"

I didn't really think it was normal, and I was a little bit creeped out that all the witches did.

"— but Susan's mom told her if she couldn't mark you for the Family before we graduate, then she'd wind up scrubbing floors for the rest of her life and would never get a coven."

"Really? That's harsh."

Priscilla nodded again. "I don't think she was serious about the scrubbing, but still. Is she still watching?"

We'd reached the steps of the classroom building. I took a quick glance back at the admin building and still saw a shadowy figure in *Prima* Rosethorn's window.

"I think so — I can't really tell who it is but I don't think *Prima* Rosethorn would be watching us all this time."

Priscilla stopped walking and turned to face me.

"Do you think you could ... I don't know, laugh or something like I told you a joke? I ... I don't know if my mother really believed that we just haven't had time to get to know each other. It might cut down on her demands for progress if she thought we liked each other a little."

"Demands?"

"Every. Fucking. Week. Every email I get from her, she wants a 'progress report' and it's driving me crazy."

I chuckled. "Okay... So tell me a joke."

Priscilla's eyes widened. "What?"

I grinned. "You can't expect me to laugh on demand — give me your best joke."

Priscilla flushed red and looked away. "Okay, let me think a minute."

"Make sure it's a good one — I'm ready for it."

"Okay — why are new covens made of thirteen witches?"

"I don't know — why?"

"Because we can't even."

I stared at her blank faced.

"Because most covens are formed when we're teens," Priscilla prompted.

"And?"

Priscilla sighed. "Teen girls can't even?"

"I don't get it."

"How can you not get it! Teen girls go into a coven in odd numbers — we can't even!"

I shrugged.

"I can't believe it — I just dissed every girl in the school and you don't get it."

I couldn't hold it in anymore — my smile widened and I broke into a laugh.

"I was just screwing with you," I said between laughs.

Priscilla's face grew outraged, then she broke into a wide grin and punched me in the arm knocking me backward.

"You asshole!"

I laughed more and went up the steps to open the door and hold it for her.

"Think that'll get your mom off your back for a while?"

"Yeah, thanks."

She paused again once we were inside the classroom building — classes were still in session, so the halls were empty.

"You, um, aren't as bad as some of the girls say."

"Do any of the girls saying that know me?"

Priscilla laughed. "Nope." She looked around and then back at me. "You know, you could maybe come sit with us sometime? I know Cassandra's a real witch, but you put her in her place a couple times already. The other girls would probably keep her off your back."

"So they can tell their moms they talked to me?"

Priscilla nodded. "Yeah."

There was no way in hell I was going to ever sit at a table with Cassandra — and much as I was kind of liking Priscilla in this exchange, she was still part of Cassandra's little clique. She hadn't been part of the group at the spellstick field, though, so maybe she wasn't as bad as the rest?

"I'm kind of happy where I've been sitting — you could come sit with us."

"With the onesies?"

"So long as you didn't pick on them," I said.

"I don't ... that much — it's mostly Cassandra and a couple other girls."

I shrugged. "I don't know — if you hang around with them and go along with their bullying, does that really make a difference?"

Priscilla flushed red. "It's ... I didn't know what she was going to do to your friend."

"Rachel?"

She nodded. "When I found out, I told her that was too much, but she's not going to listen to me." She licked her lips. "Is she okay?"

I nodded.

"That's good."

"Why does Cassandra pick on them so much anyway?" I asked.

Priscilla shrugged. "I don't know — she wasn't always like this, but once she came into her power? It's like she's always angry — and if she isn't angry, she's sad. It's weird. I mean, we all change, right? Our resonants change us when we come into our power, but Cassandra? She didn't used to be like this at all."

"Well, she's like it now," I said. "And I think it sucks." I shifted my backpack on my shoulder to a more comfortable position. "I need to get back to class ... but it was nice actually meeting you, Priscilla."

She stepped back and lowered her eyes. "You too."

She turned quickly to head off.

I had a sudden thought and figured it couldn't hurt — I'd been flirting with Katrina in potions pretty regularly and we'd been getting along, maybe if Priscilla liked me a bit more word might get around that I wasn't some ravening animal.

"Hey, Priscilla?"

"Yeah?"

"I think your mom's probably wrong."

"About what?"

"I don't see how the Hearsts could possibly have any witches prettier than you."

# CHAPTER THIRTY-THREE

HALLOWEEN MONTH WAS OVER, BUT NOT HALLOWEEN.

The faire, which had resumed after we knew Sam wasn't going to blow up all over the place, stopped on the thirtieth and most of the day on Halloween itself was spent tearing everything down and storing it away for the next year — All Hallow's Eve itself being reserved for the witches and their own rituals.

A month of running kids, heavy carts of supplies, and rampaging werewolves had done a number on the grass of the quad and sports field — I thought it would take more than the next year for it to recover, but then saw a couple teachers and some students pushing mana into what grass was left and it quickly filled in the bare and worn spots despite the late-Fall temperatures.

The cafeteria staff made up box lunches for everyone so we wouldn't have to stop working for so long, and what I'd come to think of as my group of friends — Sam, Rachel, Hannah, and Brittany — found a clear spot between the buildings and sports field to sit down and eat away from everyone else.

It was a clear day and it was still warm in the sun, despite the time of year.

The conversation ran mostly about the tasks of cleaning up the faire until I caught Brittany and Hannah whispering and giggling with sidelong glances at me.

"What?" I asked.

That only set them off giggling more.

"Do you know what's got into them?" I asked Sam.

Sam shrugged.

"No clue," she said, then reached behind me to tap Rachel on the shoulder. "You?"

Rachel jumped. "No!" She blushed bright red and turned, putting me more between her and Sam. "I mean, no, I don't know what they're giggling about."

I was about to ask Rachel and Sam what had gotten into them, too — they'd both been weird for the last month.

Rachel seemed to be avoiding Sam for some reason, even going so far as to sit on my bed rather than Sam's when she was visiting us in our room, which had become a real rarity anyway, and she'd switched seats in History to the far end of the row next to Hannah. But she also kept asking if Sam was okay — if she was feeling all right or acting different. Asking me, not Sam, because she hardly spoke to Sam anymore.

Sam was being even weirder. Every time I got back to the room after classes, she'd ask me what Rachel had done in Potions and Rituals — if I thought she needed any help with Potions, since Sam was in a more advanced class, or just what I'd talked about with her in those classes.

*Freaking girls, right?*

"So, is it true Priscilla's mom made her show you her boobs?" Hannah asked.

"*What?*"

I looked at Sam — I'd told her what happened with Priscilla and her mom, but she'd promised to keep it quiet. I had trouble believing she'd break the promise, much less ... embellish the story like *that.*

"Wasn't me," Sam said, holding up her hands in defense.

"Who told you that?" I asked, then realized what the question sounded like without a denial. "No, that didn't happen, but who told you it did?"

Brittany shrugged. "It's all over school. *Sororix* Hearst got you in *Prima* Rosethorn's office and had Priscilla strip so..." She broke up giggling again.

"You could see the goods," Hannah finished for her.

Sam smacked me on the shoulder.

"How could you not tell me that part!" she cried. "Were they perky?"

"It didn't happen," I protested. Not that I'd put it past Priscilla's mom — hell, if I expressed an interest, she'd probably have all the eligible Hearst witches do a naked lineup for me... *No! Stop thinking about that!*

"Come on," Hannah said, "we all heard you and Priscilla get called to the *Prima*'s office."

"There was no stripping, no goods — who told you that?"

"I heard it from Amber," Hannah said. "She said she heard it from Nadia."

"I heard Bella and Grace talking about it in the locker room," Brittany said. "But also, Taylor and Emma." She frowned. "And Jenna and Charlotte."

"Oh, my God," I moaned, putting my hands over my face.

Sam smacked me again. "Goddess, not God — you're a warlock now, so learn how to curse right. 'By the Maiden's rosy pink nipples' would be good for this one, I think."

"You're not helping."

"Were they soft and puffy," Sam asked, "or hard and crinkly? I bet Priscilla's got some real erasers."

"Kill me now," I mumbled.

"Yeah," Hannah said, "which do you prefer?"

"*What?*" I couldn't believe we were having this conversation and a quick look showed that they were all grinning and leaning forward like they couldn't wait to hear what I said — all except

Rachel, who was sitting quietly with her head down. "Why are you even asking?"

Hannah shrugged. "I could get some mileage out of the information — since you're looking to join a Family, everyone's wondering what you're looking *for* and who might have an advantage."

"I'm *not* 'looking' ... wait, advantage for what?"

"Getting you into their Family, of course," Brittany said. "It was bad enough when you were just a free warlock, but now that they know you're a *trinitara*? The moms are *really* pushing things."

I sighed. I guess I should have expected there to be rumors, but it wasn't right they were talking about Priscilla like that.

"Look — yes, *Sororix* Hearst gave me a pitch for joining her Family, but *there was no stripping*."

"Missed opportunity, that," Sam muttered.

"No opportunity. No. She showed me a *house* — nothing more."

Hannah frowned and pulled out her phone.

"What are you doing?" Sam asked.

"Checking urban dictionary — I don't know what house means."

"It means a fucking *house!*"

Hannah shook her head. "All this is about that doctor show ... wait, second page ... *ew!*"

She gave me a disgusted look.

"Whatever it is, it wasn't that!"

"Yeah, I'd say that too," Hannah said, wrinkling her nose.

"Stop — everyone stop." I took a deep breath. "I am not looking. I am *not* joining a Family. And even if I was looking or open to it, I *would never* hook up with some girl who's just doing it because her fucking mother wants her to, without knowing each other at all! That's ... just dishonest. Horrible and disgusting. I can't even think about it without —"

"Rachel?" Sam asked, cutting me off. "What's wrong?"

Rachel's shoulders were even more hunched and they were shaking. She covered her mouth with her hands and I heard her sob.

I reached out a hand. "Rachel?"

"*Leave me alone!*" she yelled, leaping to her feet and running toward the sports field, leaving her lunch and books behind.

---

"WHAT WAS THAT ALL ABOUT?" Brittany asked.

Hannah shrugged.

"Was she upset by all the teasing?" I asked. "It was getting kind of graphic and she's pretty shy."

"Maybe," Sam said, frowning. "Wait, don't the Winthrops practice Purity?"

I honestly was looking forward to when I could spend at least one day without asking someone to explain a thing everyone in the school already knew about. Today was not that day.

"What's Purity?" I asked.

"It's, um, a traditional thing," Brittany said.

"That didn't help."

"Okay, so, you know how I said next semester we get to go into town?" Sam asked. "And how a lot of the girls will meet guys from the mundane college and ... gather a few wild oats, so to speak?"

I nodded.

"The Winthrops ... don't. They go to their covens pure — pure in spirit, pure in thought, and pure in deed, they say."

"Oh ... wait, she can't even think about it?"

"Nope," Hannah said. "Not even a little tending of their secret garden. I don't know how they —"

She broke off and stared at me, eyes wide and I could see a line of bright red rise up her neck to her face like a thermometer. I think she'd forgotten I was a guy for a minute and was now embarrassed — as was I, because now I was sitting with three hot girls thinking about them "tending their secret gardens".

I hate magic school.

"I'll go see if she's okay," Sam said, standing, but with the way she and Rachel had been acting, I didn't know if that was a good idea.

"No, I think I'll go check on her," I said, standing as well.

"I should go, she needs comforting," Sam said. "You're — well, if she does have a crush on you, you being there isn't exactly going to get her mind out of the garden."

"Rachel has a crush on Noah?" Brittany asked.

"You were one of the ones with all the sexy talk," I told Sam, standing and gathering up Rachel's lunch so I'd have an excuse to find her. "I'll go."

"How did I not know Rachel has a crush on Noah?" Brittany continued as I walked away.

---

RACHEL WAS up in the top row of the bleachers.

"Leave me alone," she whispered when I sat down beside her.

I offered her the food she'd left behind.

"Not hungry."

I set the box on the seat away from Rachel and stayed quiet for a minute.

"Please leave me alone," Rachel whispered finally, hunching her shoulders more.

"Nope," I said. "My friend's upset and I'm going to find out why."

"It's nothing."

"Not nothing if it's got you this upset — everybody's worried about you, Rachel. Sam was ready to come after you too."

Rachel's head snapped up and she scanned the bleachers and field.

"She's not coming, is she?"

*What was up with these two?* I wondered. They hadn't had a fight that I knew of, and I think Sam would have told me. Sam certainly wasn't mad at Rachel, and Rachel didn't seem mad. She seemed almost scared, but that didn't make any sense either.

"No, I came instead — so what's wrong?"

Rachel's head hung again.

"I can't say."

"Why not?"

She was silent for a long time.

"You'll hate me," she whispered.

That was unexpected. And serious. I couldn't imagine what Rachel thought would make me hate her.

"Sam, too," she added.

Now I was really confused — something that would make both Sam and I hate her?

"Neither of us will hate you," I assured her. "Here — tell me why you think Sam'll hate you and I'll tell you if I think so too."

Rachel bent over and hugged her knees, sobbing.

"I gave her a love potion."

I WAS TOO stunned to speak, but I knew I had to quickly. If I didn't, then Rachel would think I was mad at her or thought Sam would be. And I didn't know if Sam would be mad or not — I was still busy trying to figure out *why* Rachel would give Sam a love potion in the first place.

"Are you ... gay, too?" I asked, not sure how to phrase it given my new knowledge of Rachel's Family and the purity thing.

Rachel's shoulders shuddered more and she pressed the heels of her hands hard to her eyes, shaking her head, then shrugging.

"No? I don't know? I'm not supposed to even *think* about stuff like that, much less figure it out!"

"Okay, the girls told me about the Purity thing, so I get not thinking about it — but why would you give Sam a love potion?"

"*It was supposed to be for you!*"

Stunned wasn't good enough — I was stupefied. And very confused.

"It was the cupcake," Rachel went on, whispering again. "The stupid cupcake I brought you on the first of Halloween — but then Sam grabbed it and I couldn't stop her and ... now everything's gone to *shit*!"

"Where'd you even get a love potion?" I asked, trying to buy time to figure out how I felt about all this. I was kind of angry, honestly, that she'd tried to give me a fucking love potion — but I also cared about Rachel and she was so upset. I stomped on my own irritation because my friend was upset.

"First day in potions class," Rachel whispered, rubbing her chest.

I thought back — yeah, I remembered the ingredients, sugar and watermint. We were supposed to make it a stomach tonic, but watermint could also be used for some kind of love potion.

"So, you made a love potion instead of a stomach tonic?" And I remembered the bottle she'd slipped into her bag and the mess she'd made. "And dumped the rest in the sink so *Magistra* Fallowell wouldn't know?"

"You hate me," Rachel whispered.

I took a deep breath.

"I don't hate you — I'm not very happy with you right now, but I don't hate you. I do want to understand why."

Then I realized what it must have been.

*Fucking* witch mothers.

I thought foster care was fucked up, but it had nothing on these so-called "Families."

I sighed.

"Your mom?"

"What? No!"

"Then why?"

Rachel wrapped her arms around herself and hugged hard, rocking.

"You were so nice to me. You saved me from Cassandra and you ... talked to me and walked me to class and sat with me in potions and —"

"Wait — Rachel, we made those potions the first day. You hadn't even known me for twenty-four hours ... why would you make a love potion?"

"I'd never met a boy before."

Oh, this was just a day full of shocks.

"What? Never?"

Rachel shook her head. "Never. The first time we're supposed to see a man in person is when we join our coven. I grew up knowing the first man I saw in person would be my warlock." She took a deep breath. "My mom was *pissed* when she found out you were here."

"Rachel, I —"

"Oh, don't say it, I know. It was stupid. I knew it was stupid as soon as the potion was finished — I was just ... stupid, okay? I just — I started having all these thoughts I'm not supposed to have and I got carried away that first day. I put the potion in a drawer. I decided not to use it."

"Then why did you?"

"You kept being nice to me!" Rachel cried, kicking her feet. "And you liked spellstick and didn't get mad when I talked about it so much and you *listened to me* and you wanted to come to a Banshee's game *and you said it was a date!*" She sobbed again, burying her face in her hands. "And then, after what Cassandra did? I thought I'd never like spellstick again and you just ... gave it back to me."

She sat up and clutched at her chest, grimacing.

"Rachel? Are you oka —"

"*Aarrrgghh!*"

Rachel extended her left arm, fingers clenched, and a twenty-foot wave of fire roared over the bleachers.

"*What the fuck!*"

Rachel lowered her arm like nothing had happened.

"Sorry — my resonant's Passion and if I get too worked up the mana keeps building up and —" She shrugged. "It's really uncomfortable." She felt at her hair, pulling the ends around to look at them. "At least I didn't set my hair on fire this time."

"Oh, okay, that's good," I said as slowly and carefully as I could.

Rachel sniffed and wiped her eyes.

"I thought … it's not a *strong* potion, I mean, it wouldn't *change* anything. Like *Magistra* Fallowell said, it just nudges something if it's already there. So, I thought … if I gave you a nudge and it did, then I'd know there was something there. But then…"

"Then Sam ate the cupcake."

Rachel nodded.

"I put it in the frosting," Rachel said. "At first, I didn't think anything happened, but then … she's different, right? You see it?"

I nodded. I couldn't deny it — Sam had been much more focused on Rachel all month.

"How do you feel about that?" I asked.

"What do you mean?"

"Well, do you *like* her?"

"How am I supposed to know? I'm not supposed to think about stuff like that!"

I laughed, then stood up and held out my hand.

"Come on."

"What?"

"Come on — we need to get back and explain to Sam why she's been pining after you for the last month."

"I can't!"

"You have to, come on."

"She's going to hate me."

"Hate you? Sam? Over this?" I laughed. "Sam's going to laugh her ass off."

---

"BUT I *LOOOVE* YOU, RACHEL!"

"Stop it."

Sam's singsong teasing *was* getting a bit annoying.

"I can't stop it — I am compelled. By the power of the potion!"

I couldn't decide if this was more annoying than the hysterical laughter that had filled our afternoon.

"Please, stop it," Rachel said, rolling her eyes. "I said I was sorry."

It was well after dark on Halloween — the day, not the month — and most of the Willowmere students weren't back from trick-or-treating yet. Sam hadn't been kidding about that — over half the girls all cast glamours on themselves to look like costumed kids and a fleet of rideshares took them over to the neighborhoods with the best candy. It was the one night the school relaxed its rule on first-years leaving campus in the first semester, but only for candy collection. Hannah and Brittany had done that, while Sam, Rachel, and I stayed back. Mostly because we needed time alone for Rachel to confess what she'd done to Sam, but also because we were going to Willowmere's Samhain ritual instead.

We were on a trail through the woods to the school's Grove and I was anxious to see what it looked like — and the ritual itself, since I'd never seen one.

"Oh ... asters!" Sam suddenly danced off the trail to a space clear of trees where a few purple flowers were still blooming. She plucked one of the purple, star-shaped flowers and hurried back, holding it out to Rachel. "Flower for my love?"

"You're crazy!" Rachel said, but I could tell she was trying to suppress another bout of giggles.

"Crazy for a kiss," Sam said, puckering her lips and leaning in.

"*Eeek!*" Rachel cried and dashed off down the trail with Sam in pursuit, both of them laughing.

I just shook my head and kept walking, happy to see Rachel laughing after the day's drama. She'd been relieved I wasn't mad at her, but terrified that Sam would hate her — now she could tell that if Sam was teasing her about it, then she wasn't mad at all.

How could we be mad? She'd literally grown up being told the first guy she saw would be her warlock, and then here I was. More than just that it'd be her warlock, but she wasn't supposed to see a guy until the actual marking ceremony — so she'd been taught the first guy she saw was going to be her warlock and they were going to have sex *as soon as she saw him*. I was probably lucky she hadn't jumped me right in the cafeteria that first dinner.

I caught up with them at the Grove, which looked oddly familiar — it was a natural clearing in the woods, with a large, stone block slightly off-center. The moon wasn't full — it was a few days past — but it was still pretty large and lit the clearing well. There were maybe fifty girls seated on roughly-carved log benches around the clearing's edges.

Sam and Rachel had taken a bench away from the others. They weren't chasing each other anymore, but I saw Rachel had Sam's flower tucked behind her ear. I sat next to Rachel, figuring I could offer some support if Sam's teasing got to be too much — or join in.

"So, what are we going to do?" I asked as I sat down.

"About what?" Sam asked.

I waved my hands. "The potion — we can't ask a teacher for help, that'll get Rachel in trouble."

Sam shrugged. "It'll wear off in a couple more weeks — watermint's a weak-ass potion. Now that I know about it, it won't have any more effect on me than watching her butt while we walk up the stairs."

"You look at my butt?"

"I'm a lesbian in an all-girls school — I look at *everybody's* butt. But yours?" Sam nodded and made a grabbing motion with her hands. "Oh, yeah. *Tight*."

Rachel covered her face with her hands and I could practically feel the heat of embarrassment radiating from her — or maybe she was going to turn into a flamethrower again.

She glanced at me between her fingers. "You don't look at my butt, do you?"

It sounded like she was half-hoping I'd say yes.

"Nah," I said, then paused a beat. "I'm a boob guy."

"I like your boobs, too," Sam said quickly. "Don't let them feel left out."

"Maiden's blush," Rachel whispered. "Is that all you two think about?"

"Pretty much," Sam said.

"Since I was about thirteen," I agreed.

"Late bloomer, huh?"

"No wonder you guys can't pay attention in class," Rachel said.

"You really don't think about it?" Sam asked.

Rachel shook her head. "No — well, sometimes, yeah, but then we're supposed to meditate or cycle mana through our shields or practice a ritual's call and response ... you know, to just stop."

"Wow," Sam said, then leaned forward to catch my eyes, biting her lip. "So, um, you've never-ever ... tended your garden?"

"What's that?"

"You know," I said, trying not to laugh as Sam winked at me. "Polished the pearl?"

"Fluffed the peony?"

"Spun the sugar?"

"Filled your diary?"

"What are you two talking about?" Rachel asked, looking from Sam to me with total bewilderment.

"Seriously?" Sam asked, then leaned close to Rachel and whispered.

The radiated heat grew in intensity.

"Oh," Rachel whispered. "No ... my mom told me that could make me explode."

I have no idea how long Sam and I sat there staring at her, but we were both clearly flabbergasted.

"What?" Rachel asked.

"Explode?" Sam asked finally. "It doesn't make you explode ... well, I suppose *he* sort of explodes, but for us girls it's more of an *im*plosion."

"What? Oh, no!" Rachel covered her mouth with her hands, shaking her head. "No, I meant because I have a Passion resonant — I have to be *really* careful. Without a warlock to drain off the mana or support my resonant stores they might grow too fast and … pop."

"Pop?"

Rachel nodded.

"Oh," Sam said, "that makes sense."

"Now I don't get it," I said.

"I told you about that," Rachel said.

"Yeah, but I still don't get it."

"I have to be careful about how excited I get about things, otherwise my store fills too quickly and starts stretching too much. Then I'd have to use *a lot* of mana or it hurts *a lot*. It's sort of like expanding your store with a warlock, but … there's no controls on it. So, I have to pick what I want to get excited about and stay calm the rest of the time. Or use a bunch of mana."

"Like the flamethrower thing you did earlier?"

Rachel nodded. "I can't really go throwing fireballs around my bedroom, you know. I'm not even that good at fire magic, it's just the quickest way to use up a lot of mana."

I thought about the twenty-foot stream of fire I'd witnessed earlier and wondered what "good at it" would look like.

"Passion runs in the Winthrop Family — nearly all of us have it," Rachel said. "That's why we don't care if someone knows our resonants and why we practice Purity — it's just safer for everyone if we don't think about *that* before we have a warlock."

Sam started laughing.

"It's not funny," Rachel said.

Sam kept laughing. "It is when I picture you going into town next semester and turning some guy from the mundane college into a cinder."

---

SAM SOBERED IMMEDIATELY as some sort of bell or chime sounded through the clearing — all the girls followed suit, stopping their chats and sitting up straight to look toward the center of the Grove.

The Grove went silent, with only the rustle of the wind in the trees to break it. A figure appeared in the trees nearest the stone block, slowly walking toward the Grove. She was dressed in a hooded white robe and carrying a tray that glinted in the moonlight, and as she came closer, I could see other figures, similarly dressed, behind her.

"That's the school coven," Rachel whispered.

I'd figured that, but Rachel seemed to like explaining things to me — unlike Sam, who liked telling me I didn't know anything — so I just nodded.

The first figure reached the tree line and turned to her left before reaching the circle of benches.

"The *Domina*, high priestess, goes deosil, that's clockwise," Rachel whispered, gesturing with her finger, "then they'll alternate — see the next goes widdershins, counterclockwise."

"Why?"

"There's no major working tonight, just a plea, so they want to keep the power balanced. Half the coven enters the Grove deosil, the others widdershins — if there was a working, they'd all go one direction, depending on the intent of the ritual."

"I thought magic was all about your will and intent — how does walking in a circle do anything?"

Rachel nodded. "It's not part of the magic, it's part of the ritual that forms the coven's intent when they work the magic — it ... gets everybody on the same page."

More of the witches were coming out of the trees, alternating their turns as Rachel described, and I was starting to wonder if I'd ever be able to look at my teachers the same. The deep hoods of their robes covered their faces in shadow, but the robes themselves were cut high on the side ... like, armpit-high. With every step the robes swayed, exposing bare skin from ankle to ribs. Their fronts were still covered, but it was a lot of skin and a lot of side-boob.

Sam leaned forward to look at me around Rachel and grinned. "Good to be a witch, isn't it?"

"Shush," Rachel said.

Sam sat back and I realized the lead witch was approaching us — they each had silver cups on their trays and were handing them out to the students on the benches before continuing on. Sam and Rachel each took a cup, and the witch paused in front of me, so I took one and tried not to stare as she turned to move on, exposing the open side of her robe right in front of me. I realized the witches were making a full circle to return to where they'd come from the forest, so every single one of them was going to walk in front of me, flashing bare skin from ankle to shoulder.

"Last to enter is the warlock," Rachel said, nodding.

Sure enough, coming out of the woods was a clearly male figure, but still clad in the hooded white robe.

"What's this?" I whispered to Rachel, holding up the cup.

It was hard to tell what color the liquid was in the moonlight, but it seemed thicker than water.

"Mead — don't drink it yet."

"Okay."

The walk continued and I amused myself trying to figure out which teacher was under which robe. *Magistra* Fallowell was easy — she was the shortest one there — but I couldn't tell any of the others with their faces hidden. Not that their bodies, the parts that showed, were all the same, but there's a big difference recognizing your teacher in the clothes she wears to the classroom versus ... not.

The coven's warlock was approaching us — he didn't look at me, but he slowed and held out his arm toward me, hand in a fist parallel to the ground. It was surprising, but so clear in intent that my own fist came up to bump his automatically. He gave me a thumbs-up and moved on.

As each member of the coven finished a full circle, they turned and walked to the stone block — I guess altar would be best to call it.

"What did you call the high priestess?" I whispered to Rachel. "*Domina*?"

"*Domina Ritualis* — the lady of the ritual."

"Oh."

The coven gathered around the altar, each with one of the silver cups. One of them raised hers toward the moon and I recognized *Prima* Rosethorn's voice.

"We call upon the Child," *Prima* Rosethorn called out, lowering her cup to her lips.

Everyone sipped from their cups, so I followed suit. The mead was cool and sweet.

The coven and all the girls watching responded, "Grant us your innocence, that we may know the joy of youth."

"We call upon the Maiden," *Prima* Rosethorn went on.

Everyone raised their cups again.

"Just barely touch it to your lips," Rachel whispered. "There's a lot more to come."

I nodded, just touching my tongue to the mead.

"Grant us your passion, that we may feel the thrill of life anew."

"We call upon the Mother."

"Grant us your fertility, that our family may be blessed with life."

"We call upon the Crone."

"Grant us your wisdom, that we may face all trials that come our way."

"We call upon the Goddess in all her aspects."

"Grant us your blessing, that we may do your will."

# THE MOTHER

"Are you drunk?"

I wasn't sure.

After the calling-ons, I noticed Sam and Rachel were doing more than just touching their tongues to the mead, so I started sipping. Then there were some blessings, after which the witches of the coven all went around the circle again, this time refilling our cups. Then came the praising, by which time sipping had turned to gulping, and finally the dancing — all interspersed with refilled cups and a bit more than gulping.

I remembered being especially fond of the dancing, but unable to really recall any details.

"Probably," I said, opening my eyes.

A white-robed and hooded figure stared down at me, as I appeared to be on my back in the clearing's grass.

It was still dark, so I hadn't slept there all night, which was good — having a teacher ask if you're drunk, maybe not so much.

I struggled to sit up, my head spinning and my vision still being a bit of a circle with fuzzy edges. The clearing was still dark and the moon still high, so I knew I hadn't been asleep long enough to miss class the next morning. I was still noticeably drunk, though — and I had a feeling that morning would bring another new experience for me, one much less pleasant.

I had only vague recollections of the night after the dancing started, because at that point the mead was flowing freely, instead of just being refilled between parts of the ritual the teachers were performing — one which, according to Sam and Rachel, was meant to reinforce and strengthen their coven bonds as well as the school's wards.

The dancing had been a new experience as well, one I'd enjoyed — I hadn't really gone to dances while in public school. Though my dancing tonight had been limited to Sam and Rachel, despite several of the other girls coming by seeming to express interest.

Both Sam and Rachel, whichever wasn't dancing closest with me at the moment, took to interposing themselves between me and the other girls, which sort of waved them off. I wasn't really disappointed by that, because most of those were girls who'd spent the entire school year either ignoring me or giving me stinkeye — and I didn't see a particular reason to start dancing with them just because they were drunk and knew I was a *trinitara* now.

Sam seemed to share my opinion, because once the evening wore on and girls started drifting away from the Grove, some of them holding hands in pairs or more, I asked her why she didn't see if someone might be interested in wandering off with her.

"None of them were interested in me when they were sober and I was a onesie," she answered with a shrug. "So why should I be interested in them now? Anyway, I was thinking I might save anything like that until after we've formed our coven." She looked around to make sure no one was listening. Rachel was a few feet away out of earshot, hands on hips and glaring at a girl who was wandering in our direction. "If you are still serious about letting someone join the coven. If I ... like them."

I nodded. "Of course, that's important."

A blinding pain shot through me and my eyes snapped back open. The teacher withdrew her finger from my forehead.

"Sober now?"

I nodded quickly, not wanting another shot of whatever the hell that'd been.

"Enjoy it now — it'll be gone when you return."

*Return?*

I looked around the clearing again with my now sober eyes, and saw that it was not the school's clearing. I recognized it, though, from previous dreams I could never quite recall on waking.

I looked at the teacher, who probably wasn't a teacher. I'd learned enough about the witches and their Goddess to take a guess at who this was.

"The Mother, I presume?"

"Idalia, dear," she said, sitting in front of me.

She sat cross-legged, which stuck her bare legs outside the front drape of her robe, and threw her cowl back to reveal her beautiful face. While Aveline had been beautiful — breathtakingly, heart-stoppingly beautiful — Idalia somehow surpassed her. The Maiden's beauty was ... not a facade, but somehow a projection, maybe? Idalia's was inherent. It was a part of her and she moved, spoke, and carried herself with the knowledge that it was so. She was beautiful in the same way Mel and the Willowmere teachers were beautiful — with maturity and confidence. Yet, while all the witches were beautiful, and all of Willowmere's teachers were MILFs, Idalia surpassed them all.

*The mother of all MILFs*, I thought, trying to keep from chuckling.

"Okay," I said, "but are there really four of you or just one?"

Idalia smiled. "Yes."

I sighed. "I should have expected that."

"Yes, you should have, dear." She leaned forward and patted my thigh, which both let the front of her robe fall open to reveal the deep cleft of her full, hanging breasts ... and made me aware, very aware, that she was touching my thigh. At least I wasn't naked.

"We are the four faces of the Goddess — her avatars, if you will. Archetypes of womanhood personified. We are independent, yet one." She shrugged, still leaning toward me, which made her breasts do things. "It's complicated."

"I bet," I said. "I certainly don't understand it."

Idalia sat back, removing her hand from my thigh. "What don't you understand, dear? We have some time, so I'll try to explain."

I eyed her warily. "You're a lot nicer than ... some of the yous. None of them offered to answer any questions."

She chuckled. "We all have our little quirks. Aurora and Viera both lack patience — for different reasons, but it's their nature. While Aveline ... well, patience and young women are not a common pairing."

"What about you?" I asked.

Another chuckle. "I'm the Mother, dear. Patience is a requirement."

"I don't understand what you want me to do — any of you."

"Didn't the others tell you what they wished of you?"

"Yeah, right. I figured out who Viera and Aveline were talking about — the witches, right?"

Idalia nodded.

"But how am I supposed to bring them back to Viera or make them ... have fun, like Aveline wants? And Aurora wants me to tell somebody something, but she won't tell me who. Now you're going to ask me for something and it's probably going to be just as cryptic, right?"

Idalia pursed her lips. "I don't think so, but we'll see." She sighed. "Noah, magic works in a very odd, but very intuitive way. Will and intent give the magic form, far more than spells and rituals. The spells and rituals are really there to help you focus on your intent. Do you *intend* to fulfill the tasks we've set you? Do you want to?"

I thought about that for a minute. I'd now been around witches long enough to know promises and agreements were a big deal to them — so they must be to their Goddess, too. But what they ... she ... they ... fuck. What they wanted made sense. The witches had strayed from their Goddess's path. I could see that in the fucked up way the Families ran things. Even *Magistra* Cassian kept saying as much in our Rituals class. So, yeah, I couldn't think of any reason I *wouldn't* want to help with that. And the Families certainly weren't any fun, so I'd be happy to accomplish what the Maiden wanted of me.

Aurora. I thought of the little girl and that sudden rush of emotion I'd felt when she said she loved me. All she asked was that I tell someone there'd been a mistake ... and I think I'd do absolutely anything to end her sadness over that.

"What is it you want me to do?" I asked.

Idalia smiled. "Clever and smart. Never make an open-ended promise, dear." She leaned forward to pat my thigh again and I closed my eyes so I wouldn't be distracted by the view. "My geas for you is what any mother wishes for her children — that you live a happy life, full of joy, and bring that to all my children."

I opened my eyes and met hers. "My mom didn't want that for me or she wouldn't have dumped me off like garbage."

Idalia winced.

"We can't always know someone's reasons, dear, or their circumstances."

"Are you saying she thought it was best for me?" I'd gotten pretty tired of hearing that from caseworkers and foster parents. Then I had a sudden thought. "Do you know who she was? Do you know who my parents are? Are they alive?"

"Oh, Noah, I don't. Some of my children have drifted so far from me that I can't see them any longer." She took a deep breath. "I didn't even know about you until Felicity found you."

That squashed the little bit of hope that had suddenly sprung up in me.

"Wait," I said. "Felicity, not Mel?"

Did that mean Felicity was a witch? But how could a cat be a witch?

"You haven't answered me, dear. Do you *intend* to help us?"

"Well, yeah," I said. Everything they'd asked was a good thing, I thought, but I still didn't see how I could do any of it.

"Then work toward that and trust your magic."

"But how?"

"We've each given you a gift toward that end. Aurora's given you a glimpse of true, unconditional love — would you share that with others?"

I nodded as I thought about the dark, empty pit inside of Sam and wished I could.

"Viera's given you the strength to perceive the truth, even when it's hidden and your mind is clouded by another's power, and Aveline ... well, her gift will certainly assist you."

"What was it?"

"I won't say if she didn't," Idalia said, smiling.

I really wished the witches' Goddess could be as straightforward as Priscilla's mother.

"What about you?"

"I have something very special for you, dear." She leaned further forward and put her hand in my lap. "My daughters' greatest desire."

# CHAPTER THIRTY-FOUR

The sensation of hard, cold ground beneath my back woke me. That and the contrast with soft, warm bodies on either side of me — and a bit on top where arms and legs were draped.

I blinked to clear my head, which didn't help a bit, as my mind and vision were still foggy from the mead.

*So much mead,* I thought, accusing my earlier self.

A bit more awareness and the soft bodies resolved into Sam and Rachel, one on either side and so tightly pressed against me that I could feel the rise and fall of their breasts as they breathed even through my clothes.

Or not, I realized, as I noted my shirt had disappeared sometime during the night.

At least I still had my pants on...

*I do still have my pants on, don't I?*

A quick check confirmed this, and that, a bit to my drunken disappointment, both Sam and Rachel were still fully clothed.

I raised my head and looked around the clearing.

The school's Grove was empty and dark save for two of the

torches still burning with low flames and a couple other bodies of passed out students littered around the area. As I held my head still to stop the spinning, a couple stumbled out of the tree line, clutching at each other for support, and staggered down the path back toward the school buildings.

That struck me as a fine idea. The empty Grove clearly meant the Samhain ritual was over and we should all get back to our rooms for a little sleep before classes started in the morning. I doubted any of the teachers, even those who'd been part of the ritual, would make allowances for mead-fuzzed answers in their classes.

"Sam? Rachel?" I whispered, nudging them both. "We should get back to our rooms."

"Mmph," Sam uttered, while Rachel squirmed closer to me.

That wasn't unpleasant — far from it — but as shy and easily embarrassed as the girl was, I thought it was probably something I should put an end to before it went far enough to really embarrass her.

Or she exploded.

"Hey," I whispered louder, nudging both girls a little harder. "We should get up and — *ow!*"

I sat bolt upright, dumping Sam off me and dragging Rachel along as dead weight by the teeth she had latched onto my right chest.

"Huh? What?" Sam asked, sitting up and holding her head.

Rachel let go as I clutched at where she'd bit me and leapt to my feet.

"You bit me!"

"Who?" Sam demanded, looking around.

"Rachel!"

"What? No, I didn't!"

"You did — look!"

I clutched at my chest, but in the dim moonlight there wasn't anything to see. Still, I could feel the indentation of tooth marks as I rubbed at it.

Sam stood, swaying, and peered at my chest.

"I don't see anything."

"Why do you have your shirt off?" Rachel asked.

I swayed a bit myself, now that the adrenaline rush of being bit was wearing off.

"I don't remember," I admitted.

"If you're too drunk to remember taking your shirt off," Sam reasoned, "then you're probably too drunk to remember who bit you." She looked around the mostly empty Grove, head wobbling and eyes blinking. "Could've been anyone — *lots* of drunk witches here."

"Yeah!" Rachel agreed.

"No," I said, pointing at the ground. "We were laying right there, both of you were cuddling up to me, then I tried to wake you up and Rachel bit me."

"Cuddling you?" Sam asked.

"I never," Rachel added, shaking her head, then closing her eyes and reaching out for something to steady herself with. "Oohhh..."

"Sounds like wishful thinking," Sam said. She looked around. "We should get you back to the room — you're drunk."

"Yeah," Rachel agreed.

Both the girls took a step, swayed alarmingly, then tilted their swaying toward me until they crashed into me from either side.

"Here," Sam said, pulling my left arm around her shoulders. "I'll help you back to the room. You're drunk."

"Yeah," Rachel said, pulling my right arm around her.

We managed three steps down the forest path before Rachel stopped walking, causing Sam and I to pivot around her.

"What?" Sam asked, once we'd finally stabilized.

Rachel was staring at my bare chest and frowning.

"Who bit you?"

WE STAGGERED our way back to the residence hall and the walk made my thoughts run in some odd directions. First, my thoughts laid out the situation:

I was drunk.

I was sandwiched between two beautiful witches.

I was shirtless, so their arms touched my bare skin, as well as their faces when they lolled against my chest.

I'd just come from a witch ritual filled with half-naked hot-witch teachers and drunk-witch dancing.

I'd spent the last two months on a campus filled with hot-witch students and hot-witch teachers.

Before that I'd been stuck at Mel's … who was, at least, on the top five hot-witch list of hot-witches. Maybe top two? *Magistra* Fallowell was really hot, but that was because of her magic. Some of that was because of her magic. Maybe Mel was number one.

Anyway, when I hadn't been stuck at Mel's, she'd been taking me to topless bars.

And one of the two beautiful witches with their arms draped over my shirtless back and, Goddess help me, rubbing her boobs against my bare chest as we staggered on, had asked me to have sex with her for the first time on the Winter Solstice in two months.

I was drunk.

And horny.

I was drunk and horny with two beautiful witches hanging off me, so this was clearly the time to evaluate my life and make some serious decisions.

All I could think about was having sex with Sam in two months.

*Two months.*

Sometimes it's worse to know something you want is coming and have to wait for it than to think it's not something that'll happen.

I watched my roommate out of the corner of my eye as we staggered across the quad, seeing her in a new light. I hadn't really paid attention to Sam as a girl since shortly after I'd come to Willowmere — she'd slotted quickly into the friend-roommate category.

After she'd drunk that potion and then asked me to mark her, I'd been too relieved that she was okay to really think about what that meant — then the whole Willowmere Halloween Faire had taken so much of our time that I *still* hadn't really thought about it.

Now I was thinking about it.

Hard.

Thinking about it hard, not ... well, yeah, that too.

I realized the next two months were going to be absolute hell.

And I was thinking drunk — in hindsight, I do not recommend thinking drunk.

I thought about the times I'd seen Sam nearly naked or in her pajamas in our room, which was basically every night, and how I'd never noticed before how sexy her damn pajamas were.

Not that she really wore sexy pajamas, but that pajamas in general are a little sexy — and I don't think there could possibly be unsexy pajamas.

And I was going to have to see that every night for two months before I could get her out of those pajamas.

*Shit*, I thought. *This is going to drive me batshit.*

No, there was no way I was going to last two months.

Maybe I could suggest something that might ease things?

Sam would be open to something like that, right? I mean, maybe she'd want to sort of ... ramp-up to the Solstice. Get used to the idea. Ease into it.

I pondered that as we entered the quiet residence building and made our way up the stairs.

Both girls were having trouble with the stairs, sagging next to me. That put more and more of their weight on my shoulders and I had to grip them tighter so they wouldn't fall down — but that also meant I had to slide my hands around their sides to grip them tighter, and as they sagged and slid down with every step my hands wound up just under their boobs.

I pondered harder.

We made it to our floor and I found myself simultaneously cursing and blessing Willowmere for not installing elevators.

Sam mumbled something as I tried to figure out how I could open the door to Rachel's room without one of them sliding to the floor and making things even more awkward and difficult.

"Where are we?" Sam mumbled.

"We're nearly at the room," I whispered. "Just need to get Rachel to bed and then we can go to sleep."

"Oh." Sam took a deep breath and straightened, which at least freed up one of my arms to open Rachel's door.

"She's very drunk," Sam said as she helped me get Rachel to her bed, then arrange her comfortably and take her shoes off. "Where's your shirt?"

"I don't know," I said.

Sam pouted. "I liked that shirt."

"So did I — Mel got it for me."

Sam tucked a pillow under Rachel's head and we left the drunk girl snoring.

"I can't believe The Blackwood picks out your clothes," Sam giggled as we walked the remaining distance to our own room.

I was too busy pondering to protest that, and I realized that I was going to have to say something to Sam or the next two months would be too much. I mean, what were we supposed to do? Just go on as roommates and friends as though nothing was changing, then show up on the Solstice and have sex?

No, that would be too weird. We'd have to find some not-weird way to work our way up to it.

"Say, Sam?" I said as I closed the door.

"Yeah?"

We sat across from each other on our beds and I realized I had no idea what I was going to say.

*Dammit!* I cursed myself. *This has to be my Lust resonance. That's the only thing that explains how I can't think about anything but sex right now. No normal eighteen-year-old guy who'd just been told he was going to get to have sex with his totally hot roommate in a couple months would be this obsessed and unable to think about anything else, right?*

"What was it you were saying?"

"Um..."

"Why are you so red? Are you feeling okay? Do you have a fever?"

Sam reached forward and put the back of her hand against my forehead.

She must've had a fever because her hand felt like it was burning me.

I took a deep breath.

"I was thinking ... that just showing up ... on the Solstice might be weird," I managed. "And maybe ... we should do something ... some things ... between now and then to work up to it, so it won't be so weird."

*Yeah, weird,* I told myself, *we both said it was going to be weird, and we should try to make it un-weird. This makes excellent sense.*

"Like what?"

*Okay, okay, what do I suggest — what do couples do first? It can't be, like, just to date — Sam and I spend all our time every day together as it is. Doing something together is just Tuesday. And it can't be romantic, because that would be weird — this is just a thing we're doing as friends, and it isn't romantic. Which is weird, which is why we need to work up to it.*

*What about kissing? Kissing is good. Weird, to think of with Sam, but good. But that's romantic and it's touching, maybe touching is too much. It would be hard to touch her like that for two months without being able to do more until the Solstice. What isn't touching?*

*Seeing! Seeing is not touching — we even say look but don't touch because we know they're not the same thing.*

*So, seeing — what can I see? What have I seen? New pajamas, I was just thinking about the sexy of pajamas. So, what can we do to ... ease forward toward the Solstice seeing ... less pajamas! That's it!*

*So, we could start with, her ... not wearing ... pajama bottoms?*

*Yeah?*

*Yeah.*

"Noah? Why are you just staring at me? And why are you grinning?"

*Okay, quick! Ask her to start sleeping without pajama bottoms because that's not touching!*

*No! She will bargain! We need a bigger ask so we can compromise on pajama bottoms! I took a business class — I need to set the negotiations anchor!*

*"I want you to start sleeping naked!"* I said, calmly and with drunken confidence in the power of my argument.

Sam looked at me.

She raised an eyebrow.

"Because..." She drew the word out in a long breath.

"Because it's not touching or romantic!" I laid out my first argument. If I'd had a mike, I'd drop it.

Sam nodded, clearly being won over by the power of my mead-fueled rhetoric.

"It is not touching and certainly not romantic," she agreed.

Getting agreement to one thing is an important step in persuasion, I remembered that from my high school business class too.

"And starting with not touching will help ease us out of the weirdness toward the event of the Solstice!"

Sam nodded again — my arguments were undeniable. This level of persuasion could only be something boosted by my Command power. Was I unconsciously using that? I didn't want to use that on Sam, but starting the path to not-weird was more important.

"Oh, no, we would not want any weirdness."

Sam grinned — clearly happy with the path my logic was taking, then she gave me a puzzled look.

"So, you want me to sleep naked, so that the ... Event —" she gave it finger quotes. "— of the Solstice..." She paused, furrowing her brow and biting her lower lip. "Will not be ... weird."

I nodded. "Exactly."

"Hmhmh, I see. To ease us into things."

"You understand."

Sam chewed on the inside of her cheek staring at me.

She nodded.

"Okay."

Sam stood up and headed for the bathroom.

"Grea — wait, what?"

I leaned forward to look toward the bathroom and Sam stopped halfway there. She looked back at me over her shoulder.

"I agree," she said, walking to the bathroom again.

I heard the water in the shower turn on, and Sam's head popped around the door frame.

"I agree, so now I'm going to take a shower."

Her head disappeared and a moment later her sweater flew out of the bathroom to land in a heap in front of the door.

"And I'm going to leave the bathroom door open," she called.

Her shirt followed the sweater.

"Now and every time I shower."

Her shoes clunked to the hallway floor.

"Until..." A hand stuck around the corner to make air quotes. "The Event."

Brightly colored socks fluttered through the air like celebratory streamers, followed by her pants.

"So, you can see me naked..."

*Oh, my God, Goddess, both of you, that was her bra — it's so lacy...*

"Any time you want from now until then..."

I nearly choked as Sam's hand appeared around the door frame again, this time holding a tiny pair of white panties. They weren't lace or anything, just plain white cotton, but I think that made it unbearably worse.

Sam dropped the panties and poked her head back into the room.

She grinned — but it was a kind of grin I'd never seen on her face before. It was a grin that promised things — I don't know exactly what things but I wanted the things.

"But you can't have me until the Solstice."

---

DO NOT. Under any circumstances. Show a woman how badly you want to have sex with her.

They are brutal, sadistic, and pure evil.

Over the course of the next two weeks, I saw a side of Sam that I never would've believed existed.

My formerly meticulously neat roommate began leaving her underthings all around the room, including the inside pocket of my jacket — which nearly gave me a heart attack when I reached in there to get a fresh pencil during Mel's class.

Sam didn't seem to care if her underthings got wrinkled or lost — which was probably because she needed them less now that she'd started stripping stark naked as soon the curfew bell rang.

The same bell meant I couldn't leave the room, so I was stuck in a small room with a beautiful naked witch I couldn't touch until the Solstice.

Have I mentioned the inadvisability of thinking drunk?

Then there were the touches, and the brushes, and the little sidelong glances under fluttering lashes.

Don't get me started on the pouting, the standing way too close to me in the cafeteria line, and always pointing her mouth so her breath hit my bare skin.

"You know," she said, popping a sucker out of her mouth as we walked across the quad.

Oh, yeah, she'd started sucking on lollipops all the time. Sam never ate candy, but now she was never seen without a damn lollipop in her mouth.

"It's really not fair," she continued.

"What's not fair?"

"You get to see me naked."

"Shush," I said looking around. "Someone might hear you."

Sam looked around. It was between afternoon classes, so most of the students were in the classroom building, but Sam and I had a special project for Mel's class we needed to use the library for all afternoon.

"Nobody's close enough to hear me."

"Hello?" I wiggled my fingers at her. "We live in a magic school — I'm sure somebody has a spell to eavesdrop on people. The teachers certainly do."

"Only in classrooms — as for everyone else? First, they'd have to care what we were saying. We're not that interesting. Well, you are, but everyone's gotten used to you."

"No, they haven't!"

Sam jerked her head to the side and widened her eyes. "Geez, narcissistic much?"

I could see the tiniest tightening at the corner of her mouth, telling me she was just messing with me.

"What's not fair about it?" I asked, really secretly hoping she'd have a reason it was remotely possible for me to agree with, so I could at least get some clothes back on her while retaining my dignity.

Think that's not a problem? You're an eighteen-year-old guy telling your hot-witch naked roommate to put some clothes on. That's the sort of thing that'll haunt a guy forever.

"You getting to see me naked..." She pushed the lollipop into her mouth almost to the end of the stick and I choked. The lollipop reemerged. "... but I can't see you naked."

Something in my throat didn't work right. Air could get out — at least in a sort of raspy, dying gasp — but couldn't get back in.

"Barg ... but, but you don't like guys," I blurted.

Sam scrunched up her nose. She hopped in front of me and put her hand against my chest to stop me, she popped the lollipop out of her mouth again, and held it up to mine.

I didn't even think, I just opened my mouth and she popped it in.

Look, if a pretty girl wants you to lick her lollipop, you do it.

"I know. *Ew*. It's gross —"

"Hey!"

"Oh, come on — you know it's true. Have you seen a penis? They're all ... bulbous and bumpy and..." She shuddered.

"I'm right here," I said.

"Am I lying?"

I had to admit I was not, myself, enamored of the penis.

"Yeah," Sam said. "But I'm willing to take one for the team ... for justice and fairness."

---

SO THAT'S how I came to be standing naked in the middle of my dorm room with my rather wide-eyed roommate Samantha sitting on her bed staring at my penis which was just about at her eye level.

That sort of statement should have a record scratch and a freeze frame after it.

Her hands flew to her mouth.

"Maiden's white cotton panties," she whispered.

"What?" I asked looking down at myself. I mean, the stress of the moment had it a little in retreat, but I thought it was still okay.

"It's —" Sam shook her head. "Are you a grower or a shower?"

"I'm," I shrugged. "Both? I mean, it gets bigger, but I think it's okay..."

"It gets bigger?" Sam shook her head. "I can't."

"It's not that big," I said. "It's, like, a little bit above average — I Googled it and —"

Sam's eyes flashed to mine. "You Googled your dick?"

"Hey! I Googled average penis size, all right? Every guy probably has."

"And what's the average?"

"Like, five or six inches, but that's erect."

Sam swallowed hard.

"Thirty percent greater is not 'a little above average,'" she said.

"It's not that big."

"It's bigger than any of the toys I've ever used."

Images of Sam using sex toys flashed across my brain and she flung herself backward across her bed to put her back against the wall.

"*Why is it getting bigger?*"

# CHAPTER THIRTY-FIVE

For almost two more weeks, Sam and I tried to drive each other nuts. Always one-upping the other on poses or something. I flexed my abs so much I almost got abs, then I found myself checking my ass out in the mirror to see just how different stances affected it — I mean, yeah, Sam was into girls, but she'd also said she could appreciate a good-looking guy, so maybe it would have an effect?

Sam ... was much better at that sort of thing than I was.

Finally, though, we agreed that we didn't need to run around our room naked anymore.

It was driving me crazy and creeping her out.

She did admit that she, also, had been thinking drunk when the whole thing started and, like me, couldn't figure out a way to get out of it. She'd been hoping I'd refuse to get naked when she suggested it so we could stop.

It was a still little weird thinking that we were going to have sex in a little over a month even though she really wasn't into guys, but she assured me it was the way covens worked. The groups were rarely formed out of attraction and affection, but rather for the optimal generation of mana. So, she figured she was ahead of the game because she liked me — not in that way — and I figured I was ahead because I liked her — yes, in that way.

"So, it's not normal for everyone in a coven to love each other?" I asked her, still trying to wrap my head around the idea of these covens.

Sam started laughing and I had to just sit there watching as she rolled around on her bed in her pajamas — which now included bottoms again.

"No," she said finally, but still gasping a little, "the most important things in the Family covens are power and alliances. When a new coven is formed, the high priestess is picked by the head of the Family — for the Prescotts, that's my mother. The new high priestess then gets to pick from all of the available witches in the Family — which usually means the most powerful, or the most complementary to whatever resonance the warlock has, and compatibility is a distant third. It doesn't matter that much anyway, because once everybody's marked and bound, they have to do what the high priestess says anyway. Well, the twelve marked witches do what the warlock tells them and he does what the high priestess says."

"That sounds kind of miserable."

She shrugged. "It is how it is. I think the smaller Families care more about the relationships, but they're always forming covens across Family lines because they don't have enough distant relations in the Family. Big Families like mine ... like the Prescotts, don't have that kind of consanguinity problem."

"Consa... Consommé... What?"

"Consanguinity, it's how you're related to someone else — it was a big thing with the royal families of Europe back in the day, I think that's why they all have no chins and bad teeth. It's having kids with someone too closely related. I think the pool for forming a new coven starts with the warlock's fourth cousins? Maybe. I've got, like, a hundred and twelve fourth cousins."

I blinked, that was a big Family.

"I know, right? And even more fifth and sixth cousins — and at that, you're really talking about the same genetic relationship as some random mundane off the street. The Families track relationships to the thirteenth — basically a who's-who back to the Black Death, and we don't bother with before that because so many people died that the relationships all got closer anyway. But, really, a new coven doesn't wind up any more closely related than a bunch of random people who've lived in the same small town all their lives."

I wasn't even sure what country any of my ancestors came from — only that Mel was some kind of relation somewhere.

"And they're all okay with having sex with the same guy?" I asked. That was one of the things I still had trouble accepting about the witches. That they could form so many of these covens and it was just normal to them. "Don't they get jealous?"

Sam shrugged. "Not within the coven. Some witches might be mad if their warlock had sex with someone outside the coven, but I don't think most would even care about that. Most warlocks aren't exactly, well, what the mundanes would consider relationship material."

"Why not?"

"Think about it," she said, making a seriously-you-don't-get-it-face. "Look, I know you're hung up on the Family warlocks not being able to leave their enclaves, but it's not like they're kept in cages. Other than the high priestess, they're the ultimate boss of the coven. They get the best of everything and they have a dozen witches at their beck and call. They have sex every day to harvest and transfer mana, and they don't even have to be nice to the witches. No dates, no flowers, no headaches."

"Sounds horrible," I said — and it did.

"So, what do you want life in your coven to be like?"

Her question took me by surprise. I hadn't really thought about it. I'd accepted that I was a warlock and would have to form a coven. I'd certainly accepted forming that coven with Sam — was looking forward to it, even, but beyond that I hadn't imagined anything.

Now I did and I told her the first image that popped into my head.

"I want us all together — at Christmas. Fine," I said, cutting her off, "Solstice, alright? All of us together. You can decorate for Solstice and I'll decorate for Christmas and we can make fun of each other's decorations."

"You stole all yours from witches," Sam said.

"Yeah, you can tell us all about that," I said, grinning back at her. "But more than those things, we'll be celebrating you and I starting our coven. On the Solstice, because you made me wait over two months after asking me to and taunted me the whole time with your nakedness."

"It was only a couple weeks of taunting, and you *asked* me to."

"I was drunk!"

"You're still responsible for what you ask for."

"Hmph."

Sam tilted her head to the side and rubbed her neck. I started to wonder if she'd like a neck massage.

*No! The solstice is still over a month away — we haven't even made it out of November yet, and the path you're on will only lead to frustration and sorrow.*

"So that's what you want out of a coven?" Sam asked. "A Christmas party?"

I tried to think of how to better express what I'd meant by that.

"I want our coven to be a family," I said. "Not like the big witch Families, but a real family where everybody cares about each other, even if they don't always get along."

"Mmhh," Sam said. "Good luck with that."

It might be unlikely, but I was still determined to try. The almost business-like approach Sam described didn't appeal to me at all.

"What about you?" I asked. "What do you want it to be like? I bet with the warlocks being jerks like you described the, um, market for your interests is pretty high?"

Sam sighed and shook her head.

"You'd think so, right? That this situation and not being able to go get a mundane guy, and there being a couple dozen witches for every warlock, that this would be a prime situation for someone of my orientation."

She sighed again.

"You would be wrong. Witches are a disappointingly conservative group."

I laughed.

"Well," I said, "we'll just have to be sure we add some to our coven who do feel the same."

"Really?"

"Of course, if I'm going to live with thirteen women, I want you all happy."

Sam caught her lower lip between her teeth, then frowned and looked down.

"But?"

She looked up at me and her grin came back.

"'Our coven'," she said. "We are really going to start something that's ours — and we, you, can think about things like that."

"*We*," I said, stressing it. "Yeah, I don't want anyone in the coven who doesn't want to be there, or doesn't like the rest of the coven — and that starts with you and me."

"Well, I don't think you can find thirteen women, much less witches, who like each other all the time."

"Sometimes, sure — but it sounds like you're saying in a lot of covens they're not even friends."

Sam shrugged. "There are a lot of covens where some of the members really hate others."

"I definitely don't want anything like that."

"Just make sure you find a high priestess who feels the same, because conflict between the high priestess and warlock *really* messes things up."

I decided to ask, since I hadn't been able to figure it out.

"Do you want to be high priestess? I mean, you're going to be the first —"

"Nope, nope, nope," Sam said quickly. "You think I want a piece of that? The high priestess is in charge of scheduling the rituals and the harvests in between." Her voice took on a needy, whiny, spoiled tone. "'Why did you schedule me for Thursday? Don't you know my favorite show drops new episodes on Thursday?'"

I had to laugh. "Okay, I get it."

"Seriously — it takes a lot of skills that I just don't want to deal with. I'm not an organizer and I'm certainly not a mediator." She grinned. "I'm more likely to be an instigator."

"But you'll help me find someone?"

"Absolutely — and it'll be easier for us, as a warlock-led coven."

"Why?"

"Because really all we're looking for in a high priestess is a good administrator. You don't have to find someone who can perform all the rituals, because you'll be the head of the coven and can appoint any of the witches to perform a ritual. That's one of the strengths of a warlock-led instead of priestess-led coven — being able to switch it up like that so the witch whose magic best fits the ritual's intent can run it."

I really couldn't believe that we were sitting here discussing recruiting and interviewing girls for what was, effectively, a harem for me — they might call it a coven, but I couldn't get past the fact that it meant sleeping with thirteen girls every two weeks, then spending a night in an orgy with them.

Sam and I started having late-night talks about our new coven — what to look for in new members, what to look for in a high priestess, and what would be different with the warlock in charge compared to how the Families worked. It was almost a relief to have stopped thinking about the upcoming sex all the time and just make plans for a life together.

Then came the murder.

## CHAPTER THIRTY-SIX

"What are we whispering about?" Sam asked as we arrived at the onesies table with our lunches.

Hannah and Brittany were already there and they were the source of Sam's question, since we'd seen their heads together whispering the whole time we'd been getting our food and crossing the cafeteria to our table.

I slid my tray on the table and sat down while Sam did the same next to Hannah.

Brittany leaned over the table.

"There's a party," she whispered.

"A party?" I asked.

"*Ssshh!*" Hannah shushed us. She quickly looked around the cafeteria. "Don't let the teachers hear."

"It's a secret party?" Sam whispered.

Brittany nodded.

"The mundane college is having a party at the Cove."

"What's the Cove?" I asked.

"It's a beach in the State Park next to campus," Sam told me.

"There's this big lake — the campus has some shoreline on it too, way back past the Grove."

"Brittany and I are going," Hannah said.

"Brittany's a first-year," Sam said. "We're not allowed to leave campus until next semester."

"Who'll know?" Brittany asked. "The party's Friday night, so there's no curfew, and we can get there through the forest behind the Grove."

"We won't have to go through the front gates," Hannah said. "We do this every year and never get caught."

I perked up a bit. I'd been on campus for two and a half months and before that at Mel's, where the only times we went out were to topless bars and clothes shopping. I admit I was going a little stir-crazy and this sounded like a safe opportunity. The biggest danger to me off-campus was some witch Family deciding to risk the wrath of both Mel and *Prima* Rosethorne by grabbing me — but the only witches at a party like this would be girls from Willowmere.

"That sounds fun," I said.

"What?" Sam asked. "You want to go?"

I shrugged. It probably wouldn't do to tell my friends I might like to meet some ... normal people. Yes, I was a warlock. Yes, I'd accepted that. But I hadn't been raised in the witch culture and while I wanted to learn and adopt that new culture, I'd grown up pretty mundane. It might be nice to attend a party that didn't have a pack of robotic werewolves.

"You could get in trouble," Sam protested.

"Like for sneaking into the forbidden section of the library and stealing a book?"

"That had a *point*."

"So does going to a party," Hannah said.

"What point?"

"Boys," Brittany blurted out, then flushed red and began paying studious attention to her lunch.

"You seriously can't wait until next semester?" Sam asked.

"That's next year," Brittany said.

"It's only two months," Sam said.

As someone who was only midway through a wait that was "only two months", I could sympathize with Brittany.

"If you can't get to a party until after the mundane Christmas, then all the good guys are taken for the year," Hannah said. "Trust me, I've seen it every year."

"So, I'm going," Brittany said, not looking up from her plate. "I have four years here before I graduate then probably wind up staying on my Family's compound full time, so I don't want to waste any of it."

Sam shrugged. "If you want to risk it, fine, but I'm out."

"Noah?" Hannah asked.

All three girls were looking at me.

---

"NO," Sam said.

I slid back into the bathroom and checked the mirror.

"What's wrong with it?" I asked, stepping back into the main room.

"Too mauve," she said, then went back to her potions homework.

"It's purple." I checked myself out in the mirror again. "I think it looks good."

"That," Sam said, closing her potions book and coming to stand behind me in the bathroom, "is mauve. Almost lilac."

"Mel thought it was the nicest shirt she bought me."

"It is nice."

"So, what's the problem?"

Sam sighed. "It's nice in the 'oh, look how handsome my ward is. He's such a nice young man', not in the 'damn, that guy's hot, I think I'll skip class tomorrow to have sweaty, sticky monkey-time with him'."

"I'm not planning to have monkey-time with anyone," I protested.

I just wanted to have a couple beers and meet people. Honestly, I was more excited about talking to guys than any of the college girls — a conversation about football or hockey instead of spellstick would really hit the spot.

"I'm not saying you have to go full-monkey." Sam left the bathroom and opened my closet. "But if you come back without any stories about at least a boob-feel or a particularly grindy dance, I'm going to be very disappointed in you."

"If you want a grindy-dance, you should come with."

"Nope." Sam pulled two shirts from my closet and held them up to me, frowning. "I've gotten in enough trouble this year, I think, with more coming when we get back from Solstice. I don't need to get caught sneaking off campus — neither do you, really. But if you're going, I expect to live vicariously through you." She nodded and shoved a shirt into my hands. "This one."

"Fine," I said, stripping off my purple shirt and exchanging it for one that was brownish — it would probably look better with my jacket anyway, since that was sort of brown.

"Hannah says the place is only a few hundred yards off campus," I said, "straight through the woods, and the seniors are going to cast some kind of spell to obscure the path. The teachers will never know we're gone."

"Uh huh," Sam said and I got the impression she didn't believe that — but Hannah said the girls had done this every year and never gotten caught. The Cove was just a short walk from the school grounds — in fact, the wards around that area had extra effects to keep hikers in the State Park from wandering onto the campus.

"Just don't get caught," Sam said, pushing me out the door.

Brittany was waiting in the hallway.

"Come on," she whispered. "Most of the others already left — if we miss meeting Ada and Isabella, we won't have any glamour to cover us."

We hurried downstairs, trying to look as nonchalant as possible.

Just a witch and a warlock out for an evening stroll before getting back to studying. Nothing to see here. Take no notice of the two dozen other girls surreptitiously leaving the dorm building and wandering in pairs and trios past the sports field and into the tree line.

*We're so getting busted*; I couldn't help telling myself.

"Nice shirt," Brittany said once it became clear we were well within the herd of students heading for the forest and wouldn't miss it.

"Thanks."

A few yards into the forest we caught up with the main group and joined them in waiting for the last of the stragglers. In total, about forty girls were milling about, then two of the seniors gathered everyone closer and started casting a spell.

I tried to watch what they were doing, wanting to get an idea of the intent they were putting into the spell and how they were manipulating their mana for it — I figured a spell that could hide forty students from the Willowmere faculty would be worth knowing — but I kept finding my eyes drifting away from them to look at trees and leaves, almost as though even the casting of the spell encouraged others to look elsewhere and not notice it.

Then they finished casting and started off deeper into the forest, gesturing for the rest of us to follow.

"Hey."

I glanced back and found Hannah coming up next to Brittany.

"Sorry I'm late — my roommate couldn't decide if she wanted to come or not and I had to stand in the doorway for, like, five minutes waiting for her to figure it out."

I started hearing music up ahead and then lights started showing amongst the trees.

"Hey."

That was from my other side and I turned to find Katrina from potions catching up with us.

"Hi." I checked on Hannah and Brittany, but they'd started

drifting away as we walked, engrossed in conversation with each other.

"Can I walk with you? Do you mind?"

She sounded hesitant, so I made sure my tone was upbeat.

"Sure!" I looked around. "No wingman? Or is it wingwitch?"

Katrina laughed, covering her mouth with her hand as I'd seen her do in potions when we were flirting.

"My roommate chickened out," she said.

Our pace slowed as the girls ahead of us bunched up at the edge of the forest. The two senior girls were holding us there and only letting two or three at a time leave the trees. The music was louder now and the lights brighter — most of the light coming from the headlights of cars and trucks parked on the edge of the party, as well as a couple large bonfires down at the lake's edge.

Finally, it was our turn and I left the trees with Katrina walking beside me.

We made our way into the heart of the party where people were dancing, talking, and generally messing around. I took a brief look at the mana being generated and found more Lust floating around than I had at the strip club. College students are apparently a horny bunch.

The Cove was a large, open space in the forest on the shore of the lake. A gravel parking lot with a road leading out made up the forest side, with a sandy beach area where the bonfires were going made up the lake side. There were some log buildings that looked like concessions, closed now, and stacks and racks of canoes, kayaks, and other beach stuff that were probably for rent when the weather was nicer.

Part of the parking lot was ringed off by cars and trucks and those were the ones with their lights on, making a brightly lit area where I saw some tables with kegs set up. Between the two areas someone had set up a DJ booth in the back of a truck and the gravel lot in front of that was filled with people dancing. The music was mostly a heavy, pounding bass with some techno sounds thrown in and very little in the way of words.

"So," Katrina asked, "uh, do you want to get a drink then maybe dance or something?"

My first thought was to forgo my plans to stick to the mundanes at this party. Our flirting in potions *had* ramped up a bit recently and maybe Katrina did want to hang out with me, more than just that her roommate had bailed on her — then I remembered the extra flirting had begun shortly after Sam's incident with the potion when word I was a *trinitara* got out. Did she really want to spend time with me, or had she gotten word from her mother, like so many of the witches, and was trying to get me into her Family?

That the question even had to enter my mind just made me sad and more determined to spend the party with normal people who didn't know anything about magic.

Not that I thought I had good odds of picking up a college girl, but at least I'd know they weren't trying to trap me into anything. It would be easy to tell the witches in this group, too, since I could just look and see if someone had shields. A quick look confirmed that, showing me that most of the girls, and all of the guys, at the party were simply mundanes — mundanes shedding a lot of mana, too, making my skin tingle as we walked through and my body absorbed it.

"I was planning to just wander around and watch people," I said, quickly cutting off Katrina's start of a smile and nod with: "We could meet up later and do some dancing if you want?"

Katrina's smile fell as she took the hint and I felt a little shitty about that. If her roommate really had bailed on her, then she'd be alone at the party — probably the first mundane party she'd ever been too — but there were plenty of other Willowmere students she could catch up with.

"Oh, okay. Um, I'll see you later then."

Katrina walked off and I almost called her back, but I didn't want to be around magic or witchcraft tonight — I just wanted to talk to normal people.

# CHAPTER THIRTY-SEVEN

NORMAL PEOPLE SUCK.

Normal parties suck.

At least that quickly became my opinion.

I tried a beer for the first time — nobody was checking IDs — and discovered I really preferred wine or mead. There were some wine coolers around, but only the girls were drinking those and I never did figure out where they came from. I wandered around with my red cup for a while, occasionally raising it to my lips but not really drinking the beer anymore.

Eventually my wandering reached the dancing and I sort of merged with that, moving my way through the crowd, half-walking and half-dancing my way toward the beach and the bonfires. A few girls started dancing with me on the way — there were more girls than guys doing the dancing — but none of them wanted to talk. They were only interested in a dance partner and most moved on pretty quickly when they noticed I wasn't very good at it.

There was a sort of greenish-brown type of mana they shed just before they turned to dance with someone else, even another girl, but

I couldn't figure out what that one meant. Maybe disappointment in my moves?

Anyway, I left the dance area for the beach and bonfires where there were a lot more couples and mixed-groups just hanging out and talking, along with some groups of just guys.

I caught a couple conversations about sports as I wandered around and joined those for a bit, but I quickly found that, one, I hadn't been following football or hockey at all since arriving at Willowmere, so wasn't up to speed on anything they had to talk about, and, two ... I kind of preferred spellstick.

It was quite a bit more intricate and complicated than the mundane sports, with each team's combination of magic creating unique strategies for offense and defense, where every game was completely different than the last. There was more action than football, since the game only stopped for penalties, and, honestly, more violence than hockey. I'd never seen a hockey player try to set an opponent on fire.

Plus, the witch players were a lot nicer to look at.

It wasn't just the sports talk I found disappointing.

All the conversations seemed a little boring. The mundane college classes couldn't hold a candle to Potions or Rituals, and the mundane college drama didn't stand a chance next to the witches.

Had I really changed so much in just three months at Willowmere that I couldn't relate to normal people anymore?

Or had normal people always been this boring and I just hadn't had anything to compare them to?

Eventually, I wandered away from the crowds and sat on the beach. There were a few others nearby, mostly couples doing what couples do.

It was colder here, away from the crowd and the fires, and I was glad for my jacket. I wished I'd thought to bring a blanket like the couples around me, but I had to put up with the cold sand I was sitting on. I was far enough away from the fires and headlights to make out the reflection of the moon and stars on the lake water.

I started feeling very alone, like I didn't fit in with either world — mundane or witches.

"Taking a break?"

Hannah came up behind me and plopped to the sand beside me.

"Pondering my place in the universe," I said, looking back to the moonlight on the water.

"Heavy thoughts for a party." She gestured at my half-empty red cup with her full one. "Refill?"

I shook my head. "I don't think I like beer."

"Then you won't miss this," she said, taking my cup in her other hand and draining it.

I raised an eyebrow, wondering how many she'd had before the full one she carried now.

"What about you?"

Hannah shrugged. "Not my scene anymore, I guess."

"No?"

"I'm a senior, so this is my last year." She took a big gulp of her beer. "Back to the Family after this."

I thought that would be even more reason for this to be her scene, since it would be a last taste of freedom before heading home to join a coven, and said as much.

Hannah shook her head. "No coven for me. Onesie, remember?" She took another drink. "Even if I do have a decent affinity — just not enough power to warrant a coven. I'm thinking of applying for a job at the school."

"At Willowmere? Why?"

"My Family doesn't treat onesies well. At least at Willowmere the teachers treat everybody the same — and the school even lets staff who aren't in a coven join in some rituals. Or at least watch them and receive a blessing after. My Family's covens are all very strict and private."

"Oh." There wasn't much I could say to that.

Hannah looked back at the mundane college kids dancing and drinking around the bonfires.

"The first couple years I liked this," she said, then faced the water and took a long drink. "Last year I met a guy. I really liked him. Too much."

"Too much?"

She nodded. "And he liked me too much. I think ... I think he was going to ask me to marry him."

"What happened?"

Hannah shrugged. "I had to break up with him."

"Why?"

She snorted. "What else?"

"Well, if you liked him and you know you're not going to be in a coven, why not keep going and see where things led? I mean, if you weren't in a coven then you don't have to worry about hiding that from him, right?"

"I don't think you understand how bad that is." Hannah took a deep breath. "If I got serious with a mundane, I'd *never* be able to go back to my Family. Even for visits. My Family wouldn't change anything about how they act and so I couldn't take him to visit ... how could I tell him he wasn't allowed to come with me to meet my 'parents'? Or that, no, you can only meet my mom? Dad? Yeah, he's alive, but I don't see him because he's always with his coven. No, it was best to end things with him."

She glanced back at the party and shrugged again.

"I don't want to go through that again. Witches and mundanes just don't work out."

"Even as friends?" I asked, thinking of Morgan and the difficulties I always had explaining, or not mentioning, parts of my new life.

Hannah shrugged. "Maybe if you never, ever wanted your friends to visit you at home. Family compounds are pretty different than mundane houses."

We sat in silence for a while. I didn't really think about things, just stared at the moonlight on the water — I suppose you could call it wallowing.

Hannah finished her beer and stacked her empty cup in mine.

"Want to head back?" she asked.

"Yeah," I agreed. I'd wallowed enough to understand whatever place I might have in the world was with the witches, not the mundanes.

We both stood. I took the empty cups to dispose of on the way or back at school.

By some mutual consent, Hannah and I didn't walk back through the main party, but instead took the shorter way between the closed concession stands toward the path back to campus. It was darker there, with the buildings blocking the light of both the headlights and bonfires. It was some sort of service path between the buildings, lit only by a single bulb over one of the concession's back doors.

As we walked, I felt Hannah take my hand. Maybe our mutual discovery that the party scene just wasn't for us had brought us closer, maybe too much beer on her part, maybe her memories of the guy she'd broken up with last year and knowing I was someone she didn't need to exclude from her world — maybe a combination of all three. I didn't even consider that she was a witch and, like all the witches at Willowmere, she'd probably received some kind of message from her mother and Family to try and snag me — Hannah had been my friend from the first day, so it never occurred to me, I just gave her fingers a gentle squeeze and walked on.

It was when we were halfway through the space between two of the concessions, fully hidden from the rest of the party when two figures stepped out of the shadows to block the way ahead of us — then I heard the crunch of footsteps on gravel from behind us as well.

# CHAPTER THIRTY-EIGHT

"Townies, you think?" one of the shadowy figures asked.

"Not invited, for sure," one of the two behind us said.

Hannah drew closer to me and I released her hand to put my arm around her.

"Do you have any magic that could help us out?" I whispered to her.

Hannah shook her head. "My affinity's Hindsight. I'm not much good at anything else."

I didn't know what Hindsight was, but if I did it would probably be telling me we should have walked back through the main party.

I had Command, which I wasn't going to use around Hannah, and might not be able to use on four guys, even mundanes. I'd also learned some spells I didn't have an affinity for — fire, where I could probably set someone's hair on fire before the other three jumped me, and Mel had been trying to teach me a little bit of glamour in order to make myself less noticeable to witches when I was off-campus, but she said something, possibly a passive affinity, was making that difficult for me and I didn't think I'd be able to hide both myself and Hannah from four guys, even if they were mundanes.

"Party crashers have to pay the toll," the first guy to speak said.

"What toll?" I started to feel relieved — I had a little cash with me and maybe Hannah had some, if they only wanted money.

"Let's start with the girl's tits. Show us."

"Not a chance," I said, moving in front of Hannah and turning so that I could keep all four in sight.

Unfortunately, that put our backs to one of the concession building's walls and the four guys closed in to make a half-circle around us.

The guy who'd been doing the talking had dark hair and a dark leather jacket and his partner had lighter hair and an athletics jacket — I figured him for football, since he was the shortest of the four and unlikely to be playing basketball.

The two who'd come up behind us were visible in the light now. One was wearing sweats — why he'd wear that to a party, I don't know. The other was big. Really big. Both tall and broad, with a round face and no discernible neck.

"This'll go one of two ways," Leader said. "You can step aside and you'll get your girlfriend back when we're done with her — or we can kick your ass first and then you get your girlfriend back when we're done with her."

Sweats came up to us and got right in my face.

"Which way you want to go?" he asked, grinning.

I hate bullies, but I was also realistic. There was no way I was getting out of this without getting hurt, so the question really was how hurt would I have to get for Hannah to get away?

Sweats was a no-brainer, because he was right in my face. The two who'd been in front of us were still more toward that direction, so that was two-to-one if Hannah ran that way. One-to-one if I could take one of them out after Sweats — maybe Leader, since he seemed to be in charge. But that would leave Hannah trying to outrun Jock, and it was all open space from here to the tree line and the path back to Willowmere. Football or basketball, he could probably catch her.

Back the way we'd come, to the beach, there were people. Couples on the beach, and if she could get farther, then the main party. Even if the mundane college kids wouldn't help her, the Willowmere girls would.

But that way led past No-Neck.

I resigned myself to spending some time in *Magistra* Fallwhistle's clinic and yelled for Hannah to run as I brought my knee up into Sweats' groin.

Sweats doubled over, so I grabbed the back of his head and brought my knee up again, this time into his face as I shoved his head down. Something crunched and he screamed. I shoved him at Leader and Jock, hoping to tangle one or both of them up.

I felt Hannah move behind me and I charged No-Neck to try and give her a clear path.

The closer I got, the bigger he seemed, until I was close enough for him to swing — which wasn't anywhere near close enough for me to swing.

I'd been hoping No-Neck was slow because of how big he was.

He wasn't — I also wasn't expecting him to be left-handed.

I tried to dodge, but he caught me with a wide, looping left hook that struck the side of my head and sent me entirely off my feet, crashing to the ground. Then a foot caught me in the gut, driving the air out of me and lifting me off the ground to crash again.

I tried to get up, managed to get to one knee, then something hit the back of my head, driving my face into the gravel, and it all went dark.

---

"HOLD HER!"

"What was that shit? What'd she do to Lenny?"

"Fuck if I know — just hold her!"

"Lenny — you okay?"

"Bitch knocked me into a fucking wall! I'm going to kill her!"

"Kill her later — hold her down now!"

"*Ooof!* Fuck I said hold her!"

"I've got both her arms, what'd she hit you with?"

"Fuck if I know but it hurt!"

*Crack!*

"Careful — don't break her jaw yet, we're just getting started."

"Little cunt hit me, I'm gonna — *ow!* Fuck! Put it out! *Put it out!*"

"Hold her fucking hands! She's got a lighter or something!"

"I am holding her hands! She ain't got no lighter!"

"Then how'd my hair get burnt?"

*Crack!*

"Fucking *bitch!*"

I was hearing everything, but I couldn't move. I couldn't open my eyes, couldn't get off the gravel.

Even with my eyes closed, though, I could sense Hannah using mana as best she could. Little spurts as her body generated it — she must have used whatever she had stored already and now was nearly out.

I saw a brief puff of fire magic, less than I'd use to light a candle, and one of the guys yelped, but I didn't smell anything more than the singed hair scent that already permeated the alley.

I heard tearing cloth and Hannah cried out, quickly muffled.

"Keep a hand over her mouth. Nice tits, little bitch."

"Hurry up and get her pants off — we don't have all fucking night."

"Stop squirming! What'd you think you were gonna get coming to a Kappa party?"

I got a palm flat on the gravel near my chest and pushed, rolling myself toward the voices and finally getting my eyes open.

Hannah was on the ground, arms over her head — Sweats was crouched there, one hand and a knee keeping her hands pinned while he covered her mouth with his other hand.

Her jacket gaped open and her shirt had been torn to reveal her breasts, her bra just pushed up so that the bottom band crossed her left breast, putting a deep crease in it.

Leader straddled her hips, groping at her, while Jock worked her pants down to her knees and kept tugging.

The big guy, No-Neck, stood by watching.

I gathered what mana I had — there wasn't much since I didn't generate my own. I still picked up some around campus and I'd gotten a good charge from walking through the party crowd, but I'd long since realized Mel was right about ambient mana not being enough. I had more than after a visit to a strip club, but not by much.

Still, I took what I had, formed my intent, and forced it out at the four men — the time for worrying about hiding my Control resonant and Command affinity had ended some time ago.

"Stop," I ordered them.

"Asshole's awake. Lenny, take care of him."

Nobody stopped.

I pushed more mana into my intent.

This time, unlike the mugger in the alley, I could see what I was doing.

Mana left my resonant stores, streamed toward the four men in long threads, but the threads were thin and glowed only dimly, and my resonant stores were rapidly being depleted.

I could make a guy run into a wall until he killed himself, but I couldn't stop these four douchebags? What was different?

No-Neck turned toward me, I guess he was Lenny.

*Shit.*

My head was still fuzzy — it'd probably only take one hit for me to go out again and then Hannah would be on her own.

Lenny took two steps toward me and I knew I'd have to take care of him first so I redirected my mana and will toward only him — the four dim threads combined into one, thicker and brighter, and that one attached itself to Lenny.

"Stop," I said.

Lenny stopped coming toward me.

"What the fuck?"

I could see Lenny struggling. His face contorted and what he had in place of a neck turned red, veins and tendons standing out as he fought against the command I'd given him.

"Carlos! Something weird's going on!"

*Fuck! What was I supposed to do if I could only control one of them?*

"Just put him out again!" Leader, who I guess was Carlos, yelled, reaching behind him to grope Hannah between the legs. She kicked at Jock as he tried to get her jeans off over her shoes and bucked beneath Carlos.

"I *can't!*" Lenny said.

My resonant stores had dropped by half what they'd started with already — I didn't have time to figure out how to do this, so ... brute force?

"Lenny —" I threw more mana into the bond I'd made with the big man. "— beat the shit out of Carlos."

Lenny turned and strode toward the group while I struggled to my feet, pouring more mana down the link.

"What the — *urk!*"

Lenny got there, grabbed Carlos by the throat, and lifted him off Hannah before slamming him to the ground.

I got to my feet and staggered a little.

"Hey! Lenny, what the fuck are you doing?"

That was Jock.

The link to Lenny felt ... better. Easier, maybe, and I thought I was probably overdoing it before. I might not be able to control four, but one was no problem ... so maybe two?

"Hey! You!" I called. "Jock!"

The dumbfuck actually looked at me.

I redirected half the stream of mana I was sending at Lenny to Jock and pushed more down both. I wouldn't be able to keep this up for long — the mana in my resonant stores was dropping fast.

"Kick Sweats' ass," I told Jock.

My intent must have been enough to get past me not knowing

either name, as Jock let go of Hannah's jeans and leapt at Sweats, knocking him backward.

I staggered toward Hannah.

She scrambled backward until her back was to the concession stand's wall and stared at me with wide eyes.

"Hannah," I almost fell as I got to one knee beside her — the beating I'd taken from Lenny and the outpouring of mana were getting to me. "Hey, we need to get out of here."

"Please don't hurt me," she whimpered.

"Hannah, it's okay — it's me, Noah. You're safe, but we need to get out of here. Here, let me help —"

I reached for her arm to help her stand.

"*No!*" She scrambled down the wall away from me. "I won't tell — I won't tell, I promise."

There were thuds coming from around us where Lenny was straddling Carlos' legs, driving blow after blow into the man's stomach. Jock was doing the same, only his blows were landing on Sweats' face.

I didn't even think of stopping them, not when I heard the *crunch* and not when I heard Lenny, who seemed to be taking my command literally, chanting "Please, dude, please shit so I can stop," his voice raspy with tears.

"Hannah," I said, staying where I was so I wouldn't frighten her again. "I can't hold them long — we have to go."

"I didn't see it," she whimpered. "I didn't see it. I won't tell."

*Fuck.*

"Hannah —"

"I didn't see you use it — I didn't see! I won't tell — please don't hurt me. Noah, please, I won't tell."

A chill went through me.

I looked at Hannah's face. Tears streamed down her cheeks, her eyes were wide, pupils huge, her lips trembling with fear.

Not of the men who'd just attacked her.

Of me.

# CHAPTER THIRTY-NINE

I BACKED AWAY.

I didn't know what else to do — I backed away from my friend.

"Hannah, I'm not going to hurt you."

"Please."

I moved back further and pointed toward tree line.

"I won't hurt you, Hannah, get back to campus." I felt Lenny struggle through the link I had with him and had to push more mana down that line as he fought me. "I can't hold them much longer, Hannah, please."

"I won't tell."

"I don't fucking care if you tell, I just want you safe. *Go!*"

I didn't use Command — I had nothing of that left, throwing everything I had into the links with Lenny and Jock — but Hannah took off.

She managed to get to her feet, hopping a couple times as she pulled her jeans up, then ran for the trees.

I stood up slowly and paused.

I didn't want her to think I was chasing her — she was scared enough already.

What had I been thinking? Mel had told me what witches thought of Control and Command. Sam's reaction was ... because she was Sam. She just didn't think the same way as most witches. Hannah did — and most witches were terrified of what I could do.

There was another *crunch* as Jock drove his fist into Sweats' face and Lenny was sobbing as he beat on Carlos' stomach.

I staggered toward the trees.

It became harder and harder to keep the links to Lenny and Jock the farther I got from them, but I didn't let go until I was halfway to the trees. I didn't think either would come after me and I didn't know if Carlos and Sweats were dead. I thought they might be, which meant Lenny and Jock were going to have more to worry about than catching up with me — even if not dead, the two were going to have a hard time explaining to the police how their two friends had been bludgeoned while their own hands showed exactly who did it.

I got to the trees — it wasn't where we'd come in from, but I thought it was close enough that I could find my way back to campus.

The forest was quiet and all I had were the thoughts of what might come next.

I CAUGHT sight of someone in the trees and paused in case it was Hannah so I wouldn't scare her.

It turned out to be two somebodies, and they turned toward me as they caught sight of me, too.

"What are you doing out here?" one of them hissed — I recognized her as one of the seniors who'd led me and the girls to the party.

"Heading back."

"You're *supposed* to meet us at the same place so we can take you back under glamour!"

"Oh," I said, "nobody told me."

The girl stared at me for a second then shook her head.

"Come on."

I followed them through the forest to the Grove, then made my way down the path back to the dorm. I didn't see Hannah on the way, but I also didn't see any mobs with torches and pitchforks, so maybe she hadn't told anyone yet.

Would she tell anyone?

I thought about trying to get into the teacher's lodgings to ask Mel what I should do, but if another teacher saw me there'd be questions and the whole thing would get out — including getting all the girls who'd gone to the party in trouble.

Maybe Hannah wouldn't say anything? I could talk to Mel in the morning.

The dorm building was dark and quiet when I got there. I crept up the stairs and to my room.

Sam was asleep as I let myself in. I was so exhausted, both from the late hour and the amount of mana I'd used, that I didn't even bother undressing — just collapsed onto my bed and closed my eyes to sleep.

Which lasted, it seemed, only a few seconds before someone was pounding on our door.

"*Sleepy-time!*" Sam yelled.

More pounding.

I rolled out of bed, glancing at the clock.

Four a.m. — I'd been asleep for a few hours, but not nearly enough.

Pounding on the door at four a.m. couldn't be good. I wondered if Hannah had told someone about my Command affinity already, but even if she had, *Prima* Rosethorn already knew. Some teachers and students might be upset about it, but the *Prima* and Mel would surely take care of things, right?

Maybe that was wishful thinking on my part.

I opened the door and found the two seniors who'd led us to the party in the hallway with about a half-dozen other girls — not Hannah, so it probably wasn't about that.

"Yeah?" I asked.

"You went to the party with Katrina?" one of the seniors asked.

I blinked, trying to clear my thoughts.

"Not really," I said, "we walked there together, but split up right after. We both got a beer and then went separate ways. Why?"

"Katrina never came back."

---

"USUALLY EVERYONE'S BACK BY ONE," Ava, one of the seniors, said. "But there was some drama and cops got called so things ended early. Everybody else made it back, though. We counted — everyone but Katrina and Hannah."

"Sometimes we miss a girl if we're both glamouring someone back and they don't want to wait for us in the park," the other senior, Isabella said.

"We found Hannah in her room, but we can't find Katrina," Ava went on. "The party's done — the cops came and blocked the whole area off. Some frat guys got in a fight and nearly killed each other and the whole Cove is shut down now. They've got some of the kids who were at the party at the ranger station, but none from Willowmere."

"I snuck over there and looked for shields," Isabella added. "Not a witch in sight — and we just got done searching the campus forest from the Grove to the park — nothing."

"Did she say anything? Was she going to meet a guy? Anything?"

I shook my head. "She asked if I wanted to get a beer and dance, but I told her we'd meet up later. I, uh, wanted to walk around alone first."

"Shit."

"I'm worried," Ava said. "If she was in the group the cops are questioning, Isabella would have seen her shields. Same if she was lost in the woods trying to find the Grove. Unless she was hiding, but why would she do that?"

"What if her shields were down?" I asked.

"Why would they be down — we never take our shields down, even if it's just mundanes around."

"What about drugs?" I asked, thinking of the four guys who'd attacked us. Could they have met up with Katrina first and done something to her?

"We don't do drugs," Ava said. "Witches can get most effects we want just by altering our body chemistries. Why would we need drugs?"

"No," I said, "what if somebody drugged her?"

Ava shrugged. "Then she'd kill him. She'd know as soon as the drink touched her lips there was something in it."

"Even if she didn't know enough magic to kill him," Isabella said, "there were enough witches there to notice if she screamed or something."

"I think we need to talk to *Magistra* Blackwood and *Prima* Rosethorn," I said.

# CHAPTER FORTY

It was nearly ten in the morning before they found Katrina.

Classes were canceled. The teachers and seniors did most of the searching off-campus, using glamour to keep themselves hidden from the police who were still hanging around. The rest of us were set to searching the on-campus part of the forest, gradually expanding the search from the path between the Grove and the State Park to include nearly the entire campus.

Even the school's announcement system sounded subdued when it recalled us all to return to our rooms. There was no official word on Katrina, just that she'd been found and we could stop searching, but the rumors were almost immediate that she was dead. We all figured the announcement would have said if they'd found her alive.

When we got back to our room I just sat on the edge of my bed, arms on my knees and staring at the floor. Sam crawled into my bed and sat with her back to a corner and her knees drawn up to her chest, while Rachel curled up at the bed's foot clutching one of my pillows.

I guess all of us were seeking some kind of comfort and Rachel felt better with Sam and me than her roommate.

I wasn't really seeking comfort — maybe absolution.

"It's my fault," I muttered.

"What? How is it your fault?" Sam leaned forward and laid a hand on my back.

"If I'd been with her, this wouldn't have happened," I said.

"It's not your fault."

"It is," I said, becoming more and more convinced of it as time went on. "If I'd stayed with her..."

Everything bad about last night came down to that one decision. Katrina's death, Hannah being attacked and finding out about my Control resonant — everything. If I'd been with Katrina, she wouldn't have been with whoever killed her. I wouldn't have been on the beach feeling sorry for myself. Hannah wouldn't have found me there. We wouldn't have walked back through the concession stands and run into those bastards.

Everything would have been fine, everyone would have been safe, now it was shit.

"You can't know that," Sam said.

"I can. She just wanted to dance. Her roommate bailed on her and she asked me to dance with her, but I was too caught up in my own shit to spend a little time with her."

Or maybe things would be just as shit.

If I'd been with Katrina, would Hannah have been on the beach by herself? Maybe she would have taken the same path back to campus and been attacked alone, without anyone to help her. Maybe Hannah would be the one dead.

It was all too complicated.

---

I ENTERED *Prima* Rosethorn's office to find her and Mel waiting for me in the sitting area.

The *Prima* gestured for me to sit — the same chair I'd sat in to talk to Priscilla's mom. I wished I could go back and have that conversation again instead of this one.

"We need to ask you some questions about last night, dear," Mel said. "I know it's difficult, but we think you were the last person from Willowmere to see Katrina, before..."

Yeah, "before." People were avoiding saying what came after "before", like it was some evil invocation.

I nodded. "I understand — but I'm not sure what more I can say. We split up right after we got there and I didn't see her again. I didn't —" I swallowed hard against the lump in my throat. "I didn't even see where she went from the beer kegs."

"Anything could be helpful, *Magellus* Ashe," *Prima* Rosethorn said. "Anything at all. Could you start from earlier in the evening — from the first time you saw Katrina yesterday?"

I told them everything I could, starting with Katrina coming up to me in the forest on our way to the party. They scrutinized every word we'd said to each other, asking me to repeat things, to be sure of the words, to tell them about her tone. Everything.

"Did she say anything about meeting someone at the party?"

I shook my head. "No, she seemed upset that her roommate wasn't coming. She wanted to hang out with me."

The questioning went on and by time they were finished I was exhausted. I could tell from their expressions that nothing I'd said had been helpful.

"Tell us about what else you did at the party, Noah," Mel said finally.

I'd been staring at my feet the whole time, but that made me look up. I hadn't had a chance to tell Mel about Hannah and I being attacked — once word got out that Katrina was missing, all the teachers, including Mel, had been busy and I hadn't seen her. I wasn't sure I wanted to tell her in front of *Prima* Rosethorne, but it didn't seem like I had a choice — and the *Prima* would find out anyway. I just didn't want to be there when she did.

So, I described everything I'd done at the party, mostly talk to mundanes about boring things, until I got to the beach and Hannah.

I took a deep breath. "We decided to head back to campus and the shortest route was between the concession buildings. Some guys attacked us there."

"What?" both asked. "You were attacked? Why didn't you tell someone before this?"

"Everything was so busy — I wanted to tell Mel, but once we told you Katrina was missing, I didn't have a chance for anything else. The teachers were all searching the park and we were stuck on campus, then the recall came and we were supposed to go to our rooms."

"Did you not think someone attacking a witch at that party might have some bearing on Katrina's disappearance?"

I did. I almost hoped they had, because then I'd know who needed to be killed in some particularly unpleasant way.

"I was going to, but ... was Katrina ... assaulted?" I couldn't think of any way else to phrase it. "That's what they tried to do to Hannah."

"Not in the way I think you mean," Mel said. "Go on, tell us what happened."

I did. Including Hannah seeing me use Command on the four attackers, what they'd tried to do to her, even how she'd reacted to me after. *Prima* Rosethorn already knew about my resonants and affinities, so I wasn't giving any of that away, and it felt good to tell someone. I hadn't even had a chance to tell Sam yet, since Rachel had been in our room all morning.

Both Mel and *Prima* Rosethorne were silent for a long time when I'd finished. I'd been pretty thorough, not leaving anything at all out.

"While we do not condone the use of magic on mundanes," *Prima* Rosethorn said, "nor the use of that affinity on anyone..." She sighed. "I cannot in good conscience fault you. Neither maintaining the Veil nor our ethics would force a witch to go undefended in the face of such things."

Mel leaned toward me and put a hand on my knee. "You did well, dear. Four attackers, even mundanes, is a lot for you to be faced with. Even Hannah, as a senior, couldn't defend herself as well."

I shrugged. Nothing about the night before felt like I'd done well.

"She hates me now," I mumbled, still trying to comprehend how I'd lost a good friend so quickly.

"We'll speak to Hannah, dear. If she didn't come running to us immediately, then she likely won't tell anyone before we have a chance to talk to her"

I shrugged again. I didn't say I was less concerned about her telling anyone than that one of my few friends here was now terrified of me.

Mel laid a hand on my shoulder. "She's known you for some months — that she didn't rush to *Prima* Rosethorn immediately means she doesn't truly think you're a danger. It was likely just the shock of it coming right on the heels of being attacked that made her react so strongly."

"I think that's all for now," *Prima* Rosethorn said. "It's nearly lunchtime — you should get something to eat."

---

I'D SKIPPED BREAKFAST — most of us had as we were searching the forest for Katrina — and didn't feel like eating still, but Sam and Rachel were waiting for me outside the *Prima*'s office.

They didn't even ask me what happened. Sam just took my arm and pressed close while Rachel took my other hand. The two girls steered me back across the quad to the residence building and toward the cafeteria.

"You need to eat something," Sam said before I even had the chance to object.

With both of them deciding my direction, I didn't bother to protest. The food didn't look appetizing to me, but I took a little — some mac and cheese and a portion of fries. Good comfort food.

The cafeteria was far less full than normal. There were even completely empty tables we passed on the way to the onesies table. It wasn't until we were sitting that I noticed what else was different.

All the girls were staring at me again. And whispering.

I'd gotten so used to it after I first came to Willowmere that I'd barely noticed when they'd gotten used to me and stopped. Now it was all back with a vengeance.

Stares and whispers — and their faces were even more hostile now than when I'd first arrived.

Had Hannah said something? Had the rumor mill already informed everyone that I had the feared Control resonant?

Brittany approached us with her tray — Hannah wasn't with her, which was pretty unusual. In fact, I didn't see Hannah anywhere else in the cafeteria, so she was probably staying in her room. Even without the shock of finding out about my Control resonant, she probably wanted to rest and be alone after just the attack.

Brittany paused a few feet away until Sam caught sight of her.

"What? Are you sitting?"

"Um, yeah," Brittany mumbled with a glance at me. She sat down and bowed her head over her tray.

Sam scanned the cafeteria.

"What's with everybody?"

"Somebody just died?" Rachel suggested.

"Yeah, but —" Sam looked around, frowning. "Why are they looking at us like that?"

"They're looking at Noah," Brittany said, not looking up.

"Why?"

"Katrina was drained and they think Noah did it," Brittany said quickly.

"What?"

Brittany shrugged. "That's what they're saying."

"Who?" Sam asked, looking like she was ready to go do something unpleasant to whoever was named.

Brittany shrugged again. "Everybody?" She glanced quickly at me, then down again. "The teachers haven't said for sure she was drained, but that's what everybody's saying."

Leave it to the Willowmere rumor mill to start spreading things before the body was cold.

"Why do they think Noah did it?" Rachel asked, then laid her hand on my arm, squeezing tightly. "He didn't."

"There're only two things that can drain a witch's mana," Brittany said. "A warlock or a vampire — and the vampires have left witches alone ever since the Hindenburg."

"The blimp?" I asked.

Rachel nodded. "There was a whole vampire clan in the cargo and ballast, trying to get out of Germany, with more ready to follow — the Council sent them a message."

"Noah didn't have anything to do with it," Sam said.

Brittany glanced up but wouldn't meet my eyes. "I'm not saying it, they're saying it."

I looked around the cafeteria again to find more than half the eyes on me with the rest very obviously not on me.

"I'm going back to the room," I said, rising. I didn't want to deal with this shit right now.

I'd liked Katrina. She was smart, funny, and from day one she'd treated me like a person, not a "feral" warlock. Sure, I didn't know her well, just a few hours a week in potions class, but we'd talked there and I'd grown to like her a lot.

Now everyone thought I'd killed her.

Sam and Rachel rose a moment later, picking up their trays as well. Brittany studied my face for a second longer, then stood too.

"You guys don't need to come," I said. "Eat your lunch."

"We're coming," Sam said and Rachel nodded.

They both looked at Brittany who seemed more willing to meet my eye.

"I'm coming," she said. "Nobody could look that upset if they did it."

"SO," Sam said as the door to our room closed behind Brittany who was the last in. I expected Rachel to come in with us, but was a little surprised at Brittany — especially since she was Hannah's sister. "What are we going to do about it?"

"About what?" Brittany asked.

"Convincing everyone that Noah had nothing to do with Katrina's death."

"Won't the teachers do that?" Brittany asked.

"If they could, they would have done it by now."

"What do you mean?" I asked.

I sat on my bed and Sam and Rachel joined me there, one on each side, and when I leaned back to lean against the wall, they both followed. The feel of their arms pressed against mine was comforting, and I'd have liked to put my arms around both of them. I knew Sam would be okay with it and I suspected Rachel would as well, but I didn't want to weird Brittany out.

"If they'd found anything with Katrina's body that could prove who killed her, we'd have heard the Council was coming already."

"The Council?" I asked.

"The Witches Council," Rachel told me. "It's like the government."

"More like the United Nations," Sam said. "They pretend to be on the same page, but everyone's out for themselves."

"Oh."

"So, I think the fact that they haven't called in the Council means they don't know what did it — which means they can't clear Noah that easily. Maybe they could question him under a truth potion — the Council would accept their oath on that."

"Maybe I should go suggest it to *Prima* Rosethorn?" I said.

Sam shook her head. "That's, like, a last resort. Families have too many secrets — nobody really likes to use a truth potion."

"Then how are we supposed to do anything?" Brittany asked.

"The teachers are going to be trying to figure out who did it and prove that," Sam said. "*We* just want to prove Noah *didn't*. So, we might see things differently than them."

"Yeah, but how are we going to see anything?"

"Well, first we need to see Katrina's body," Sam said, holding up a hand to stop their protests. "The first step is to prove *what* killed Katrina. If it was a vampire, then Noah's in the clear, but if it was a warlock we have more work to do."

"Wouldn't the teachers be able to tell if it was a vampire?"

Rachel shook her head. "A vampire bite isn't always clear and a lot of them learn to disguise their bites even from witches"

That confused me.

"Wait, wouldn't a vampire attack be pretty obvious? I mean, if there's no blood in the ... body," I finished, wincing at the thought of Katrina like that.

"That's not how vampires work." Rachel shook her head. "They don't drink blood — it's more of a ... filtering thing."

"How's that?"

"Vampires feed off of mana, not blood. That's why they prefer witches to mundanes, and why witches blew up that blimp to keep more of the creeps out of the country. What they do is their fangs first inject something that attracts mana to the blood, then they drain your blood with one fang while they filter out the mana and then put the blood back with the other fang. That's how they get your mana into them. It's the loss of mana that kills someone, not blood loss."

"Oh."

"If we can find evidence it was a vampire," Sam said, "then we're done. If not, then we're going to need to investigate more." She frowned. "We'll need Hannah."

"Why?" I asked.

I didn't think it would be a good idea to ask Hannah to help me right now.

"So, she can help us," Sam said, then frowned. "We'll need a way to get off campus and into the State Park, too."

"Ava and Isabella will help with that," Brittany said.

"The two seniors who cast the glamour last night?" I asked.

"Yeah — they take their job of guiding us on and off campus safely pretty seriously. They're pissed about what happened to Katrina — and they have some ideas about what to do to whoever killed her once we catch him."

Sam nodded, as though everything was settled. "Okay, Rachel, you go get Isabella; Brittany, you get Ava; and Noah and I will go get Hannah. Meet back here and we'll get started."

## CHAPTER FORTY-ONE

The others left and Sam was ready to go get Hannah, but I held her back.

"What?" Sam asked once we were alone.

I told Sam the whole story. I was expecting her to think it was a big deal, but she just shrugged.

"Okay, let's go talk to her."

I blinked. "Did you hear what I just said? She knows I have Control and a Command affinity – I don't think she'll want to talk to me."

"I'll talk; you just sit there and look harmless."

"I don't know if this is a good idea – she was pretty freaked out."

Sam snorted, grabbed my hand, and dragged me out of the room.

"Hannah freaks out all the time. I'll talk her down."

We went downstairs to the seniors' dorms and found Hannah's room.

"Hannah!" Sam called out, knocking on the door – not loudly enough to be heard by any of the girls in nearby rooms, but definitely enough to be heard by Hannah. "Hey! Hannah! Open up, we need to talk."

"Go away!"

"We need to talk, Hannah, it's important!"

"I don't want to talk to anyone right now!"

"Hannah, if you don't let me in, I'm going to tell the whole school what we did at my thirteenth birthday party."

Hannah didn't answer right away.

"What did you do?" I whispered.

Sam glared at me. "It's an effective threat because it's *a secret*."

"Oh."

"I mean it, Hannah!"

There were muffled curses and the door opened a crack.

"You *swore* —" Hannah broke off as she saw me and would have slammed the door if Sam hadn't wedged her foot in it.

"He's not going to hurt you," Sam said. "He's not going to make you do anything, either."

Hannah stared at Sam, eyes widening.

"You know?"

Sam nodded. "I promise he won't hurt you. We need to talk — it's for Katrina."

I wasn't sure what Sam thought we needed Hannah for, but I hoped she wasn't just using that to get us in.

"I —" Hannah's shoulders sagged and she opened the door. "I suppose if I say no, he can just make me."

"It's not like that," Sam said, tugging me in and closing the door behind us.

Hannah's room was much like Sam's and mine, except she and her roommate had bunkbeds instead of two singles. That gave them space to have a small, two-person couch in the space the other bed would be in, and they had a midsized TV on a swinging arm that could be viewed from the couch.

Hannah gestured to the couch, then sat on the lower bunk. She looked down at her feet.

"I haven't told," she said quietly, and in that I heard the echo of her the night before, whimpering over and over her promise not to tell anyone.

"Good — so, what's your problem?" Sam asked.

"What? You know what —"

"What? Say it."

Hannah looked at me like this might be some kind of trick. Like I was testing her promise not to tell anyone.

"Eyes here," Sam said, pointing at her own. "Don't worry about him — now, tell me, what's the problem?"

Hannah swallowed hard and mumbled, "He has Control."

"I can't hear you."

"He has Control!" Hannah said, sitting up and pointing at me. "And Command!"

"Which he used to save your butt last night, right? And which, in three months here, he hasn't used on anyone."

"How do you know that?" Hannah asked. "My mom says the warlocks who were really good with Command could make you do something and think it was your idea."

"Come on," Sam said. "This is Noah we're talking about —"

"Thanks Sam," I said.

"— he's not that good."

"Hey!"

"I'm not saying you're *bad*, but you're a first-year, not some Svengali mind-melder. Besides, that's not how Command works — it can't make you think differently."

"How do you know he hasn't used it on you?" Hannah asked.

"He has."

"*What?*"

Crap — why did Sam have to tell her that?

"I asked him to."

"*Why?*"

Sam shrugged. "I wanted to see what it was like."

Hannah stared at her.

"Crone's bunions, you're worse than Brittany when you get curious about something. But *why* would you trust him?"

"*Nobody's* as curious as Brittany," Sam said. "I trusted him because of how I found out. Do you know why Noah and I are partnered in Intro to Spellcasting?"

Hannah shook her head.

"*Magistra* Blackwood was going to do it, because he's ... you know, a *boy*, but I offered." She shrugged. "I could see all the other onesies were paired up and you know none of the dualies would want to partner with me — so I asked Noah; I figured, how bad could it be?"

"Right here."

Sam stuck her tongue out at me.

Hannah frowned, thinking.

"Wait — if you partnered with him for shield work, then you'd see his resonants. You've known since then?"

Sam nodded.

"Since the *first day* of school?"

Sam nodded again.

"How could you find that out and trust him on the first day?"

Sam put her hand over mine — which was in my lap and very close to something that suddenly took notice. Her eyes softened and she pursed her lips before turning back to Hannah.

"Because he was worried I'd be hurt if he said no without a good reason — and he didn't want to lie to me. Rather than do either of those things, he told me a secret that could literally get him killed."

Hannah looked from Sam to me and back several times.

"That's —" she said, finally, "— that's..."

"Trustworthy?" I offered. "Noble?"

"*So fucking stupid!*" Hannah's brow furrowed. "What kind of *idiot* would tell a secret like that to someone he'd just met? That's even dumber than what *she* did trusting you."

"He's a guy," Sam said. "Hannah, think about what happened last night and what you're really scared of. This is *Noah*."

I waited for her to drop the other shoe and take a dig at me, but she didn't.

"He's not a Family warlock," Sam went on. "He wasn't raised in the Families — in a lot of ways, he's just a regular guy. A good guy."

Hannah stared at me and I did my best to look harmless.

"You really trust him?"

"Yeah. More than you'd believe. He saved my life, right?"

Hannah took a deep breath. "Yeah."

She was quiet for a long time, then looked at me. "Um, about last night —"

I didn't want to talk about that, not when it looked like Hannah was going to be okay with me. Or, if not totally okay, then at least willing to overlook that resonant.

"Hannah," I said quickly, "that big guy hit me so hard ... I don't remember a thing from the time he connected until I woke up this morning. It's a complete blank."

Hannah's eyes got watery. "Thank you."

The school's announcement system picked that time to blare, "Noah Ashe, please report to *Prima* Rosethorn's office immediately."

"Maybe they have more questions about last night," I said.

"You go," Sam said, "we'll meet you back in our room after."

I nodded, gave Hannah what I hoped was a nice smile, and went through the door. As I closed it behind me, I heard:

"What was it like?"

*PRIMA* ROSETHORN'S outer office was empty except for her receptionist, who motioned me to the sitting area to sit down and wait.

After a few minutes of sitting there and her shuffling through papers, she looked at me.

"Noah, you can go in now."

I was kind of curious how *Prima* Rosethorn let her know she was ready for me, since I hadn't heard or seen any sort of notice.

I suppressed a sigh of relief as I entered the *Prima*'s office and saw Mel was there too. *Prima* Rosethorn was sitting behind her desk and Mel was in one of the two chairs in front of the desk — I stayed standing until *Prima* Rosethorn spoke.

"Have a seat, Noah."

I sat and Mel gave me a look that I hoped was supposed to be reassuring.

"Did you have more questions for me?" I asked.

"Much the same questions, I'm afraid."

"What does that mean?"

*Prima* Rosethorn pursed her lips. "We've just received word that multiple Families are sending representatives to monitor our investigation into Katrina's death. Which presents us a problem with you, given the manner in which she was killed."

"Me?"

"Yes. I'm sure the school rumor mill has it widely known that Katrina was killed by the draining of all her mana."

I nodded.

"There being only two things who can kill a witch by draining — a vampire or a warlock — and you being the only warlock on campus will raise certain concerns amongst those representatives."

"*We* believe you had nothing to do with it, dear," Mel said, "but these witches will have no reason to trust you."

*Prima* Rosethorn nodded. "Yes, we would like to put their concerns to rest as soon as possible — which is why we'd like you to agree to us questioning you again in a slightly different manner."

"You don't have to agree," Mel said. "No one will force you — but if we can tell those who doubt conclusively you weren't involved, that you were questioned in this way, and satisfied us that you had no involvement, it would go a long way toward avoiding any trouble their concerns might cause."

*Prima* Rosethorn nodded. "And better the two of us question you in this way than waiting for those representatives to arrive. If they wished to be present, or, worse, ask you questions themselves, it's possible your secrets would be revealed."

"Questioned in this manner" had a slightly ominous ring to it. That sort of concerned me. These were witches, after all, and witch history had a lot of suspect questioning methods in it. Sure, the witches were usually the targets of those methods, but that didn't mean it wasn't what they had in mind.

"What sort of methods?"

Mel laughed. "He thinks we mean the Inquisition," she said.

*Prima* Rosethorn raised her eyebrows. "We're not talking about some sort of torture; besides, such methods aren't very effective."

Mel laughed again. "Arguably they're very effective, in my experience — not so much for getting a truthful confession, but for getting actual information from someone who has it? Quite."

Both *Prima* Rosethorn and I stared at Mel for a moment.

"What? Am I wrong?"

*Prima* Rosethorn cleared her throat.

"A discussion for another day, perhaps." She turned her attention back to me. "No, what I have in mind is a simple potion which would ensure that your answers to our questions are truthful."

Like Sam had mentioned. "Some kind of truth serum?"

"A potion. Magic," Mel said. "You won't be compelled to speak or be forced to answer questions, but the magic will ensure anything you do say is entirely truthful."

"It will also lower your inhibitions for a short time," *Prima* Rosethorn said, "making you more willing to offer up information. Which is why we'd prefer not to give the Family representatives a chance to question you directly."

"Sure," I said. "I didn't do anything to Katina, and if something can prove I'm telling the truth, then I'm willing to do it."

Maybe this would even be enough to settle the rumors going around the school, too.

"Thank you, *Magellus* Ashe," *Prima* Rosethorn said. She pulled a potion bottle from her desk and slid it across to me. "If you'll drink this — the effects should last no more than a few minutes."

I reached for the bottle, but Mel laid a hand on my wrist, stopping me.

"Remember — the potion will not compel you to answer, but if you do, the answer must be the truth. You are allowed to have secrets, just not about this. So, you are not required to compromise anything else."

"True," *Prima* Rosethorn said. "That's why Melaina is here — as the closest you have to a guardian or Family. If it was another student, we would not do this without a representative of her Family here to ensure that Family secrets are kept so."

I nodded that I understood and Mel took her hand from my wrist — it wasn't like I had any secrets, anyway. Well, my plans with Sam were a secret, so I'd have to be careful not to say anything about that. I lifted the potion bottle and unstoppered it — the stench of its contents hit me even before I raised it to my face. Was there some rule that most potions had to be nasty?

"It is not the most pleasant," *Prima* Rosethorn acknowledged.

I scrunched up my nose, took a deep breath and raised the bottle to my lips — then paused.

"Um, this is, like, for one person? The whole thing?"

"Yes," Mel said, chuckling. "It is one dose, not intended for an entire coven to share."

"Just checking."

Another deep breath and I downed the potion — it was thick and syrupy, and tasted like soapy feet. No, I have no idea what soapy feet taste like, but this tasted like soapy feet.

It also burned.

My lips, my tongue, my throat, and then my stomach all felt like they were on fire as I could trace the potion's path.

"Ugh," I said, trying to generate enough spit to clear my mouth and eliminate both the taste and the sensation.

The burning sensation started spreading from my stomach

through the rest of me — but at least that seemed to distribute the burning as well, and it eventually settled down to a slightly too warm feeling covering my entire body.

"It should take effect immediately," *Prima* Rosethorn said, "so we'll get right to it. Noah, did you know Katrina Cartright?"

"Sort of," I found myself saying. "We took potions together and she sat at my table but we didn't see each other outside class — she had nicer boobs than Sylvia and she wasn't a bitch to me so we talked and flirted a little bit."

I was babbling. I knew I was babbling. Everything I said was truthful, but I wasn't sure why I felt it necessary to say so much.

"That's enough," *Prima* Rosethorn said, and I felt the babbling stop.

It's weird to say that, but I could feel the babbling like a physical thing inside me.

"Try to concentrate on short, truthful answers," Mel said. "As well as the actual topic of the question."

I nodded, but I wasn't sure I was going to be able to concentrate on anything — the just too warm sensation covering my body had changed to a tingling. My lips were numb, and my vision was a little blurry. It felt like I was drunk, but Mel and *Prima* Rosethorn wouldn't get me drunk, would they?

I blinked a couple times trying to clear my vision and looked at Mel.

"Are you feeling all right, Noah?"

"I'm feeling ... fantastic! Really, really good, actually."

And I was — it felt like I was floating, not sitting in a chair, and waves were rolling through my body. Like massaging hands running over me from top to bottom. I looked at Mel and *Prima* Rosethorn, waiting for the next question.

While I looked at them, I noticed that Mel was looking particularly lovely today. She had on a tight knit sweater and a pencil skirt, both of which clung to her generous figure. The skirt rode up to mid-thigh as she was sitting, and I wondered how high her hose went — if they were pantyhose or stockings? Maybe a garter belt? Her long dark hair was draped over her shoulders flowing over her ample breasts. Those breasts filled and stretched her sweater like balloons. Sweater-balloons.

"Pretty," I murmured, staring at the sweater balloons.

"Noah?"

"Balloons," I murmured through a grin.

Mel frowned.

"Let me see that bottle," she said.

"Pretty, pretty," I said, handing it to her.

Mel sniffed the bottle, then set it on *Prima* Rosethorn's desk with a sigh.

"I assume you got that from Lisandra?"

"Of course," *Prima* Rosethorn said. "Is something the matter?"

"Did you happen to tell *Magistra* Fallowell who it was for?"

The *Prima* and *Magistra* Fallowell had talked about me. Tiny, delicate, beautiful *Magistra* Fallowell.

*Prima* Rosethorn shook her head. "I asked her to send several over this morning, once it became clear we might need to question some students."

Mel sighed.

I liked the sigh. It did things to the sweater balloons.

"Noah? Noah? Noah!"

I raised my gaze to Mel's face, watching as she said my name. Her mouth was very pretty too.

"Pretty," I said smiling.

"What's wrong with him?" *Prima* Rosethorn asked.

"This particular potion is designed to merge with the mana a witch generates. The merging allows her to burn off the effects of the potion rather quickly, which is why it only lasts for a few minutes ... on a witch."

"But warlocks don't generate as much mana of their own. All their mana is in their resonant stores, so there's nothing to bind up the potion," *Prima* said, lowering her head and shaking it. "Willowmere is not having a good year with potions, it seems. What effect will it have on him? And, whatever it is, I'll remind you this is the natural result of adding a warlock to the school when there hasn't been one here in so long. No one thinks to consider their differences."

"We can discuss that later," Mel said. "For now, we can expect the effects to last on him for an hour or more — perhaps two — and be much stronger than on a witch, especially the reduction of his inhibitions, which makes someone more comfortable telling the truth."

"So, no lasting ill effects?"

I reached out a finger to touch Mel's pretty lips, but she swatted it away and gave me a glare.

"Not to anything but his dignity," she said.

"So perhaps we should finish the questioning, and then put him somewhere safe for it to wear off?"

"Safe and alone."

"Very well, *Magellus* Ashe? *Magellus* Ashe?"

I turned to *Prima* Rosethorn — she was quite attractive too, though older looking than Mel. She was still a handsome woman, with a good figure, even though the clothes she wore weren't as tight as Mel's.

"You're pretty too," I said, not wanting *Prima* Rosethorn to feel left out.

Something about that felt inappropriate, but I didn't care. It was the truth.

"Yes, we'll skip the preliminaries and get this done with as quickly as possible. *Magellus* Ashe, did you kill Katrina Cartwright?"

I shook my head emphatically. "No. I liked Katrina. She had sweater pillows."

*Prima* Rosethorn sighed. "Do you know anything about the circumstances of Katrina Cartwright's death?"

I shook my head again. "No, I think I know she was found in the State Park forest, and that she was drained of mana — you told me that — and that it's very sad."

"Did you see Katrina Cartwright after your arrival at the party last night?"

"No — I wish I had. I wish I'd danced with her. Maybe she'd be alive if I hadn't been selfish."

*Prima* Rosethorn drew in a sharp breath. "I … I believe that's all I care to ask him in this state."

Mel nodded. "It should be sufficient for us to assure the Cartwrights that we can conclude he had nothing to do with Katrina's death."

"Should we put him in the infirmary until this wears off?"

"Katrina's body is there," Mel said quietly. "I don't think it would be kind to leave him in the same room with her — nor do I think he should be in the infirmary when her Family arrives. Especially in this state."

"You said it will wear off in an hour or two?"

Mel nodded. "Possibly more, depending on his metabolism."

"Then perhaps if you escort him back to his room, he can remain there — we can ask *Magella* Prescott to use the library for a few hours before returning to their room."

"That would be best," Mel said, standing.

Standing made her skirt slide back down her thighs, that was disappointing, but it also put her butt at my eye-level.

"Pretty."

# CHAPTER FORTY-TWO

MEL AND I LEFT *PRIMA* ROSETHORN'S OFFICE.

"I'm sorry, Noah," Mel said once we were out on the empty quad. "I should've checked which potion she intended to give you to see if there were any side effects for warlocks. I expected her to do that check herself, but I sometimes forget how very long it's been since warlocks attended Willowmere."

"That's okay," I said, falling a step or two behind her so I could watch her butt. I knew that was inappropriate, but I couldn't seem to help myself. "I feel really good."

Mel snapped her fingers.

"Up with me, if you will, dear," she said causing me to jump and skip a couple steps so that I was beside her again. "At least it's chosen to interact with the least harmful of your resonants."

I thought about what she said. Apparently, I'd been right to blame the potion for how I couldn't seem to stop staring at Mel's attributes, but did that mean there'd been a chance for it to affect either of my other resonants? What would've happened if it had bound to Control? Would I have started trying to boss Mel and *Prima* Rosethorn around? Or if Pain, would I have tried to hurt someone?

"The effects should last no more than an hour or two longer," Mel said. "We just need to keep you away from others until it wears off, or you'll wind up babbling about how pretty all the girls are — or answering all their questions with the absolute truth, as I don't think it would take them long to figure out all the effects of the potion."

I shuddered at the thought of having to answer any questions the girls might put to me — I knew how a group of guys would take advantage of a girl they found in this position.

"Noah," Mel said as we were halfway across the deserted quad, "what you said in *Prima* Rosethorn's office — about being selfish and Katrina possibly being alive if you'd stayed with her? You do know that's not the case, don't you? We can't what-if our every decision when something bad happens to others.

I nodded. I did know that — but I didn't feel that. I think the feeling would take a lot longer.

"I know — sort of," I said. "If I'd stayed with her, if I hadn't gone at all — it might be different, you know? Or if Ada and Isabella had made a mistake with their glamour and we got caught? It's like all these things that could have changed it."

"There are any number of things one can look at that way. If Willowmere had no tradition of students sneaking off campus to the Cove parties in the first place? If the staff didn't overlook such things? Should we blame *Prima* Rosethorn for Katrina's death?"

I stopped walking. "What? *Prima* Rosethorn knew?"

Mel sighed. "Do you really think the school wards wouldn't notice dozens of students crossing them? The tradition's been in place since the first time the mundanes held a party at the Cove. Decades." She chuckled. "Most of the faculty attended Willowmere themselves, you know, do you suppose they've forgotten?"

Did everybody except the students know what the students were up to?

"Why?" I asked.

"Because it's fun. It's rebellious. Half the reason first-years aren't allowed off-campus in the first semester is to build up resentment for the restriction, then see which students decide to rebel and go to the Cove. The girls have fun, the faculty learns something about them, and it's ... it was quite safe."

Mel resumed walking and I followed.

"The point, dear, is do we go all the way back to the first girl who snuck off campus and started the tradition and blame her for Katrina's death? Some things are no one's fault but the one who did the act."

I nodded, but it still didn't change what I felt.

We entered the dorm building and got at least as much attention as I had when I'd left earlier. I wondered if Mel returning with me would add a positive or negative spin to the rumor mill.

"Here we are, dear," Mel said as we reached my door. "I suggest you lie down and have a nice nap while this wears off. *Prima* Rosethorn will ensure Samantha understands not to return for at least two hours."

I slid between Mel and the door facing her.

"Well, if she won't be back for a couple hours, why don't you slip inside with me and we can make the most of the privacy?"

*Oh, no,* I thought. *Was that me? Did I just ask that? What the hell is wrong with me? Did I just suggest...*

"Hhmm," Mel said, her face becoming thoughtful. She licked her lips and raised one hand to rest her fingertips on my chest, then leaned toward me. "That is a very ... interesting suggestion. How might we spend that time?"

*Oh, no, is she... Would she really be into it? And had I managed to trigger her interest with such a lame fucking line?*

Mel leaned forward, her lips suddenly inches from mine.

I quickly glanced around, the hallway was empty with all the girls either in their rooms or down in the common room and cafeteria. Thoughts of rolling around my narrow bed with Mel flashed through my head ... even if she was four thousand years old or something like that, she was still probably the hottest woman on campus.

I closed my eyes and leaned toward her.

The door latch clicked, the door behind me opened, and Mel pushed me backward into my room.

"I'm going to spell the latch so that it won't open from the inside for two hours, dear. I don't want you running amok with your irresistible charms amongst the girls."

Mel pulled the door shut and a moment later I saw a sparkle of light through the door's edge and a click from the latch. I tried to open the door but it wouldn't budge.

"I'm not sure if I should be disappointed or not," I murmured.

I turned around, stripping off my shirt for a nap, and found five heads staring at me from around the short entryway's corners.

Hannah, Brittany, Rachel, Ava, and Isabella were all crowded at the head of each bed, trying to stay out of sight of the doorway.

"We hid when we heard *Magistra* Blackwood's voice outside," Hannah said. "If she saw us in here, she might suspect something's up."

I'd forgotten Sam had told the others to get Ava and Isabella then meet us back in our room.

"Good thinking," I said, trying to think of a way to get them out quickly so I could lie down alone and stop embarrassing myself.

I froze, remembering. The door was locked, and spelled not to open for two hours.

"What did *Prima* Rosethorn say?" Brittany asked.

"She asked me questions. She seemed to believe me," I said, fighting the urge to try and quote my entire conversation with *Prima* Rosethorn verbatim. I managed to convince myself that I truthfully answered the intent of the question, if not literally, but it was really hard.

"That's good," Rachel said. "Where's Sam? Did she not come back with you?"

"Sam is in the library for at least two hours."

"Why?"

I struggled, I tried so hard, to find a way to phrase my answer, but both mind and body betrayed me, because all I could think about was being locked in my bedroom for two hours with five beautiful girls.

"Because *Prima* Rosethorn gave me a truth potion that made me tell the absolute truth for the next two hours and has the side effect of making me feel drunk and horny."

Ava and Isabella stared at me. Rachel turned bright red and her hand rose to cover her mouth, while Brittany couldn't seem to stop blinking and Hannah's mouth kept opening and closing like a fish gulping air.

"See? I have no filter. I answer every question and can't stop looking at pretty boobs."

My problem now was that I'd entered the room and there were five sets of pretty boobs kneeling on the beds and I couldn't pick which set to look at. I decided to be fair and give them all equal time.

"Oh," Isabella said, face growing nearly as red as Rachel's.

"I should go to sleep for the next two hours," I said.

"Yes!" Brittany said.

"Absolutely!" Hannah agreed. "We'll go back to our rooms now and you let Sam come get us when you're feeling better."

I moved out of the way as they rushed past me, heading for the door, but knew it was no use.

I entered the main part of our room while they clustered by the door, Hannah rattling the doorknob and trying to open it.

I sat down on my bed.

"Mel spelled the latch not to open for two hours so no one would have to be in here with me in this state."

I kicked my shoes off as the girls crept slowly back into the main room.

"This is not fair," Brittany said.

Ava nodded. "We did try."

"Try what?" I asked.

"We tried to leave," Isabella said. "We tried to do the right thing, but you can't expect us to sit in your room for two hours with you like this and not..."

"Not what?"

The five girls sat on Sam's bed and stared at me intently.

Hannah narrowed her eyes.

I stared back — well, my stare was a little lower than theirs, but I did stare.

The silence stretched on long enough to make me a little nervous and I raised my gaze to the girls' faces.

They each had an intense, almost hungry look, staring at me intently. Ava's tongue wet her lips. Brittany's lips were slightly parted and she breathed deeply, making what I'd just been staring at even more distracting. Rachel's brow was creased, as though she was worried, and Hannah ... I think I might have been safer when Hannah was afraid of me.

I edged back on my bed to put my back against the wall. Part of me did it to put more distance between myself and those piercing gazes — a different part decided that if I was going to be trapped in the room for two hours with five girls who looked like they were about to devour me, I should at least get comfortable.

What was this? What had gotten into them?

Was it my Lust resonant?

I knew if the mana in my resonants got out of balance it could affect me — did the truth potion interacting with that somehow give off a fuck-me vibe the girls were picking up on? *Magistra* Fallowell had the Allure affinity — had the truth potion triggered that in me, too?

Was ... was there going to be a perilous orgy?

I took a deep breath and braced myself to welcome the peril.

"Girls?" I asked, slowly and carefully. "What are you doing?"

Rachel held back a bit, frowning more, but the other four girls leaned toward me. Ava put a hand on my bed, and as though that was some kind of signal, the others did as well. Leaning forward ... shirts draping open to expose cleavage and bras. Isabella's bra was pink lace, very sheer, and exposed her —

"Remember we did try," Ava said.

Rachel remained sitting, but the other four came closer, putting their other hand on my bed, moving in unison like a pack of hunting cats, stalking me.

"We tried to leave," Hannah said.

"We tried to be good," Isabella purred.

It was a purr; I can't describe it any other way.

"Um, could we maybe talk about this?" I asked.

If it was some combination of the potion and my Lust resonant working on them, I didn't want something to happen that they might regret — the look on Ava's face made my mouth go dry — or that I might not survive.

"No!"

The girls pounced, turning to sit on my bed, making it bounce as they seated themselves and leaned in toward me.

"Who do you think is the prettiest girl in the school?" Hannah asked.

"No, no," Brittany said. "Who do you have a *crush* on in school?"

"Oh, forget that," Ava said. "What's The Blackwood really like?"

"Yeah, yeah," Isabella demanded eagerly. "Is she really as powerful as they say?"

I nearly bit my tongue in half to keep from speaking. I clenched my jaw and tried to concentrate — because even if I wasn't compelled to answer, the damn potion had me so loopy that I almost couldn't control myself. There was no way this ended well — no answer to any of those questions that wouldn't get me in trouble with somebody, and I just knew worse questions were on their way. The only thing going in my favor was that the questions were coming so fast I didn't have a chance to babble before the next one came.

"Who in this school would you least like to be stuck on a deserted island with and why?"

"No, no, who would you *most* like to be stuck on a desert island with and why?"

"Do you have a crush on anyone?"

"Have you ever kissed a girl?"

"Who would you *like* to kiss?"

"Have you ever *more* than kissed a girl?"

"Who would you *like* to more than kiss?"

I closed my eyes and covered my ears with my hands. I'd have chanted "la-la-la-la" if I thought it might help.

"Guys, come on," Rachel said. "This isn't fair."

"We're just having fun!"

"No, you're not," Rachel said.

I felt movement in the room and opened my eyes to find myself staring at Rachel's butt — she'd stood up and pushed the others off my bed, putting herself between us, hands on hips and staring them down.

"*Magistra* Blackwood wouldn't have locked him in here if she didn't think he needed to be alone — what do you think she's going to do when she finds out you all took advantage of Noah's condition to embarrass him?"

"We're not trying to embarrass him, we're trying to solicit valuable information."

"If there's any doubt," I offered, "you're embarrassing me."

"See?"

I resisted the urge to grab Rachel's butt — it was just so firm and cute, and she was adorable when she got wound up. I was sad that the only time she stood up to others was to defend somebody — or yell at a spellstick game — and not to stand up for herself. She was always so quiet and shy when it was about her.

I hoped defending me didn't make her explode.

Hannah huffed.

"So, what are we supposed to do for two hours, just sit here?"

"Yes, that's exactly what I expect you to do." Rachel turned around. "Noah, you need — what are you doing with your hands?"

My hands were raised to my chest level — her butt's — with fingers curled and ready to grab something. I quickly straightened my fingers and raised my hands higher.

"I was going to grab your butt," I said, entirely truthfully, "but I surrender to your fierceness. What do you want me to do?"

Rachel looked at my hands, which I'd raised so that they were now level with her boobs.

She blushed and stammered, "I — you —" she took a deep breath. "You should lie down and sleep this off." She turned around to face Hannah and the others again, covering her butt with her hands. "And you all, sit there and be quiet and let him sleep. I don't care if you take a nap, or do your homework, or just sit there and stare at the wall, but leave Noah alone."

She sat down on the edge of my bed, apparently fully prepared to stay there and guard me while I slept the potion off. Which seemed to me an awfully good idea, so I did lie down and close my eyes.

# CHAPTER FORTY-THREE

The sound of a door closing woke me up.

I opened my eyes to find Rachel exactly where she'd been when I fell asleep, sitting on the edge of my bed glaring at the other girls who were all on Sam's bed with either laptops or books. Aside from Brittany who seemed to have fallen asleep leaning against her sister's shoulder.

Sometime in my sleep, I'd stretched an arm out and my fingertips were touching Rachel's thigh — I figured if she hadn't moved it while I was asleep then she didn't mind.

"Sorry I'm late — *Prima* Rosethorn said Noah needed some time to recover from a potion and sent me to the library," Sam said, coming into the main room. "Did I miss anything?"

"*Prima* Rosethorn gave Noah a potion that made him tell the truth for two hours," Brittany said.

"And stare at our boobs," Ava added.

"I'm pretty sure that was just Noah," Rachel said. "He does that."

"A truth potion? Really?" Sam asked. She bounced onto my bed beside Rachel. "What'd we find out? Dish!"

"Nothing," Isabella said, clearly disappointed.

"What? How not?"

"Rachel wouldn't let us."

"Why not?" Sam asked, glaring at Rachel.

"It wouldn't be fair," Rachel said. "They were trying to take advantage of him."

Sam put an arm around Rachel's shoulders, drawing her close.

"That's so sweet — we really need to work on your corruption-level." Sam sighed. "Okay, missed opportunity." She turned her attention to Ava and Isabella. "Anyway, we wanted to talk to you two because we're going to try and clear Noah of Katrina's murder and could use your help. Plus, if we're looking at things that way, we might find some evidence the teachers are missing."

Ava glanced at Brittany and Rachel. "They told us — count us in."

I was a little surprised that Ava and Isabella were so quick to agree — and, now that my head had cleared and I could think about it — that they hadn't seemed to suspect me when I'd first come back to the room.

"You believe I didn't do it?" I asked.

"Most of the seniors do," Isabella said. "You're a first-year — there's no way you could hide something like that from *Prima* Rosethorn and the rest of the faculty, so if they haven't locked you up, you probably didn't do it."

"It's only the lower grades that are freaking out about you," Ava added.

"We're more mature," Isabella said.

I remembered the questions they'd asked before Rachel intervened and had to question that.

"Good," Sam said. "We have two paths to investigate. First, we want to check Katrina's body for any hidden vampire marks, since a vampire could have done this. Second, we want to check out where she was found — that's where Hannah comes in."

"Why her?" Ava asked, making me glad that I didn't have to for once.

"Hannah's got Hindsight," Brittany said.

"Oh," the other girls said together.

I sighed, resigned to my place in witch society. "What's Hindsight?"

"Do you remember the replays at the spellstick tryouts?" Rachel asked, then when I nodded, "That's Hindsight."

"Which is a big part of why we believe you didn't do it," Ava said. "The teachers would have cast Hindsight on the scene first thing and there's no way a first-year warlock could keep them from seeing him do it."

Isabella nodded.

"Ava, you and Isabella are the best glamours in the school," Sam said. Both girls nodded as though simply acknowledging a known fact. "I think it would be best to split up and do both things at once, rather than some of us waiting around or all of us trying to sneak into the same place."

Everybody nodded agreement.

"Isabella, you, me, and Rachel will sneak into the clinic to look at Katrina. Rachel's the closest thing we have to an expert on vampires, since the Winthrops know a lot about them." Rachel flushed a little, but didn't object. "Then Ava, you take Noah, Brittany, and Hannah into the State Park. Hannah, we need your Hindsight there."

The girls nodded, but all looked a little nervous.

"Any thoughts before we get started?" Sam asked and all the girls shook their heads.

"Sounds like a plan," Ava said.

I scooted around to get my feet off my bed and sit like everyone else.

"Um, I'd just like to say I appreciate you all going to bat for me like this."

Sam, Rachel, Brittany, and even Hannah gave me small smiles, but Ava and Isabella shared a look.

"Ava and I are doing this for Katrina," Isabella said. "We might not think you had anything to do with it, but if we find out you did, I'll kill you myself."

It was a fair point.

---

THE FOREST WAS bright with sunlight streaming through the leaves as we passed Willowmere's Grove and made our way toward the State Park.

That felt wrong to me — we were on our way to the scene of a murder. We should have been walking through gloomy shadows with an eerie wind blowing, not sunlight and birdsong.

Our group was far less upbeat than the forest. Ava led the way, quietly keeping up her glamour to conceal us. We crossed the wards to leave the campus without incident and I wondered if the wards had notified *Prima* Rosethorn. Was four students crossing different than forty? Would *Prima* Rosethorn be too occupied with other things to notice, or would she let us go?

Either way, we crossed the wards and no one stopped us.

Other than a brief tingle of mana from the wards, there was no sign of the change, only a gradual thinning of the trees until we reached the tree line around the State Park's Cove.

I saw yellow police tape blocking off the space between the concession stands where Hannah and I had been attacked by the four frat guys, but there was no police presence left. I thought that must mean none of the four had died — if it had been more than assault the police were dealing with, they'd surely still be processing the scene.

Still, we stayed inside the trees and worked our way around the Cove's parking lot to where we'd heard Katrina's body was found, just in case.

I caught Hannah staring at the concession stands as we walked.

I'd stared at them too, but Hannah couldn't seem to tear her gaze away and her face was haunted. That was understandable, given what had happened — and almost happened — the night before, but I didn't think it was good for her to dwell on it that much, so I stepped forward, blocking her view of the concessions as we walked.

Hannah looked me in the eye for a few steps, then returned to looking forward, but her hand reached out and clasped mine.

I gave her hand a little squeeze and when she didn't let go, I didn't either, but Brittany, walking on her other side, caught the little exchange and looked at me quizzically.

Things were getting complicated, I guess.

I'd told Sam what had happened the night before — and *Prima* Rosethorn and Mel, of course — but no one else, and if Hannah hadn't told anyone, even her sister, then I wouldn't either, which would leave Brittany wondering what had suddenly happened to get Hannah holding my hand as we walked toward a murder site.

A minute later, Ava stopped.

"I think this is near where they found her," she whispered.

I looked around — nothing in the forest would suggest there'd been a murder. I'd expect there to be signs of a struggle, broken tree limbs, crushed plants, even blood — but things were as peaceful as if nothing had happened here.

Ava looked expectantly at Hannah.

"Um, that's not how it works," Hannah said.

"What do you mean?"

Hannah licked her lips and looked around.

"I'm not very strong yet," she said. "I mean, I have a lot of mana — for me — right now, after what happ ... just, from stuff."

I caught Brittany giving her sister a worried look. I thought Hannah might be referring to us being attacked, but didn't know what that might have to do with how much mana she had.

"But I need specifics," Hannah went on. "I need to be within about twenty feet of where someone was and know when they were there — by about five minutes."

Ava looked around, clearly frustrated.

"The teachers found her body," Ava said. "We don't know exactly where or when she died. Did we come out here for nothing?"

"I'm sorry," Hannah said. "Once I have a handle on the past, I can follow someone, but I have to stay within twenty feet of them, and I need a starting place and time"

"You have no idea how infuriating playing hide-and-seek with her was," Brittany muttered.

"Like knowing where someone's going to hide ahead of time isn't cheating," Hannah shot back at her sister.

"This isn't a game!" Ava yelled. "What are we supposed to do now?"

"I'm sorry," Hannah said. "I — I'm not that strong."

I gave the hand I was still holding a squeeze.

"Hey, we'll figure this out," I said, thinking about it. "How long can you follow someone or whatever once you find them?"

Hannah shrugged. "That's easy — a couple hours."

I nodded. "Okay, come on."

I tugged her hand and led her out of the trees into the parking lot.

"What are you doing?" Ava hissed. "Someone might see us! I can't maintain a glamour out in the open like that!"

I shrugged, still walking and pulling Hannah along. "So? What's the worst that could happen? They'll tell us to leave."

"What? No! There was a crime here last night!"

I knew she was talking about the frat guys beating each other up, not Katrina.

"So?"

Ava sputtered. "The mundane police could be watching — you know, surveillance! Waiting for someone to come back to the scene or whatever!"

I paused and grinned, thankful that for once I knew something the witches didn't.

"I think you watch too many TV shows. It was a fight — the cops aren't going to be looking for anything more complicated than that."

I started leading Hannah into the parking lot again, looking around to get my bearings.

"What if they told?" Hannah whispered to me.

"Even if they were stupid enough to try telling the cops someone hypnotized them into beating up their buddies or something, they'd know if the cops found us, we'd tell them about what else those assholes tried to do. No way are they going to want that kind of heat."

I was certain those guys would keep their mouths shut about what happened. At most, they might try to find me and get some revenge, but I doubted even that. Lenny and Jock were probably still in jail, while Leader and Sweats were probably still in the hospital.

"All right," I said when we'd gotten to what I thought was the right spot. "Brittany and I left the dorms at quarter of eight because we were all supposed to meet just past the Grove at eight. Ava, how long is the walk through the woods to the parking lot here?"

I figured Ava would have a better idea than I did, since I hadn't really been paying attention during the walk to or from the Cove, while she was one of the pair leading the group.

Ava looked around the parking lot and up at the sky like she was expecting a SWAT team to rappel down from a helicopter any minute. I thought it was hilarious how concerned she was about the mundane police when she was perfectly okay with sneaking a bunch of us off campus. *Prima* Rosethorn was way scarier than a SWAT team.

"Twenty minutes," she said.

"Right, so eight twenty we'd be at the trees there," I pointed, "and Katrina and I came straight here. The beer kegs were ... there." I pointed again. "So, between eight twenty and eight thirty Katrina and I were both right around here."

The space was more than twenty feet across, but I didn't think I could get things any closer.

"Is that close enough?" I asked Hannah.

"Maybe?"

I squeezed her hand before letting it go. "You can do it. Do your witchy thing."

Hannah gave me a smile, then closed her eyes and held her hands to either side, palms down.

She turned in place, brow furrowed, while she mumbled to herself, then shook her head and took a couple steps forward.

"Sometimes I can search by moving around," she whispered.

"Straight ahead," I said. "That's where the beer kegs were and Katrina went that way."

Hannah nodded, not opening her eyes, and took a few more steps forward.

"You got this," I whispered to her, just before she opened her eyes and pointed.

"There."

A few feet ahead of us, a ghostly image of Katrina appeared.

"Mother's tears," Ava whispered, one hand to her mouth.

I had the same feeling. It was disturbing to stand there and look at the image of someone you knew was already dead.

"She's talking to someone," Hannah said. "Let me see who."

A moment later a second image appeared next to Katrina.

"Noah?" Brittany whispered.

I nodded.

"Yeah, this is where we split up."

I swallowed hard, watching as the ghostly Katrina's lips moved, followed by my own. I knew she was asking if I wanted to get a beer and then dance. I was telling her later.

My eyes burned. Then burned even more as my image turned and left Katrina behind, while the girl's shoulders slumped and she turned to walk in the other direction. I hadn't even noticed her reaction — if I had, would I have changed my mind? I wish I knew.

For over an hour we followed Katrina's image around the Cove. Through the parking lot, to the dance floor where she danced for a while. When it looked like she was interacting with someone, Hannah would show us who. Ava made a note of the time and place in case we wanted to follow whoever Katrina had talked to later.

As we neared two hours, I wondered if Hannah might need some rest. We wanted to find out what happened, but I didn't want her pushing herself too far.

"Do you need a break?" I asked her.

Hannah shook her head. "I'm good — barely down half my mana."

She'd said a couple hours, but we'd passed that and she'd only used half her mana?

Hannah must have seen the question on my face, because she looked around to be sure Ava wasn't close and then whispered, "My resonant's Regret — that's where Hindsight comes from." She shrugged. "It's pretty full right now."

Shit. I started wondering if the witches had *any* good resonants. The best I had was Lust, and even that kind of sucked a lot of the time.

Katrina's shade left the dance floor and went down to the beach, past the remnants of the bonfires, and stood for a long time staring farther down the beach.

Maybe she wasn't looking at the spot where I'd sat, I told myself. Maybe Katrina hadn't stood there and stared at me — sitting alone and then talking with Hannah. Maybe I imagined the look of hurt on her shade's face as she turned and walked back toward the parking lot. Maybe Katrina hadn't spent her last hours in pain because I'd rejected her. Maybe I'm not an asshole.

I glanced at Hannah as we followed. Regret as a resonant? I'd be a fucking nuclear reactor right now.

Katrina wandered back past where the dancing had been, past the beer kegs, past where I thought the cars had been set up to shine their lights on the party. She sat on one of the parking curbs and hugged her knees.

After several minutes she looked up and frowned. She looked around what must have been complete darkness.

And then she ran.

"WHAT?" Ava asked as we hurried to follow Katrina's running image. "What is she running from?"

"I don't know," Hannah panted. She was having to both run and maintain whatever concentration her Hindsight required. "I'm looking but I can't see anything!"

"Well, *she* can see it!"

Katrina clearly could.

She kept looking back, almost at us, and her face was a rictus of fear. Eyes wide, she ran. Into the trees not far from where we'd started. Deeper into the forest, then she tripped, sprawling to the ground.

In some weird juxtaposition of the past and present, I could see the disturbed leaves and furrowed dirt as her shade sprawled across the forest floor, scrambled to her feet, and then —

"Oh, Goddess," Ava breathed as we came to a stop.

Katrina's image was lifted off the forest floor and slammed into the trunk of a massive tree. Her hands grasped at her throat — near her throat, as though clutching at a ghostly, invisible arm that held her there.

"I can't —" Brittany turned away, tears streaming down her face, and covered her mouth with her hands.

I don't know what we'd been thinking.

Rush into the forest, have Hannah replay a murder, and not expect to see something this horrifying?

"What's doing this to her?"

"I don't *know*," Hannah cried. "I can't see anything — it's like there's nothing there!"

Katrina struggled, but as she did the glow of her image began to fade.

Not all at once — it started at the edges. Her head, her arms, her legs, all started going dark.

"What's happening?" Ava asked.

"I don't know," Hannah whispered. "I've never seen anything like this before."

That scared me. Something Hannah's magic couldn't see — something the witches hadn't seen before.

I looked around the forest, wondering if it could still be here, watching us.

"It's her mana," Hannah whispered.

"What?"

Hannah swallowed, lips trembling, as the last of Katrina's image faded.

"Where'd she go?" Ava demanded. "What happened?"

Hannah continued to stare at the place Katrina's image had been.

"What happened?" Ava nearly yelled, stalking toward her.

"Hey!" I said, stepping between them. "Give her a minute!"

"A minute? I want to know what the fuck happened!"

"And Hannah's probably never seen someone die before!" I blocked Ava as she tried to go around me. "Give her a fucking minute!"

"It's okay, Noah," Hannah said behind me. She put a hand on my shoulder and pulled me back from Ava. "I'm okay."

"Are you sure?"

I heard retching and spun around — it was Brittany. She'd stumbled over to some nearby bushes and was spewing into them. A glance at Hannah showed she was close to doing the same, and, honestly, if I hadn't had Ava making me mad, I'd probably be on my knees. My stomach was roiling — more than from the guy in the alley, more than from the sound of Sweats' cheekbones breaking under blows the night before.

I was sure Katrina had never hurt anyone. She'd been nice to me, the feral warlock, on my first day — from the moment she met me.

I turned back and stared at the tree where she'd died.

Somebody needed to pay for this. Somebody needed to *hurt*.

"What happened to her?" Ava asked, quietly now. I think she'd gotten the message that we were all upset and doing the best we could.

Hannah took a deep breath.

"It's mana — what we saw was mana. That's how Hindsight works. I ... put my mana into the past and it finds the traces of the mana I'm looking for. Then it sort of ... paints it in the present."

Hannah was trembling and I worried she might collapse, so I put an arm around her and gently led her to a fallen tree to sit.

"But we didn't see who attacked her," Ava said.

"Because there was no mana there for mine to bind to ... the space was empty. A void."

"That's impossible," Ava said. "Everything has mana. Fucking *rocks* have mana."

Hannah nodded. "I know. But it didn't. There was nothing there ... even after it took Katrina's."

"So, a vampire, then? Draining her?"

Hannah shook her head. "Vampires have mana — they take it from others, but they still have it."

Ava looked at me, eyes narrowed. "A warlock? With a glamour to hide —"

"You can't hide from Hindsight!" Hannah was trembling worse now. "A glamour *is* mana! I'd still see that. You can trick Hindsight, make it think you're something else, but there's never ... nothing."

"I want to go home."

We all looked at Brittany who was kneeling by the bush she'd thrown up in.

"I don't want to be here anymore. I want to go home."

# CHAPTER FORTY-FOUR

I SAT ON MY BED, BACK AGAINST THE WALL, WITH HANNAH NEXT to me, but on the bed's edge.

I was rubbing her shoulders. She hadn't asked, I hadn't offered, but when she'd sat down and then Brittany laid down with her head in her lap and Hannah stroked her sister's hair, I'd started.

I think we all just needed to touch someone — to have some tactile reminder that we were alive.

Maybe seeing death makes you want to reaffirm life.

Sam was sitting on the bed near Brittany's feet and was rubbing the girl's back while Rachel was on the floor between the beds, holding the hand Brittany had draped over her shoulder.

Ava and Isabella were on Sam's bed, holding hands and staring at nothing like we all were.

The girls who'd gone to look at Katrina's body were in a similar mood to us, having made a similar discovery — death isn't cavalier.

"Did you find anything?" Ava asked after we'd told the others what we'd seen in the park.

Sam shook her head.

"There were a couple marks on ... her body," Rachel said. "On her stomach — like needles, I think?"

"Or bug bites," Sam said.

Rachel nodded. "Yeah."

"So, no sign of a vampire bite?" Ava asked. I think Ava didn't want to believe what we'd seen — what Hannah said it meant — and was still pushing for vampire.

Sam shook her head.

"It wasn't a vampire," Hannah whispered.

"What, then?"

Hannah shrugged.

"It wasn't Noah, at least," Brittany said.

"We can't prove that."

"The teachers know it," Rachel said.

"What?"

"The teachers know it wasn't Noah. Not just think it, *know* it. One of them has Hindsight, I'm sure — they'll have seen the same thing Hannah saw. They know it couldn't be Noah."

"But will they tell anyone *why* they're so sure?" Hannah asked. "Without that, people will still doubt. Even with the truth potion, a lot of the girls will think he might have tricked it."

"Why wouldn't they say why they can be sure? No warlock could hide from Hindsight like that."

"This is something new," Hannah said. "Something *bad*. Look, *everything* has mana. Everything that happens is mana interacting with mana. Everything you feel, touch, taste — it's all mana. But this ... thing ... doesn't have any. Our mana can't interact with it ... it just disappears."

"So don't let it touch you?"

"Don't you get it? If it has no mana, mana can't affect it. Shields are useless. Wards are useless. Spells are useless." I could hear her swallow. "Magic's useless."

Hannah shook her head. "That can't get out. Witches would panic that there's something out there immune to magic — I mean, lots of things are resistant, but nothing is immune. Goddess, everyone would panic — witches, vampires, fae, the Rom ... everyone. They'd panic, get careless. Even enough to pierce the Veil."

Rachel drew in a sharp breath. "It could destroy the Veil," she whispered.

---

*PRIMA* ROSETHORN SPOKE to us at dinner.

All the teachers were there in the cafeteria with her, and, as Hannah predicted, they said nothing about some new creature, without any mana of its own, that had drained Katrina's.

Only that the staff was looking into it, the Council was looking into it, and that they were one hundred percent confident that no one on campus had been involved.

That's where everybody looked at me, even most of the teachers.

Classes were canceled for the next week, and over the next few days we saw a lot of strangers arrive and leave. Some of them were Katrina's Family, retrieving her body — others I heard were representatives of other Families, concerned about leaving their daughters at Willowmere, but I didn't see anyone I knew missing and didn't hear about anyone being withdrawn from school.

I'm sure some of the visitors were representatives or investigators from the witches' Council, but we didn't hear anything more about the investigation — only that things were progressing.

The school even offered grief counseling, just like a mundane school would. Or maybe different — maybe they used magic. No one I knew went, so I don't know.

Classes the next week started somewhat subdued, but, over a few days, slowly returned to normal. It's funny how fast you can get used to something — even something horrible. The first day back in potions class was hard with Katrina's empty seat at our table, but by the end of the week — it was just empty. By the end of the second week of December, things were almost back to normal, with just the occasional thought about what had happened.

I was busy not having morbid thoughts about how easy it was to get over someone being murdered when Sam's phone rang.

"Hello?"

I looked up from my laptop and the rituals paper I was writing. Sam didn't get calls often — in fact I didn't think she'd gotten one the whole time we'd been at Willowmere.

"Sure — here." Sam held the phone out to me. "It's Morgan," she whispered.

I took the phone quickly, realizing I'd forgotten to call Morgan to confirm getting together over the Solstice break with everything that had happened.

I took the phone.

"Morgan?"

"Hey."

"Hi — I'm sorry I didn't call you. Some ... things happened here and it's been a little crazy."

"What things?" Morgan asked, concern in her voice.

"Ah — one of the students here died." It wasn't something I wanted to talk about, but I didn't want to lie to Morgan.

"Oh — did you know him?"

"Her, and, yeah, we had a class together."

"Oh, Noah, I'm sorry." She paused. "Do you need to cancel getting together? Do you need time for something?"

"No! No, I want to see you — I miss you."

"I miss you, too — so, still the twenty-third?"

"Yeah, I was thinking of that coffee shop you like? The one next to the pet store? We can meet there and figure out what else we want to do."

"Okay, that sounds good."

Morgan's voice was a lot brighter now that we had a solid plan. I think she'd been worried I was going to bail on her.

"And maybe we could get together after Christmas, too?" I asked. "If you're not busy? Before school starts again?"

I wanted to make sure I didn't make the same mistake with Morgan that I'd made with Katrina — getting too wrapped up in what I wanted that I missed the important people in my life. Not that I *didn't* want to spend time with Morgan, just that life had a way of filling up time.

"Yeah! I'd like that — maybe I could come up and see your campus? You never said what school you're at?"

"Oh, um, it's called Willowmere," I said, trying to come up with a reason Morgan couldn't visit.

Knowing the name wasn't a big deal — Willowmere had a website and was accredited with the mundanes and everything. That was so any mundanes wondering about the campus wouldn't be suspicious — of course, all the mundane degrees and classes listed on the website were fake, but none of the witches would be looking for mundane jobs after graduation, so it didn't really matter.

Morgan visiting, though, would be ... complicated.

First, there'd be the very obvious fact that the entire school was inhabited by nothing but girls, even the faculty, so why was I here?

Second ... no, I was pretty sure I'd get stuck trying to come up with an explanation for the first one and we'd be there for a while.

"Maybe, yeah," I said, trying for noncommittal.

"Cool — um, who was that who answered the phone?"

"That's Sam, I told you about her."

"You told me your roommate was named Sam; you didn't say Sam was a girl."

"I didn't? Oh, well, yeah, she's a girl."

I glanced at Sam to find her with an amused look and a raised eyebrow.

"Soooo..." Morgan drew out the word. "Girlfriend?"

"No ... not ... girlfriend..."

Sam was biting her lip and her shoulders were shaking with

restrained laughter. She might not be able to hear Morgan's side of the conversation, but my side was more than enough.

What was I supposed to say?

*No, not my girlfriend ... she's gay. But we're going to have sex next week and then our relationship will be more permanent than marriage — with my lesbian friend. But not my girlfriend. No.*

"I see." Morgan paused. "So, you move out and first you move in with an older woman, but 'it's not like that', and now you have a girl for a roommate, but 'not your girlfriend' ... you know, I never asked about it, but are you sure you're not gay?"

I choked, coughing. Sam looked at me with a clear, what-the-fuck face.

"I'm not gay," I assured Morgan when I could speak again, setting Sam off into silent contortions as she tried not to laugh out loud.

I was really beginning to understand why the witches didn't have relationships with mundanes anymore. This was really annoying, and it would only get more so if, when, I grew my coven. I wondered if the witches had any protocol for telling a mundane what was going on — surely it had happened before, and I'd like to tell Morgan. She might not believe me until I could prove it like Mel had to me, but once she believed it, I was sure she'd keep it secret.

"Not that there's anything wrong with that," she said, "just that it would be good to know."

"Why?"

"Um ..." Morgan hesitated. "No reason? Just, you know, we're friends, so I'd like to know."

"Well, I'm not — not that there's anything wrong with that either." I realized what might settle the matter. "Sam's gay."

"Oh, she is?"

"Yeah, yeah, so that's why her being my roommate isn't ... weird."

Sam rolled her eyes.

# CHAPTER FORTY-FIVE

Solstice break started with the campus emptying itself of students.

Sam and I walked together across the quad to the school's gravel driveway, where she got into one of her Family's big, black SUVs for the trip home to their estate while I caught a cab from the waiting line to the train station.

There were a couple other students I saw at the station, boarding trains to their destinations — I assumed either their Families' Solstice celebrations were happening too far away to drive, or they were some of the smaller Families who didn't have a fleet of cars and drivers. While I recognized them from Willowmere, I hadn't really interacted with any of them so didn't try to talk to them. Instead, I waited quietly for the train, thinking about the school break and how I was going to spend it.

I still hadn't told Mel that I was going to spend the actual Solstice night with Sam, but she didn't seem to be someone who got overly into holidays or that sort of thing.

Sam was going to tell her mom that she was going to spend the Solstice with Mel and me. She figured that would make her mother think she was trying to get close enough to me to mark me, so her mom wouldn't object — or would probably encourage it. The plan was for me to tell Mel that Sam had invited me to the Prescott's Solstice celebration. We decided that it would be best to tell Mel that after the break started, so there was less chance she tried to speak to Sam, or worse, contact Sam's mother.

Me riding the train alone was a calculated risk.

Mel had needed to return home a few days earlier to take care of some things she didn't specify, but we hadn't wanted me to miss the last few days of class before the break. *Prima* Rosethorn taught Mel's classes while she was gone. Everyone seemed to think the witch Families would still be preoccupied with the implications of Katrina's death and not be willing to take on both Mel and Willowmere to get at me, so it would be safe.

Which it was — the train ride was peaceful and uneventful, and I even got quite a bit of studying done. Mostly in potions, which I still didn't quite get. The whole idea that the ingredients themselves weren't magical, but only held the mana we put into them, but at the same time, the ingredients mattered because of their association with particular effects. It was almost as if the beliefs of generations of witches had formed and restricted the magic in some way — if it was only the intent, then I should be able to put any intent and enough mana into, say, parsley to have any effect I intended, but parsley would only work for things like protection or fertility — the witches had a lot of ingredients about fertility.

Even after reading the chapter several times, I still hadn't really grasped the idea when the train pulled into the station.

I stuffed my books back in my backpack as the train came to a stop. Outside the station, I caught a cab to Mel's brownstone.

I climbed the stoop and put the key in the lock, happy to be home — then paused, realizing that I really did feel that way about the place, not just the happiness part, but the home part. Mel's brownstone seemed to exude an aura of welcoming that made me feel something, for the first time in my life, that fit with what other people seemed to mean when they said home. Even the building's wards seemed to reach out to me as I approached and give me a welcoming hug.

It was an odd sensation and I kind of hoped that I'd never get used to it. It was too special to let become commonplace.

Then I opened the brownstone's door and felt like someone had punched me in the nose.

Cinnamon and nutmeg, mint and chocolate — they seemed to roll through the open door like a wall of fog. The scents were overwhelming — not unpleasant, but there was so much of them that I staggered.

"Is that you, Noah?"

I took a deep breath, trying to breathe through my mouth until I got used to it.

"Yeah, Mel," I called, closing the door behind me and setting my backpack by the stairs to take up later.

"I'm in the kitchen, dear."

I walked back to the main room and saw a scene of utter chaos.

The kitchen, kitchen island, dining room table, and living room were all covered in some sort of massive baking effort.

There were cloths covering the island, dining table, coffee table, both chairs, and a third of the couch, all with either cooling racks, baking supplies, plastic storage containers, or other things I didn't immediately recognize. Mel had three stand mixers in the kitchen and she was putting cookie sheets into the oven.

"Did you have any trouble with the train, dear?"

I shook my head. "None. I did most of my potions paper for the break, but I still don't get the whole attributes thing."

Mel grabbed another two cookie sheets off the counter and slid them into the oven.

"Don't worry, it will come to you.

Mel turned to slide two more trays of cookies into the oven. I reached for one of the cookies she'd just set on the cooling rack, but

Felicity hopped up onto the island and smacked my hand with her paw.

"Those are still too hot, dear," Mel said, not turning from the oven. "Try the ones on the dining table, they've cooled a bit. But first hand me those two trays."

I grabbed the two trays of cookie dough balls from the island and stepped around it to hand them to Mel, who took them and slid them into the oven — I opened my mouth to ask just how big the inside of the oven was, then closed it as I thought better of the idea. Whatever magic Mel had going on in the appliance would probably just confuse me.

I went over to the dining table and sat down to grab a couple cookies — before I took even one bite, Mel was beside me setting down a glass of milk.

"Thank you."

Mel patted my shoulder. "You're welcome, dear."

I had to resist the urge to stuff an entire cookie in my mouth after the first bite. They were absolutely perfect — a slightly crispy edge, with a soft center that combined with the edge to give it a little bit of chew, and chocolate chips still warm enough to coat your entire tongue.

Okay — I did shove an entire cookie in my mouth.

"What's with all the cookies?" I asked after I swallowed my first with a gulp of milk.

"Evelina has invited us to the school's Solstice celebration and I don't want to show up empty-handed."

"Oh," I said, feeling my stomach sink.

Mel turned from the counter where she was preparing another batch of dough in one of the stand mixers and crossed to the island, setting her hands one atop the other there.

"Is something wrong?"

I flushed, kind of hating that I was going to have to lie to Mel after everything she'd done for me, as well as after having just eaten one of her fantastic cookies. Our whole plan had been that Mel wouldn't have any particular plans for the Solstice and now she wanted to return to the school for a party?

"Um, Sam has kind of asked me to spend the Solstice with her," I said — phrasing it so it wasn't quite as big a lie. I was going to spend the night with Sam, after all.

"With the Prescotts?" Mel asked, eyebrows rising.

I quickly stuffed a cookie in my mouth and mumbled something around it.

It still wasn't really a lie, right? I would be spending the Solstice with a Prescott — I just hadn't corrected Mel's plural assumption with the singular reality.

I grabbed another cookie and glanced over at her, then quickly away — Mel's lips were rather thin and her eyes narrowed. Felicity hopped up into my lap and rubbed her cheek against my arm, so I tried to distract myself from Mel's expression by dipping a finger in my milk and holding it for her to lick.

"I see," Mel said.

"It's just that — Sam and I are really good friends, and she asked me if I'd like to go, and I didn't think we'd have any real plans, since I've never had a Solstice-thing before, so I said yes..."

Mel nodded slowly.

"I ... could maybe ... tell Sam I have to change plans?"

I wasn't sure why I'd even suggested that, because Sam had been pretty excited about the idea of doing it on the Solstice for witch-reasons, and I really didn't want to tell her we had to do it a different day, but I could feel Mel staring at me.

Felicity bumped her head against my hand so I dipped out some more milk for her to lick.

"No," Mel said, "that won't be necessary — you should spend Solstice with your friend rather than a room full of teachers and school marms who have nowhere better to go."

"Are you sure?"

"Absolutely. Just watch the mead and don't get into any trouble."

"Trouble?"

"The Prescotts are not known for their restraint," Mel said. "Samantha excluded, I'm sure. And you are, after all, still a rather valuable, unmarked, *trinitara* warlock. I'd expect there to be certain ... offers made."

My face flushed hot, and I snuck a quick glance at Mel, who seemed to be smirking.

"Oh. You think they might try ... something? I mean, how bad are they?"

"They'll make you an offer, certainly, but there's no need to look so frightened, dear. The Prescotts are too well known to try anything untoward, especially with the protections I and Evelina offer. Still..."

"Um, still?"

"You've met Samantha's mother."

"Yeah." Well, I'd seen her, which was about as close to meeting the witch as I cared to get.

"Julia Prescott is the public face of the Prescotts because she's the nice one."

# CHAPTER FORTY-SIX

SAM USED HER KEY CARD TO OPEN THE DOOR TO THE HOTEL room. She was wearing a skirt and buttoned blouse today instead of her usual tight jeans and irreverent t-shirt, because she wanted her mother to think she was dressing up to spend Solstice with me and Mel.

We went in, and it really wasn't just a room, it was a whole suite with a small kitchen, sitting area, and a door to a separate bedroom that was slightly ajar and showed a king-size bed.

I gave a low whistle. "This is nice," I said.

Sam grinned. "I put it on my mother's credit card — probably the last thing I charge, because I'm pretty sure she's gonna cut me off after this."

Her comment made me think again about what we were doing. It was a big thing for me — to be tying myself to her, basically forever — but I'd reconciled myself to the fact that I couldn't hide from the witches and they'd keep trying to mark me and bring me into these Families of theirs, so I needed to do what was necessary to remain independent. And if I had to tie myself to thirteen witches, Sam was the best start I could think of.

She'd been a real friend to me since I arrived at the school — maybe the first real friend I'd had other than Morgan.

She was risking more than I was though. She fully expected her mother and the rest of her Family to disown her — well, unless one of them managed to mark me later, in which case they'd get her back and probably pretend like nothing ever happened.

"Do you want a drink?" Sam asked, running a finger over the minibar.

"No," I said. "I'm good."

Sam took a deep breath and then grabbed my hand.

"All right then."

She turned around and led me to the bedroom, then let go of my hand and backed up to the bed. My mouth went dry.

With a dramatic wave of her arms, she jumped backward onto the bed, landing on her back with her legs hanging over the edge, her arms outspread, and face toward the ceiling with her eyes closed.

"All right, stud-boy, do me!"

I stared at her.

She cracked one eye open. "Awkward?"

I laughed. "Yeah, awkward."

Sam sat up and I went to the bed and sat beside her.

"Look, you don't —" we both said together.

I chuckled and she shook her head.

"We don't have to do this, if you don't want to — if you've changed your mind," Sam said. "Like, if you wouldn't want me in your coven, or you don't think I'm attractive enough, or —"

I reached over and took her hand.

"I can't think of any witch I'd rather start a coven with, and you're beautiful."

"Really? Not cute?"

"I learned that lesson."

Sam nodded. "Excellent — I knew you could be taught."

"Brat," I said, nudging her with my shoulder.

Sam giggled, but then we both sobered again.

"Um, I've, well," I tried. "I've been thinking about it since you suggested this — well, at least since I learned what it really meant we were going to do —"

"Ooo — did I get you worked up?"

"Yeah, pretty worked up and you know it. But even so, I know I'm not ... the sort of thing you want. So, I want you to know it's okay if you change your mind — I won't get mad or anything. We'll still be friends — best friends."

Sam sighed and pulled my hand into her lap and covered it with her other hand.

"I've known all my life that I liked girls," she said. "And I've known just as long that I want to be part of a coven and I want to have kids — and I don't think you realize how important kids are to witches these days. Girls aren't going to make that happen and I can't be part of a coven, doing rituals, if I restrict myself to girls. So, I guess I'm ... well, not fully-bi, but situationally-bi?"

"I'm the situation?"

Sam grinned. "You're *my* situation." She paused. "But I won't be mad either ... if you changed your mind. I know I'm not what you —"

"Hey," I cut her off. "I told you I wanted my coven to be a family — you're my family."

Sam sighed. "We're doing it again, aren't we?"

I nodded. "Yeah, we could spend all night trying to make sure the other one's okay with this."

Sam caught her lower lip between her teeth. "So, how do we start?"

I grinned. "You don't know?"

"No, I've never done this before."

"With a guy?"

"With anyone. What about you?"

"With a guy?"

Sam smacked me on the shoulder. "With anyone!"

"Um, no." I looked at her. "Well, how about we start with a kiss?"

She smiled and lowered her gaze. "Okay."

I turned toward her, put my free hand against her cheek to turn her face toward me, and leaned in.

It was weird and not weird at the same time.

Her lips were soft, and tasted like strawberries. I could smell peaches, too, and I knew that was the scent of her body wash — it was a familiar scent, after all we lived in the same room and I'd smelled that every time she took a shower, but now it had an extra, almost intoxicating, effect. My heart sped up and I was very aware of my hand in her lap clasped between both of hers. My fingertips were touching her thigh and I felt sure her skirt must be about to catch fire from how hot she felt against my hand.

After a bit I broke off the kiss, and looked at her. Her eyes were closed, lips barely parted, and the corners of her mouth quirked up in a smile.

"That was nice," she whispered.

"Yeah," I said with my voice cracking a little.

"I'm still going to pretend you're a flat-chested chick with a strap on."

"Brat!" I said and shoved her back to fall on the bed while she laughed.

I lay down beside her, pulled her face toward me again, and kissed her.

Her hands were at her side now, and as I rolled toward her into the kiss, one was touching me mid-thigh. She tensed for a moment then relaxed and I felt her fingertips barely stroking.

I opened my lips and gently probed with my tongue and her lips opened in response.

Our tongues met gently, tentatively, then more firmly. I rolled more toward her, propping myself up on one elbow and laid my free hand on her waist. She gasped, but didn't break the kiss so I gently caressed her side from chest to hip.

I silently thanked my foster-mom for being addicted to romance novels. While I might not have gotten any real action in high school, I'd had a lot of spare time to read. And while I knew those were unrealistic fantasies for middle-aged women, I thought I'd been able to separate out a few practical things that made those stories appealing and had real world applications.

After a bit more kissing, I trailed my fingers gently up from her side and over her belly. I slid one finger into the gap between the buttons of her shirt and let my fingertip stroke her bare skin.

Sam gasped. She arched her back pressing herself up into my hand, and let out a long breath.

Still kissing her I moved my fingers to the bottom button of her blouse and gave her shirt a little tug to free it from her skirt. I figured that made it clear where I was going next, so she could object if she wanted to, but if anything, her tongue became more forceful and energetic against mine.

I fumbled the first button a couple times, but got the hang of it, then undid the bottom three buttons of her blouse and let the fabric drift away down her sides to bare her stomach. I laid my hand there and started idly tracing designs with my fingertips. Sam moaned low and long, her breath coming hot where our lips met.

I ran my hand up under her shirt, over her ribs, until I touched the fabric of her bra. Sam took in a long slow breath, air hissing between her teeth.

The sound made a shudder roll through my body and I felt a strong satisfaction. Something deep inside me clicked — I'd made her do that; I'd drawn that sound from her. I felt proud and wanted to get more from her. Play her body like an instrument, and see what music we might make. That was a line from one of Karen's romances that had stuck with me.

When Mel had told me my primary resonance was Control, I hadn't fully understood — I'd understood that I could make people do things with that power, but not how I'd fill it. There were urges filling me now that I thought must have to do with that — to roll over on top of Sam, pin her beneath me, and see what other sounds I could draw out of her.

But I also didn't want to scare her by going too fast — and I knew this was about more than just our bodies, too, it was about merging our magic.

I broke off the kiss and opened my eyes.

"Can I look at you?" I asked, knowing she'd understand I meant her magic.

Sam bit her lower lip again and nodded. "Can I?"

"Yeah."

I lowered my shields and looked at Sam as she lowered hers. We'd done this before, often, for Mel's class, but this was different. It was somehow more intimate than doing it for class.

When we'd first merged our shields for class, looking at Sam was like looking into a dark void. The mana she generated was muted and dim. Looking at her now was like seeing a rave when the lights were out and there were glowsticks everywhere.

Her body was a dark void with glowing strands twisting and turning about, with a different color for everything she was feeling. They started deep within her, floated to the surface, and then faded quickly as they left her body. Some of those that floated off came to me — not all, but a few. My body sucked them in, absorbing the mana, and I could feel my own resonant stores start to fill with mana — but slowly, and I felt an urge to stuff them full with the magical energy I saw in Sam.

I didn't know what all the colors meant — I couldn't remember all of the rapid-fire set of emotions Mel had thrown at me when we were trying to figure out my resonants. I figured Sam was feeling a lot of what I was — nervous, anxious, and all the rest.

She didn't shed the mana that matched my resonants, not one of them, anyway, and I saw some of the strands she generated sucked into her own resonant stores.

Her primary resonance was still empty and achingly dark. It broke my heart to think of how that must feel.

Her secondary was mostly empty too — the resonant for Pain I'd given her.

Her third, though, made me smile — Lust, glowing bright and visibly filling as I watched.

I began to understand the witches a bit better — their seeming obsession with harvesting power. Just looking at Sam's power, I felt an aching hunger deep inside of me, equal, almost greater, than the one in my pants.

I felt the urge to drain her, to take all of that power for myself, and disappointment that she didn't have more for me to take. Ideas for ways to increase the mana she was generating and fill those quicker started flashing through my mind.

I ran my fingertips along the lower edge of her bra and watched to see what would happen.

More Lust floated up, mixed with another color — a light green that made me think of spearmint. The spearmint wasn't captured, it floated off Sam's body and my skin tingled where some shadow of it came to me.

Then I realize some of the spearmint was being captured. Strands of pink Lust when they touched the spearmint wrapped around them and dragged them to her resonant store.

In class, they'd talked about complementary resonants, where even if a witch didn't have a resonant for something, if it was somehow related to one she did have, then she'd still gain some additional mana from it and it wouldn't all be shed.

I thought the spearmint might be ... Pleasure, maybe? That was related to Lust, right?

I experimented, trailing my fingertips from Sam's chest down her belly noting how the spearmint brightened as I got to the more sensitive skin, and even more when I gently used my nails — at its brightest, Sam bent her head back and moaned.

*This is so cool,* I thought. *It's like having the cheat codes.*

I trailed my fingers back up to the edge of Sam's bra and she shivered. This time I ran my hand over her bra letting my palm fall to cup her breast. I could feel the hard nub of her nipple pressing against my hand through the thin fabric.

Sam moaned again and arched her back into the pressure of my hand.

Since her back was off the bed already, I decided to take advantage of that and slid my hand around her side to her back where I felt at the bra's clasp.

I fumbled it a couple times, the thing was complicated, then figured it out. Her bra came loose and she collapsed back to the bed as I ran my hand back up her side and underneath her now loose bra to cup her breast again, this time skin to skin. For all Sam's complaints about their size, it seemed to fit perfectly in my hand as I gently caressed, feeling her nipple harden even more against my palm.

I watched the Pleasure and Lust she was generating spike again, and I swear I started salivating at the thought of tasting that power. If I didn't know vampires were real, I'd wonder if warlocks were actually the root of vampire myths, as I felt the sudden urge to bury my teeth in her neck.

*I didn't think I was this much of a pervert,* I thought — but the thought quickly faded as Sam moaned again.

I pushed her bra up, exposing her to me, and spent a bit of time just looking. Yes, small, but beautiful, with pale skin topped by pink — her nipples were small too, but prominent and growing more so now that they were exposed to the cool air of the room.

I took the little nub of her nipple gently between thumb and forefinger and gave just a little pressure.

"Oh," Sam sighed.

I grinned.

I squeezed a little harder, watching the spearmint brighten. Then harder still, because the spearmint and cotton candy kept coming.

I squeezed until dim strands of red, a cherry-red, started appearing and filling her Pain resonant. I figured that was the limit — and reduced the pressure, but then I saw those red strands were being picked up by the pink as well — entwining with both pink and the green — and Sam hadn't stopped moaning. If anything, she'd grown louder and started squirming beneath my hands.

I squeezed just a little bit harder.

"*Oh!*" Sam moaned, as the cherry brightened and single strands began filling Sam's secondary store, as well as entwining even more so with the pink.

*That's ... unexpected*, I thought. *Does her having Lust and Pain ... mean that she likes it?*

I pinched harder.

"*Oh, Goddess!*"

*Well, I don't want to hurt her...*

Louder moans and she clenched her fingers, one grasping the bedding and the other the inside of my thigh.

But if she liked it, it wasn't hurting her, was it?

I squeezed her nipple a little more and she threw her head back, her face contorted, so I hesitated and let up on the pressure a bit.

"Don't..." Sam moaned. "Stop..."

Was that: Don't. Stop. Or don't stop?

I released her nipple, despite the cheat codes telling me she was still enjoying it.

"Is that too much —"

"Don't stop! *Don't stop!*" Sam screamed, fumbling for my wrist and dragging my hand back to her breast. "Goddess, this is so much better when someone else does it!"

I grinned as I caught her wrist and drew both her hands above her head, wrists crossed. I held them there with one hand while I brought the other back to her breast and grabbed her nipple again, squeezing harder than before and pulling up, stretching it.

"Go... Go... *Goddess, yes!*"

All signs pointed to her liking that, but I was still a little worried — the skin of her breast was stretched taut and it looked painful. You know, it looked like that should hurt a lot even if she was enjoying it, and I didn't want to leave a bruise or leave her sore afterward so she might regret things she'd enjoyed in the heat of the moment. I released her nipple and she cried out, but then I covered her nipple with my mouth and the moans started again.

The little nub was hard and had a rougher texture than her skin as I ran my tongue over it.

While I worked on her nipple with my mouth, I trailed the fingers of my right hand down her side, across her belly, to the edge of her skirt. Sam kicked her feet against the side of the bed, raising her hips to press against my hand.

As much as I wanted to tease her more and build things up until she begged —

*Where did that come from? Beg?*

I couldn't explain how the thought of her begging me to move on and fuck her already turned me on, but that made my own situation worse, as my cock was already harder than it had ever been, and folded uncomfortably inside my pants.

I took my mouth from Sam's breast and trailed little kisses and licks down to the edge of her skirt.

Her belly trembled against my lips.

Now I just had to get her skirt off.

I needed both hands for that, but as soon as I started to release her arms, Sam moved them, so I got a grip on her wrists again and planted her arms firmly against the mattress.

"No, just leave them there," I whispered, then released her wrists and trailed my fingertips down her arm so I could concentrate on her skirt. I wanted her to be still and concentrate on what she was feeling, so her body would keep generating that delicious mana.

Sam was generating the grey mana of Control now, as I'd told her to do something and she complied — and I swear those strands felt different, better, as she shed them and my resonant sucked them in.

I tugged at the edge of her skirt, but the band wasn't very elastic, so it must have some sort of catch — I felt around the side and then slid my hand under her. She arched her back and rolled toward me a little bit and I felt the zipper at the back of the skirt, pulled it down, and then found a second little catch at the very top. I fumbled that until it came loose and Sam immediately started squirming and kicking her legs to get the skirt off.

I sat up, keeping one hand on her belly because I didn't want to stop touching her, and tugged at the skirt. Once it was at her knees, Sam's kicking guided it rest of the way until she flung it across the room and spread her legs wide.

That was all the invitation I needed.

I trailed my hand down her thigh to her knee and then got off the bed to kneel between her legs. Sam thrust her hips at me, but stayed on the bed with her arms stretched above her head.

I noticed again that she was keeping her hands where I told her to, and was surprised at how satisfying I found that. The position did ... something. She looked so exposed and vulnerable.

Starting at her knees, I ran fingertips up the inside of both her thighs, stopping at the silky soft crease where her thighs and hips met — that was just at the edge of her panties and she squirmed from side to side, trying to get my hands to pass that border, but I moved with her, keeping my fingertips where they were.

Her panties had a damp spot and I felt a little relief at that.

I knew that she was doing this for reasons other than desire — because she wanted to be part of a coven, to get away from her Family, to try and find a place in the world, so I'd been worried a little. I really wanted this to be something she enjoyed, not just something she accepted — and all the moaning could have been faked. Well, I didn't see why she would've faked liking her nipple squeezed so hard, but what did I really know? Seeing the mana she generated, even knowing what it meant, was still so new to me, that maybe I didn't trust even that.

The dampness soaking through her panties and the heat I felt even with my hands a few inches away reassured me that I was at least making it good for her.

And then I just couldn't wait any longer to tease her more — I wanted to taste her and then I wanted to be inside her.

I grabbed the top of her panties and pulled them down, sliding backward out of the way so she could close her legs enough for them to come off.

I got them past her knees and she lifted one leg out of them.

"Please," Sam whispered, spreading her legs and grinding her hips as though there was something she desperately wanted just out of reach.

I took a moment to appreciate the view. Sam had shaved, leaving just a triangle of curly red hair rising from the top of her slit. The sides were completely bare and her lips opened like a blooming flower as she spread her legs, exposing her glistening, almost dripping, opening.

Sam moaned and kicked her feet, trying to get her legs around me. She got one foot behind my head and tried to pull me toward her, but I resisted, grinning even more as she whined at that.

"Please," she whispered. "Noah, please? I want to feel you touch me."

That was all the encouragement I needed. I didn't waste any more time. I grasped her legs high up on her thighs and pushed them farther apart, making her lips spread even wider, then dove forward, plunging my tongue into Sam's pussy.

I licked, starting at the bottom, driving my tongue as deep as I could, and licking up until my tongue covered her clit, where I swirled it back and forth.

Sam screamed — truly screamed, and if I hadn't been able to see the thick, thick and bright, threads of Pleasure forming in her, I would've thought I'd done something to hurt her.

As it was, I knew she liked that. So, I did it again.

And again.

Over and over, long deep licks from bottom to top, then spending some time working her clit before repeating.

Sam bucked her hips with each stroke, pushing herself hard against my face and driving my tongue deeper and harder against her.

Her juices tasted sweet and tangy and I lapped them up eagerly.

Hormones and writhing hips seemed to be approaching a peak — at least I couldn't imagine how there could be much more without something giving. Sam was straining, muscles tense. Her stomach rippled and her arms strained as though there was really something holding her hands above her head.

I gave her one more lick, then concentrated my tongue on her clit while I slid a finger inside her — that got an even bigger reaction, and I added a second finger, not plunging them in and out, but reaching inside her and massaging the upper wall of her channel. She was wet and warm around my fingers, and the flesh I was massaging felt puffy and swollen.

The more I licked and massaged, the louder Sam got — until she let out a long, low, guttural groan, and her body tensed.

Her pussy clenched around my fingers, holding them tight, and I knew she was coming.

It seemed to go on and on, and I found I could almost control it — if I lightened the pressure on her clit or slowed my massaging fingers, Sam would start to relax, still clenched around me, but easing a bit; while if I increase the pressure and speed her reactions increased again.

I played with that for a bit, dialing her up and down at my whim, and wondering if, with some practice, I could get her to eleven.

I grinned at the thought, and at the satisfaction I was feeling at controlling such obviously pleasurable sensations.

Finally, my own desire grew to the point I couldn't take it anymore. Sam's moans, the taste of her, the feel of her tightly gripping my fingers all combined to give me an erection that was now causing me physical pain.

I undid my pants with one hand, still not letting up on Sam, and pushed them down to my knees, then rose up to stand between her spread legs.

Sam whined as my lips left her clit. Then again, as I withdrew my fingers.

"More, please, more," she moaned. "Don't stop."

*Shit*, I thought, *the condoms are in my backpack.*

"I have to — get the thing," I said, taking a step back.

"What ... thing?" Sam whined.

"The thing," I said again, hoping she wouldn't open her eyes and see me waddle across the room with my pants around my knees to get one. "I left them in my backpack."

"Oh." She hooked her legs around me and pulled hard to draw me back. "No ... it's okay."

"But —"

"Witches know their bodies — it's safe," she gasped. "And besides ... children are a blessing."

I let her draw me back toward her until the head of my cock brushed against her lips again, thinking about what she'd said. Not having to use a condom because she knew when it was safe was one thing, but it made me think about what I was getting into starting a coven. It wasn't just magic and sex, it was starting a family too — and I was just eighteen.

Did I really want to start having kids — and kids with maybe thirteen girls even. I looked down at Sam, whose face was scrunched up as she tried to pull me closer and closer to her with her heels, and thought about being inside her, my seed filling her, taking root, and then watching her swell with my child.

Did I want that? Was I ready for that?

"Fuck, yeah," I whispered. Maybe not this time, but I wouldn't be upset if it happened.

Sam stopped whining and gasped when I pressed the head of my cock harder against her folds.

I entered her slowly and gently until just the head of my cock was inside her, resisting the urge to slam my hips forward. I wanted to take her, hard and fast, and, I'll admit, almost brutally, but this was her first time and I wanted it to be as an enjoyable as possible for her. There'd be time, I hoped, to take her the way I wanted later. Given her reaction to having her nipple pinched, hard and brutal might be a thing she wanted too. But later, not now.

I also remembered why we are doing this in the first place. Something that had slipped my mind in the thrill of watching Sam's reactions and seeing her body. It was so different now than when we'd been teasing each other with our nudity. That had been like a game. Yeah, it had turned me on, but this was so different — this was seeing her and knowing I could have her. I'd almost forgotten that I was supposed to be marking her. That meant I needed to think about more than the physical.

I looked at our mana, and extended my resonants toward hers as I had after she took the potion. The sensation as I touched those was very much again like what I felt now from my cock entering her. It must've felt the same for Sam, and was a surprise to her — she'd been unconscious after the potion, after all — because her eyes flew open.

"*Fuucckk! What is that?*"

I grinned and eased deeper inside her with both my cock and resonants, coordinating the motions as one — it felt every bit as good as I'd suspected it would. Better, even.

Sam closed her eyes again and threw her head back. "Fuck yes, Maiden's dripping ... *whatever that is keep doing it!*"

I eased everything deeper still, until our resonants seemed to fully connect with an almost audible click that sent a physical tremor through us both. At the same time, I fully filled her with my cock, a little disappointed that about an inch of me was still outside.

"*Oh! Goddess, I'm so full!*"

I slowly withdrew until I was almost out of her, then pumped forward again — I didn't want to do that with the resonants, because I needed to stay fully connected to mark her, but I knew I was going to experiment with that another time.

I grunted with frustration as I realized I couldn't get all of myself inside her — I was hitting the back wall of her channel, leaving maybe an inch of my cock outside her. I wanted more. I wanted to feel myself inside her to the root, feel her pressed tightly against my belly and thighs. At the same time, that impact was driving me crazy with the knowledge that I was completely filling her.

I thrust again and the motion pulled a high-pitched whine from Sam as I withdrew, followed by a low moan as I entered her again.

*"Eeee ... ooooh ... eeee ... oooh!"*

I withdrew and entered her again.

*"Eeeee!"*

I noticed that her face scrunched up, scowling, lips drawn back in a grimace on each "eee", then softened on the "oh" as I filled her again. It was one of the most adorable things I'd ever seen.

Sam's reactions were so entertaining that I almost didn't notice how it felt to me, but when I did, it was everything I'd thought it would be. Her pussy gripped my cock like it didn't want to let go — warm and wet with a delicious friction as I pumped into her.

My resonants seemed to be physically throbbing, and I could feel the mana Sam had stored pulsing against them, tickling — at least the two, and I was reminded again how empty and sad her primary was.

I couldn't think about that right now, though, because I needed to start the marking.

I'd learned the process, at least the basics, but they seemed more like guidelines than instructions, because they said it was different for every warlock depending on their resonants and affinities, and I'd have to act almost on instinct the first time until I learned what it all meant to me.

Like so much of the witches' world, nothing was hard and fast, only driven by intent.

I knew I needed to drain Sam's mana almost completely, and that scared me a little, especially after what something had done to Katrina. I needed to drain her so much that she couldn't resist the marking, but not so much that it hurt her. Again, the only thing I'd been able to learn, was that warlocks were supposed to instinctively recognize the limit.

I started pulling on Sam's mana through our connected resonants, getting a trickle at first from Lust and Pain, but nothing from Love, of course. I could tell how much more satisfying all three would be.

The mana coming to me increased as I pulled harder, turning

from the pink and red Sam stored to the bright yellow of refined mana as it entered me and filled my own stores.

I kept up the physical act while increasing what I drew magically until I felt resistance to what I was taking. It became like sucking on a straw in a too-thick milkshake. I was pulling and pulling harder and harder, but nothing was coming through.

I worried about pulling too hard and hurting Sam, so I eased off on the pressure.

"Don't stop!" Sam yelled as I thrust into her again. "I can't ... not fight it ... take it! Take me!"

Yeah, everything I knew said marking, even voluntary, was a struggle between the witch and the warlock for supremacy. Her body was fighting me, instinctively, and at any moment she could start trying to draw my power from me.

I snarled at the thought.

*No fucking way. She was mine!*

The intensity of that feeling surprised me, but I used it to overcome my reluctance and pulled hard against her resonants.

Sam screamed — truly screamed, and I almost stopped again, but this was normal. The marking between witch and warlock was a contest of wills where each tried to rip the others power from them. Even when it was consensual, like this, our instincts were to resist and then try to control the other. After the first time, once the connection was made, it wouldn't hurt at all, but the first time would be painful for whoever was losing the contest.

I felt Sam resist and pulled harder, sucking mana from her into myself. The sensation for me wasn't painful, in fact it was quite pleasurable, I just felt guilty at what Sam was feeling, because now her Pain resonance was filling without the sort of pleasure I'd seen before.

I kept pulling harder and harder until her resonants were almost empty, then pulled more, sucking in every bit of mana she continued to generate.

Sam's screams had stopped some time ago, and she lay still, almost lifeless, beneath me.

That was when I knew it was time and I started pushing that mana back into her. The refined, trebled mana that filled my own resonants.

That changed what Sam was feeling and her eyes flew open — she should now be feeling what I'd felt when I took the mana — like three simultaneous orgasms, as mana flowed out of me into her.

Now was when I had to figure out how I, as a warlock, would mark my coven — apparently it was supposed to just come to me, but the examples were like a touch or a kiss or something physical that would place my mark on her. The witches mark those bastards in the Inquisition used to check for.

I suddenly realized Sam and I hadn't discussed where I would put that mark, and I thought, since I was going to be adding a mark to her body, she might want to have some say in it.

"Where..." I gasped, the sensation of flooding mana back into Sam and my continued thrusting into her had me out of breath. "Where ... should I mark?"

"Anywhere! I don't care!" Sam threw her head back, eyes closed. "Oh, *Goddess*, it's too much — I'm going to —"

Sam's pussy clenched around me and I knew I needed to do it now. Her resonants were already full and stretching with the mana I'd taken from her and trebled. They wouldn't hold much more, and with her orgasm tightening her pussy around my cock, that wasn't going to last too much longer either.

I moved without really thinking about it — the decision to mark her now driven by some instinct, and I lowered my face to the top of her left breast and bit.

I don't know why I bit, I just knew it felt right, and I added mana to the bite with the intent to mark her as mine.

Sam screamed again — the good kind — and the walls of her pussy clenched so tight around me that I had to force my way back in with each stroke. That set me off and if my mouth hadn't been latched on to the upper globe of Sam's breast, I would've screamed too as I came, pumping stream after stream of my seed into her with every thrust.

---

I PANTED, coming back to myself from wherever the most intense orgasm of my life had taken me.

My jaw ached as I raised my head up and unclenched my teeth from Sam's flesh — I licked my lips and tasted blood.

*Oh, shit.*

I quickly raised my head and looked at Sam's breast, seeing that I had, indeed, broken the skin a little, but before I could apologize, I saw it quickly heal and the indentations of my teeth filled and darkened to form two curves of delicate, brown moles in the shape of my bite.

"Cool," I said.

"You ... had to ... do it ... there?" Sam panted.

"You said you didn't care."

"That's going to show every time I wear a bikini."

"Good, then everyone will see that you're mine," I said ... and realized what I'd said. "I don't know where that came from," I added even as a thrill of possession swept through me and my cock twitched inside her.

"You saying that should not have turned me on as much as it just did," Sam chuckled.

I groaned as I got my elbows under me and raised myself off her to look at her face — she still had her eyes closed and the corners of her lips dimpled in a smile. Strands of sweat-damp hair covered her face.

"Let's rest a bit before we start talking about turning each other on again," I said, pushing myself farther up.

Moving made me aware of just how awkward a physical position we were in now, with Sam's butt at the edge of the bed, her feet on the floor, and me half collapsed on top of her. I was still inside her, but was starting to slip out as my knees weakened.

I was reminded of a line from a comedian I'd once seen: sex is just a dirty, sweaty, sticky mess ... when it's done right.

We'd done it right, I guess, because we were all of those things — Sam's hair was wet with sweat and I was sure mine was as well, our bodies were sticking together wherever we touched, and I could feel things dripping from where I was still inside her.

I got my feet under me and managed to stand — Sam pouted and whined as I slid out of her.

"Let's get more comfortable," I said, climbing up on the bed, pulling out the pillows to stack them, and then leaning back against the pile with a long exhalation.

I looked at Sam who was still laying there like she wasn't ready to move yet, her arms stretched above her and her legs hanging off the bed.

"Um, Noah?"

"Yeah?"

"Can I move my arms now?"

"What do you mean?" Sure, I told her to keep her hands there, and it had been kind of hot, but we were done, at least for the moment.

"I can't move my hands from where they are."

"Why not?"

"Because you told me not to."

I laughed. "It was kind of hot that you kept them there, but we're done for now."

"No, I mean I *can't* move my arms because you *told* me not to."

"What — *fuck*!" Had I? I must've unknowingly used Command when I'd told her that. "I'm so sorry, I didn't mean to do that, I didn't real —"

"Noah!"

"What —"

"Tell me I can move my hands again."

"Fuck." I concentrated and tried to use just a little of my affinity with Command to undo what I'd said earlier. "You can move your hands however you want now."

Sam sighed and tension I hadn't seen went out of her shoulders as she brought her arms from over her head and onto her belly.

"Sam, I am so —"

"*Hush!* You're harshing my afterglow."

"But —"

"*Sshh!* Cuddle time."

I shut up, but I felt awful — I needed to practice Control more, because I never wanted to use that on anyone, especially anyone I cared about.

Sam rolled onto her stomach and dragged herself up the bed to lay beside me. She pressed her body along mine, flung one leg over my thighs, and rested her head and left hand on my chest and stomach. My arm went around her naturally, fingers spread from her tailbone to her side.

"I didn't tell you when it happened, because I knew you'd react this way — all guilty and apologizing — and we were ... in the middle of something."

"But —"

"*Sshh!*" She poked me in the stomach. "Listen to me, it's okay. I was a little scared when I realized what happened, but that only lasted a second and then I remembered how much I trust you. I knew that if I said something you'd let me go — but also get all weird, so I didn't say anything. That was my choice."

I was silent for a moment, trying to think of what to say.

Sam snuggled closer to me. "Besides, it was hot."

I froze. "What?"

Sam took a deep breath.

"It was hot — and it helped me get past the thing."

"Thing?"

"You know," she waved her fingers at my crotch. "The thing."

"Is that what we're calling it?"

"Yes," Sam said, "in fact —"

She reached down and very carefully with the tips of thumb and forefinger, touching my dick as little as possible, she bent it from where it lay flat on my stomach and tucked it between my legs.

"Close your legs?"

I laughed, complying.

"Better," Sam said, settling her face back on my chest. "Yeah, I was really nervous about having sex with a guy, more than just doing it for the first time at all, and it was sort of like not being able to move meant I ... couldn't do anything about it, so it wasn't my fault." She slapped my stomach. "Stop that!"

"What?"

"Feeling guilty and thinking I regret anything we did tonight — you might not generate much mana, but I can see exactly what you're feeling." She took a deep breath. "Before we started, I was worried about how it would feel having sex with a guy — now I know how I feel about getting fucked into oblivion by my Noah, my warlock. And that's fantastic because they're two different things. Do you get that?"

I thought I understood what she meant, so I tried to keep the doubts out of my head.

"Your Noah?"

"Yeah — my Noah, my warlock — you're as much mine as I am yours now, buddy, and don't forget it."

I smiled at that.

"Okay. So, um, you ... thought it was hot?"

She turned her head to bury her face in my chest.

"Yeah."

"Good to know."

I felt her smile, but it still bothered me a little.

"You're not even a little weirded out that I can do something like that? I am."

Sam propped herself up and turned so she could look at me, her brow furrowed.

"What do you think marking a witch for your coven does? Do you really not know how much control that gives you over us, even without your double-special Command thingie?"

"Well, I figured it meant being head of the coven — like you said the high priestess is head of the coven if she marks the warlock, right?"

"Noah, in the Family covens the high priestess controls the warlock and through him the other witches of the coven. For you, if you don't let a high priestess mark you and you mark her instead, then *you* control everyone."

"Right, so head of the coven. I get that. What does that have to do with my Command affinity?"

"Witches aren't afraid of Command because of what it does inside of a coven — they're afraid of it because you could use it to control witches who *aren't* in your coven. You don't need it for what's already yours."

I still wasn't getting it and Sam must have seen that confusion on my face.

"Noah, a witch you've marked into your coven *can't* disobey you. It's inherent to the coven bond — just as if the high priestess is in control, neither the witches nor the warlock can disobey her."

"What do you mean?"

Sam took a deep breath. "I should've realized you didn't know this about how covens work — after all, you know nothing." She licked her lips. "We, both witches and warlocks, are *compelled* to obey whoever marks us." She reached out and laid her hand on my cheek. "I'm sorry, I didn't realize you didn't understand that. There are limits and intent has a lot to do with it — the coven bond can kind of tell if you're saying 'hey, would you get me a beer' or '*go get me a beer, obedient wench*', and if we don't like something you tell us to do it doesn't change how we feel, we still don't like it — we can tell you that, we can argue with you or complain, but if you insist —" she shrugged. "— we have to do it."

Shit, I hadn't known that and I should've done the research to really understand what this meant before I'd agreed to do it — but there was so damn much I didn't know about witches. It didn't help that the idea of having that sort of control over someone made my stomach tighten with pleasure and anticipation. Maybe there was something wrong with me, but I liked the idea at the same time as I was very nearly horrified by it.

"Stop overthinking it," Sam said. "It's a physical compulsion, not mental or emotional."

"I don't know if that makes it any better."

"Hmph. Let me think of a good example." Sam was silent for a few seconds while I tried to adjust to the idea. "Look, a particularly unpleasant warlock *could* use the bond to tell one of his witches to give him a blowjob, even if she really didn't want to."

I winced — that really wasn't an example I was comfortable with.

"*But*," Sam went on, "he'd have to be very specific about a few things."

"Like what?"

"Like 'don't bite it off,'" Sam said, then ignoring another wince. "Or, 'don't dig your nails into the dangly-bits and rip them open.'"

I cringed, trying to sink into the mattress.

"'Don't set my ass-hair on fire,'" Sam went on. "That sort of thing. Don't get me wrong, it can be abused — and it is. A lot. But it's very specific and immediate control."

She put two fingers over my lips.

"This is nothing new for witches. We know exactly what we're getting into by forming a coven and we're okay with it — it's right there in the title, even, *Domina Ritualis*. *Dominus*, in your case."

"What's that? I thought Rachel said that was for rituals."

"Mistress of the Ritual — or Master of the Ritual. It applies to the coven all the time, not just during rituals. We usually just shorten it to *Domina*..." She paused. "*Dominus*."

I grunted, struggling with the idea.

"What's wrong, *Dominus*?" Sam asked. I could feel her grinning.

I could also feel my face heat.

On the one hand, I was a modern guy in current year and I was really uncomfortable with the idea of Sam or anyone else being compelled to do whatever I told her to. It was somehow even worse than my Command affinity, because it sounded like it was something inherent in the bond, not something I had to consciously do. On the other hand ... the idea was setting off a lot of involuntary muscle contractions below my belly button.

"Maybe," I said, "we could not use that title? I mean, this isn't first century Rome or something, right? We could be like a modern coven, sort of?"

"Hhmm." Sam raised her head to look at me. "Maybe you're right."

"Good."

"We should be modern and not use that old Latin." She snuggled closer to me and keeping my dick between my thighs was becoming a little uncomfortable. "I'll just call you Master."

"What? No! That's not what I —"

"As you wish, My Lord."

"*What the hell?*"

"*Dominus* — it's either that, master, or lord, pick one."

I closed my eyes and rubbed my forehead.

"What's wrong, Master?" Sam asked, in an obviously fake tone of concern. She threw her leg over my hips and rolled on top of me, pouting. "Do you not want to be my master? Do you not want me?"

Now she actually managed to look hurt, and even though I knew she was entirely faking her distress, I had the urge to wrap her in my arms and make everything better.

"Of course, I want you — I just —"

She lowered her face to nuzzle at my neck, then nibbled on my earlobe.

"Not want me to obey you, Master?" Her breath was hot against my neck and tickled my ear — far hotter in my brain, though. "Obey your every wish?" She trailed kisses over my throat to my other ear and nibbled there, too. "Fulfill your every desire?"

"Sam —"

She shifted her hips to slide her lower lips over my cock, which I realized had escaped from between my legs and was getting hard again, and I moaned.

"Sam, we should talk about —"

"I'm busy, Master." She swiveled her hips to catch my cock and ease it inside her. "I've waited my whole life to have a warlock, so, if you want me to stop and talk ... you'll have to order me."

# CHAPTER FORTY-SEVEN

I DIDN'T GET ANOTHER CHANCE TO TALK MORE WITH SAM ABOUT the coven bond and its compulsion until the next morning when we left the hotel.

Yes, that's a long time.

We were busy.

"I feel kind of bad," Sam said as we walked — it was a sunny day, cold, but pleasant, and we'd decided to walk a few blocks before catching a rideshare to Mel's.

"Why should you feel bad? I'm the one who —"

"You didn't know what you were getting into — not really. I did. Did you even really understand that a coven-bond is permanent? Like, life-permanent?"

"Yes, that I knew."

I did, but it was a big step and maybe I hadn't thought it all the way through — though, even if I had it wouldn't have changed my decision. I didn't *mind* being tied to her, and I certainly wouldn't have denied forming a coven with her.

"It only gets stronger with time, you know?" she asked.

"What does?"

"The bond. Have you noticed you can see through my shields?"

I nodded. That was something I'd noticed last night — even with her shields up after the first time, I'd still been able to read the cheat codes and see everything she was feeling through her mana.

"There aren't many secrets in a coven," she said. "We'll always know what the other's feeling, we'll always know where the other one is —"

"Wait? Like a party map in a game?"

"No, you don't get a HUD or something out of it — you're such a guy." She shook her head. "More like ... direction and distance. It'll be weak at first, but it gets stronger with time or concentration." She wrapped herself around my arm as we walked. "Other things, too."

"Like you having to do what I say," I said, frowning. That was the part I really had trouble with.

Sam sighed.

"But that's exactly why I wanted to form a coven with you instead of some warlock my mom picked for me. Just like with your Command affinity, I trust you — if you asked me to do something and I said I really didn't want to, what would you do?"

I shrugged. "Not make you do it, I suppose." I thought about that for a minute. "So, will you promise me you'll tell me if that happens? So, I can take it back?"

She squeezed my arm and I could feel her warmth and softness through my jacket.

"Yes, Master."

"Don't —"

She looked up at me with wide eyes, lips trembling.

"I don't want you to order me to stop, Master."

Sometimes she was as big a brat as Morgan was.

"Shit," I muttered. "Can we go back to *Dominus*?"

At least that wouldn't make passers-by look at us weird. Maybe.

I stayed quiet for about two blocks, letting her bask in her victory, because she really did have me there.

"So," I said, finally, "hypothetically — if I told you to go make me a sandwich..."

She slapped my shoulder.

"Such a guy."

---

I SPENT the ride back to Mel's brownstone thinking of ways to tell her that I'd marked Sam.

Well, she was probably going to know as soon as she looked at us, because she just knew things, so really, I spent the time thinking of things to say after she calmed down from finding out.

"How mad do you think she's going to be?" Sam asked.

I shrugged. "Pretty mad, but she'll get over it."

Mel was the one who'd told me I needed to form a coven, after all. Could she really be that mad at me for starting one?

"She might get over it with you, but how mad is she going to be at me?"

I pulled Sam close. "Well, we're a coven now, right? So, we're sticking together. If she's mad at you she's gotta be mad at me."

We got to Mel's brownstone and paused at the door.

"This is it," I said.

"I wonder who's going to be maddest at us — well, I know my mother's going to be the absolute maddest, but between The Blackwood and *Prima* Rosethorn who do you think?"

I shrugged. "Only one way to find out."

I unlocked the door and we went in.

"Is that you, Noah?" Mel called.

"Me and Sam," I answered.

"I'm in the kitchen, dear — there are fresh cookies."

"The Blackwood ... *bakes?*"

"I can hear you," Mel called.

"*Eep!*" Sam jumped.

I heard the tinkling of a bell and Felicity came trotting around the corner to greet us.

I reached down and gave her a scratch behind the ears while she rubbed against my hand and purred.

I stood up and started into the house, Sam got behind me and grabbed my arm, peeking around my shoulder.

Mel was in the kitchen, with her long dark hair up in the frazzled-looking bun she wore while cooking. She had on her typical jeans and V-neck top, both tight, no sweater since the kitchen was cozy from the oven's heat, an apron around her waist and a towel draped over one shoulder. The house smelled like fresh-baked cookies again, just chocolate chip this time, and I took a big whiff.

"You're just in time for a fresh batch," Mel said, opening the oven door and reaching in for a tray of cookies, which really exhibited how tight those jeans were.

"The last batch wasn't enough?" I asked.

"Those were left at the school last night, these are for us."

I walked up to the island and leaned against it, keeping it between us and Mel as a sort of physical barrier. Felicity hopped up on the counter and started rubbing against my arm. It was calming as always.

Mel turned around from the oven, stared at us for a moment, then dropped the sheet of cookies to the kitchen floor.

"What have you done?" Mel stared at us, then before I could start to explain, "Oh, do you have any idea how much trouble this is going to cause?"

"How can she tell?" Sam whispered. "I have my shields up."

"The two of you reek of sex," Mel said.

"But we showered," Sam whispered. "Twice."

"Yeah, but then we —"

"Oh, yeah."

"Will the two of you stop whispering? If I could hear you in the other room, I can certainly hear you now. And there's no way that much sex didn't end up in one of you being marked. Since I know

Noah's affinity, I assume it wasn't him who was on the receiving end. Which means your mother is going to be furious, young lady."

"Good, I hope she has an apoplectic fit and swallows her tongue."

"So do I," Mel said, "but that doesn't change the trouble this is going to cause. Evelina is going to want to expel you both."

"We didn't do it at the school," I said. "We are of age, away from school, so there's nothing she can do about it."

I hoped that was true.

Mel sighed. "There's nothing she can do about it officially, dear. Unofficially, I'm sure your lives at Willowmere are going to become quite interesting."

Since she was back to calling me "dear" I figured Sam and I weren't in any particular danger.

I shrugged. "We'll deal with it."

Mel bent and picked up the tray of cookies, coming to the island where the cookie racks from previous batches were. She set the tray down and grabbed a small spatula to start taking the cookies off the tray and place them on the cooling racks.

"Don't look at me like that," she said. "The cookies didn't touch the floor, just the bottom of the pan. I'm certainly not going to waste them."

"She doesn't seem very upset," Sam whispered.

Yeah, she didn't. She didn't even seem particularly surprised and I noted the cookie sheet had fallen absolutely flat so that none of the cookies would spill. Almost as though she'd staged it.

"That's because she knew it was going to happen," I said, suddenly realizing what it was I knew I didn't know, or didn't know I knew. Just, suddenly, a lot of pieces came together.

"What?" Both Mel and Sam said at the same time.

I started pacing, staring down at my feet while I worked through it in my head. I pointed at Mel.

"There is no way you would've let me go off to spend Solstice with the Prescotts," I said. "I was too nervous at the time to figure it out, but you agreed way too easily."

I frowned, realizing something else.

"Not only did you know we were going to, but you wanted us to."

Mel raised an eyebrow. "Whatever makes you think that?"

"Because you knew what we were up to and didn't stop us." I narrowed my eyes. "You are *not* the sort of person who'd just let me do something you disapproved of or thought was a bad idea."

Mel took the bowl of cookie dough from the stand mixer and brought it over to the island. She pulled three spoons from a drawer and offered them to us.

"You're granting me credit for a great deal of perception, dear. Perhaps I was simply preoccupied with my cookies?"

"No, you wouldn't have let me go if you didn't know. Or you'd have invited yourself along to the Prescotts' Solstice party."

"That would be rather rude."

"Would it stop you?"

"Of course not, dear."

Mel scooped up a big spoonful of cookie dough, popped it in her mouth, then scooped out more and offered it to Felicity.

"Cats can't have chocolate," I pointed out, as Sam scooped up some dough of her own.

"*Pfft!*" Felicity hissed at me before daintily nibbling at the dough Mel offered her.

"She'll be fine, dear."

"Who picked Sam to be my roommate?" I demanded, suddenly certain there'd been more going on than just letting me go to meet Sam.

"Whatever do you mean, dear?"

"Yeah," Sam asked, "what do you mean?"

"When she and *Prima* Rosethorn were making the plans for me to go to Willowmere she sent me out of the room so they could talk about the details. One of the details was a roommate. Who picked Sam as my roommate?"

Mel shrugged. "Evelina proposed several options and we discussed them. I can't really recall how we decided on Samantha."

I had some doubts about Mel's faulty memory, but I wasn't prepared to outright call her a liar.

"And you hardly argued at all when I wanted to partner with Sam for shield work," I went on.

"She swore an oath," Mel said.

"Yeah, you *really* didn't want anyone to know I was *trinitara*, much less had the Control resonant — but you just went along with it."

Mel shrugged. "It was a good oath."

I narrowed my eyes.

"Oh, very well," Mel said, tossing her spoon into the cookie dough. "Yes, I strongly suspected what you and Samantha were up to. If you wanted to keep it secret you should have been more circumspect."

"What?" Sam said. "We didn't do anything until last night!"

"There's a certain look a young woman gives someone she's chosen to become intimate with, dear, even before the act. You've been looking at Noah that way since you recovered from your rather foolish potion adventure." Mel frowned. "And the Winthrop girl, as well." She turned to me. "Will she be next?"

"What? Rachel?" I stammered, looking at Sam.

Sam shrugged. "I told you I like her butt."

"Will she be next to join your coven, dear? I'm nearly certain she'd be willing."

"Wait, what, no!" I held up my hands. "Stop, you're trying to distract me."

Mel frowned. "You're being far more perceptive than I'd expect. Has something more than a marking happened?"

"No. And I'm not marking Rachel!"

I said that. Those were the words that came out of my mouth, but it certainly wasn't what I felt.

Now that someone had said it, I realized that I absolutely wanted to mark Rachel. So much that my jaw ached even thinking about it. I wanted the shy little witch under me and to have one hand fisted in her hair to keep her from hiding her face while I entered her. I wanted to tear the walls of her reserve down and see all the passion she'd shown at the spellstick game focused on me. I wanted — I wanted Sam there with us, but those images were confused. In one I made Rachel pleasure Sam while I took her from behind … in the other, Sam was restrained, unable to move while she watched Rachel and I together.

"Noah, dear, you're growling."

I blinked.

*Where the fuck had that come from?*

"Whatever the fuck put that look on your face, I want it," Sam whispered.

I blinked again, then checked my resonants, but they were all evenly filled, so I had nothing to blame that reaction on but myself.

I shook my head to clear it, then glared at Mel.

"Stop trying to change the subject. You set this up! Sam and I."

Mel sighed. "I told you from the beginning, dear, that you must form a coven to become independent from the Families. Attending Willowmere, aside from the protection it offers, was to allow you to meet the witches there. I simply made sure you had the best possible choice for a roommate at Willowmere, someone you'd be spending the most time with. Anything after that is entirely your own doing."

I turned to Sam. "Doesn't this bother you?"

Sam shrugged. "What? That she thought we'd be a good match and put us together?" She shrugged again. "We are, aren't we?"

"Well, yeah, but — wait, you had to have known she's gay, right? I asked Mel.

Mel shrugged. "What difference does that make if she wants a coven?"

Sam nodded. "Told you."

I rubbed my eyes, trying to figure out just how deep Mel's machinations went. "You said I'd have to build up a super powerful coven to defend against the Families and stay independent."

"You do," Mel agreed.

"You had to have known Sam was a onesie, too — sorry, Sam."

Sam shrugged, doing disturbingly distracting things with her spoonful of dough. "I got better."

Mel shrugged. "What of it?"

"You couldn't have known she was looking for that book, or that she'd drink all of the potion — so why would you think a onesie was a good match?"

Mel chuckled. "Noah, dear, you are a *trinitara* warlock of the Blackwood line — if Samantha hadn't already been a *trinitara* yesterday, she *would* be today. You would not have been able to resist opening her dormant resonants during your marking. The coven bond always wants more power."

"Wait," Sam said. "Are you saying Noah did that to me? It wasn't the potion and all that raw mana?"

Mel and I had kept that even from Sam because of how dangerous the knowledge was. And Mel was right, having experienced that with three resonants, I wouldn't have been satisfied with one or two. Any inkling or instinct that it was possible would have been hard to resist.

"Yes, dear," Mel said to Sam. "The raw mana brought on by the potion made it more difficult and dangerous, but the act itself was Noah."

Sam's eyes got big — whether from the knowledge I could do that or Mel elevating her to "dear", I don't know.

"Would've been good to know before I almost blew up the school," she muttered.

She wasn't wrong. I wondered what would have gone differently if I'd told Mel about Sam's plan ahead of time — would she have just told us about this then and sent us off to get a room?

"That's what makes a 'onesie', offensive as the term is," Mel said, "an ideal candidate for your coven, dear. There's far more power generated when the witch and warlock have compatible resonants. Being able to mirror two of yours into the witch ensures a quite powerful match — the only better match would be a witch who has all three of your resonants."

Sam's eyes got even wider. "Crone's gnarled knuckles," she breathed. "An entire coven of *trinitaras*?"

Mel shrugged. "It's not unknown — though it has been a very long time. And you should keep that secret until your coven is powerful enough to defend itself — that ability will be sought after."

"You should have told me," I said.

"Told you what, dear? That you should seduce your roommate? Witches do meddle, it's in our nature, but there are lines even I won't cross."

Sam nodded and dipped her spoon back into the cookie dough.

Felicity must have decided she wasn't getting any more cookie dough and hopped off the counter to hurry into the next room.

I lowered my gaze, trying to figure out what had me so upset about this.

"I guess I'm just trying to figure out how much meddling you've done," I said.

"What do you mean, dear?"

"It's — ever since this happened to me, that I found out I was a warlock, I mean, it's been like the decisions were all forced on me."

Mel opened her mouth, then closed it, cocking her head to one side, waiting.

"Then when Sam and I ... well, *we* decided to form a coven. It wasn't forced on me, it wasn't that I had no choice like so much has. Now it feels like you nudged that along, too."

I was starting to feel angry about it, the more and more I thought.

"And it *has* to go back farther than just when you brought me back here after I was attacked. I mean, I've known Felicity for *years*. Maybe I was too busy catching up with witches and magic when I first got here that I accepted you didn't know she was visiting me, but I'm really supposed to believe a cat, even one as special as Felicity, stumbled across me one day and then kept the fact that I was a warlock from you until *just* when I needed someone to rescue me from that alley?"

I put my palms flat on the counter.

"Okay, I'll believe Felicity is smarter than the average cat. She understands a lot, she's very intuitive, but how did she even find me? My foster home is *miles* from here. I'm supposed to just believe she happened to be roaming miles from home one day and stumbled across me? And that she knew enough to wait? That it was her decision not to tell you about me? That's too much for a cat."

"Cats do roam, dear."

"You know what I think, Mel? I think you came across me and sent Felicity to check on me once in a while. I think you've been 'meddling' for a lot longer than you've told me. I either believe that, or I believe Felicity did it all on her own. And I don't see how Felicity could."

"You should," someone said behind me, "because Felicity is far more clever than you seem to think."

I turned around and screamed.

# CHAPTER FORTY-EIGHT

"WHAT THE EVER-LOVING FUCK?"

I hopped up on the kitchen island and nearly scrambled off the other side.

There was a cat in the living room doorway. A girl. A girl-cat. A cat-girl.

A little over five-feet of black-furred, white-spotted, sleekly-moving ... very clearly naked cat-girl.

My dick twitched and began expanding in my pants.

*Not now*, I told my dick.

*But ... naked cat-girl ...* my dick insisted.

"What the hell?" I said, letting my dick do whatever the hell it wanted, because it was going to anyway.

The naked cat-girl came around the island to stand beside me and Sam.

"Felicity, Noah," Mel said, gesturing. "Noah, Felicity. Now you've been properly introduced."

"How is there a cat-girl?" I asked.

Mel sighed.

"She's not a cat-girl. She's a witch ... who has spent far too much time over the years in the form of a cat."

Felicity shrugged — a lithe, shimmying, very naked cat-girl shrug.

"No, no," I muttered, pacing between the kitchen and living room. "This is too much." I looked at Felicity. "All those years you were really a person? You've been in my lap! I've ... I've rubbed your belly! I've..." I froze, staring at her, then whispering, "I've seen your butthole."

Sam and Mel started laughing.

"Stop it! This is serious!" I stormed over to Mel. "How can you be okay with seeing her butthole all the time? And it wasn't at a distance, either, *it was right here!*"

Mel and Sam kept laughing while Felicity just stared at me, face ... blank like a cat's.

---

IT TOOK a few minutes of being laughed at, but eventually I calmed down enough to return to the kitchen.

Felicity — the cat-girl — had taken one of the island stools and was busy spooning cookie dough out of the mixing bowl, the tip of her tail twitching slightly as she daintily nibbled the dough with very white, very pointy teeth.

She was still very naked.

Sure, fur covered her — everywhere but the very tips of her breasts, which were...

Wait.

Felicity-cat-girl had two breasts, each with one nipple.

Two nipples.

I counted.

One, two nipples.

But when I'd rubbed Felicity-cat's belly there'd been...

Therapy. I was going to need therapy.

I was okay with magic — with witches, vampires, secret patriarchal enemies, even having scary magic powers some people might want to kill me for.

But years of rubbing transmogrifying cat-girl nipples was a step too far.

*That* I was going to need professional help with.

I was still upset, too.

I was sick of surprises, sick of things being sprung on me with no warning, sick of things being kept from me, sick of being meddled with and manipulated, even if it was for my own good or whatever.

Fine, maybe it was best that I hadn't been told about magic until I aged-out of foster care, but since then, someone could have told me Felicity was a real person, not just a smart cat. It had been *six months* and no one found a chance to catch me up on that?

Hell, I'd thought last night with Sam was the first nipple-touching I'd ever done and...

Therapy.

I took a deep breath, but it didn't help.

It was all too much and I needed some time to process it all.

"I think I need to think about things for a little bit," I said.

"Noah?"

Sam looked worried, but I really needed some time alone to think about ... everything.

I realized I'd had very little, if any, time to do that since I'd woken up here at Mel's. Everything had moved so fast. The closest I'd had was at the lake party, and I'd spent that time thinking about the differences between mundane and witch worlds — not trying to process everything that had happened to me.

"Yeah," I said, standing, but not looking at anyone. "I'm going to take a walk and ... think. I'll be back in a while."

I left Mel's.

THERE WAS a park a couple blocks away, and I felt the need for fresh air and open space. Someplace where I wasn't smelling fucking cookies and it didn't feel like things were pressing in on me from all sides.

I don't know how long I was there, sitting on a bench and watching the squirrels and pigeons — and fighting thoughts about how funny it would be to bring Felicity here and watch her try to catch the damn things. I didn't want to have good thoughts about Felicity right now.

Even if I accepted that she and Mel couldn't have told me anything before I turned eighteen — which I guess was the right choice — they'd still had *six months* to tell me Felicity wasn't a fucking cat.

I wasn't unhappy she wasn't a cat — that was pretty cool, actually, and I wanted to have some conversations with her. Given everything I'd told her over the years, she probably knew more about me than anyone in the world and her opinion would be interesting.

But *six months*?

"Hey, you."

I heard Sam's voice behind me, but didn't turn around. At least she hadn't been involved in keeping things from me, so I couldn't be mad at her — that would be awkward after we just tied ourselves to each other for life the night before.

"Hey."

She came up behind me and started massaging my shoulders.

"Oo, tight," Sam said.

"That's what he said."

Sam's hands stopped massaging.

"Did you really? Did you really just make a sex joke when you're so upset you had to run out of the house without giving anyone even a chance to explain?"

I shrugged and she started massaging again.

"You are such a guy."

"I didn't run," I said.

"You walked at speed."

I grunted. "Are you here to tell me I'm an asshole for running off?"

"Not really, but what set you off?"

I sighed — that was what I was trying to figure out.

"Sometimes it seems like I had more control over my life when I was in foster care and had a CPS caseworker. At least Mrs. Dexter would have told me if she was a cat. I'm not saying everything is bad — I'm not saying *anything* is bad — but I'd like to have a little control over things and I don't. Not where I live, not where I go to school, not how I support myself, nothing."

"What about me?"

"You're the one thing I *do* have control over." I winced. "Sorry, I didn't mean it that way, I meant —"

Sam's hands slid from my shoulders to my chest and her lips brushed my neck.

"But what if I want you to mean it that way, *Dominus*?"

I sighed.

"I *meant* that the decision to be with you was the one thing I think I did have control over — and I wouldn't change it. But that whole '*Dominus*' thing is one of the things I mean — is that you, or is that some more magic controlling things? Because you never talked about stuff like that before."

Now it was Sam's turn to sigh.

"Oh, we're being serious, I guess." Her arms tightened around me. "So, is your magic affecting me? Yes, of course it is. You gave me Lust and Pain resonants — to save my life, so if you feel guilty about it that means you'd rather I be dead, so just put that shit out of your mind right the fuck now. Our resonants affect us — that's the way it works. I've always been ... sexual, but, yeah, I've really noticed it since I took that potion. Which is why I'm going to be jumping you six times a day, because, Maiden's moans, that's been on my mind the last two months — and more now that I know how good it is."

She nudged me in the back with her knee.

"Scooch."

I slid forward on the bench and she sat behind me, spreading her legs around me and pressing close to my back.

"Better — my back was hurting from bending over. So — *Dominus* thing."

"I know you're mostly teasing me with that."

Sam was silent for a minute. "Maybe ... not?" She took a deep breath. "It really is the title for who's in charge of a coven and I may be teasing you a little with the other meaning, but I've ... looked into that sort of thing before. A little. I'm the curious sort. But, yeah, again, my interest has been a little more piqued the last couple months. Especially since last night. Is that all me or your Control resonance working on me through the coven bond to up the power for the coven? Both, probably, and *that's how covens work*." Her hands moved back to my shoulders, massaging again. "You're going to need twelve more witches to form a coven and you're going to be giving each of them one or two resonants — because it would be fucking unfair *not to* when you can. That's going to change them. They're going to change you. We're all going to change each other. So, am I different than I was two months ago? Yeah. If you don't like the difference, tell me, but if I don't tell you I don't like it, then just fucking enjoy it, okay?"

I chuckled. "Yes, *Domina*."

Sam smacked me on the back of the head. "*Ew!* That is not me. Don't even joke about it."

I laughed.

"Good, now you're in a better mood, so let's talk about Felicity."

"Fine. I just don't get why she couldn't tell me sometime in the last six months. I mean, it's not like I don't *like* cat-girls."

"Noah, Melaina told me some things before I came to find you. Felicity's ... fragile."

"Felicity?" That I had trouble believing. The cat, girl, cat-girl, witch, cat-witch, whatever, was independent, self-assured, bossy ...

fragile wasn't something that occurred to me when I thought about Felicity.

Sam nodded. "She is. Melaina said she hasn't shown any form other than cat to anyone else in a long time. She hasn't *talked* to anyone but Melaina in ... a long time. Longer than you'd believe, probably. When you left ... it broke something in her."

"What?" I started to stand up. I didn't want to hurt Felicity, I'd just wanted an hour or two alone to figure things out. I needed to get back to Mel's and fix this.

Sam caught my shoulders and pulled me back down to the bench.

"Melaina's comforting her, I think it'd be best to give them some more time."

"Shit. I didn't mean to hurt her; I just wanted some time to think."

"I know — and Melaina does, too. You had no way to know how hard it was for Felicity to show you something other than her full-cat form. Especially with me there too — I think because we're a coven now Felicity sees us as one thing, maybe. She has a lot of self-esteem issues that make her afraid of people."

"*Felicity?* She's the most —"

"As a cat," Sam interrupted me. "Whatever you know about her is how she presents *as a cat*."

"Fuck."

Of course. If she went around as a cat, then that was the perfect way to hide from people.

"I tried not to listen but there were a lot of words like stupid, worthless, and ugly thrown in with the crying."

I bent forward and buried my face in my hands. "Fuck me."

I really didn't need to fuck up this badly again so soon after Katrina.

"You couldn't know," Sam said, seeming to read my mind.

# CHAPTER FORTY-NINE

We walked back to Mel's brownstone. Sam kept her arms wrapped around one of mine and I kind of marveled at how quickly I'd calmed down and stopped being upset once she started touching me. It was as though she'd cleared my head and let me really think about things.

The brownstone door was unlocked, so we just went in and found Mel in the kitchen cleaning up the aftermath of baking.

She stopped when she saw us enter and went awkwardly to the island. She set her hands on it, one clutching the other, and looked down at them. It was weird to see Mel uncertain or apologetic — even when she apologized, she usually did it from a position of strength and certainty.

"I tried to convince Felicity to show you sooner, dear, but she was too afraid."

"Why is she so afraid? We've known each other for years — the only thing I was upset about was how long it took to tell me."

The teapot I hadn't noticed on the stove top started to whistle.

"We should sit for that. Samantha, dear, there are tea things in that cabinet, would you get them, please?"

"Of course, Melaina," Sam said, going to the cabinet.

Apparently, we were having tea. And apparently Mel and Sam had worked out Sam not calling Mel The Blackwood all the time, though why I rated Mel and Sam was stuck with Melaina, I didn't know.

"Call me Mel, dear, you're family now."

"Can we work our way up to that?"

Ah, that explained it, then.

Mel set the tea to steeping — teabags weren't something I'd ever seen in her home — and we stayed gathered around the island while we waited.

"You're feeling better, dear?" Mel asked me.

I nodded and Sam laid one hand over Mel's on the counter — I raised an eyebrow at that, because it was a little unexpected given how awed she seemed of the older witch.

"Are you certain *you're* okay?" Sam asked.

Mel looked at her with a puzzled frown, then looked down at their hands. Sam quickly jerked her hand away and her eyes went wide, as though she hadn't realized she'd touched Mel, but Mel reached out and took Sam's hand, staring at her for a moment.

"I'm fine, dear, but thank you. That's going to be a real asset to Noah's coven."

"What is?" Sam asked.

"You don't know? Look inside, dear."

Sam's eyes went distant and impulsively I looked for her mana as well, even though I was sure she'd have her shields up. I could see her resonants even though her shields were in place due to the coven bond.

Sam's eyes went wide. "Oh!"

"What is it?" I asked.

I noticed something else was different. There was a dim, line of manna from Sam to me and also from Sam to Mel.

"I — I have an affinity," Sam whispered, her eyes widening more and a slow smile creeping up her face.

"What is it?"

Sam shook her head. "I don't know — I'm not trying to do anything. But it feels ... comfortable."

"It's Harmony," Mel said. "It'll work best on your coven sisters and Noah — less so on someone whose shields are up or knows enough to resist it."

"Harmony?"

"It's one of the passive workings," Mel said. "Which is why you didn't realize you were doing it. It comes from your Love resonant — it will help those close to you in conflict. Maybe even make them more willing to listen and work things out. I think most covens would like to have something like that available."

We all got a cup of tea and moved to the living room where Mel sat in her regular chair and Sam and I took the couch.

"I have Felicity's consent to tell you this," Mel said, "so I'm not telling tales out of school — and she's currently sulking behind the couch, so she's free to object or correct me if she wishes. She is being a bit unreasonable."

A muffled "*pfft*" sounded from behind me.

"I met Felicity in Salem," Mel said, taking her first sip of tea.

"Salem Salem?" I asked.

"Yes, dear, the Trials."

That would mean Felicity was over four hundred years old. I'd accepted such things about Mel, but Felicity, too?

"She was orphaned a few years before the Trials," Mel went on, "and taken in by another family — not witches, the Family coven structure wasn't in use then, and another witch family wasn't around to take her in. The family that did take her in ... was not kind, even before the Trials. They had a daughter of their own, and when the Trials started, she accused Felicity of witchcraft. It was nonsense, of course, Felicity hadn't even come into her power yet. She was held for trial for several months, and repeatedly questioned, before she escaped."

We learned about such questioning in *Magistra* Nightingale's class and I had a sudden urge to wrap Felicity in a hug and reassure her that I'd never let anything like that happen to her again. I don't know where the feeling came from, just that it was overwhelmingly strong — maybe because of all the times I'd been sad in foster care and she'd comforted me even as a cat.

"How?" I asked. I knew it was probably a very personal question, but I hadn't heard of anyone actually escaping the Salem Trials.

"By changing into a cat, of course," Mel said.

"But shape shifting takes a huge amount of power," Sam said, "and she was still a teenager? Untrained?"

Mel nodded.

"She came into her power in the dungeons — oh, the mundanes will say it was a simple jail, but once the questioning starts, it's a dungeon. Her resonants are Fear and Despair, you see — not the most pleasant for a witch, especially not a witch with no one to explain it to her, more especially in a situation where they would be generating so much mana and reinforcing each other."

I shuddered, thinking about spending months in a cell being "questioned", which was really a euphemism for tortured, and having to rely on the fear and despair I felt from that for the opportunity to escape. No wonder Felicity preferred to spend time as a cat.

"Body magic isn't normally an affinity that comes with either of those," Mel went on, "but circumstances sometimes shape our magic. And our magic often shapes our selves."

We were all silent for a few seconds before Mel went on.

"I found her wandering the edges of the village," Mel said. "And got her away from there before I went back to see who else I might be able to save." She took a sip of her tea. "She's been with me ever since — mostly as a cat."

"Four hundred years?" I asked.

Mel nodded. "Nearly that, yes."

Four hundred years ... four hundred years without showing herself to anyone but Mel, and she'd picked me. And I couldn't handle it. Well, I could have handled if she'd shown me the same day Mel had shown me that magic was real — then it would have just been one more amazing thing. Or before I'd started at Willowmere? Probably no issue then. But today it had been one more weird thing just when I thought I might be getting a handle on the weird things, coming on the heels of both my failure with Katrina and marking Sam, and I'd been overwhelmed for a moment. But a moment's all it takes sometimes.

"Let's let Noah have some time to himself, dear," Mel said to Sam. "Come, we'll go down to my workroom and have a look at your new affinity. There are some tricks I can show you."

Mel rose and made her way to the stairs; confident Sam would follow.

I saw Sam was frozen, eyes wide.

"The Blackwood's workroom?" she whispered.

"You'd better go," I said, "she doesn't like to be kept waiting."

"But ... but, personal instruction from The Blackwood?"

I nodded. "You should get used to it, you're family now."

Sam's eyes got even wider.

"Go," I whispered.

"*Eep!*"

Sam hurried to the stairs and I looked around the empty room before deciding I needed to at least try to talk to Felicity.

I got up and slid a small table away from the side of the couch so I could have room to sit down next to the open space behind it.

I took a quick look into the space, but couldn't see Felicity and I didn't think she'd appreciate having me shine a flashlight or something at her in there, so I sat with my back against the wall.

"Hey, Felicity," I said quietly. "I'm sorry I upset you. It was just a little bit of a shock and there was a lot of other stuff, not you, that's built up, so I felt like I needed some space to think things out. I want you to know I'm not angry or upset with you and I never meant to hurt you."

I heard a rustling behind the couch, so I just kept talking — I'm not even sure what I said other than wanting to reassure Felicity that I cared for her and wasn't angry. I talked about some of the memories I had of her coming to me as a cat. Especially the times I was upset and how much comfort I'd gotten from her. I wanted her to know that I appreciated what she'd done for me over the years.

After a bit of time, I slid my hand behind the couch.

"It always made me feel better when you rubbed your face against me or I could pet you."

I felt a twinge of weirdness now, knowing that she was a person and not just a cat, but I kind of figured if she spent so much time as a cat, then maybe I should still treat her a little bit like one.

"I know you're upset, and I'm a little upset too still, so maybe it would make us both feel better ... that is if you want a little neck scratch or maybe behind the ears?"

I heard a faint, rumbling purr, and then a light pressure of fur against my hand. I stayed still until it became firmer and then moved my fingers to work them gently into her fur.

"I really do care about you, Felicity — one of the things that bothered me the most about having to leave the foster home was knowing I'd probably never see you again. And now, knowing you're a person, I'd hate losing you even more."

The purring grew louder and Felicity's head filled my hand as she rubbed against my palm. I realized Sam had said something really important in the park that I hadn't known before. She'd said Felicity loved me — I should've realized that, because she watched over me for years, to keep me safe, comfort me, and got me to Mel as soon as she thought it was safe.

"I love you too, you know. More now that I know you're a person."

Felicity started rubbing her head farther up my arm as I lightly scratched the fur along her side, her purring was practically vibrating the couch now.

"I mean, with Mel maybe being my many greats grandmother or whatever and you being with her for so long, it's like we're family too, right? Like you're my aunt or some —"

"*Mrowr!*"

"*Fuck!*"

# CHAPTER FIFTY

"What did you do to her?"

I wasn't sure I deserved the accusatory tone in Sam's voice, after all I was the one standing at the kitchen sink running water over an arm that looked like I'd shoved it into a garbage disposal.

"Nothing! We were just talking — well, I was talking and she was purring and I was scratching her and then she suddenly went batshit!"

"Well, you must've said something."

"Stop flinching," Mel said, holding my arm under the water.

"It hurts!"

"And it will keep hurting," Mel told me. "Until I've got these cuts cleaned and bandaged."

"Will it get infected?"

Mel stopped cleaning my wounds and stared at me, face blank.

"Are you suggesting Felicity doesn't keep her claws clean?"

"Um, no?"

"Good. If there's any infection it will be because you didn't take care of your wounds."

"Can't you just heal it?" I asked, thinking of how quickly the injured spellstick players had been healed.

"That depends."

"On what?"

"On what you did to Felicity. It's possible you need to suffer a bit."

That didn't sound at all fair.

"So, what did you say to her?" Sam demanded.

"Nothing! Well, nothing bad. I was talking about all the times that her visits made me feel better, and how much I cared about her, even loved her — and how if I was related to Mel and she'd been with Mel for so long, then it was like we were family too and she was like an aunt or —"

*"You what?"* Sam and Mel demanded together.

"What?"

Sam shook her head and walked into the other room while Mel roughly jerked my arm back under the water.

*"Ow!"*

"Oh, Felicity, sister, I'm so sorry," Sam was saying in the other room — far louder than she needed to be for Felicity to hear her, so she must've been intending her words half for me. "He really does know nothing, so he didn't mean it. He's just a *stupid boy*."

---

AFTER MY ARM WAS BANDAGED, Mel got dinner in the oven, then made up one of her guest rooms for Sam.

"The two of you may do as you will," she said. "But I'll be able to tell Judith Prescott truthfully that I provided you separate rooms."

Dinner was roast chicken with mashed potatoes and gravy and green beans sautéed with garlic and butter. Mel fixed a bowl for Felicity and set it on the table, but Felicity didn't come out to get it.

"I'll leave it in the refrigerator," Mel called toward the couch as she cleared the table after we'd eaten.

Dessert was chocolate chip cookies with a scoop of ice cream — even the ice cream was freshly made. Mel had some kitchen appliance that could turn frozen pints of ingredients into a creamy texture.

It was awkward to sit on the couch with our dessert — at least for me — knowing that Felicity was behind us.

"Maybe Sam and I should stay in a hotel until school starts," I suggested. "I feel bad that Felicity's dinner is cold."

"She knows how the microwave works," Mel said, nibbling on a cookie.

"Still —"

"You're still safest here until you can return to Willowmere. Even if you go out during the day, it's best others have the reminder of where you live. And whose protection you're under."

We had started to watch a movie with the dessert, but I couldn't get into it. My feelings were all a mess — I was feeling guilty about Felicity, and anxious to get Sam alone, even if I wasn't entirely sure we'd have a repeat of last night.

I mean, she'd *said* she was going to jump me six times a day and she was still being very touchy, but I was a guy and all. It'd been necessary for marking her and forming the coven, but maybe she saw that as a necessary evil, and would want that coven-schedule thing where the warlock only harvested mana from each witch in the coven once every two weeks.

If so, that was going to be ... rough.

I certainly wanted to do it more than once every two weeks — although, if our coven had been full, then I guess it wouldn't be so bad with twelve other girls to cycle through. I still wasn't used to the idea — and how would it even work if the girls also didn't want to wait two weeks between sex? I figured Sam would be open to joining me and another girl, but would we have to judge potential coven members on whether they would be cool with that too? I knew I still wanted at least one witch in our coven that Sam could love and be loved by in return, maybe more than one.

I got more and more nervous about things as the evening went on

— maybe Sam would actually want the other room Mel had made up. She'd been very affectionate and touchy-feely all day, hardly ever leaving my side and always leaning against me or holding my hand, but would that really mean —

*Geez — things are already so complicated with one witch, what am I going to do with thirteen?*

Midway through the movie — some romantic comedy where everybody misunderstood everybody else — I decided it was time to go ahead and go to bed for the night. I could read, or study, or probably just lay there and stare at the ceiling.

"I'm going to bed," I said, standing. Sam had been leaning against me and had to sit up. "It's been kind of a long day — I feel like getting some rest."

"Me too," Sam said, hopping up.

"Have fun," Mel said, running a finger along the inside of her bowl to get the last of her ice cream and sticking it in her mouth before pulling it out with a loud pop. "Don't worry — the walls here are thick."

I flushed red and started to say something like we weren't going to — but then stopped, because, one, I didn't want Sam to think I didn't want to; and, two, I really, really hoped we would.

My hopes got stronger as Sam followed me into my bedroom, and then pretty certain as she closed the door firmly behind us and wrapped her arms around my neck to start a deep, passionate kiss.

I would have been happy to just keep the kiss going and explore her body with my hands as we stood there, but Sam had other ideas — she shoved me toward the bed so hard that I stumbled and fell back.

"Get your clothes off, *Dominus*," she nearly snarled as she pulled her shirt over her head and began stripping off her jeans.

I didn't hesitate — I sat up on the bed and tried to catch up with her — but that did seem an awfully bossy thing to say to your *dominus*.

I really hoped the walls were as thick as Mel thought they were, because I had a feeling we were going to be very loud.

SAM and I watched each other undress, then she strode toward me and shoved me back down on the bed so I was in roughly the same position as she had been the night before, except for my hands were free. She straddled me and stared into my eyes, then frowned — she looked down at my chest and sighed.

"What's wrong?" I asked. I wasn't ripped or anything, but I thought I looked okay.

She sighed again. "It's just ... maybe, when they start teaching us more body control, you could —"

She raised her hands from my chest and cupped them a couple inches away from me, wiggling her eyebrows.

"I am not growing boobs for you," I said firmly.

Sam pouted. "I'm not talking, like, humongous things. Just ... a little B-cup? No, As – I don't want yours to be bigger than mine. Nobody else would even notice."

"No."

She waggled her eyebrows again and cocked her head. "You could play with them whenever you wanted."

I raised my own hands and cupped her breasts. "I'd rather play with yours whenever I want."

Sam closed her eyes and threw her head back, pressing into my hands.

"Point," she moaned. "Very much point."

# CHAPTER FIFTY-ONE

"Try the mauve one," Sam said, reaching into my closet at Mel's place.

"That's the one you told me not to wear!"

"To a college party, this is different."

"Yeah, it's different because Morgan isn't going to care what I wear — we lived together for five years. She's seen me at my worst."

"She *hasn't* seen you in six months," Sam said while I changed shirts ... again. "You should look like you're doing well, not living on the streets or something."

I looked at my bed where the shirt I'd been planning to wear before Sam's "help" was piled up. To me, it looked identical to the one I was putting on, except for color.

"I don't think I looked like I was homeless or something."

Sam snorted, then adjusted my collar, snugged each button, and tugged the purple shirt down firmly. It's purple. I don't know what the hell "mauve" is.

"You're living with Melaina Seraphina Blackwood," Sam said firmly. "Do you want to make The Blackwood look bad?"

"No, I don't want that."

"Besides, you're my warlock now. Get used to me making sure you look good, because I want *all* the jealousy."

For being *Dominus* of my coven, I seemed to be getting told what to do quite a bit. I'd thought living under the control of the State's Child Protective Services and in a foster home had me accustomed to being bossed around — they had nothing on Mel and Sam, even if I was supposed to be the one in charge of Sam through our coven bond. I suppose I could have just told her to stop and worn whatever I wanted, but she seemed to be having fun. I guess there's magical control shit and then there's the power a girl you care about has over you. Guess which is stronger?

Sam nodded. "Yeah, that one."

"Okay, let's get go —"

"Not the cocoa one," Sam stopped me as I reached back into the closet for my jacket. "Not with mauve — wear the black one."

"The brown one's warmer —"

"Not the cocoa one! Not with mauve. Mother's frown, you're such a guy." She pulled my black jacket out of the closet and handed it to me. She waited until I put it on, then straightened something that wasn't crooked. "Perfect, let's get going."

We went downstairs. Mel was in the kitchen, looking through the cabinets and checking things on her laptop. She'd been busy researching Christmas since the day before when she'd realized I'd spent my life celebrating that instead of Solstice — and after she'd questioned me about it and found out how much Christmas in a foster family usually sucked.

Then she started watching Christmas movies and I was a little afraid.

"Do you have your card and phone, dear?" Mel asked as we passed through the kitchen.

The two days since the Solstice, and Sam and I forming a coven, had seen a lot of changes around Mel's.

I'd always been reluctant to ask Mel for anything, since she'd done so much for me already, but Sam had no such reservations now that we were a coven. She told me the workload could be divided more evenly once I had more witches, but until then, she'd take care of things. Apparently being *Dominus* didn't mean you had to control everything, it mostly meant letting the rest of the coven serve you by taking care of things so you didn't have to.

I had mixed feelings.

Taking care of things included letting Mel know that our coven needed some seed money — a tradition amongst witches for the Families involved to set a new coven up properly. We weren't likely to get anything from the Prescotts, who Sam still hadn't told about being marked by me, but she thought Mel would see it differently.

The next thing I knew, Mel was reaching into a desk drawer and handing Sam and I credit cards — they had Mel's name on them, but with chips and tapping, nobody checked that anymore — to "tide us over" until the authorized user cards she ordered for us came. And those were to "tide us over" until we could get our own coven accounts set up and there was someplace for her to transfer funds.

I objected to that, saying I didn't want to take all Mel's money, to which Mel asked if I was planning to purchase a small country or, possibly, a Fortune 500 company, and Sam said we'd need to have a talk about the effects of compounding over several hundred years.

The end result was that I had a credit card in my wallet, instead of the thirty-four dollars in cash I had left after aging out, and my own phone, so I could order our rideshare myself instead of asking Sam to do it — which didn't stop her from doing it before I could, because I was *Dominus*.

"I have both — thanks, Mel!" I called, hurrying out the door because Ricardo was two minutes away in a black Volkswagen Jetta.

We slid into the back seat and were on our way — a lot more comfortably than the bus and subway I'd been planning on taking.

Sam sat close to me, touching me from heel to shoulder. She'd been doing that ever since ... the Event of the Solstice, which she insisted on calling it. I was never going to live that down.

It was weird to drive through my old neighborhood — it'd only been six months since I'd last seen it. Maybe the place hadn't really changed, but it seemed so different. I guess I'd gotten used to Willowmere.

The difference didn't bother me, though, it just was — and the knowledge that I'd be seeing Morgan again in a few minutes made me oddly optimistic about the future, as though she was an anchor to my old life, and maybe a bridge between old and new.

There was a lot still ahead of me — us, I corrected myself, giving Sam's thigh a squeeze — but I thought it would be okay. There was college to finish — assuming *Prima* Rosethorn didn't kick us out of Willowmere, but I figured Mel would just verbally assault her until she gave in. We still had to tell Sam's Family that they'd lost their new *trinitara* witch and wouldn't be getting her back, because she was all mine. I still needed to make up with Felicity, but Sam assured me the cat-witch just needed some time, and no little abject apologetics from me, and it would work out. I didn't know everything I had to apologize for, but that was okay — I think if I was going to live with thirteen women in a coven, then I should probably get used to apologizing for no reason. And there was still Katrina's murder, and the presence of some undetectable, mana-eating creature, hanging over us and every witch at Willowmere — we hadn't forgotten about her. I was no less determined that whoever killed her was going to pay, but until we could discover more, there was little we could do but move on with our own lives.

It was a lot, but I thought we could handle it.

Ricardo pulled over about half a block before the coffee shop and we piled out.

"Are you sure you don't want me to go hang out somewhere until you're done?" Sam asked.

"No, I want you to meet Morgan — she's been a big part of my life."

Sam hugged my arm as we walked. "And we'll keep it that way."

Sam and I had started spending a lot of time talking late at night in bed ... after other things. Some of that was me telling her my concerns about Morgan and my promises to be there for her when she aged out in six months. We hadn't figured out how to handle that, but I had come to believe it was "we" who would be. Sam was quick to show me that whatever came, we were facing it as a team now. It was a new experience for me, having someone I could count on so much.

"Oh, here," Sam said as we neared the coffee shop, handing me the bag she was carrying. "You should carry this so it doesn't look like it's coming from me."

The bag had my Christmas gift for Morgan in it.

I'd wracked my brain for weeks trying to come up with something … something that cost less than thirty-four dollars, then Mel gave me the credit card and I knew exactly what to get Morgan.

I didn't want Morgan to feel like I'd forgotten her or she wasn't a priority to me — I'd fucked up too often like that lately — so the bag held a new cell phone. That way we could reach each other without leaving messages or dealing with the creepy Gabriel.

As we entered the coffee shop and I started scanning for Morgan, Sam suddenly grabbed my arm and pulled me to the side.

"*Hsst!* There's a witch here!" she whispered sharply.

I was surprised, but not too worried — I was with Sam, so any witch who didn't know us would assume we were part of the same coven. It might be odd for a warlock to be out in public, but accompanied by a witch, no one would assume I was up for grabs — and if they did know who I was, the protection of both Willowmere and Mel should keep all but the most predatory witches at bay.

"Where?" I asked, mostly unnecessarily, because I was already scanning the room for shields and mana — then I saw her.

No shields, because she was untrained, and resonants not really visible, because she hadn't yet come into her full power — being in her eighteenth year, but still six months away from her birthday.

Morgan was a witch.

# AUTHOR'S NOTE

Hi — and thank you for reading!

I hope you enjoyed reading *Warlock* as much as I enjoyed writing it.

It seems to be traditional in this genre to say things like "as soon as I get X reviews, I'll start writing the next book" — not my style. Book 2 is already in the works, but if you'd like to further support my work, the best way is to leave a review and rating on Amazon or Goodreads — reviews are the lifeblood of independent authors and help other readers find new books.

I also have a Patreon (DanielKensingtonAuthor) if you'd like to make a bit of more tangible support. We're still fleshing out what the Patreon will offer (what the Patrons want).

Some of the ideas I have for the Patreon rewards are: alternate points of view for the sexy-times scenes in the books (from the girl's point of view, for instance), expanded sexy-times scenes including some things cut from the books, extra sexy-times scenes not included in the books, and...

Yeah, the Patreon's gonna be pretty smutty, I guess.

Don't worry - the books in the series will have plenty of smut, but I can't every night's activities in there or that's all it'd be. :) And anything that first appears on Patreon that's necessary for the continuing series will be included in the books.

Probably some tiers that can vote on options for sexy-times scenes and certainly a tier that can request specifics or custom scenes — canon or not — and if there's enough interest, maybe some commissions of artwork to represent some of the girls or scenes.

So, I'm pretty proud of *Warlock* — I have established book series in other genres under a different name, which I'm also proud of, but this is my first foray into the Harem genre and I think I did a decent job.

Part of what went into *Warlock* was the inclusion of some BDSM elements — somewhat tentatively in the first book as Noah comes to grips with his own desires, but to become more later in the series. I'm including that because it's been a large part of my own life and when I started reading in this genre, I felt it was something that wasn't represented enough — and because it's really fun and opens up some interesting dynamics between the characters.

Not all of Noah's relationships, coven or otherwise, will be full-on BDSM dynamics, but most will have some elements, especially around control-issues, because ... well, he has Control. It's a big thing for him.

Looking forward to book 2 and seeing who the next member of Noah's coven is.

I should address the cliffhangers, I guess. I know some readers really don't like them, and I understand, but one thing I found in writing this book is that it takes a lot of words to cover just one year in magic school, and I tend to write longer, multi-book story arcs to begin with. Book One is already over four hundred pages and almost a hundred and forty thousand words, which is big. I suppose I could have cut some things, but that's not my way of writing.

So the cliffhangers and unresolved plot threads aren't really intentional, but they're a natural result of this story and will all be addressed in future books.

Daniel Kensington
Orlando, FL
9/29/2024

Printed in Great Britain
by Amazon

f799738a-7a38-4553-bf1c-57625d9d336eR01